For my Friend
Bonnie
A beautiful creature
Spent who sees
me as I wish I could
Love
Winchuchala

HEBE JEEBIE

by

WINCHINCHALA

People With Wings Productions
A Word-Art Artists Organization

A People With Wings Publication   Boston

HEBE JEEBIE

by

This is # _54_ of _1500_ copies.

Winchinchola

WINCHINCHALA

A People With Wings Publication   Boston

Book front cover art: "Just what is it that makes today's homes
so different, so appealing?" Collage, 1956 by Richard Hamilton
Printed with personal permission of the artist, Richard Hamilton.

Library of Congress Cataloging-in-Publication Data

von der Vogelweide, Winchinchala.
        Hebe Jeebie/ Winchinchala von der Vogelweide.--1st ed.
        Special Limited Edition, numbered and signed by the author

ISBN 1-889768-29-4
I. Title

                                96-070538
                                CIP

FIRST EDITION: August 1998

10 9 8 7 6 5 4 3 2 1

REPRODUCTION PERMISSIONS AND ACKNOWLEDGEMENTS:

Book front cover art: "Just what is it that makes today's homes so different, so appealing?" Collage,1956 Richard Hamilton. Printed with personal permission of the artist, RICHARD HAMILTON.

CANOVA sculpture of Hebe. Devonshire Collection, CHATSWORTH. Reproduced by permission of the Chatsworth Settlement Trustees.

Van Cliburn, May 20,1958,(211) released for one-time editorial reproduction "NEAL BOENZI/ NYT PERMISSIONS" NYT Pictures, The New York Times Company 229 West 43rd Street, 9TH Fl, NYC 10036.

Collage, "CHOJO" 1996,(233) by MASATAKA ONO, designed for this novel and reproduced by personal permission of MASATAKA ONO.

Photo: CARTIER brooches: SIOUX CHIEF HEAD and SQUAW HEAD (365) Reproduced courtesy of: "Collection Ancienne", CARTIER: Geneva.

Photo of Hotel Del Coronado reproduced by permission of hotel.

Drawings:Horse(27);House(144 & 325);Count d'Entrecoeur (348) by the author, Winchinchala, used with permission.

Cherokee (Indian Love Song), Words and Music by Ray Noble Copyright (c) 1938 The Peter Maurice Music Co., London, England Copyright Renewed and assigned to Shapiro, Bernstein & Co., Inc., New York for U.S.A. and Canada. International Copyright Secured. All Rights Reserved. Used by Permission.

A PHOENIX TOO FREQUENT, CHRISTOPHER FRY,1949 Oxford University Press, "by permission of Oxford University Press."

"Times Square", WINCHINCHALA, Primary Poetry, PONDERING PURPLE volume 4: 1999, People With Wings Boston, Massachusetts.

From COMING OF AGE IN SAMOA by Margaret Mead. Copyright 1928, 1955, 1961 by permission of William Morrow and Company, Inc.

From THE POETRY OF ROBERT FROST, edited by Edward Connery Lathem, Copyright 1944, by Robert Frost, Copyright 1916, (c) 1969 by Henry Holt and Company, Inc.

From LADY CHATTERLY'S LOVER by D.H. Lawrence. Copyright 1928. Bantam Doubleday Dell, New York.

Front Bookplate Design adapted from HERALDISHCER ATLAS edited by Hugo Stroehl. Copyright 1909 by Hoffmann:Stuttgart.

Strauss notes HARPER's WEEKLY, July 2, 1872 and July 13, 1872.

Volapük words from the COMPLETE COURSE OF VOLAPUK by I. Henry Harrison. Copyright (c) 1888. BOSTON: Carl Schoenhof.

PROLOGUE and PERSONAL ACKNOWLEDGEMENTS

Finding time to write is difficult, especially when one must work two, three, four jobs; get divorced; fall in love; become a vegetarian; undergo surgery; denounce love; become a carnivore; meet therapists; have an emergency root canal; do laundry etc. But writing is something a writer must do more than any other; eventhough, leisure time, time with people and immoderations are sacrificed. It is a congenital addiction, a passion which is cathartic yet fulfilling. Hebe is one of several works written in the infirm, holiday and "down-times" of almost a decade.

Over the years, I have been asked many questions about my writing. 1. "What's the book about?" 2. "Is it autobiographical?" 3. "Why do you write?" 4. "Who is your publisher?" To answer in reverse order: I am self-published because mortality has reared its head in my middle aged life, and I realize that another nine years may not be mine to continue to try to find representation and a publisher. Given that the corporate publishing system which has evolved makes it discouragingly frustrating to be read, even by a reputable agent unless one is published, I decided to join the ranks of the many privately funded such as Mary Baker Eddy, Edgar Allan Poe, Rudyard Kipling, Henry Thoreau, Leo Tolstoy and John Grisham etc. After all, I write because I love to write. I have since I was eight. Creating characters, unraveling the intricacies of their lives and loves is truly exciting for me. To share them with people is another variety of joy.

Being human is, after all, a conditon both mysterious and complicated. Parents often complain about children having come without instructions. Guess what? No one got any. We're all making up our actions as we go along, or following someone else's example. No one knows what to do. We often admit that. "I don't know what to do." The lack of knowing is the one key which opens life up to an infinity of possibilities if we use it. And that is what I like to write about, people exploring the unknown.

I do not like to write about myself, and I have not here. This book is a work of fiction set against historical events of the 1950's. Any fictional character's resemblance to persons living or dead is entirely coincidental, and incidents in which they interact with celebrities are the product of my imagination.

However, considerable: insight, inspiration information and time have come from quite a few very real people. I offer my sincerest thanks to all: friends, librarians, archivists, etalii who answered my curious, impulsive inquiries, served as readers or provided me with the minutia of facts and detail needed for Hebe. In no particular order of importance of contribution or other preference, I would like to acknowledge the following: Ben Lippencott: Newport Historic Society; Mark S. Young III: archivist/ historian of the Tennis Hall of Fame and Museum at the Newport Casino; Albert Curtis III:Evergreen Colorado; Sea Wolfe: Council Chief for Chappaquiddick Tribe, Wampanoag Indian Nation; Masa Ono:Japan; Jodi A. Hullinger; Attorney Diane W. Spears; Lauren Ash Donoho + Judith Bond: Hotel Del Coronado, San Diego, CA; Robert G. Gardner:Cambridge, MA; George Peabody Gardner Jr.; Andreas Voswinckel: Hamburg, Germany; Jean Keddy; Mia Thurlow; Gay: Gay's Flowers; José Gurría: Mexico City; Loretta Girón; Tim Walsh at Lewis Siegal's "Marty's" Allston, MA; Mary Jo Mc Nally: Pierre Hotel, N.Y.; Brian Cole, Grip Inc.; "Banjo's" Autoshop; James W. Curtis: Cape Cod; Anne Tilney Brune; Mrs. Nancy Moore; Madame Claudine Depierre-Bovier and Olivier Depierre, Geneve; William Morris Hunt; Florence Harth:Caracas Venezuela; Yann Janic Chevry, France; Jacqueline S. French and Nancy M. Osserman; the Myopia Hunt Club; the spirits of seven generations of ancestors before me; the Boston Public Library: Social Science Reference.

Special Thanks to:

Rune Waldekranz of Sweden, for a decade of encouragement and constructive literary criticism, most of all for understanding.

Bill Shakespeare and his wife Francesca for their generous and loving hospitality and kindness, Bill's detailed historical Brookline information and Francesca's direct reader's commentary.

Frantizek Daniel (Frank) and Samson Raphaelson (Raph), my dearly departed Columbia University professors who long ago handed me the reins of the wild horse writing and taught me how to believe in myself and "wride" with confidence.

Devonshire Collection, Chatsworth: photograph Courtauld
Institute of Art.

In Loving Memory of Joy

Notice of Intention of Marriage—Form

Commonwealth of Massachusetts

Health Department—Registry Division

City of _____

Int. No. _____

Cert. No. _____

Notice of Intention of Marriage

To the City Registrar of ———, *Massachusetts*

The following notice of intention of marriage is hereby given in compliance with law:

GROOM	BRIDE
Name _____	Name _____
Age _____ Years Color _____	Age _____ Years Color _____
Place of Residence, ⎱ _____ Street and Number ⎰ _____	Place of Residence, ⎱ _____ Street and Number ⎰ _____
Marriage, first or more ⎫ _____ Divorced, place and date ⎬ Widowed, place and date ⎭ _____	Marriage, first or more ⎫ _____ Divorced, place and date ⎬ Widowed place and date ⎭ _____
Occupation _____	Occupation _____
Birthplace ⎱ Town and State ⎰ _____	Birthplace ⎱ Town and State ⎰ _____
Father's Name _____	Father's Name _____
Mother's Maiden Name _____	Mother's Maiden Name _____
Date Blood Test was done _____	Date Blood Test was done _____
Name of Physician _____	Name of Physician _____
Address of Physician _____	Address of Physician _____

I, We, hereby depose and say that there is an absence of any legal impediment to the marriage, that this application is made with the full consent of both interested parties, and that all the statements herein contained and subscribed to whereof I, we, could have knowledge are true.

Applicants: _____

_____

_____ COUNTY, ss. Subscribed and sworn to before me, this _____ day of _____,

19___.

Marriage License issued _____ 19___

Marriage Certificate returned _____ 19___

_____ ⎰ *City Registrar*
⎱ *Assistant Registrar*
  Designated Clerk

To THE HONORABLE THE JUDGES OF THE PROBATE COURT IN AND FOR THE COUNTY OF SUFFOLK:

RESPECTFULLY represents _____ *Hebe Gourdin* _____
that She is a minor of the age of _____ *twelve* _____ years, and a resident of Boston, _____, in said County of Suffolk; that she desires to marry _____ *Marie d'Entrecoeur* _____ of Boston, _____ in the County of Suffolk, _____, who is _____ *twenty nine* _____ years of age and that her ~~father, mother,~~ (guardian,) consents hereto; she therefore prays that an order may be made allowing her to marry the said _____ *Marie d'Entrecoeur* _____

Dated at *Boston* the _____ 20ᵗʰ *of August* day of _____ *1959* _____
A. D. 19

_____ *Hebe Gourdin* _____

I, _____ *Clair deLune White* _____ being the ~~father, mother,~~ (guardian) of said minor, consent to granting the order asked for in the above petition.

Clair de Lune White

ONE

THE END

A Wedding?

215 Warren Street
Brookline, Massachusetts
August 29, 1959

"A new beginning is not always considered the beginning of
the end, but the end is always considered a beginning. Right?"
asked Hebe, the willowy young bride standing in the bathroom. A
monarch butterfly fluttered around the room and she held out her
suntanned finger to attract it. A handful of friends held her
gown away from the floor, so she could pee. A gangling figure
with a mane of frizzy hair, she wasn't a particularly beautiful
bride. A, tall child of only twelve and a half, she looked as if
she were playing dress up in the spectacular House of Worth gown.
She was not. She was about to descend the Italian marble stairs
of Mrs. White's home to the cloister garden to marry a handsome,
wealthy, European, noble man. Her little band of foreign friends
were as different as they could be in background and appearance,
and each had her own opinion about marriage.

Nell, a platnum-blonde Flemish sylph almost twenty, longed

to marry, preferably someone with a title. Holly, a young oil painter from an old Yankee family with splatters of paint on her white gown, didn't think it necessary for anyone to get married. Rosalita, a pint-sized Mexican high school student, whose right arm was shorter and smaller than her left; thought the opposite, that everyone should get married, that it was the main goal of life. Bozena, a chubby, teenager from Poland, herself recently wed, wasn't sure with whom she agreed. And the thirty-year-old ballerina, Rem, married, for the third time, thought that it was romantic in theory, but was usually more of a useful institution. Regardless of their varying perspectives, they were all swept up in the nuptial preparations.

Rem was the one who responded to the bride's philosophical question, speaking loudly above the water running in the sink and the tub in an effort to help, Hebe, relieve herself. "This is a time for biological functions, not intellectual functions Hebe. Please. Concentrate! Everyone is waiting downstairs. This is our third trip up here."

"Doesn't she look sort of like one of those big parasols you might see in a summer carnival in Trinidad?" asked Holly, tipping her head and moving it back to better see her subject.

"I think this dress looks just like whipped cream," said Bozena dreamily, lighting a cigarette. She handed it to the Mexican girl.

"I never been to there, but I think she looks like she's never gonna pee," she remarked rolling her eyes at the ceiling and tapping her foot energetically.

"I should be the one getting married," pouted Nell.

"I thought you were married," muttered Rosalita a little suprised looking at Nell's golden band."

"No. It's my great-grandmother's. But I plan to use it when I get married and become a countess."

"Well, I'll tell you one thing," began Rem, quickly changing the subject, "We can not have a beginning or an ending by staying in this bathroom. My God Hebe, I think Congress took less time to vote Hawaii into statehood."

"Watch out! The water from the tub is going to splash on the dress!" warned Holly closing the shower curtain. "What a story; If you had told me a year ago that I'd be a bridesmaid for a twelve-year old, I'd have laughed in your face. Rem, are you sure this is legal?"

"Hey, I'll be thirteen in November," the bride pointed out a little defensively. "I think I'm just nervous. Rem can I have a glass of water please?"

"You mean, may I," she corrected extending her long, thin, white arm. "Yes, you may. Here, have the rest of my champagne," she said, then gave the facts. "I'm positive it's legal. My attorney said all that was needed was consent. Her grandmother signed her over to me. I'm her legal guardian. Therefore, it's all in accordance with the law." She fanned herself with her flimsy, chiffon dress end. "It's getting too hot in here. Are you sure that's the cold water you're running?"

Hebe plunked herself down again. So much had happened in such a short period of time. Her leg smarted beneath the large, white gauze bandage covering the six inch wound that had nearly cost her her life. The words of the nurse ran through her head, "You're a lucky little girl. If you had lost just a couple more drops of blood," she paused. Well, you wouldn't have met your pretty Miss Barbie doll." That was three weeks ago.

Now, she was getting married. Certainly, she had dreamed of her wedding day, she hadn't quite expected it to arrive so soon, or for her betrothed to be nearly a stranger. She thought he would be someone special, a man she truly loved as much as Rem loved Bob. She wanted to marry a man without a mustache. Her groom, patiently waiting at the altar downstairs, had a mustache; it tickled when upon meeting her, he kissed her cheeks. Rem told her she wouldn't have to kiss him again, or do anything else, and she was glad.

The merry commotion of the crowd of guest below, playing the piano and singing, clinking glasses, even the voices of the girls swarming around her sounded far far away. Finally, she relieved herself, and they all applauded. Her light tulle and silk gown was lowered and smoothed.

"That isn't rubbing your leg, is it, Darling?" Rem asked sweetly. She shook her head. "Are you ready to carry on then?"

She nodded; even though, she didn't want to go downstairs. She would much rather have gone to her favorite place, to bed, to dream in quiet warmth and comfort. Her misgivings and youth were covered with the veil. Bravely, she placed one foot in front of the other in step with the Wedding March. Filled with fears, she descended to her new beginning, not for tradition, not for title, not even for love, but for independence, to break free from the uncaring forces and hurtful hands which had been spinning her life in a circle of chaos for five long years.

TWO

THE BEGINNING

Family Details

Hawthorne Street
Cambridge, Massachusetts
Tuesday: August 31, 1954

Indulging in the cottony limbo between slumber and wakefulness, Hebe held her eyes closed attempting to postpone the
arrival of another day. She was just a child, and each day
coming meant another one lost to the unstoppable passage of time
marching relentlessly toward autumn, toward school days. Once
she welcomed those days, catching falling leaves, wearing soft
sweaters and getting new construction paper. That welcome
changed when she started the first grade last year. School days
became glum and meant rushing into a cold room, being teased by
the other children and told what to do by teachers. The end of
summer was drawing near. From the border of consciousness, snug
in her down feather bed, Hebe found it possible to imagine it a
day closer to the middle of the summer, a hot, July day when the
whole family would pile into their big Packard and head off for a
picnic on Cape Cod at Grandmother Wilkinson's. She listened
carefully for the sound of the car being pulled around to the
front. Instead, her ears were filled with the disheartening

sound of rain. She sighed a big sigh. Rainy days were the worst for pretending it was still summer. Suddenly, a boom exploded through the air pulling her to an upright position causing her stomach and hands to tremble. Rudely, she was hurled into the almost-autumn day.

Throwing aside the sheet, she scampered to the window. In her seven and a half years of life she had never seen such rain. It wasn't drops; it was sheets of grey-white water unfolding from the sky, billowing, flapping and tattering in violent, whistling ululations of the wind. Frightened, but mesmerized, Hebe stood in front of the vibrating window pane looking into the street. She yelled out, "Mama! Mama! Mama, come quick. Look at what's happening in the street!" The giant oak in front of the house kow towed in the power of the wind and wiped the patent black top of a neighbor's Buick shaking in the street. Hebe ran to the French doors of her room and back to the window in a panicked shuffle. "Mama!" she cried out again. No reply. Transfixed to the cool, wooden planks of the hardwood floor she stood. Another boom jolted the apartment. Pale gold lightning flashed, branch-like through the sky and touched the houses lining the horizon. Sirens unwound wails of emergency in the distance. "Mama!" Hebe mouthed in a silent scream as fear-filled tears spilled onto her small face. Just as she was about to run into the other room, a square, yellow, torpid taxi came to a stop. Its reflection jumped-ed around in the water rushing in a shallow river in the street.

The driver got out and struggled with the wind on his way to the passenger side. He clung to his cap with one hand and the cab with the other. The blowing wind riveted him to the ground; he buried his head in the bend of his elbow, shoved his cap under his arm and pressed on. Rain pelleted his face, but finally he reached the shiny, chrome handle, jerked on the door and opened it. His hat blew down the street, a pair of women's legs popped out of the cab. Hebe recognized them as her mother's, and a smile of relief inched across her face. She tapped on the glass and wimpered "Mama!" Her mothers enormous, baby-filled figure draped in a powder-blue sundress bent forward dangling her pink-gold cross from her neck as she grappled the driver in an arduous attempt to get out. Art, the sandy-haired man who had just moved in downstairs, darted out to greet them with a large, black umbrella like a hotel porter. In the blink of an eye, the wind had not only turned the umbrella inside out but had sent it tumbling down the street.

Hebe knocked on the glass. "Mama," whined her small, worried voice. She jumped up and down and ran to the French doors, then back to the window again where she watched as Art slipped and almost fell. Hearing Hebe's noisy knocking the threesome looked up. Hebe's mother's eyes widened and maternal instinct yanked her tongue out in a command which was instantly whipped down the street in a gust of damp leaves. They approached the curb, a lumbering, twelve-limbed beast, then stopped. It waved its arms, contorted its faces into horrible expressions and stretched its mouths around muted words. It communicated fear. It communicated danger.

Hebe wanted to run to the beast, to be enfolded in the comfort of its bosom, protected by its authoritative voices and powerful endarms. A siren sounded. It sent her running straight to her closet to grab her favorite dress, to her bed for her stuffed dog, Rivet and finally, to the wall under the desk as she had learned in duck-and-cover practice at school. Quivering there in the tiny space by the wall, she waited, unwittingly holding her breath for her mother. "Those big, scary, Russians are coming?" she thought. She just didn't know. An image of a bomb mushrooming in the sky that she had seen in a magazine flashed through her mind. Thunder cracked. She held her legs and tried to become smaller.

In the street below, rain splashed in the flooded gutter. The murmur of voices and the sound of her mother's enervated ascent on the front steps pulled her out from under her dusty caché. The brass key clicked in the hall lock. Hebe stood, embraced her stuffed dog then kissed his lifeless, brown face announcing, "Mama's coming. Hear?" Thunder boomed. Lightning sizzled into the oak in front of the window. She saw the giant,

flaming, zigzag stab an electric, blue-yellow blow through the
leaves and into the trunk. She watched helplessly as the spray
of leaves, glass and rain burst into the room over her. No time
to cry out. The branch knocked her down, knocked her out, knocked her right back through the cottony limbo between slumber and
wakefulness and into the black heart of unconsciousness. Beyond
the twighlight, she heard her mother calling her name. "Hebe!" it
repeated over and over and over. Then all was quiet.

    Projected through the blackness her legs began girating;
peddling furiously; running. But she didn't feel anything
beneath her feet. Each step simply collided with molecules of
space as she ran deeper and deeper into a tunnel. The tinkling
of brass bells brought down a light rain of golden coins. A
beautiful white gown billowed all around her. She strained to
see it; it felt so soft, almost fluid. But the force of falling
was pushing her face toward her ears. She fought for air. All
she could do was hold onto the edges of the billowing dress and
fall. Down and down she went until a current caught her and she
caught her breath. For a few seconds she was suspended in the
air. Then, without any notice, she began to drop again. She
thought she saw a cord to hold onto and she stretched out her arm
to catch it, but all she got was a coin. In the breezy, black,
nothingness, she rode airwave after airwave straining her eyes to
see. All at once she felt secure; her legs straddling a horse as
soft as a kitten. It's large muscles moved its sweat damp fell
against her naked thighs. Running on air his hooves were silent.
A loud, sucking sound emptied the space. Gravity reached up and
yanked her down. A body of water became visible. She heard a sea
sloshing onto a shore. Another cord. She caught it. The horse
disappeared. Holding so tightly to the cord, pushed the golden
coin into her hand. Even though it became hot from sliding down
a few feet, she held on. Just above the water, she stopped. Her
heart raced. She saw herself in the beautiful white gown in the
reflection. It vanished. She closed her eyes and opened them
again. Everything was blurry, but she could see.

    She was in her room, the edge of the blanket firmly clenched in her hand. To her amazement, she also felt the warm coin in her palm. Slowly, she peeked in; there it was, just as it was in the dream. However, it wasn't a golden coin; it was a shiny, new silver dollar. She smiled and looked around. The tree branch filled the window frame; its boughs stretched into the room near her bed and rested on the sparkling splinters of the window pane on the floor. The leaves rustled in a damp zephyr that sighed through the broken window. She sighed along with it because she was unable to pretend that it was not the end of summer now.

Usually a gargantuan Zenith television enshrined in a veneer cabinet sat in a prominent position in the living room. It was strangely at the foot of the bed, its glowing, orange tubes visible through the vent holes in the sides. Facing it was evidence of her mother's vigil, a rocking chair half-filled with a knitted baby-comforter in the making, one of D.H. Lawrence's novels and an empty glass. The announcer blared out the emergency bulletin about Hurricane Carol's damage to the east coast. "Hurricane," thought Hebe outloud. "I knew it had to be something bigger than rain." She toyed with her coin.

Her mother's face appeared in the squares of the French doors as she walked by in the hallway. Hebe attempted to lift up her head; it seemed very heavy. She felt her heart beating in her temples. She decided to be still and burrow a little deeper into the warmth of her bed to enjoy the smells of morning; strong coffee, sweet bacon and fresh cologne. Her mother would return; she always did. Mother was a magically recurring image in her life that unwittingly concretized reality and imparted a sense of security in her; even though she felt guilty that she didn't always like her mother. She tried to remember the very first time she had seen her, but could only remember the last time, just a few moments ago when she went by the bedroom door. This made her get up to see where her mother was right at that moment. The room was cool. She sat up and rubbed her head where it hurt. Through her bushy mane of dark-brown hair she felt a bandage. She didn't go much farther than the end of the bed. Too woozy. So she just dangled her slim, olive legs over the end and reached into

the green leaves of the branch with her toes. In a puddle was a
wet piece of paper.

Just then, the French doors swung open and her mother
reappeared filling the frame with her gravid form. In one hand
was one of Hebe's favorite dresses which she had grabbed from the
closet just before the tree hit her. It was damp, wrinkled and a
little soiled from having been on the floor. In the other hand
she had a glass of orange juice. Hebe could smell it. Neither
spoke. Hebe looked at the dress and looked away; she felt as if
she had done something wrong. She put her hand on the bandage.

"Why a little girl would mop up the floor with her favorite
dress is a mystery to me," said her mother in her cool-roast,
British-bent Boston accent. Automatically Hebe reached around
for her security, her stuffed dog, Rivet.

"I didn't mop up the floor..." she began.

"Oh, don't bother to try and explain. Let's just hope the
cleaners can help. Or maybe we'll just have to throw it away,"
she teased unkindly causing Hebe to gasp. "Oh, Hebe stop. You
know I'm just playing." Then she smiled. Even though it was a
superficial smile, it lit up her face; its arrival coincided with
that morning's first burst of sunrays which played on the leaves
of the branch. The sunlight illuminated the blonde hairs on her
milky cheek and formed tiny rainbows in the beads of spray in her
light-brown hair. Hebe tipped her head and looked at her.

No matter where or when she made her inevitable reappear-
ance; in front of school, in the aisle of the supermarket, or in
her room in the morning, she was beauty parlor fresh. Wordless-
ly, she floated across the room in the nimbus of her négligé.
Hebe kicked the leaves nervously and asked, "Are you angry?" She
wanted to tell her about how she had seen her from the window,
how her knees knocked together and the dream. She wanted to show
her the silver dollar, but she didn't dare. At any moment her
mother could get ugly-angry and lash out at her with venemous
words and smarting slaps, so said nothing.

"Juice," her mother asked. But before she could answer,
Hebe's father's voice pulled her mother into the hall again.

"Gaye, where's my white shirt?"

Hebe drank in her father's voice like a delicious elixir. She was so happy that he was home. He was always very interested in the tiny details of her life; he listened and asked questions. She followed her mother, a small, silent shadow in bare-feet, to search for her father's white shirt.

In the bathroom, she watched her mother's eyes trace the well-toned muscles of her father's long, brown back. He was scrubbing a shirt on a washboard in the tub. Her father was a Cheyenne Indian, but he told everyone he was a Cuban. No matter what he was called, he seemed to be a perfect human; everyone liked him. Hebe had heard men say," That Gordy Gourdin, now that's a man's man cause he's a lady's man if ever there was one." And when ladies saw him, they would speak in softer, but higher voices, flash their eyes and place the ends of their fingers to their mouths. "Oh, is that you're Daddy?" they would ask. "Aren't you a lucky little girl. If you ever have a son, he's for sure going to be a great-big, fine man too." Then they would ask glancing nonchalantly around, "Is your mother with you today?" It didn't matter if he dropped Hebe off for ballet, took her to watch him play tennis, out to buy cigarettes in the corner store or a family gathering; there was always a pair of lady's eyes on him, even if it was her mother's, as they were now.

"Gordy, what on God's green earth are you doing?"

"I'm washing my shirt."

"I can see that," she answered flatly. "You have twenty others in the box from..."

"I want this one." He turned around and he saw his daughter. The washboard fell into the stream of water and splashed it all around. He swept her up in his arms as carefully as a newborn filling her with joy and releasing all the pent up news and emotion she had stored. Out it came in a torrent of babble which ended with the words, ".....silver coin except it looked gold in my dream." She stuck it up in front of his face.

"Oh wow. Did you really bring that back from a dream?"

"For Heaven's sakes Gordy. Don't fill her head with silly

nonsense." She tried to snatch the coin from Hebe's hand, but he was faster in closing the child's hand around the dollar. They laughed at being faster than Gaye.

"Mama doesn't believe in magic. And that's incredible because she's carrying an elf or a fairy in her stomach."

"Gordy stop! She'll soon believe in make believe worlds."

His brown eyes danced and his white teeth gleemed as he let a laugh escape from his heart. "Make-believe worlds Gaye? Go inside of anyone's house. They're all different. Each person creates what he wants. Why do women wear these?" He held up a padded bra. "And what about all of this?" He pointed to her make-up on the shelf. "Isn't that make believe too?" He paused and took the coin from Hebe's hand. "How do you know where this coin came from? And even if you do, why is it so difficult for you to play along with us. Just because your mother packed you off to a boarding school and treated you like a stranger, you don't have to treat my daughter the same way." He shook his head from side to side and tutted.

"Oh Gordy, what do you know?"

"When is the my little brother coming?" asked Hebe from beneath their conversation. No answer. For the moment, her parents' ears were child deaf. They were preoccupied, pulling the tug-of-war rope of adult conversation over the mud puddle of dispute. From his self assured footing Gordy yanked for blind faith. From Gaye's confused side, she pulled for a logic. She was stubborn and loud and insistant. He? Strong and reasonable and amused as he moved toward the door. In the hallway, he snapped his shirt with a final, loud wet bang, then, began to work his way into the damp, wrinkled garment. Gaye gasped in disbelief. "You're not serious!" Immobilized by incredulity, she watched as he buttoned it up and stuck his little package of Lucky Strikes in the pocket. He always did things that upset her mother, things her mother said, "One just doesn't do." He drank red wine with fish; sometimes ate spagetti for breakfast in the backyard; wore sneakers with his suit, and liked to waltz with his wife without any clothes on. She hadn't seen them, but that's the story she heard their maid telling another on the phone. She didn't believe it until the girl said, "Well, the wife didn't want to. Said, 'One just doesn't do that.'" Then she knew it was true. The idea made her laugh. "Mommy and Daddy dancing naked. How does he think of these crazy things?" She wondered if he were having fun annoying her as he was now, with the shirt.

"See you at 6:00. Take good care of my girl." He hugged Hebe. She giggled feeling the cold, clammy shirt on her arms.

"Gordy! Gordy what will the neighbors think?" asked Gaye her words falling on the closing door. "They will think I am crazy. Me. Gordy you have many other shirts. They will think we don't have a laundry maid," she continued going to the living room to speak through the window. Hebe thought this was very funny, but she didn't dare let her mother see her amusement. She watched as Gaye hung out of the living room window into the nacreous light of September's second morning, a giant, radiant flower begging in a stifled voice, "Come back." She toyed nervously with the cross dangling from her neck. Gordy did stop for a moment, but only to light one of the cigarettes.

"Bye Daddy!" called Hebe. He smiled and waved. She waved back. He waved again at Gaye.

"Yes, I am a little crazy. How else could I love you?" She did not wave back. He continued down the street and disappeared around the corner. Only the trailing tendrils of grey smoke lingering in the humid air heard Gaye's final plea for him to come back, "Gordy!"

She picked up the nearest available projectile, a crystal ashtray and hurled it against the wall into a fountain of sparkling globules, and she burst into tears. "He is mad Hebe! Your father is mad." Anger and frustration smoldered in her pale, green eyes; she began to cry. Suddenly, she lashed out and slapped Hebe across the face. "Don't you dare laugh at me. Wipe that smirk of your face. You were not supposed to be up ghosting around after me in the first place. You little sneak." Tears were streaming down Hebe's face. As usual her mother had managed to obliterate any mirth that happened to drift into their lives, into her heart. Past experience had taught her that reacting only escalated matters, so she stood quietly sobbing with her hand soothing her smarting cheek, waiting for whatever would come next. Gaye sniveled into a handkerchief which she produced out of the sleeve of her bathrobe. "Oh, what is wrong with me," she muttered to herself before kneeling down to Hebe and giving her a cool embrace. Looking right into her eyes, she asked her very nicely, "What would you like to have for breakfast more than anything else in the whole world?"

Hebe's face lit up, "Pancakes!" she responded softly.

"Pancakes it will be then," her mother said taking her by the hand and leading her off to the kitchen.

It was a languid, chilly, pancake-perfect day. After breakfast, Gaye suggested that they make fudge. They did, a huge square of it that filled the house with its rich, sweet, aroma for the rest of the day. The day passed in a series of images like the falling pages of an oversized book: Gaye unfurling the newspaper commenting about a movie, The Caine Mutiny; Tinker Bell fluttering around in bold, coloring-book outlines; a monstrous, red and black truck that reached into her room and removed the branch; Gaye opening a bottle of beer; tongues of bleached clothes being sent through the ringer; Rivet going around and around in the washing machine; a river of yellow knitting flowing over Gaye's stomach; Gaye opening a bottle of beer; the bloody bandage being changed on her head; bright red fillet tips on the cutting board; velvetty pink roses, the last of the summer, survivors of the storm, scattered about the yard in mud puddles; veils of sheets and curtains strung out above the lawn to dry; Gaye opening a bottle of beer; Howdy Doody's smiling freckled face on the television and the hands of the clock on the wall. All seemed to wait for the big hand to touch six and Daddy's key to unlock the front door.

Gaye did not seem to think it was necessary to speak to Hebe, and she did not. "Children should be seen and not heard," she would say whenever Hebe wanted to share something with her.

Every now and then they would exchange a little smile. As six
o'clock drew closer and closer, the clock seemed to tick louder
and louder. Hebe's head began to ache a little.

Finally, six o'clock struck. Gordy's brass key clicked the
lock and opened the apartment. As if figurines in a giant music
box responding to the lid being lifted, Gaye and Hebe sprang into
motion. Gaye drained the rest of her amber calming beer into her
glass, stood up and covered her maternity dress with an apron.
Hebe ran into the pantry to play the regular game of hide and
seek with her father. The wait was sweetened by the taste of
fudge she got from the side of the pan cooling there. He seemed
to take a long time. She started to count the canning jars full
of greenbeans, then she heard laughter on the other side of the
door. She strained to hear the voices. They stopped. Her every
sinew tingled with gleeful anticipation. She hid her face in her
hands attempting to further conceal herself in the nook. Nothing
happened. The tense hush was broken by a glass thudding on the
table and Gaye's vexation laced greeting, "I didn't hear you say
you were bringing anyone home Gordy."

"I didn't know myself. Surely there's no problem. This is
my good friend from MIT" Hebe heard her father whisper, "Hal?"

"Hans," came a deep, gentle voice.

Hebe knew her mother was about to be aggravated and her
father about to do playful things to make her smile. Never
bothered himself, he was a master at extracting high spirits and
laughter from people. He told wonderful tales from his simple
life and liked to hear about other people, so he brought them
home. There had been an opera singer, a magician, a navy officer
and the accordion player with his instrument neither she nor the
neighbors will soon forget. But the most annoying to her mother
was a slim, green-eyed, Cuban club singer who Gordy claimed he
was watching over while her brother, his friend, took care of
some business downtown.

She remembered her mother saying, "Gordy she's got every
man in Boston watching over her, she doesn't need your particular
attention. Get rid of her!" He did, but he also got rid of

himself in the process. Hebe wanted to see who it was this time
and she pressed her face against the keyhole, but someone was
standing against the door.

"It's a nice night. We'll eat on the back lanai," suggested
Gordy clapping his hands together loudly as was his habit when he
was a little nervous. She heard their shoes shuffle away then
glass breaking. Through the keyhole she saw her mother throwing
things into the sink and decided to stay in the closet. Crash!
More breaking glass. Then one pair of shoes scuffed back into
the kitchen. Gordy's voice poured over her mother's choler like
a soothing lotion, "Where's little Hebie Jeebie?"

"You know perfectly well where she is. Why do you insist on
playing childish games with her? And why do you bring people
when you know the maid is off? When are you going to grow up."

"Never, I hope. A person has to grow older, but a person
never has to grow up. You can be a child at any time. Watch!"
He jiggled the pantry knob; Hebe lost her breath.

"I have no help Gordy. How in the world are the dishes,"
Gordy piled all the china and silverware for the meal into
the table cloth, pulled the four corners together and toted it
out like a bundle of wash. Quickly, she tip-toed out of the
pantry and slinked down the hallway to the bathroom. She was
certain no one saw her. Even though it was still dusk, the
windowless room was pitchblack. She started to move her hand to
look for the light and hit a glass. The orange juice she had
left there in the morning. Then she heard a sound come from
behind the shower curtain, a strange rumbling ferocious sound
which froze her feet to the floor next to the toilet. She opened
her mouth to scream, but no sound came out. Its loud growl and
roar filled the tiny room and the shower curtain was ripped
aside. Hebe screamed a blood-curdling scream and threw the juice
in the direction of the sound. It stopped and she heard her
father laughing and spitting out the orange juice. Her heart was
in her throat, "Daddy, you didn't scare me. I knew it was you,"
she lied.

"Will you too stop clowning around?" asked Gaye from outside

as Gordy picked Hebe up and carried her out. Her river of chat
about her day had began to flow. Gordy listened attentively.

Outside, she saw the man, Hans; he was tall and thin with
blonder hair than Bobby Ohlsen, the boy who sat next to her when
they made butter in kindergarten last year. Hans was taking a
picture of Gaye while she opened the cover to the tureen full of
stew. "Pregnant women are so beautiful; the epitome of woman, a
mother. I will call this one, American Mother."

"How about American Father?" asked Gordy sitting Hebe in a
chair and slipping his arm around his wife's waist.

"Gordy," said Gaye pulling away from him, "What's that in
your hair? It smells like orange juice."

"It is!" he confirmed then pulled her apron over his head to
dry it off despite Gaye's protests.

"Click! Flash!" The camera captured them.

Hebe hee hawed, Hans spun around and "Click! Flash!" took a
picture of her too.

"This is my daughter Hebe," Gordy said proudly.

"Hebe, as the Greek goddess of youth, or is it just short
for Hebie Jeebie?"

"Both. Gaye was visiting her father in England and she saw
Canova's Hebe at," he snapped his fingers trying to remember.

"Chatsworth, home of the Duke and Duchess of Devonshire, as
a guided visitor, not a guest. I thought it would be a good name
for a girl, that or Hesperides. We didn't think about Hebie
Jeebie at the time. I think you were the first one to call her
that," Gaye reminded him gently.

Hebe was very hungry. She sat up in her chair with her
hands folded on the edge of the table doing her best to be seen
and not heard since they had company.

"Very nice," complimented Gaye on her posture and sat with
her hands in a similar position in preparation to say a prayer.
Gordy grabbed a biscuit and put it on his bread plate. He handed
the basket to Hans. Gaye with her lips pursed together, glaring
at her husband.

"Gordy, a prayer?"

Gordy didn't pray; instead he asked Hans about his religion.
"I'm a scientist."

"Oh a Christian Scientist," Gaye remarked.

"No. My countrymen are Calvinists, but I am interested in
various theories of origin. In fact, did you ever think that
perhaps we come from....."

"Ha Ha Ha," interrupted Gordy waving his hand in a negative
motion," Let's not talk about that stuff now."

"What stuff?" asked Gaye her eyes gleaming with interest
encouraging Hans to continue.

"I believe it's entirely possible we come from." He gestured
to the flannel-hued sky with his enormous square-shaped hand.

"Of course. We come from Heaven. What's new about that?"

Hebe was delighted that for the time being, Gaye had
forgotten about the prayer and had begun serving dinner.

"No. No. American mother, I don't mean Heaven, I'm talking
about outer space," clarified Hans snatching her polite smile
from her face. Gordy clapped his hands loudly as if he had heard
a joke and laughed. It was superficial at first, but long and
loud and infectious enough to spread to Hans and even Hebe. In a
few seconds, it was genuine and the two men were splitting their
sides and gafawing into their napkins.

"Oh honestly, I should know better than to listen to you
two." She turned and gazed at Hebe about to put a spoonful of
stew into her mouth.

"Not without a prayer."

"Oh Gaye. Don't be so hard on her," Gordy sputtered out.
He folded his hands for a split-second and bowed his head with,
"Bless the meat and let's eat," which sent Hans into a second fit
of laughter. Hebe siezed the moment and filled her very hungry
mouth with stew. Gaye's glare prevented her from either chewing
or swallowing. She just held the stew in her mouth. "Go ahead
and eat your stew Hebe," said Gordy seeing her imprisioned in
immobility by her mother.

Her little teeth eagerly obliged, but after she swallowed
she, strangely, no longer felt like eating. Gaye shot a hurt

glance at her as if she had betrayed her, then shot a look at
Gordy, who was still sharing the laugh and said, "What a poor
example you are setting. So boisterous at the dinner table."

The men stopped and caught their breath. Hans lit a
cigarette. Gordy agreed, somewhat patronizingly, "Yes, Gaye.
Yes, as always my Dear, you are right." He looked at her and
their contrasting beliefs ran two diaphonous beams of dogged
defiance across the table between their four pupils. They met in
an almost visible line of tension just above the porcelain salt
and pepper shakers, a couple in Dutch traditional costumes. The
ceramic Dutch pair were usually puckered up to one another on
their tiny bench. Recently used, they sat on opposite ends of
the bench in the center of the table. Hebe returned them to
their kissing posture truly hoping it would break her parents
angry spell. She looked at her mother and father. She saw that
her effort had failed. She turned to Hans.

Hans, also excluded now, had Napoleonically inserted one
hand in his shirt, and he leaned back casually in a smoky, cloud
of reticent interest observing his host and hostess. He rubbed
Hebe's head and smiled a smile which his elastic face stretched
to his ears. Shyly hung her head over her stew and ferreted for
a vegetable. Hans' hand gently rubbed her back and she again
looked at him. "What big eyes you have. And so dark. Isn't it
difficult to see out of such dark eyes?" She squinted at him a
little baffled by his remark, but said nothing. "Come on we'll
get them to talk again," he whispered with a twitch of his head
toward her parents. "Gordy, what's this? No music?"

Gordy snapped his fingers loudly in the air breaking the
spell of disagreement, jumped up and darted into the apartment.

"I forgot! Perfect! Great idea!" Gaye sat down unfolded
her napkin onto her lap and punctilliously began arranging the
things on the table: fork, knife, plate, glass, salt, pepper.
She removed the little Dutch woman from the bench, used it and
placed it on the table by the bread.

An instant later, under Gordy's zeal, the Victrola's metal
wheels were rotating in stubborn, squealing orbits across the

polished parquet and came noisily crashing onto the weathered, oak, porch boards.

"What a great old music machine," Hans exclaimed.

"Isn't it? It belonged to Mr. Wilkinson, Gaye Lee's father. I always always admired it, and he left it to me. Wait 'till you hear the sound. It's actually very good."

From behind the lustrous mahogany cabinet doors Gordy brought out one of Gaye's happy faces by producing a record cover with "The Blue Danube" scrawled in shapely, cursive letters.

She emanated her pleasure further with a flurried clapping of hands and a squeel of delight, "Oh Gordy, you got it!"

Carefully, he placed the bulbous tonearm on the thick disc and allowed Strauss to one-two-three out of the tiny neck into the lilly-shaped ebony horn. Out, out, out the waltz flowed into the vast space of the night and the storm-damp yard beyond the porch. Hebe mimicked Hans as he conducted with broad motions of his arms and sighed a sigh of enjoyment.

Magically, the music assuaged the meal's inimical beginning and formed an atmosphere of serenity. Contemplating the white balustrade surrounding the square porch, Hebe envisioned a river boat from a page in a "Huckleberrry Finn" which her father had been reading to her. Hans' chain of cigarettes provided the billows of smoke necessary to steam through the meal to the clearing of the dishes, a mountain of whipped cream on strawberry shortcake and down the riverlets of brandy in the giant snifters. He stamped out the last of a chain of cigarettes and they all glided for a while on the surface of the river of time beneath the sun-veined, grey sky of dusk along the banks of the backyard alive with things chirping and buzzing.

All through the journey, Hans kept glancing at Hebe from the side of his eyes and raising his eyebrows in playfull, flirtatious movements. Hebe kept sneaking sips of brandy from all the glasses. And once when he looked at her, she flushed and asked, "What does that mean?" while imitating his gesture.

"You know, you look like Carmen," he noted.

"Carmen who?" asked Hebe. "My name isn't Carmen," and she

wrinkled her nose in disapproval.

"I know," Hans laughed. "you will be a real heartbreaker.
Come. Let's have one more photo."

Hebe drank in his attention and his last sip of brandy. The
flash went off immortalizing her with a sparkling booze mustache.

Gaye and Gordy had begun a routine dialogue about his day at
the office. Rapt in his total physical reenactment of the event,
she gazed at him cooing tenderly. The antiseptic properties of
the alcohol annihilated the germs of discontentment previously
between them and a magnetic field replaced the tug of war rope
they had held in the morning. Moving to a wicker settee by the
wall, they unwittingly sat in the pose of the Dutch salt and
pepper shaker lovers. Hans took a picture of them as if he had
read Hebe's mind. She sat next to him. They leaned forward and
back at the same time in harmonious magic. She looked at him and
he at her, and, suddenly, they both stuck out their tongues; this
concretized the magic in Hebe's mind. She adored Hans.

"Watch!" he commanded. She did. He balanced a lit
cigarette on the end of the table. With a quick slap on the
table with his palm, he sent the cigarette flying into the air
and caught it with his mouth. In the manner of monkey see and
monkey do, she tried the same thing with an unlit cigarette. She
slammed the table much too hard, startled herself and sent the
cigarette rolling off the table, off the porch and into the
darkness. She looked at Hans, genuinely amused by her failure as
he sat against the curtain of the night. How very white his skin
looked in the half-light of the yellow, porch lantern. His long,
blonde hair hung around his head like a rag doll.

"How old are you?" she asked.

"Almost twenty-four," he replied rather proudly.

"Holy cow! That's really old."

"And you are a really cute, little girl," he stated inviting
her up onto his lap and lighting another cigarette. Together,
they glanced at her parents on the bench by the wall.

"Oh, don't worry. Sooner or later they'll remember you're
here. They do that to me all the time. Sometimes, my mother does

it to me even when she's by herself. Twice, she left me in the
supermarket. She said, 'I don't know why I'm always forgetting
you.' I guess, I'm forgetfulable," she concluded struggling over
the word and shrugging her shoulders.

"No, you are not forgettable. It is an excuse grown-ups
make because they get embarrassed. You know?" Hebe looked at
him for a long time then she shrugged her shoulders again.

"Hey, I bet you can't blow this out," she challenged
striking a match and holding it up. He did rather easily. She
held up another, farther away. The moist vapors of his smoke and
brandy laced breath wafted over her face and made her blink. She
was totally intoxicated by this stranger, Hans. He drew her near
to his chest for warmth and nestled his head in her hair.

"You remind me of my little friend Nell."

"Where does she live?"

"Amsterdam."

"Shhh," said Hebe holding her finger to her lips. "You
shouldn't let my mother hear you say damn. She'll be mad."

Hans chuckled and clarified, "Amsterdam, is one word. It's
the name of a city, in Holland. That's where I come from."

"I've never been to Holland. I've been to "The Bogs",
Grandmother's house on Cape Cod, and Newport lots of times.

"Maybe one day you'll come and visit me."

"I would like that. Is it far away?"

"Oh, very."

"That would be fun. I could meet your friend."

"Actually she's my neighbor."

"I know someone else who comes from Holland."

"Who? Is he a friend of your father? Maybe I know him."

"Probably. My father says all people from Holland know him.
His name is Rembrandt. Do you know him?"

Hans laughed. "Not personally, but his works."

"I don't like his paintings."

"Oh no?"

She shook her head. "No. There are no pretty colors, and
the people are not cute."

"That's true. Maybe, you will grow up to be an art
critique."

"No, I don't think so. I want to wear white gloves. I will
be an elevator operator or a lady like my grandmother."

"If those are your choices, I hope you will be the lady.
Hans kissed the back of her small hand. Coquettishly looking in
his eyes he said, "Charmed, I'm sure," in a mature voice.

They noticed the record needle scratching over and over, but
her parents hadn't. Gordy had his finger in one ear and the
other ear pressed against Gaye's pregnant stomach.

"Do you want a little brother or a little sister?"

"A brother of course."

"Oh pardón, of course," echoed Hans. "You know, I have a
little dog, but he got lost in the hurricane."

"That's terrible," she reached up and gave him a sympathetic
hug. "Don't worry, you'll find him. My dog is out there," she
added pointing to the hurricane-puddled lawn. Hans placed both
of his index fingers in his mouth and blew out a high, shrill
beckoning whistle. A car in the distance screeched to a halt.
The crickets stopped chirping. Gordy and Gaye looked up. A
heavy silence plunked down for a moment.

Then a man's voice from the yard called out cautiously,
"Gaye? Is everything all right?" All eyes turned to her mother.
Gordy stood up, Gaye pulled at his shirt.

"Everything's just fine," Gordy replied in a clear, firm,
assertive tone. All four leaned over the railing and saw the
shadow of a man among the many back lawn garden shadows. the
person stepped back from the lower patio into the gauzy shafts of
the porch's lantern light. It was Art, the downstairs neighbor
who had run out to meet the taxi with the umbrella. Caught in
the light, his steel-grey eyes were orange and his shiny shock of
hair looked as if it would burst into flames. He shuffled his
feet a little nervously and puffed his cigarette causing the
ember to glow. Hebe thought he looked like the devil; she got a
shiver of fear and folded her arms around herself. She didn't
know why, but she felt uncomfortable when he came up, which

usually seemed to be when her father wasn't around. She just
didn't like him. Last summer he often visited her mother at her
grandmother's on Cape Cod. It was at that time, Hebe noticed that
he didn't smell. His absence of odor and mysterious appearances
made her suspicious of him.

"I thought you went to California," Gordy said in a flat
voice bereft of friendliness.

"I came back," retorted Art in a nonchalant monotone.
"Didn't Gaye tell you?"

"No. No she didn't." Gordy dropped his arm from around
Gaye's waist.

"Shall we invite your friend up for a drink?" Hans proposed
cheerfully.

"He's not my friend. He's a friend of Gaye's." He turned
and cut a jealousy-laced glance at her making Hans at once aware
of some tension.

"He helped Mama from the cab the other day," chimed in Hebe.

Gaye's eyes pierced right through Hebe's head and Hebe, then
she asked accusingly, "What did you whistle like that for in the
first place?"

"Oh, sorry; that was me," confessed Hans with a comforting
hand on Hebe's shoulder. "I was trying to call the dog."

"Art will you get my dog from the clothes line please?"

"I ought to hang you up down there with him," Gaye joked.

A smile wormed it's way through Art's thin lips. Slowly, he
crushed his cigarette jewel in a silver pocket ashtray, and
swaggered to the edge of the patio where the clothesline hung.
His movements were stiff and military-like. His whole being
seemed as creased as his sharply pressedchino slacks. He climbed
up several rungs of the sturdy rose arbor-ladder and handed up
the toy dog, but he didn't come quite high enough to show his
face. He hung there for a moment; stealthy, cat-like while they
issued their collectively muttered thanks, then he disappeared
down the rungs and into the shadows with a dismissive,
"Good-night."

"So this is your famous dog. I guess he doesn't eat very

much," remarked Hans gently handing him over to Hebe.

Gordy handed Gaye the end of the tug-of-war rope argument they had pulled in the morning and they began to yank it back and forth over her relationship with the downstairs neighbor, Art.

Under a light drizzle of words, all filed into the kitchen where Gaye loosened her grip on the rope long enough to command, "Hebe, go to bed." In the bat of an eye her hand went limp and fell from Hans' and she started toward her room. "Don't forget your prayers," Gaye called after her.

"I told you I don't want her to recite that idiotic prayer. 'If I die before I wake,' what kind of bullshit is that to put into a little girl's head before she goes to sleep? Don't you agree Hans?" He turned to look at Hans who was holding Rivet. Just then Hebe's face appeared in the door frame.

"I forget my dog."

"Go to bed!" shouted Gaye.

"You don't have to yell," her father almost whispered. "Look at the innocence and tell me you can find logic in your prayer."

"It's better than not believing in anything like a heathen."

"Indians do believe in something; the power of all mighty nature and the spirit of.."

"Don't start that with me," Gaye said cutting him off. "You don't believe in Indian religion either. I swear you're some kind of a Communist or something."

Hans bent down to hand Rivet to Hebe who had become quiet and stood cutting her eyes to her parents and down at the floor. "Do you want to see my room," she whispered offering to spare him from getting involved in their quarrel. Accepting the opportunity to exit gracefully, he picked her up and carried her out. Resting her head against his chest realized he was so big she could stretch her legs out to the other arm, so she did.

"What are you doing?" he asked amused.
"You're even wider than my father," she remarked. Hearing something break in the kitchen, Hans jumped. She patted his shoulder and mimicked words which she had heard before, "It's OK, sometimes grown-ups get angry." She kissed his cheek and smelled

the nape of his neck with childish closeness.

"Do you like it?" he asked.

"Yes. I like it all."

"All?" he asked curiously.

"Yes, your mouth smells like brandy, your hair like smoke and your neck like limes."

"It is limes. You have a good nose."

"I cheated. He told me." She held up the stuffed dog, Rivet.

"Then he has a good nose." He placed her on her bed which much to his surprise was set beneath a large circular mosquito net.

Seeing his curiosity, Hebe said, "Daddy brought that for me from Cuba. It's a souvenir, but it helps me too. I'm allergic to the bugs. See?" She held out her arm and pulled up her sleeve and showed him several welts on her arm from where some June bugs had bitten her on the beach.

"Oh I see."

"Wait here," she said politely. She crossed the room and turned on a phantasmagoria by a door going into a bathroom. The heat of the lamp sent the pictures of clouds in the sky and ponies prancing in the leaves around the ceiling and walls of the room as Hebe got ready for bed. Hans smoked and relaxed. Among the curiosities on her night stand was a framed photograph of Canova's Hebe in the Chatsworth sculpture garden. He was examining it closely when she returned.

"If you go to Paris, you can see his 'Cupid and Psyche' in the Louvre. He was one of the greatest. Look how lovely she still is. Not bad for 2000 years old."

"Maybe that's why she is the Godess of youth," she pointed out matter-of-factly as she crawled into bed. "Will you come see us again Mr. Hans?" she yawned.

"Sure," he muttered tenderly tucking her in. He leaned back and watched her; he didn't want to leave. He remembered how he used to do the same thing with his sister, just a little older than Hebe. She had died in a car accident a few years ago. He never spoke about her and he tried not to thing about her. Hebe's sweet, sleeping face pulled him toward her. He laid his head on her chest and heard her heart racing her off to dreams. Gently, she placed her small, coffee-colored hands in his silky blonde hair.

"Good dog, Rivet," she muttered in her sleep. Hans placed Rivet in her arms glad she was not still awake. Suddenly, Gordy appeared in the doorframe.

"Hey, thanks," he whispered. "I've never seen her take a shine to anyone like that. Do you have a kid?"

"Come on Gordy, I'm just 24."

"So what! I was nineteen when she came along."

"Nineteen!"

"You know the war just over," he began. His eyes staring into the air as if he could see the days about which he was speaking," I don't remember all the details, but I know Gaye had been faithfully waiting for me. And it was hard for her, you know me being so dark. People like me don't often mingle with women from Beacon Hill. At least not on a permanent basis, andnever in public."

"This segregtion you have here is so strange to me. Europe is different. Go to any club, Moroccans, Africans, Orientals. In Paris so many of your black people come for freedom. It's a great paradox this running away from the 'Land of the free,' to find freedom. And you! You are home here, an Indian. If anyone should feel,"

"Oh it isn't really about that. There's always a reason for people not to like one another; degrees of intelligence; amounts of money; how you worship your God. Anything. I remember in Paris it was all about your address."

"Ja. That's so true."

"Arrondissement," they said together.

"Then how did you meet her?"

"Stockholm."

"Stockholm?"

"Yeah. I was on shore leave, and she was there on her

senior class trip. She went to school in Switzerland, you know.
I saw her at a play, <u>Miss Julie</u>.

"How can you fall for someone at a Strindberg play?"

"She had on a mint green blouse with this delicate lace
trim." Gordy ran his big, masculine fingers gracefully around
his collar. Then his face lit up, and tossed his hands in the
air. Wow! After the war, what a celebration we had, all of us.
Gaye-Lee and I rendezvoused in Sweden. We got married there the
first time."

"The first time?"

"It was just the two of us. For the family thing, we got
married here." Gordy searched through his pockets and he produced
a silver dollar which he put under Hebe's pillow.

"Hey Gordy,"

"Yeah?" he said taking a cigarette from Hans and lighting
them both up.

"Come and put one under my pillow later?"

"Sure," he smiled and said, "Just don't be in the bed when I
get there.

"Gordy, I miss you," Gaye sang out sweetly pulling the men
back into the kitchen.

Sometime later, Hebe came out of her deep sleep for an
instant and heard the sound of the adult's voices playing the
familiar, melodyless tune of night talk in the key of
disharmonious cacaphony to the rythm of hissing bottle mouths,
clinking bottle caps and ashtrays, banging class bottoms and
laughter.

The Dream Horse

THREE

LIFE GOES ON

Inner Conflicts

Sunny days were expected. The weather's changing was a
constant. In fact, everything in Hebe's life seemed a constant:
mother, father, Rivet, breakfast at 7:00, lunch at 12:00, dinner
at 6:00, the pages of books she had read a hundred times, and her
clothes were all the bits and pieces that made up the
kaleidoscope of existence which fell into the predictable
patterns of her very small world. A noisy bluejay sang out a
message, waited for a response, then sang out again. Hebe opened
her eyes and saw the puffy cumulus clouds of a bright sunny day.
She turned her head and looked at the French doors awaiting the
appearance of her mother, master of ceremonies who began the
drama of each day by opening the doors. She inhaled deeply;
something was amiss. The air was not redolent of morning; there
was no fragrant, smoky bacon fat, coffee aroma, spicy after
shave. There was no radio, no murmurs, no parents talking. The
unfamiliar atmosphere gave Hebe an insecure feeling. She grabbed
her toy dog Rivet and stuck her thumb in her mouth. She looked
the dog square in his black, glass eyes and asked, "Do you hear
anything?" A bird peeped. She put on her yellow, seersucker

robe and sniffed audibly through the rooms of the house for the
smells she was accustomed to. Approaching the kitchen the
peeping of the bird grew louder and louder.

Entering the kitchen, she was greeted by a surprising, but
well-known sight, Grandmother Wilkinson's delicately-shaped
silhouette. It leaned out of the kitchen window humming at the
birds and listening for a response. On her head rested a
generous, nest-like hat made larger still by the flowers on it.
She had succeeded in deceiving one unwitting sparrow who sat
chirping from her bonnet until Hebe interrupted with a stifled
greeting, "Grandmother?" She turned and presented her beautiful
face framed, of course, by her hat and her striking silver-
threaded, light brown hair swept up under it. There were fine
lines around her perfectly round, grey violet eyes which didn't
light up seeing Hebe, but remained expressionless.

"Yes, I am," she answered without moving.
Hebe rushed to her and gave her a big hug. And, in return, her
grandmother patted her gently on the back not sure what to do
about such demonstrative behavior. "Children are not my strong
suit," she was often heard to say. "Your mother and father have
gone to the hospital to get your new brother or sister." They
walked to the stove together where her grandmother's bosom formed
a small fragrant canopy over Hebe's head. She peered into the
pot and stirred the oatmeal on the stove. "I'm not certain this
will be edible Hebe dear. What time does the maid arrive?"

"Oh, Celia's not with us anymore?"

"And why not?" she asked in a voice which made Hebe think of
the Queen of Hearts. "She had excellent references," she uttered
to herself. "What fault could Gaye have found this time?"

"Mother said she never smiled and," Hebe stifled a giggle,
"And she moved her rear end too much when she did the housework."
She bent over to show her.

"A demonstration is not necessary, Hebe. She should have
replaced her before she let her go. Well, I guess this will have
to do."

Hebe took a long look at the gluttenous mass sticking to the

middle of the dish and lied, "It looks delicious," then suggested
Let's make some toast too."

Her grandmother quietly agreed. She never raised her voice,
or told her what to do; in fact, she rarely spoke at all. Being
only seven and a half, she hadn't quite figured out the meaning
of her grandmother's favorite expression, "Children should be
seen and not heard." Hebe thought it meant her grandmother
thought children were cute. And she mistook her soothing, calm
cordial voice for kindness.   Her grandmother tucked up a stray
strand of hair as she looked at her reflection in a spoon. Then
she asked Hebe whether she liked her new hat.

"I think you are beautiful."

"Oh, don't be silly." Grandmother Wilkinson stole a glimpse
of herself in the spoon again.

"I hope Mama gets a boy at the hospital," Hebe said as if
her mother really had a choice.

"Most little girls want sisters," remarked her grandmother
watching Hebe eat.

"Not me. I want a big, strong brother so he can beat up Pia
and her stupid friends," she retorted her voice tightening with
bitterness.

"Oh don't tell me you're still thinking about those silly
children. Just wait, I will convince your mother to send you to a
proper private school; Windsor would be out of the question. You
should know Hebe, not all children are like that. Some of them
are much better bred than that. Their parents teach them
properly. Stick with people who have similar, or better
backgrounds, and you won't have any reason to dislike anyone
anymore than they dislike you."

"How come you didn't tell mother that?

"Don't be cheeky." She took a breath, then tacked on in a
murmur to herself. "Perhaps you'd enjoy Beaver Country Day or
someplace abroad, anywhere where little girls learn how to keep
their opinions to themselves," she said dismissing the subject
and returning her attention to the window. "Look, there's one of
those damn noisy bluejays."

Hebe's face flushed just thinking about the first day of
school last year and the horrible opinions which were revealed,
not just then, but during the summer as well. She had spent
nearly the entire season with Grandmother Wilkinson on Cape Cod.
Her mother often went off to the little social events which her
grandmother had arranged for her to be invited to in an attempt
to "keep her in touch with the joys of fullfilling one's social
duties." She never thought her mother looked particularly
comfortable dressed in so many clothes on the hot, summer days.
Solemnly, Gaye followed orders from Grandmother on which outfit
was correct, whom to speak to and whom to snub. Interestingly,
Art often played chauffeur to them on their outtings. He would
pull his big, black cadillac up to the front, step out, lean
against the door, adjust his hat and light a cigarette. Usually,
he came and went without Hebe seeing him, like a snake in the
garden she thought. But sometimes he did see her. He would tip
his hat and say "Good-afternoon Miss Hiawatha." She always
wanted to tell him that Hiawatha was a boy and he was making a
mistake, but she knew she shouldn't try to correct a grown-up.
Besides, she didn't like him; he was always so clean, so pressed.
And he didn't sweat. Had not smell. All living things had a
smell, garbage stank, flowers and ladies smelled sweet, even the
pond smelled like a pond. How could he have no scent? She
didn't trust him, and she tried to keep her distance.

Hebe was always left behind with the Irish maid, Kathleen
who was either too lazy or too busy to bother with her, Hebe
never could figure out which. Thus, she whiled the way the hours
as she pleased. There was a small weathered wooden shop at the
end of the long dirt road which had jars and jars of penny candy
and hand-churned icecream. This was her first stop when she had
pocket money; otherwise, she went directly to the pond in back of
the house where she would sit among the splendor of the golden
hay and listen to the song of the crickets. As if she were an
integral part of the landscape, birds landed near enough to
touch, grasshoppers popped around her and an ocassional butterfly
alighted on her arm. Once, having fallen asleep, she awakened to

see a large bunny sitting very calmly next to her. There beneath
the vault of the blue sky, but a speck in the field's summer
song, Hebe thought she was in heaven. Then, from what seemed to
be the middle of the water, she heard someone call, "Hey! Hey can
you hear me?" She got up and looked to see no one. Again the
small voice called, "Over here!" She looked left and saw a
rowboat. Standing in it was a girl not much older than herself.
She was wearing a pretty white dress and a straw hat which was
clearly too large for her. It spun to resettle in whichever
direction she moved her head, and had twisted her long
straw-colored hair into tangles.

"What are you doing there?" she asked in a friendly voice.

Hebe glanced back at the flattened grass where she had been,
cupped her hands around her mouth and shouted the honest answer,
"I'm sitting."

"Me too," the girl hollered back looking at her row boat
seat. " Do you want to sit together?"

No sooner had Hebe agreed than the girl maneuvered the boat
to the tall grass by the bank. She identified herself as Anne
Atkinson. Hebe told her her name and pointed to her
grandmother's gables just visible above the trees. "My
grandmother knows that lady."

"That's my grandmother," Hebe said smiling, pulling off her
shoes and socks and her dress before laying it flat on the grass.
She got into the boat in just her underwear. Anne's curious
gaze, made her feel awkward. But, then Anne got up and said,

"That's a good idea," and stripped down as well, and laid
her dress on the bank next to Hebe's. The spontaneous, copycat
gesture made them equals in their playful wrong doing, and bonded
them in an instant childish comradery. Off into the pond they
rowed, their faces shining with pleasure, saying nothing. The
intense heat of the late July sun pulled Hebe's hand up to shield
her eyes; she wished she had a hat too. She noticed Anne's face
was quite freckled and red despite the hat. Suddenly, while they
were just sitting there, Anne asked, "Do you want to come to my
birthday party?"

"O.K.," answered Hebe in a lazy voice before pointing out a little bunch of salamanders in the pond.

"My mother will put you on the invitation list," Anne remarked from beneath her hat. The water was green from the reflection of the trees, and they dunked their arms in it attempting to capture one of the salamanders. It refreshed their thirsty skin, so they hung there a while after the salamanders had passed. Then, Anne positioned her hat to completely cover her face. With that the two young girls both fell asleep as the small cradle-of-a-craft rocked and wended it's way to the center of a perfect Winslow Homer-scene.

A short while later they awoke to the crinkle and tickle of the willow branches. The boat had drifted under the tree, almost right back where Anne had picked Hebe up. "That was really fun," Hebe said putting on her clothes and yawning. They shared a warm hug, then Hebe waded to the grass.

Anne stayed in the boat and Hebe handed her the lacy white dress as she agreed. "I really had fun too. I hope you can come to my party." Her dress on, but by no means in place, she slapped the big hat back on her head. For a moment they just stood there beaming at each other. Then Anne asked Hebe if she could give the boat a little push. When she did, she slipped in the mud and fell right into the water. "Oh no! Your dress!" cried Anne sympathetically.

"It's o.k. My mother's not home yet." They laughed and waved good-bye.

Hebe was mistaken. Her mother and grandmother had already arrived home. She walked into the kitchen and stood slightly dripping onto the linoleum tile floor. Gaye's face turned red when she saw her daughter, and Hebe automatically winced and pulled away from her fearing a slap. Her mother's hand seemed to reach right through her arms and grab at her hair. She pulled her to the floor and struck her repeatedly.

"Look at you. You look disgusting."
Then she kicked at her.

"That is totally uncalled for Gaye-Lee. Stop it!" her

grandmother demanded shrilly. "Hebe run along upstairs."

She thought she was going to be sick on the floor, but she pulled herself up to a sitting position. Neither woman moved to help her to her feet. They stood glaring at one another.

"Run upstairs!: her grandmother repeated. Her voice was stern and admonishing; and her eyes remained fixed on her mother instead of at her. She felt invisible.

Getting to her feet she mentioned, "I was invited to a party by a girl."

"What girl?" Grandmother Wilkinson eyed her suspiciously.

"Anne Atkinson," she blubbered

"Anne Atkinson,"she echoed. "From across the way?"

"No," said her mother putting her ice tea down.

"Why not? Why not let her try and make friends?"

"Mother don't be ridiculous. As soon it was even rumored that I was going to marry Gordy, your precious social register dropped me."

"My. You act as though I made up the rules and,"

"I don't really give a good God damn, mother. I don't need them.

"But how will you be invited anywhere if you are not in the book."

"Mr. and Mrs. Gourdin is in the city directory."

"Oh really. You are who you are, a Wilkinson, a Hapsburg."

"Why? Because you are the great, grand niece of some second cousin twice removed who once shared a train car with.."

Her Grandmother's Queen of Hearts voice nearly shouted, "How dare you speak to me this way. I am your mother! One day you will understand what I'm trying to tell you. Your just angry because you've been excluded, but if things work out between you and Arthur, that will all change," she muttered fanning herself.

"Well, Hebe is Gordy's child. There's the proof of my blunder. What am I supposed to do, kill her?

Hebe flinched when she heard the words. She didn't mean to eavesdrop. She was exhausted and sat on the steps leading to the upstairs. Her limbs stuck out from her pond-rinsed dress like

cinnamon sticks. Long, black spirals of hair sprang away from
her sun-red face.

The sight of her made the women yell in unison, "Go
upstairs!" And she scrambled off like a hunted rabbit.

"No one ever said she would be a debutante. I warned you
not to marry a...heathen."

Refraining from slapping her own mother, Gay-lee glared at
her. "How dare you. He's a genius."

"He's a playboy."

"Like my father," she shot back.

"Don't talk about your father like that. Why half the
paintings in the museum are from his family's collection.
Chairman of the board for two companies, member of the best clubs
in New England, and..."

"That was Uncle John."

"It's all in the family, Dear."

"No it isn't, mother. And what's so great about the people
in your clubs anyway?"

"Nothing. It's just that we have more money and better
back..."

"You make it sound like a pedigree kennel."

"How rude. How utterly rude. I think you owe me an apology,
and your father. He was well-loved Gay-lee.

"Especially by the ladies club."

With that remark, the matriarch bristled, turned on her heel
and calmly walked upstairs.

The sound of footsteps pulled Hebe out of the tub. She
locked the door and disappeared in the privacy of the noisy
running water and the mountains of bubbles. Her grandmother was
right; she had no friends. Anne seemed like she would be a great
friend and now she knew she would probably never see her again.
Everyone seemed to hate her.

Several weeks later when school began, she was filled with
the excitement of the first day and the prospect of making a new
friend, or at least seeing a little girl she had met on her
street named Rena. First, she ran into Pia, her eleven-year-old

sister who was just about the same height as Hebe who was only
going on eight.   Seeing the dusty, nut-brown girl Hebe had
become, Pia confronted her menacingly as if she hadn't met her,
which she had.   "Who are you?"

Hebe smiled, " I played with your sister Rena. Remember? I'm
Hebe, Hebe Gourdin."

"No you're not. Or maybe you are. My mother said your
father is a nigger, or worse an Indian." She cackled and started
to yelp the way Indians do in the movies and all the children
began to laugh and yelp and hit their mouths.

Hebe shuffled her feet on the ground and felt her heart
beating fast from fear and embarrassment. She reached out for
friendship again, ignoring the comment. Everyone was quiet.

"Where's Rena?" she asked her weak voice cracking a little
from nervousness. She wanted to look up for a teacher, but she
was so intimidated that she couldn't move her head that high.

The girl's big face curled up in her superior attitude as she
snarled out, "My little sister is not allowed to talk to you
anymore, so don't bother looking. Get lost!" And with that she
turned her back to Hebe and flung her long braids over her back.
The red, taffetta bow at the end snapped into Hebe's eye.

"Ow!" she cried out.

Pia turned around and laughed. "Look at the little Indian
baby crying." She began to whoop Indian style again, then she
stopped, hooked her arms with the girls on either side of her and
spat in Hebe's face.

Hebe was suntan as she defended herself, "I'm not a nigger.
I'm suntan."

In a flash the girls were on Hebe and holding her down as
their leader Pia pulled up her skirt and pulled down her
underpants. Most of the children in the crowd that had gathered
in the schoolyard giggled, some gasped because her unexposed
bottom was even lighter than Pia herself.

"It is a tan!" remarked one of Pia's accomplices letting go
of Hebe.

"Are you calling my mother a liar?" asked Pia.

There was no time for anyone to respond. The humiliation
had turned Hebe's little right hand into a hard ball of knuckles
which she threw straight into Pia's face. The energy transfer
had begun; Pia gave it back to her full in the tummy. All the
air rushed from her lungs. She coughed and the ground seemed to
come up under her knees. As Pia bent down, Hebe grabbed her two
braids and yanked her to the ground with her. She had a bow in
each hand. She threw them aside and rolled on top of the girl
scratching, biting, kicking.

"You half-breeded dog!" shouted Pia. Then she bit Hebe
causing her not only to scream, but to become enraged.

Animal instinct had broken out of the cages of the little
girls bodies in pretty dresses as they intuitively attacked and
protected themselves in a rare display of girls' playground
pugilism. The brass school bell began ringing and ringing louder
and louder over the cheering children; and the earth began
shaking beneath them. The teachers had arrived. The girls were
attacking one another with such wild flailing that the female
teachers hesitated to step in and two men had to yank them apart.
But there was no power on earth which could overcome the ignorant
of innocents in a prejudiced world and bring them back together
again. Henceforth, they were repelled by one another.

From that day on Hebe was no longer Hebe to anyone except
her teacher. They called her Half-breed, Pow Wow or Tonto. At
recess, she sat out from skip the rope or hopscotch. Sometimes
the teacher would sit next to her and try to encourage her to
play, but she felt it was better not to risk insult and
rejection. If she just didn't interact with the other children,
they didn't bother her. She began to enjoy being alone. The only
time it hurt was on special ocassions.

Halloween that year, there was a party at Mary Beth Haley's
house. After school a gaggle of Studebakers, Packards and Fords
honked in front of the high black gates of the playground. The
students piled in and the cars roared away. There was no room
for her. She sat down on the curb in the quiet, grey, aftermath
of their noisy, rainbow-costumed departure. Hot tears ran lines

of sadness through the doll face her mother had painted on her that morning. Emptiness filled her small body with a weight which made getting up seem an incredible effort. An acorn fell at her foot and she picked it up. Carrying the acorn in her hand and her small and broken spirit in her heart, she walked into her kitchen.

Her mother turned to greet her child, but she saw a broken individual. Hebe dragged herself over to the table and into a chair. Her mother sat opposite her sipping a beer, her brow knit with concern. She waited for a story, perhaps a puppy her child had seen hurt or something. No story came. She broke the silence herself, "Hebe, what's wrong? Did something happen?"

Hebe looked up at her and spoke with a small trembling voice while she shook her head hopelessly from side to side. "Mama, I'm a dog. A half-breed dog."

Gaye put her hand to her mouth and winced. "I knew this would happen," she mumbled to herself. She got down on her knees in front of her daughter who buried her face in her elbow sobbing. Not really being demonstrative, she didn't reach out to hold her, and she had no idea what to tell her. She searched her mind for words. She tried the truth, "Hebe, there is a good side to people and a bad side. Whoever said those words to you is just showing you their bad side." She touched her daughter's arm seeing her body convulse with sadness, then asked, "Who said that to you?"

"It's everybody Mama! No one likes me. I wish I were dead."

These words pulled Gaye's arms around her little doll-faced daughter, and she, herself wept from guilt. "I would be so sad if you were not here. Who would keep me company while I wait for Daddy? You must never, never think like that." She used the dish towel to wipe Hebe's tears, and eventually got her calm by washing the doll make-up off with a warm cloth.

Hebe presented her with the acorn, "Look I brought you a piece of nature. Isn't it pretty."

"Hebe, the next time something like this happens, I want you to say to those people," she hesitated. "Tell them you are not a dog; you are a person, one of the best. Why look at Will Rogers; he's a Cherokee Indian. There's Tarzan Brown of Boston Marathon fame." She stopped and thought for a moment. "Oh, the beautiful ballet dancer, Maria Tallchief. Danced around the world, she has. No one would call them dogs. You have to speak up for yourself."

The opportunity to say her piece arrived at Thanksgiving when the class read about the arrival of the Pilgrims to Plymouth. When they got to the part about the Indians, a boy giggled and whooped patting his hand over his mouth.

"Does your father talk like that?" he shot across the room at Hebe.

She jumped up out of her seat, "Indians don't talk like that."

"They do so. In the movies you see how stupid they are."

"That will do children," interrupted Miss Brahms, the teacher.

He sobered his face and raised his hand, "How. Me Tonto, Hebe's father," then led the class in laughter.

Hebe started to bolt across the room, but Miss Brahms restrained her. She retorted anyway in a big loud voice giving the names of the Indians her mother had told her about and their accomplishments. "And, my father does not talk like that. He went to MIT. He has his own office and his own secretary."

"Thank you," said the teacher. "Now, please, take your seat."

She did. She felt good inside. She had stopped them. She thought. Christmas, she got no present under the tree on the desk at the back of the room. Someone had to have gotten her name; they had all written them on a pieces of paper and put them into a hat. She bought paints for someone. No one had bought anything for her. But worse than Christmas, was Valentines Day.

She saw her mother coming down the street as she was coming home. She said she was going to the store and she wanted her to come along. "Please, let's go down the other street. I want to see the puppy," she pleaded trying to get her mother to change

direction. But her mother was in a hurry. She buttoned Hebe's
top button of her overcoat, took her hand and off they went
crunching through the snow. There on the battered, grey trash
can on a pile of snow was Hebe's pink Valentine's box. There was
no mistaken; her name was written on the side in large letters
sprinkled with red glitter. Seeing it, Gaye picked it up and
asked, "Didn't you want to keep it for next year? You worked so
hard making it. Where are your Valentines?" She tutted and
looked down the street then at Hebe. "Sometimes I think it would
have been better if you hadn't been born," she muttered half to
the street. Hebe shuffled in the snow and brushed the
accumulating powder from her coat.

     "Well, we can't leave it sitting out here." Gaye was
wondering what to do. It was cold and she was in a hurry. Hebe
pulled off the top and began ripping it up. They ripped it up
together and put it in the can where it became refuse as
insignificant as all the other. Their faces burned from the cold
February air. She gave her mother a little smile then dusted the
snow off her hands. For the first time she could remember, her
mother held her hand all the way to the store. Her mother had a
very serious look on her face, and when they arrived she asked
her, "Don't you love me anymore?" Gaye didn't answer.

     Crash! The sound of the pot top falling into the sink made
her jump back into present time reality. She found herself
sitting at the table with the bowl of gluey oatmeal in front of
her. Grandmother Wilkinson came into the room. "Good night!"
she exclaimed. "How long are you going to keep company with that
oatmeal? "Even your little doggy is bored," she noted picking
Rivet up from where he had fallen out of the chair. Hebe
laughed.

     "Did Mama get the baby yet."

     "Soon. Very soon," she assured her, adding under her
breath, "I hope so for her sake,"

     Art appeared at the back screen door, "Good afternoon Mrs.
Wilkinson," Art said politely tipping his hat, knocking gently.
His face was that of an obsequious young person showing off his

knowledge of manners. Propriety dictated his behavior, his gait, his choice in clothing and even the length of his laughter at jokes. He was correct to the point of tedium, and the delight of Mrs. Wilkinson.

Her grandmother's face lit up. "Oh, Mr. Higginson! You certainly don't have to enter through the back door." She unlatched it, and in he marched with a bunch of flowers and a roll of very large white papers. He sat in a chair which Hebe considered to be her father's chair and spread them out on the table excitedly. "Look Eleanor. This entire side of the house which faces the beach is glass."

"Gaye will just adore it." She put her hands to her face admiring the idea while her head tipped from side to side trying to make sense of it from the blueprint. "I'm sure you'll go down in architectural history next to Morris Hunt and Bullfinch."

Art's face reddened with the honorable compliment and he shuffled his feet, ""Well, maybe one day. I'm just redesigning this one, and we'll probably stay in it." He turned to Hebe, "Where are my manners? Hello, Miss Hiawatha."

She greeted him without looking up from her cereal, "Good morning Mr. Higginson. Who's Morris Hunt?"

"Hunt's an architect, a very accomplished man. In fact his grandson lives right here in Boston. Ask anyone in the arts at Harvard. They all know him." He lit a cigarette, then flashed a big smile. The phone began to ring and Grandmother Wilkinson excused herself and went in the living room to answer it. She looked at Art's elegant, hand resting near the crystal ashtray, she studied his ring, so she didn't have to look at him. It said Harvard veritas. It was a very pretty ring, but she didn't tell him. "That's my father's chair," she pointed out.

"Oh really?" he asked rather cooly, but still smiling.

"Yes, really," she confirmed sassily imitating his manner of speaking without moving his jaw.

Before things could go any further, Grandmother Wilkinson came in the room glowing with the news, "It's a boy. A son." And all rejoiced.

- 43 -

"I told Gaye we would come right away."

"I had a feeling this morning that today would be the day,"
Art said picking up the bouquet of flowers and putting it to his
face."

In a flash they stood ready to go. Hebe looked up at them
and asked, "What about me?"

"Don't worry. I've asked Mrs. Jones downstairs to come up
and check on you. Children aren't allowed in the maternity ward.

"Babies are children," noted Hebe.

Grandmother Wilkinson ignored her observation and hinted to
Art, "I hate to impose Mr. Higginson, but could you
possibly...No,I really shouldn't ask. I'll take a cab, or..."
she hesitated politely.

Art stated, "Consider it done. It's Friday, I will pick you
up along with my mother at the Chilton."

She beamed with his understanding of her routine, then
turned with a list of commands for Hebe. "Your father will be
home in a few, short hours. Don't open the door. Don't plug
anything in. Don't turn anything on. Don't cook. Don't walk
around the house barefoot. Don't hang out of the window like a
fool. Just sit quietly and read to Rivet." Hebe watched the back
door close. Her Grandmother's face appeared in its small, round
porthole window for a minute while she adjusted her flower
adorned hat. Then she was gone.

Hebe was alone. She let out a little scream of frustration
and began a minor rebellion. She turned on the radio. She turned
on the television. She pulled the hoover out of the closet and
began to vacuum the floor. She pulled off her socks and threw
them in the air. Suddenly amid the din, the phone rang. She
squeeled and jerked around as if the caller were someone calling
to scold her. She ran through the list of things not to do in
her mind as she undid all the things she wasn't supposed to be
doing, put her socks back on, and finally decided she could
answer the telephone. Too late; the caller had hung up. She
sighed and rested between the sofa's arm and back, she liked the
way it seemed to hug her. The bright light grew in the room and

intensified the colors, made them sparkle, and eventually became so overpowering that all the colors disappeared. She went to the pane and watched a large cloud covering the sun.

Forbidden to hang out of the window, Hebe smartly opened her favorite doors in the house, those to the small balcony overlooking the street. They were a pretty yellow, and arched at the top with long, brass handles. The view of the street they provided was perfect and she could remain unseen behind the boughs of the trees. There, she had spent many hours beneath the green canopy of leaves as an innocent voyeur trying to understand the complicated talk of adults stopping below and birds alighting above.

Today, she went out looking for some sign of her father or something interesting to watch. Nothing moved. Not one car passed. Not one person's footsteps sounded on the sidewalk. Not even a leaf flitted on the end of a twig. The world was lying at anchor in the peace-filled port of 3:00 o'clock. After a while, the rag man and his horse drawn cart clopped by, then there was a man in a grey hat carrying a brown bag. He snapped his fingers and turned back then walked the other way twice. Seconds later the pony-like rythm of a woman's pumps clopped on the sidewalk. Hebe peeked under the leaves and saw her tossing her head from one side of the street to the other searchingly. "Dan," she heard her call out in a guarded voice. It sounded like Mrs.Jones the downstairs maid and she was tempted to call down to her. However, the repeated admonishments she had heard from her mother in the past echoed clearly in the present and kept her quiet. Silently, anxiously she waited to see which direction the woman would take. Finally, to Hebe's relief, she hurried in the direction the man had taken and out of sight. She strained her ear to hear the end of the mystery, but all that ensued was a bellow of silence. She lingered beneath the music of the leaves rustling, sweeping shadows light into the room behind her.

Eventually, balcony sitting became prosaic and Hebe went in herself vanishing from the view of those spying on her spying. Purposefully, she climbed onto the glossy black piano and pulled down the white, leather, photo album with pictures of her parents wedding; she enjoyed looking at them. It was like a fairy tale; everyone so dressed up standing on the flower covered lawn of a mansion in front of a carriage with white horses. She had never ridden a horse, except in her dreams, but she wanted to. She thought the riders looked so elegant on the backs of the graceful giants. There were crowds of people, many were anonymous, some she knew well, all of her grandparents and various others to whom she had been told she was related. And there were her father's parents, the Indians. Though in a far corner, their dark faces and simple clothing commanded attention. She had never met them. She wondered where the people were as she scrutinized the the dresses! The dresses were dreamy. How like a princess her mother looked, not just in the wedding album, but in all the photographs of special ocassions.

Taking advantage of being abandoned, she flew into the usually forbidden land of Gaye's dressing room releasing the lightly perfumed air of the soft velvet, noisy taffeta, whispering chiffon, organdy, and silk dresses of her teas and balls and cocktail parties. She closed her eyes, and she saw herself, a belle, waltzing beautifully to the envy of her imaginary coterie. She donned a pale, cloud-like strapless with tulle puffing out from its waist and actualized her fantasy by winding up the victrola, playing Strauss and dancing what she thought was a waltz, but which was more a dusting of the floors with her hem. She felt the music vibrating through her body, and would have gone on all afternoon had there not been a knock at the door.

It was a very hard knock; the music was so loud. She snapped out of her trance and looked around to see that there was far too much of her fantasy in the room to hide. Then to her horror, the door opened. It was Hans. He surveyed the scene, muttered, "Uh oh," raised his eyebrows in his friendly manner and added, "I hope I'm not interrupting anything," and turned down the music.

"I remember you," she blurted out in a voice that was both

welcoming and relieved.

"Your father asked me to come and see if you are O.K. He had to go somewhere," he said. "I didn't know you were entertaining," he remarked fluffing up her tulle.

Embarrased, she rushed to put her fantasy away by hanging up her mother's dress and washing off her face. It seems she had tried on many dresses, and had opened every container on her mother's vanity in her primping. Hans helped her put everything back in its proper place.

The afternoon they spent together was just as much fun as waltzing, even more because her fantasy partner was not a stuffed dog, but a person, one who conversed with her, interracted with her, made her feel as if she were important, a friend. Hans had brought not only his motor scooter but also his lost dog, Lucky. Together they went to the icecream shop and the Franklin Park Zoo.

The puppy barked incessantly at the animals, sadly no ponies. She rolled down the hills and swang on the swings, and Hans snapped photographs and smoked a pack of cigarettes. In fact, it was the search for cigarettes which ended their expedition. But the best was definitely last, when they rode up and down the hills in the park before leaving. Hans heightened the thrills by warning her only seconds in advance, "O.K. we're going to go down now." Then hollered in excitement with her. But Hebe felt secure snuggling against the warmth of the puppy, Lucky, which she held between her and Hans' body. He lapped at her arms while the wind whisked their eyes shut and took their breath away. Her cheeks were hot from the sun; her skin itched from tumbling in the grass; and she was exhausted to the point of tranquility from the unexpected afternoon of fun. Hans suggested that they meet again sometime soon, and she eagerly agreed. She was happy; she had found a friend. Even though it was September, she had had a perfect summer's day.

Brother Jude

What did a Jude look like? She knew what a Joe, or a
Dennis, or a Phillip looked like.   She had never even heard of a
Jude.   But there he was, a fragile bundle of green knitting
behind the bars of the clean, white crib. Peeking under the edge
of the blanket she could see him, his hairless head, his wrinkled
skin. He had a small, inchoate face with navy blue eyes that,
she was told, didn't yet see. She didn't believe it. He had tiny
hands with fingernails which were not even a fourth the size of
her own. And, by no means, could he be mistaken for cute, the
word everyone uttered upon seeing him. No, so far a Jude didn't
look like anything other than a newborn baby, and the arrival of
this little person changed everything about the people in the
house and even the house itself.

It took on the essence of diapers, sour milk and baby
powder. Old mahogany furniture was moved out of the study,
Jude's new room, and new white enamel-painted things were brought
in a dresser, a rocker and even a high chair. They were all
either adorned with delicate brass knobs or stenciled with
matching, child-like designs which complimented the walls which
had been painted pastel yellow a few months ago. A wardrobe and a
desk were crowded into Hebe's room. She didn't like the way they
blocked the light from shining on her pillow, on her face in the
morning. The wardrobe seemed to be the problem, so she tried to
move it. It wouldn't give one iota. She complained as sweetly
as she could, as politely as she could, as pleadingly as she
could. Each time she got the same disinterested response which
ended with her being shushed and told, "Children should be seen
and not heard," and finally she gave up and solved the problem by
putting her pillows at the foot of the bed and sleeping, in
effect, upside down. No one seemed to care about it, or anything
elses that she did. All of the adults attentions went to Jude;
they spoke in soft cooing voices and walked very softly when they
were around him. He didn't have to do anything special to make

them smile and look very pleased, if he moved the smallest muscle on his face, or made an expression, any expression at all, they responded.

When they were away from Jude, her parents argued about the baby, the way he should be handled. She couldn't remember the last time she had heard one of them call her name; she felt not only unheard, but unseen.

Then one morning she awakened to find a little bunch of brilliant, summer flowers on the dark, ugly desk. A note card hung from it which read, "We still love you Heebie Jeebie," and it was signed "Love Daddy". Next to it was a box of Droste Cocoa and a letter, but it wasn't from her father. It was from Hans!

It was written on a brown paper bag in flowery, cursive, almost feminine writing.

> Dear Hebe and Rivet,
> How's my favorite girl? I miss you. I
> have been very busy researching for a
> project, but I'm going to come to see you
> soon. If your parents give you permission,
> we can go horse back riding.
> I hope you like the cocoa.
>   Lots of Love,
>   Hans and Lucky

She was elated; the possibility of riding a horse and a letter a real friend. She read it over and over and over. Sometime during the umteenth reading; she heard the Blue Danube waltz playing and she saw Hans sitting on the back porch catching the lit cigarette in his mouth. She smiled to herself and decided to write back to her friend. She examined the box of cocoa again and licked the brown dust off her hands without really noticing the bitterness of the sweetly given unsweetened mix. She offered thanks for the gift and her hope that he would come soon, then drew a big heart on the bottom of the page and colored it red. She folded it up and placed it in an envelope.

As she was writing his name on the front, the muffled din of her parents heated discussion in the living room became audible.

She stood outside of the living room door among the satin-smooth cherry wood furniture and listened for a moment trying to muster the courage to knock. Grandmother was showering in the bathroom, and the maid, Kathleen, whom she had lent to her mother was humming in the kitchen. Her parents were alone; that was almost never a time to interrupt. But, she wanted to give her father the note for Hans, so he would know how much she cared. A sense of urgency possessed her; she listened for a moment to enter.

"I should have seen this coming," she heard Gordy say in a low and unhappy voice. "People like you just don't marry people like me. Mesalliance. Wasn't that your mother's word?"

"But I did, Gordy. We did. We have the license and the photos. How can you..." Gaye let out a nervous, trill of laughter, her words sounded as if they were meant to be comforting, but her father interrrupted her.

"If you had really married me Gaye, if you really did, we wouldn't be having this conversation. A marriage is about two spirits which were one finding each other, coming together against all odds, and fitting together. It isn't about a God damn piece of paper or pictures, or big words like committment...,"

"Gordy, what are you saying?" she asked innocently.

"Don't take me for a fool Gaye!"

For a moment neither said anything and Hebe siezed the opportunity of quiet to open the door, very carefully, just as her father looked her mother square in her face and said, "I know he's not my son."

Catching sight of Hebe standing there Gaye gasped and snapped, "Go to your room!" Feeling the tension, watching them argue in a way she had never seen before, Hebe began to cry.

Her father pulled her into his arms and reprimanded her mother, harshly. "I told you before, don't yell at her. She's just a little girl." Gayes eyes scanned her daughter's face and for that moment, she felt her mother hated her.

"Yes, she's _your_ little girl,"

"And the other one?" he asked kissing Hebe's face.

"I will not discuss this in front of the....," her mother began indignantly.

But her father cut her off. "When a person can't give a fast, 'No,' the answer is, 'Maybe.' Gaye, I can live with a lot, being talked down to by your society friends, waiting for you at back entrances," he raised his voice as Gaye gasped as if about to utter some words of defense and continued punctuating his speech with his hand," your mother's surreptitious invectives, being blamed for your father's heart attack. That hard, old Yankee, heart of his didn't stop on account of you marrying beneath you, or out of your race. He was most gracious to my mother at the wedding. And after! He completely funded the new well on her reservation. I'd say his death and the color of my skin are unrelated. The truth is they took him from Mrs. Phillips house around 3:00 a.m. Rather late for a cognac, wouldn't you say?" Gaye's eyes widened in pain from the words he flung at her like stones. Again she opened her mouth to say something, but he stopped her, "I'm sorry, I know that has nothing to do with anything here and now. All I'm telling you is what you know. I've put up with a lot for your love, our love," he corrected himself, "but Gaye...that little maybe, I can't live with that maybe." He put Hebe down. Something was terribly wrong; she clung to him, even while he put on his jacket and stepped into the hall toward the door.

From the living room Gaye called after him," I can't believe you'd talk to me, your wife, in such a way, ask such a question," and she sniffled into a handkerchief. Then, she slammed the living room door.

Gordy picked up his confused weeping daughter and wiped away her tears. "If you want a fire to die down, you take away the wind," he said holding her close to his chest. She felt his body trembling. "I'm just going out for a little while. We'll let the fire go out." She cocked her head a little puzzled by his

words, but she agreed. He breathed a big breath and she breathed
a big breath. When at last she returned his smile, he promised,
"I'm going to go to Bailey's to bring back ice cream. What
flavor do you want?"

"Peach."

He put her down, and all he said before his face disappeared
behind the front door was, "Don't worry. Everything is going to
be fine. I'll be right back. Peach."

But as many times before, he didn't come right back. The
three generations of women sat through a dinner in which only the
utensils, their eyes, and the maid spoke. The women's eyes
glanced disapproval, and the eagerness to end the meal. Hebe's
eyes watched their looks being tossed across the steaming food.
She tried to interpret them. She could not. She wanted to ask,
but she heard the most probable response in her head, "Children
should be seen and not heard." She couldn't even bring herself
to ask for more water. She knew she should not speak at all and
that tonight was probably not a good night to leave any lima
beans on her plate. There were eleven and a half left. When
there were seven, Jude cried out and both mother and grandmother
responded by rushing away from the table. She picked up all the
beans with her spoon and divided them between her mother and
grandmother's servings since they hadn't eaten all of theirs yet
either. Then, she went to her room to watch the ponies on the
phantasmagoria run around the walls, to bury herself in the
secure powdered warmth of her bed.

In the morning, not quite completely awake, Hebe stumbled
into the kitchen, opened the freezer and stood on tip-toe to see
inside. There, prominently perched on a metal, tray of ice cubes
was the frost-covered testimony of her father's faith and love, a
quart of peach ice cream. She felt warm all over despite
the icy air in her face and the cool kitchen linoleum beneath her
bare feet. She pulled it out and smugly marched down the hall to
show her mother and thank her father. She looked at the clock;
it read eight. Her father would be gone, but she still wanted to
her mother to see. Much to her delight, she heard both of their

voices as she approached. She barged gleefully into the bedroom with her father's love for her clasped firmly in her two hands and nearly shouted, "You remembered. Daddy!" Then an involuntary, barely-audible, scream of shock escaped from her throat.

There was the snake, Mr. Higginson with his arm coiled around her mother goo-gooing at Jude! For a split second the adults were flash frozen statues wearing expressions of shame and surprise at seeing her. They raised their eyes in unison as Hebe backed out of the room and pulled the door closed before anyone had a chance to say anything.

"Hebe!" her mother called sweetly after her. She just stood there. "Hebe Jeebie this is your mother speaking. Answer me."

"Yes, mother?" she asked obediently from the other side of the door.

"You came in here for a reason. What was it?"

Hebe looked down at the icecream in her hands and called loudly through the door, "I wanted to know if you wanted any of this icecream that Daddy brought."

"That's very thoughtful of you, but no thank you."

"But Daddy knows we love...," she began.

"Hebe don't let the icecream melt. Take it to the kitchen," commanded Gaye in a no nonsense voice.

"Are you going to school with me for the first day?"

"Yes, I'll tell you when," she answered flatly dismissing her.

Over icecream in the sun lit kitchen, it occurred to her that things were going on in the night while she was lost in dreamland. In the eight short hours of darkness, big decisions had been made, things were happening. Art was in her mother's bedroom, dessert was being allowed for breakfast. And what about school? She knew she was supposed to have started. Was it a miracle? Had it been cancelled during the night while she was dreaming? She vowed to stay awake that night. However, this was unintentionally made difficult by Grandmother Wilkinson.

She had to spend the entire day shopping, that is to say walking, with Grandmother Wilkinson who seemed oblivious to the public transportation system, cars or taxis. As they had many times before, they walked all the way from their house, on Hawthorne Street behind Harvard Square, to Louisburg Square atop Beacon Hill. It was on these outtings that Hebe learned to love Sterns department store because it was there that her grandmother invariably stopped. Her grandmother's head, as far Hebe was concerned, would not be her grandmother's head without a dark face-framing, appendage fixed to it since she had never ever seen her without a hat. The same was true for all of her older lady friends; therefore, it was not the least bit surprising for them to visit the milinery department, and run into one of her fellow hat fanciers, whereupon she would send Hebe to a chair with her customary comment, "Children should be seen and not heard," thus allowing Hebe to sit with enthusiasm. She couldn't quite figure out how her grandmother actually acquired her assortment of hats because she didn't witness her purchase any. She just stood there chatting, tittering into the fingers of her gloved hand. Then she would thank the salesgirl, who did nothing that Hebe could see, and summon her with a toss of her hatted head to go marching off to the next place, predictably a bookshop.

She didn't think her Mary Janes had previously seen quite that many miles in one day; she was exhausted. Yet she was determined to stay awake and see what life went on after 9:30 at night. Waves of fatigue brought on by the peregrination to and from Beacon Hill, the evening's heavy meal, and purloined sips of sherry caused her to sink deeper and deeper into the comfort of her beloved bed. She began to consider postponing her investigation into night life until tomorrow. Somewhere far away she heard the back door open and the voices of Art and her mother, a cork being launched from a champagne bottle. She shook her head sparring with the Sandman, attemting to ward off the sounds of an approaching dream. She shook her head again to stop herself from falling into the tranquilizing arms of another mystery-filled night. A cool, refreshing breeze came through the chink in the window, shaking the branches outside. The large moon poured a shimmering mercury light over everything; her

hands, the leaves, the clouds, the mane of her horse as it
charged toward the lighted wire of the horizon. Holding onto his
strong glowing, crest, the fresh, cool autumn air whipping her
hair she felt the rythm of his powerful body beneath her. The
exhausting day and the need to stay up were banished from her
mind. She rode the pony past the moon and into the black clouds
of Morpheus. She didn't want to sleep; she wanted to know what
happened at night.

Hebe was very upset with herself when she awakened late the
next morning. Waking up meant that she had fallen asleep.
Immediately, it was apparent that again decisions had been.
There were cardboard boxes everywhere. Men in overalls were
wrapping things and packing them into wooden barrels. One of
them rubbed her bushy head, "Well, good morning sleepy head," he
said cheerfully before removing the large oil painting, "The
Hunt" from the wall. She loved this painting of the red-jacketed
riders poised in the field with their hounds. She thought one of
the two women riders, sitting side-saddle in a full-skirted dress
looked just like her. For this reason, Grandfather Wilkinson had
always told her that one day it would be hers. Why were these men
taking it away?

She almost ran into the kitchen. Her mother looked
unusually beautiful. It wasn't a new dress or her hair, it was
something in her eyes. Jude was in her arms and she was in
Art's, in a perfect pose of a happy family. Observing them, she
didn't see how she could possibly fit in anywhere. They were
very close together and though only a few feet away, seemed far
away from her. Sensing her presence, Art looked up. He let go
of his smile and her mother.

"What are they doing with our things?"

"Good morning," Gaye said with a glare.

"Good morning," she echoed. Then, quickly repeated, "What
are they doing with our things?"

Art and Gaye exchanged a communicative glance, then Gaye
spoke, "We're going on a little trip," she informed her.

"With the furniture? Without Daddy?" Her voice was shaking in disbelief. Her head reeled. She looked up at Art through the thin haze of his cigarette smoke fogging out of his rascally grin.

"Sure Hiawatha. Like the time we went up to the mountains together. Wasn't that fun?"

The world and all that was familiar to her had changed in the long blinking of her two eyes. She was being told about it as if it were a book in which she was a central character, yet she had not been allowed to read. Last night, the pages had turned to a new chapter. How did this happen? What would be next? A hundred questions wanting to come out of her mouth at once and the shock of hearing the news that the family was leaving the only place she had ever known as home, without her beloved father, inflicted her with a temporary aphonia. Queasiness welled up inside or her, the floor swayed like the deck of a ship. She watched concern cross her mother's face, then Hebe swooned into Art's arms which he had quickly unfolded to catch her.

Time sped up to the blurr of a pinwheel in the wind, and things were happening right before her open eyes. The Rockingham dessert dishes, only released from their glass cages on the rarest of events, were packed; the oriental rugs rolled up the piano lowered from the balcony to the front lawn.

Art's black Cadillac waited for them at the bottom of the back steps. Colorful as a lifesaver wrapper they fluttered down to it. Gaye in a bright red, well-tailored suit with a small belt accenting her waist held a baby-blue, swaddled Jude and beckoned Hebe to, "Come along." She had chosen a yellow sundress to wear for the simple reason that she knew her mother hated it. She kept glancing back at the door of the house as she left it for what she understood to be the last time. She held Rivet up for a final look as well. Then she ran around to the front, to the doors, her big, yellow, arched doors to the world. She wanted to take them along. Just as she was about to overcome her muteness and tell one of the moving men not to forget the doors, Art called out in a kind voice, "Hey, Hiawatha. We're waiting for you."

Slowly as a trickle of molasses she went to the idling
vehicle then stood by the rear door which Art held open. She
turned her head back and forth from the house to the car. Getting
in meant going away forever. Life, her life was out of her
hands. She wanted to see her father. Her eyes scanned the quiet
dawn for any sign of him; there was none.

"Hebe," her mother pleaded rather nervously. then she
threatened her, "Get in the car and I mean this instant, or
else."

Undaunted, she stood shuffling her foot in the damp grass.
Art stooped down to her and tried to bribe her with an offer of
pancakes. "We'll get some for your little doggie too. O.K.
Hiawatha?" He reached out to stroke her forearm affectionately
and escaping his touch she got into the car. He closed the
door. Behind the barrier of the front seat she watched him lean
over and give kiss her mother on the cheek. The recreant kiss
released her from her speechlessness. "Stop calling me Hiawatha.
Hiawatha was a man," she announced to her lap. Despite her
mother's protests, she rolled down the window and stuck her head
out and watch life as she knew it pass away in a blear with the
elms and the historic, wooden houses. Maybe not. Maybe they
were just moving around the corner. She didn't know. She didn't
ask. She didn't care. She just sat there in the back of the car
unheard, unseen.

Both adults kept consulting their watches indicating a
previously scheduled itinerary lay somewhere in their minds or
the glove compartment, and they were pleased with their following
of it as far as Hebe could tell from the look on their faces.
Art stopped in Harvard Square by Harvard Yard to have a passerby
take one last picture of him in front of his Alma Mater by a
brass plaque on the red brick wall bearing his family name.
Propriety pulled his hand out of his pocket and caused him to
nervously flick away his cigarette before he unwittingly raised
his eyebrows and his entire countenance into an expression of
complacent condescension only begotten by the well-bred and

privileged. The passer-by rolled his eyes at the gesture,
quickly snapped the photograph and escaped further obligation by
claiming the need to catch a bus.

A motor scooter putting into the square turned her head
toward the vision of the force capable of stopping the seemingly
incongruous course of events, her father and Hans. Their motions
were languid and cheerless as they strode away from the Vespa.
They searched the streets with their eyes. "Daddy," she cried
shoving open the heavy car door, jack-in-the boxing out and
dashing across the street. At the same time her mother objected
with a resounding, "No! Stay here!" Safely in her father's arms
tears began to wash her confusion down her face in large drops.
Uncharacteristically silent, his brow knit with concern, Gordy
wiped them away. His chestnut-tone face softened into an
expression of adoration for his little daughter whose stared back
at him, her liquid, black eyes deepening with total devotion.

He set her down on the curb as gently as an irreplaceable,
porcelain doll, and she clutched his powerful hand and tried to
sashay with optimism as the men escorted her back across the
street. From a distance they looked like any other group of
friends in any other square. Indiscernible were the traces of
the crossed ties among husband, wife, lover, and friends. The
bystanders' view was of four acquaintances, but the air seemed to
be the wiser. With the coming together of Gordy Gourdin, his
daughter Hebe, his friend Hans and Mrs. Gourdin, Mr. Arthur
Higginson and the baby Jude, Harvard Square held it's history
-dewed, breath and the venerable, red-brick buildings in Harvard
Yard verily bristled and recoiled from the shameless, public
airing of infidelity. An autumn zephyr rushed a long, strong,
shush through the ivy on the curving wall as the conversation
grew loud. When all was said and done, Hebe, for reasons
mysterious to her, found herself again saturninely situated in
the soft leathered back seat of the luxurious automobile, Art at
the wheel and her mother and Jude by the passenger side.

Outside, Her father placed the palm of his hand flat on the
window for support as he leaned down to the front to speak with

Gaye. Hebe put her cheek next to the large hand, she could feel
its warmth through the cool pane. Through the rain of sorrow
pouring out of her eyes she saw the hand; it was an important
ever recurring part of her life. Daily it assumed innumerable
positions while performing paternal tasks of care and love: it
sometimes brushed her teeth; brought the blankets under her chin
before she slept; danced over the piano keys to accompany the
family in song; fought with tweezers and glue to operate on her
little crystal horse when one of his ears was chipped in a fall;
tossed her mother's finest chiffon shawl in the air to explain
the ways of wind currents; split the logs into pieces more
manageable for her small hands, so that she may participate in
making a fire in the fireplace; held the shiny new silver dollar
she brought back from her dreams. When he moved it to wave
good-bye, it left a partial handprint. Her mother had refused to
roll down the window and talk. She just hung her head over her
lap averting Gordy's eyes. The car moved away from the curb. An
invisible tether between father and child drew her against the
window.

"Mother, we're leaving Daddy!" she blurted out stating the
obvious. "Mother!" she repeated screaming. He was getting
smaller and smaller, and the only reason she could see for his
shrinking was the car was moving forward. "Stop the car!" she
commanded. "Mr. Higginson?" she began, then paused gasping for
air. "Please..," her voice was high and pleading and frenzied as
she watched her father's farewell. His cheeks had pulled his
lips up into the special smile he had reserved for Grandmother
Wilkinson when she gave advice. It was something he could apply
and wipe off, like a lotion applied to the face. His eyes were
dark with grief. From behind the car she heard Gordy's
tenor-pitched voice sing out the parting words.

"Bye Hebe Jeebie. Be a good girl. I'll see you soon."

She spun around in the seat and knocking off Art's hat placed
her hands over his eyes.

"Let go!" he shouted.

"Oh Dear Lord!" exclaimed her mother who was helpless to

assist Art because she was holding the sleeping baby.

"Hebe, I can't see. We're going to have an accident," he pointed out trying to maintain control of the car. Unintentionally, by leaning toward the rear, checking to see if she was achieving the desire affect, her grip weakened. Art wrassled her loose and flung her into the corner, then reached up and ran his fingers through his hair. Her mother's hand slapped her bare calfs and thighs so forcefully that Hebe's legs were covered with deep red welts. Each time her perspiration damp hand made contact she asked, "What is wrong with you?" Hebe felt a terrrible weight on her chest; she couldn't take a breath. Everything blinked red and black. "Oh Dear; her face is turning blue! Art, something's wrong." She heard her mother's words echo and she saw her face. It was far away, but she too was sobbing. Then there was nothing.

Projected throught the blackness her legs began peddling furiously; running, but she didn't feel anything. Each step simply collided with the molecules as she ran deeper and deeper into space. A beautiful white gown billowed around her and there was the tinkling of brass bells. She pushed her thighs together and felt the horses ribs beneath her, and she breathed a breath of relief. She knew she was dreaming, but she was cognizant of what was going on around her. She was with a friend. She released her fears, rested into the comfort of his bare back and rode airwave after airwave through the familiar comfort of her nocturnal purlieu guided by an inexplicable flickering light. The expected sound of water drowned out the silence. Slowly, the animal walked to the water's purling black-lacquered surface. In her reflection, she saw she was wearing a wreath of pink flowers holding slender, white lighted candles. The light threw a golden aura around her white dress and the lovely Arabian. As if he were aware of her adoration, he proudly tossed his mane and snorted. While she dismounted, he nibbled the irridescent white jewels on her dress. Curious, she licked one herself; it was sugar! The horse curled back his downy lips and smiled. The roar of the water began to soften as she leaned against her

- 60 -

velvety felled friend in the cool aired sanctuary somewhere on
the periphery of reality. Thirsty from the breeze in her face
and the sugary candy she began to smack her lips. She kissed the
horse and said good-bye because she was going to return to her
room, the way she always did when she had this dream. All she
needed to do was close her eyes. When she opened them she would
be nestled in the downy comfort of her bed. She closed her eyes.

But when she opened them, she found that her logic had not
followed through; she was not in her room at all. The sky,
around her was tombstone, grey, a blear. She was in the moving
car, her head cradled in the bend of her mother's arm. She was
rocking her back and forth, and talking even though she knew she
was not conscious.

"Everything is going to be all right Hebe. One day, when
you grow up, you'll understand."

Hebe closed her eyes, not to escape back to dream land, but
to relish her mother's rare embrace, prolong it for as long as
she could.

FOUR

ETERNAL SUMMER

The Garcia's

Los Angeles California
Sunday, October 24, 1954

    The dazzling, brilliance of the fine, white gem of Los
Angeles set in concrete lolling in the mid-morning sun, burned
away the foggy, memory of the preceding day's grey dawning in
Boston and the airplane ride which had been an unpleasant series
of turbulent cat naps and jaunts to the lavatory to throw up.
The day's events were even further dimmed, and actually physically obliterated by Art and Gaye moving the hands of their watches
back three hours to California time.

    Flown into this eonian summer, she was blithe. But, she
didn't want to be blithe. She wanted to be miserable, for her
mother's benefit to make her suffer for having yanked her away
from her father and her life. However,in the sweeping spotlight
of the west coast's eternal sunny season, Hebe found a cheerful
squint into the warm rays more natural than a scowl in any
direction. She kept close watch, and when Gaye cast an eye her

way, she put on a wry, little countenance.

The glare from the sun on the windshield was blinding and Art was unable to see, so he pulled over to buy sunglasses. The car, a black, monstrosity equal in size and ugliness to his Boston Cadillac, was so big, and shiny and new that it announced the promise of a generous tip, and immediately called to duty, the gas station attendant tanning his face by the side of the carport. He snatched his red cap off his head and used it to dust off his clothes, then whisked himself up to the car pulling a servile smile up under his dark glasses. Every person in sight, on the street, in every doorway, under every tree and in every car was wearing sunglasses, except Art. She was amused that Art looked foolish using his hand to block out the sun before he went into the dark shop next to the station. Putting her hands to her face to giggle, it occurred to her that her own eyes were uncovered, and she ducked down in the seat. Gaye turned to see what she was up to; Hebe moped. Having given up on trying to talk to her newly obnoxious daughter, and growing increas-ingly impatient with her antics, she just tutted and turned to see Art. She beamed as Art modeled his beautiful new sunglasses in front of the car and demonstrated their effectiveness by lifting his face directly to the sun and flinging his arms out to the side like a performer. He hardly looked foolish now; in fact, he looked quite handsome. He got in the car and presented Gaye with a pair for herself. They had speckled frames with dark, green lenses and it was apparent by the way she admired herself in the sunvisor mirror that she didn't have to be told that they complimented her looks; nevertheless, Art did tell her.

"Doesn't your mother look spiffy?" He asked Hebe placing his hand in her mother's hair bringing a blush to Gaye's already heat-reddened cheeks.

Now that she alone in all of California had no sunglasses, self-consciousness welled up in her. She nodded her head in agreement and stared covetously at Gaye's glasses.

"Oh, I almost forgot," Art reached in his jacket pocket and produced yet another pair with tortoise shell rims. He looked at

Hebe with a smile in his small round eyes in the rear view mirror
as he adjusted it, and handed them to her over his shoulder.

"For you Hiawatha."

"Jeepers," she exclaimed breathlesssly, neglecting to
reprimand him for calling her by the male name of Hiawatha. She
accepted them with childish impetuosity and gave a wholehearted,
"Thank you very, very, very, much Art." She placed them on the
bridge of her small nose and gave a genuine Cheshire cat grin of
satisfaction while imitating Art and modeling them for her
stuffed dog, Rivet. Art and Gaye watched. "Now, am I
beautiful?" Hebe asked her mother.

There was a pause in which Gaye studied her daughter with
her wild coif of Medusa screwing out from her head, parts of it
remaining homeless in the space around her, other parts winding
down in front of her face and the large sunglasses. She sighed a
hopeless sigh, but Art spoke right up.

"Why whatever do you mean Hiawatha? You were an attractive
little thing to begin with."

She contemplated being called a thing.

"My mother was right. It makes all the difference in the
world being with someone of your own kind. That was thoughtful
of you to buy something for her," Gaye said witnessing the change
in behavior the gift had produced in her daughter. She then
leaned over and pecked Art lightly on the cheek.

"No point in dragging the old Yankee parsimony all the way
out here to the west coast."

Between the split in the front seat, Hebe saw Art slide his
hand up her mother's thigh. She desisted from reaching through
and slapping it away as her hand had often been when it ventured
onto forbidden between meal sweet temptations. That smooth,
white, square-fingered hand was touching something that belonged
to her father as far as she was concerned. Without moving it,
Art leaned over Jude who had begun to whimper and tenderly kissed
the rumpled skin on the back of his hand.

"Your mother is a very wise woman," he said to Gaye sliding
his hand in reverse down the entire length of her stockinged leg.

"A little money, a letter of introduction, a quick phone call to the right person," he stopped in mid-sentence, pulled his arm back and lit a cigarette and exhaled. In the soft, controlled voice of one who is absolutely certain of his message, he continued, "The world and everything in it really only belongs to a handful of people. Haven't you noticed? Oh sure some people own some things, but all the castles; the priceless art; the precious heirlooms; the bottles of 1929 Veuve Clicquot waiting to be drunk, proud, flashy steeds," Gaye's eyes were transfixed to Art's as she steadily rocked the baby. "Face it, even history is ours; after all, we created most of it. Why knowledge itself, Latin, Greek, philosophy, the wisdom of the ages. We don't mind sharing it. You know among ouselves," a knavish laugh trilled in his throat.

"Alter ipse amicus, said the Romans."

"But I say alter ipse amoris." A nuage of tenderness wafted over him. "We belong together Gaye-Lee.

Hebe was uneasy seeing her mother look at this man, Art, their downstairs neighbor, with the adoring gaze she once gave her father. Her own sunglasses which had moments ago been too large and teetered on her face, seemed to be pinching her nose, and became all around ill-fitting and uncomforatble. She took them off and tried them on the dog. They fell to the seat. She left them near the crack. The car merged with the other cars and brought them closer to the end of their journey and the beginning of a new life.

When the blanched repetition of the highway and the monotonous lovliness of the novel, pastel-painted, stucco houses on the carpets of green grass wearied her and her dog, Rivet, Hebe was again intrigued by her sunglasses, and resorted to the pleasurable sureveilance of herself in them. She adjusted her posture to be as mature as possible to match the grown-up contour they gave her young face. Thus occupied, she hadn't noticed that they were slowing down until they had come crunching to a sandy halt. The cerulean ocean was flowing to greet them just beyond their new home.

The beach side of the enormous double A-framed structure was made from the bottom half of assorted colored bottles which had been sliced in two and assembled into the image of a river running through the woods. In the various places where light would naturally appear through the canopy of the trees in the image, clear glass bottoms were used. The picture was very realistic, but when the sunlight poured through the red, brown, green, blue, it transformed the house into a gallery of lights and gave it, in effect, the holy atmosphere of a cathedral. The giant, multi-colored fingers of colored light ran vertically through the vast room sometimes changing color in mid-air as they collided with one another, but touching everything from the rafters below the forty foot ceiling, to the catwalk about thirty feet up the walls, to the polished oak floor boards below. They even reached out to adorn the grass beyond the windows on the other walls, and held the indubitable guarantee to infuse the swimming pool and scenery on the opposite side of the house when the sun set. The family stood in quiet rainbowed amazement of the phenomenon. It was wondrous to see, but the idea of living in such light was questionable.

"Now we know why they said we could have it," Gaye began putting her sunglasses back on chuckling.

"I saw the glass on the blueprint, but it didn't mention anything about color, or bottles," he added a trifle baffled, testing the edge of one of the bottles facing inward for smoothness. "It certainly is unique," he said stepping back and placing his hands in his pockets to appreciate it.

"Yes," Gaye agreed putting her sunglasses back on, "Perhaps, for convenience, so we are not forced into boredom, or insanity by seeing it all the time, well we might try some sort of drape," she waved her hand in a sweeping motion suggesting one that would cover it in its entirety.

Thus with much ado from the astounded workmen, a stupendous velvet, cream drape was installed, and removed in the same day when its color proved incapable of inhibiting the midday window's effulgence. The fabric merely became a canvas on which the

colors displayed themselves before seeking their diffused paths
into the room. Only three days later, with increased grumbling,
the workmen replaced it with one in burgundy which, while not a
complete success, was not a complete failure. It allowed for
various hues of restrained, romantic, lavender light to suffuse
serenity throughout the entire room which Gaye decided was
acceptable.

At that time another curtain was being hung. It was
invisible, but just as heavy and suppressive, drawn by
circumstance more than intention, and it dropped down between
Hebe and the rest of the family.

It started with meals. Art had to commute a long distance
to work, so he had breakfast early and dinner very late. Gaye
chose to eat with him since Jude was on a bottle feeding schedule
and two of the baby's meal times coincided with Art's which were
too early and too late for Hebe to eat, according to Gaye. In
addition, the few, fine pieces of furniture they brought with
them were lost in the spacious new "dream house," which is how
Hebe heard Gaye refer to it in her frequent telephone chats with
Grandmother Wilkinson. Thus, Gaye was merrily absorbed with
decorating which meant having designers come to see the house
over cocktails, and going to see this or that in places that,
"didn't want to have children brooding about," or so she told
Hebe. And then there was Art, himself. More than her own baby
brother, or the house, her mother did things for Art. It was:
"Art won't like that," "Art wants it this way," "I'll have to ask
Art," "Art said this," Art said that," "Art, Art, Art!" Hebe
began to hate the name.

In school, which she had begun to attend without incident,
she had been asked to choose between art and music. "No art!"
she almost shouted at the startled teacher. The alienation and
hostility of former school days still on the top of her thoughts,
she kept her distance.

Sometimes everone would arrive home and carry on without
taking notice of her, or calling out to see if she were there.
She would press her face up against the glass barrier of the

sliding doors leading to the patio and look at them billing and cooing over the baby, Art pressed and sharp as ever and her mother coiffed and radiant. Lately, she always appeared as she had when she was the most beautiful Hebe had ever seen her, last New Year's Eve, sparkling like the star atop the Christmas tree, so pretty to see, so far from reach. Hebe began to think that when she was at home she was invisible, and she began to act accordingly by walking softly and never speaking. In one way, she didn't mind because her mother no longer scolded her or hit her or even lost her temper. In another way, she loathed their apparent indifference to her, and she sometimes ached to have her mother's arms around her as they were the day she told her about Tarzan Brown, the famous Indian runner, or when she passed out while leaving Boston. However, nothing about Hebe or her existence was capable of winning Gaye's attention anymore; she was so preoccupied with everything else. Hebe tried going far away in order to be missed, but going out of sight, or even far down the beach where she was admonished not to go, only provided her with a longer lonely walk home.

And so her day consisted of going to school and coming home to the glorious, eternal summer days which she passed by the pool, or the ocean front reading. Sometimes Max, a neighbor's dog, a jaunty, Irish setter would come and invite her to play by running up to her then making a false start for the ocean with a little bark. Whether she went or not, his game was always the same, to terrorize the ocean once and for all. Down the beach he would charge to the edge of the foam and arf his arrival at the ebbing waves. He would walk out into the water in his canine ignorance in search of them, then seeing one swell, or feeling it would dash for the sand. Usually, it splashed over his furry red rump sending him beyond its reach for a few seconds to shake off before charging after the wave woofing with all his might, and from his dog's perspective causing it to retreat. For hours on end he would do this to her amusement. She wondered why he stopped when he did. In fact, she asked him, "What happened? Give up?" She deduced he had because he was only a dog with no

more knowledge about the behavior of the ocean than the ocean had
of his. When he stopped, he would thump into the sand beside her
and pant. Sometimes he sat upright and seemed to be imitating
her just sitting and letting her mind wander over the sound of
the sea. It wandered to Boston. Even though she knew the
weather was cool there and getting cooler, she wanted to be
there. She wanted to see "The Hunt" spotlighted over the
wainscot in the hall, not hidden in the basement. She longed for
the big, yellow doors opening onto her private, street theatre,
to wake up in her old room and smell her father's Agua Lavanda
and the smoke of morning bacon. More than anything she wanted to
see her father, to fill his ears with her daily adventures as she
used to. She missed him and Grandmother Wilkinson; she missed
her life. And there on the sands of her much wished for never
ending summer, she cried from unhappiness.

However, she was not alone. There was Margarita, the
Mexican cook and housekeeper. She was quite a bit shorter than
Hebe, with heavy, jet-black hair and soft cocoa-colored skin; she
came with the house. She just appeared one afternoon shortly
after the family had arrived and in very broken English,
accompanied by deliberate, experienced hand gestures, she asked
her mother what she would like to have for meals that week,
showed her where she was to write these things in the future and
began most cheerfully to attend to cleaning the house. Gaye
liked the idea, but wanted to know more about where this woman
had come from. However Margarita's English was too minimal to
respond to Gaye's numerous inquiries with anything other than a
smile. Her small, chubby body burst into an unstoppable,
methodical cleaning routine involving rags, brushes and assorted
cleansers. Art made one of his bragged-about contact phone calls
and was informed that she had been in the employ of the former
owners who promised that she could resume work for the new
occupants, if they didn't object. She was unaware they hadn't
even been consulted and offered the opportunity to refuse her.
The kitchen had already begun to sparkle and she was down on the
terrazzo floor scouring, in a position Gaye had never even

imagined assuming in order to clean, on all fours. Impressed by her zeal and her apparent inability to interfere or waste time in idle chat as Gaye had seen her mother's maid Kathleen do, she agreed to try her out.

"No, that's fine. She can stay. That is she can be our housekeeper, I'm assuming she resides elsewhere," Art stated and hanging up informed Gaye, "The son is a mechanic, her sister a seamstress and I didn't quite comprehend by whom or when, but it appears that the grass will be mowed and the grounds other-wise manicured. Margarita had stopped and was kneeling in front of her washbucket with the forlorn look of a stray animal whose finder was deciding whether or not to keep it. But when Art extended his hand to her in welcome, her smile returned to her face. "Gracias, Señor," she said in a low thankful tone. "Martini?"

"If it's good, I don't think a trial period will be necessary," he said pulling his hand away and discreetly wiping the dampness from her hand on his handkerchief. The Martinis were excellent, the best he had ever tasted. Gaye concurred and Margarita's job was secured.

That particular evening, the family dined together in the sticky, ocean breeze of the terrace, and they were served by Margarita. No one knew exactly what they were eating; even though she explained several times. Each time she began with a clear triplet of understandable words in English and each time she followed them with a hundred in Spanish, then smiled and clasped her hands together and ask, "Eez good, si?" And on that point they were all in accord. Beans were identified and they recognized the rice, but it tasted like roses. It was an exotic meal, but "A winner," Art deduced. More important than its delicousness was the fact that it complimented the wine Art had selected. They drank a toast, Hebe included. Gaye was as rosy as her red satin cocktail dress. Her high spirits flung her arms around her daughter.

"We're going to be so happy here," she said placing her booze-warmed cheek next to Hebe's.

And they were. Of course each had an obstruction to total
satisfaction with the new perfect life. Hebe longed to be in
Boston. Art wanted his project for a new museum to be accepted.
And Gaye wanted an uncolored window and for Margarita to wear a
uniform. She had entertained a fantasy that her help in
California would dress properly. Assuming the maid would be
happy to recieve a uniform, she presented it to her. It was
black with a little white collar and an apron Margarita obliged
Gaye by putting it on, but she still didn't resemble the maid of
Gayes's dreams. Plump as she was, the uniform had to be very
large to accomodate her width, but she didn't have the height to
take it up. She looked like a big, black pillow with white lace
trim and sandalled feet. In addition, she could not live without
her rebozo, a shawl-like piece of cloth which she needed to
function. She used it for everything. To rest on the couch it
was folded neatly into a pillow. If the weather turned cool, she
wrapped it around her shoulders for warmth. In the supermarket,
it was a basket for groceries; in the garden, it held bulbs; in
the house, it carried almost everything; laundry, dishes, even
Jude. To carry Jude and work at the same time, it was tied to
form a sling-hammock around her body. It was part of her, and
now it was part of the uniform, a red, purple and green, cotton
woven shawl. She also refused to part with her hat made of black
felt. It came down to her ears just above the long plaits of
hair that hung on either side of her head. Gaye didn't know why
she wanted to wear the hat which she thought ridiculous, but in
the end it didn't matter why. Margarita won, by repeatedly
replacing the hat on her head when Gaye removed it saying, "No
hat please."

"Si, sombrero, por favor," Margarita said with a jovial
chuckle that shook her body as if toying with the hat were a
game. After about the fiftieth time, she placed the hat on
Gaye's head. Defeated, Gaye removed it and placed it on
Margarita's head.

"Gracias Señiora," she said with a big smile and shuffled on
into the kitchen. The black uniform was never seen again after

that day.

"She just doesn't look like a maid," Gaye would complain to
Art whenever she had the chance.

"You mean she doesn't look like Kathleen, and she never
will. She's just not Irish enough to look like a maid, or Polish
or French enough for that matter. But, I know you agree she's
worth her weight in gold."

Gaye did agree, but she still wished her maid looked more
like what she thought a maid should look like.

Art's big complaint was the lack of social clubs in San
Diego, not country clubs or private associations, "but real
clubs" founded on tradition and lineage. "Everyone is so casual,
If I say I met Charles Sweeney, no one as much as bats an eye.
But let some pompous, second-generation, nouveau riche son of a
theater chain mention that he just caught a glimpse of Marlon
Brando or Raymond Chandler and everyone is all ears."

And Hebe, though home, wanted to go home, back to Boston,
back to the set of constants she knew as life. Slowly, things in
California were concretizing themselves as part of her life,
making that wish one that confused her. For now there were things
in California she would miss if she were to leave.

Jude was one. He had finally developed facial features and
was constantly testing out his ability to create expressions, or
simply focus for that matter. One eye would look ahead while the
other looked for its mate, then together they would try to focus
on an object. During the whole process, his tongue darted
gleefully in and out of his mouth sending saliva down his chin
and cheeks. Finally, seeing something, he squeeled, wriggled
his whole body and threw his feet out in the air as if he were
stamping them. Hebe tried to throw her eyes out of focus and
then back to partake in the excitement; she only succeeded in
crossing her eyes. In the meantime, Jude had become fascinated
with consuming his toes. She was completely captivated by his
baby charms, and she couldn't imagine life without him.

School was also becoming a positive part of her life. Since
almost everyone was tanned, and there were a couple of Mexican

students, her color was not an issue. They just assumed she was
Mexican, and she was not eager to inform them otherwise. Once
when she was sitting in the cafeteria she heard two sixth graders
talking.

"She's something strange, Look at her."

"No. She's just another Chicano."

"I heard her name is Gordo or something like that."

"Of course, you idiot. Just her mother is Mexican."

"Oh, how do you know?"

"I've seen her."

They had probably seen Margarita dropping her off at school
as she sometimes did on her way to do the shopping. Margarita,
despite her energy, was a peace-filled person who spread her
calming energy on those who came near her. She was also very
affectionate. She embraced Hebe when she saw her and made a big
fuss about how "Que cute," she looked. The best part of
Margarita's affection was the expression of slight jealousy it
brought to Gaye's face. Hebe hoped her mother was paying close
attention so that she might learn how to hug. Once near the
maids soft cheek, Hebe caught the scent of Agua Lavanda, and she
said, "Margarita, you smell like my father."

"Dios!" she exclaimed. "Your padre wear Agua Lavanda. My
son, Tony too. You will see. He is in the Mexico with my
brother."

But Margarita didn't always communicate in broken English.
On the way to school one day Hebe was overcome with melancholy.
She sat with her head hanging down weeping a puddle into her
skirt. Margarita pulled the car over and took her in her arms and
let her cry outloud onto her shoulder as if she were a little
baby. "I'm sorry," Hebe said repeatedly.

Margarita laughed and said, "Sorry! Sorry for what. Tears
are meant to come out. And the way we get them out is to cry.
For goodness sakes, we don't hold back our laughter. Why should
we hold back our tears?" And she rubbed her back in slow
soothing strokes and gave a wise chortle. Hebe sniffed and
pulled back and looked at her somewhat bewildered.

"You speak English," she remarked.

"Of course. I'm in America. Well that's what some people
say for your United States anyway. Why not? Oh, I know what you
are thinking. I don't speak so well in your house. Well,
sometimes it's best not too put all your cards on the table.
Entiende?" she asked. Hebe shook her head back and forth.
"Well, it's just part of my job. The people get nervous if they
think I can understand too much. My ignorance is my job
insurance in a way." Hebe kept shaking her head from side to
side because eventhough she was speaking in English she
understood her less than when she spoke in Spanish. "My language
is not why we stopped," she said changing the subject and kissing
her on the cheek. "Why is it raining in my old car today?"
Reminded of her sorrow, Hebe broke down and told her all about
how she missed her father. Margarita assured her that what she
felt here in California, he felt there, wherever he was, only
doubley because he was much bigger than she was, and she
suggested that they sit down and write him a letter. From that
day on Hebe gained a cheerful disposition hearing Margarita
approach or knowing she was around. She was delighted that the
pupils thought Margarita was her mother when she dropped her off.

She actually enjoyed going to school and being there. It
was clean and bright and new compare to the old one in Boston.
The windows were so large, she felt as if she were studying right
outside. When they opened them in the morning one palm leaf
insisted on popping in. Everytime the teacher put it outside it
snapped back in until finally it was allowed to stay. She
thought it very pleasant to sit in the sun next to a large leaf
and read her book in class.

And though she was segregated from her family at home and
hadn't yet made any friends at school. However, she did make one
at home when she met Margarita's daughter. One day, as she tip-
toed through the house past the lump of Magarita snoozing on the
couch, she saw a girl standing looking out of the patio door.
Had she not been wearing pumps, they would have been about the
same height. She was skinny with budding bra-free breast visible

beneath her soft shell sweater. She was casually draining all
the empty wine and champagne bottles into two separate glasses.
All the while she kept stealing glances over her shoulder at
Margarita who had begun to snore softly. Hebe startled her when
she came in dripping wet through the door from the pool. Their
eyes met. The girl smiled. Hebe brushed past her and pulled a
bottle of wine from the wine rack in the lower cabinet and
plunked it down. "That's disgusting. Why don't you just open a
new bottle?" She got the cork screw. "You must be Margarita's
daughter. I've heard about you."

"And you must be Hebe. I've heard about you too, but my
mother talks about you like you was a baby or something."

"I'm not," Hebe said with a giggle and began to open the
bottle herself.

"You are crassee," remarked Rosalita watching her struggle
with the cork. She looked back at Margarita who stirred on the
couch, then reached out enthusiastically to help revealing that
one of her arms was considerably smaller and shorter than the
other one. She saw Hebe look at her arm. "I was born this way.
God made me different. Isn't that great?" she asked seriously
and holding out her arm looked at it and smiled, quite pleased
with it. Just then Margarita sat up sleepily from her siesta.
Seeing her, Hebe grabbed Rosalita by her hand and with the bottle
and corkscrew they breezed out of the door and blew down to the
cabana-striped umbrella Hebe had planted on the beach earlier and
sat down. They took turns pulling to get the stubborn cork out
of the bottle, but finally Rosalita gave it a mighty tug and it
popped out.

"Hebe," came Margarita's voice from the patio. Hebe showed
her face from under the umbrella and waved. "Hebe, you left
water all over the floor. Next time you clean up after
yourself," she scolded.

Hebe stood up and cupped her hands over her mouth, "Sorry.
I will." She watched as Margarita waved and went back in. "Your
mother's wonderful."

"Your mother's gorgeous."

"I'd rather have your mother."

"Why?"

"Oh, I don't know." She took another sip of the wine and
looked at the label then said in an artificial voice, "Excellent,
don't you agree?"

"What are you doing?" Rosalita asked.

"I don't know. That's what all the grown ups do. They take
a little then look at the glass, smell it and stuff. Then they
say things." She polished off her glass as did Rosalita. They
looked at each other already tipsy, giggled and raised their
empty glasses to one another and then roared in uncontrollable
laughter when they both uttered the same word, "Dahling." An old
man with a cane and a canvas fishing hat tottered slowly by and
looked curiously under the umbrella at the girls cutting off
their boistrous haw-hawing. But as soon as he passed by they
burst forth again even louder than before. Hebe got up but was
pulled to the sand by her mild intoxication. She tried to gain
her composure. Suddenly she seemed very distressed and whispered
loudly to Rosalita, "Give me the bottle. Do you think he saw?"
she asked turning her head toward the old man.

"No. He would 'a said something."
She followed Hebe who took the towel wrapped bottle and
zig-zagged down to a piece of driftwood on the beach where she
buried it with several other wine bottles. Rosalita stared in
disbelief.

"I like wine, but it's better if you mix it with orange
juice, or something."

"I've had vodka with orange juice, but never wine." They
were sitting on the piece of driftwood in the blazing sun.
"Let's go in the ocean," suggessted Hebe. And impulsively the
two charged off in an inebriated pre-adolescent gust of exhilarated running, tumbling and prancing down the stretch of beach.
Into the cool blue water they went playfully splashing and
frolicking in their first day of friendship.

Coming out if the water, Rosalita screamed, "My clothes!"
pulling her ocean drenched skirt away from her body and they

laughed until they were choking as she peeled off all but her underpants.

"You dummy," remarked Hebe causing her to chase after her and tackle her. She pulled off Hebe's bikini top and they rolled around in the warm, gritty sand. Finally she pinned Hebe down and lay on top of her.

"I give," shouted Hebe under Rosalita's cool wet body, her hair dripping into her face.

"I'm not a dummy," she said holding her harder.

"O.K. you're not a dummy," she conceded.

And with these words Rosalita let go, but remained on top of her. She looked down at her barely visible breasts on Hebe's flat chest and said happily, "Hey you know what this means? We're bosom buddies." They stood up and rubbed their nipples together, in a little wiggling dance, then walked arm in arm back to the water to wash off. In the water, beneath the naked blue sky, bees were buzzing in Hebe's head and the world became a pulsating yellow and white for an instant. From behind the fading veil of Chablis she exchanged a smile with her bosom buddy.

*****

Arithmetic usually confused Hebe, but the next day, it absolutely made her sick. She sat in class gazing out the window and pictured herself among the palms walking with her father or Hans. Why hadn't they called? Homesickness magnified by her hangover welled up inside of her and tears trickled out and onto her #5 subtraction problem. She slid the Thanksgiving turkey drawings she had colored in the morning class out from beneath the confusing math paper and began again to work a brown pencil over his plump, feathered outline. Completely absorbed, she didn't hear the teacher call on her, but she did hear the class laughing. Seeing her pale face when she got her attention, the teacher kindly asked her if she would like to go to the nurse. Hebe looked around the class at the other children. It was as if they were sitting in a fog, as if there were two days occurring at once, one inside and one outside. "Thank you," she said meekly and left the room.

Art came to pick her up. He had an angry tense look on his
face and she assumed he was in this mood because he had been
called away from work to come and get her. She felt sorry that
she had caused him trouble and she sat close to the passenger
side door. He reached over with a caring pat on her leg and
assured her that they would be home soon without changing his
expression. Without another word he steered them there, turned
off the ignition and toyed with the keys. Her mother's shouting
made her realize that she was probably not the reason for his ill
temper. "O.K. Hiawatha, just go inside and up to your room."

These simple instructions were not as easy to follow as they
sounded because in the multi-colored lights of the room she saw
Margarita being assailed by Gaye near the kitchen counter. It
was packed with pumpkins, bags of potatoes and cranberries and
the large gobbler half stuffed. In front of the holiday fixings
stood seven sand-mudded wine bottles. Gaye had a drink in her
hand and her manner of speaking made it clear that she was not
only angry but drunk. Hebe stopped in her steps.

"I thought you said you were sending her home."

"Not until she owns up to this."

"Señor," Margarita beckoned to Art. "No se nada."

"Speak English God dammit!" shouted Gaye striking her with
the palm of her hand across her face stunning Margarita more than
hurting her. Seeing her beautiful Margarita, singer of songs,
maker of cookies, mother of her bosom buddy being humiliated,
falsely accused and slapped, Hebe sprang across the room her arms
spinning like a small windmill and pommelled her mother. She
grabbed her child by the arms and pushed her to the floor.

"That will do Gaye," Art interrupted more loudly than she
had ever heard him speak. He helped Hebe to her feet.

"I drank the wine," she confessed in a shout. "Leave her
alone."

Margarita, vindicated but surprised whispered, "Was you
Hebe?" in disbelief. Gaye turned to Margarita, who dodged
another attack, and headed for the door with Art right behind her

offering apologies for his wife. Knowing her worth, he was
trying his best, even speaking Spanish.

Gaye spun around, grabbed Hebe by her hair and began to slap
her repeatedly. "Drinking wine! You're only seven years old."

"I'm almost eight," she announced and searched for her
mother's face. It was gone. In its place were the blazing green
eyes and flaring nostrils of a monster. She covered her own face
with her free hand and noticed that her nose was bleeding, or her
mouth. Alarmed, she screamed.

Art caught Gaye's arms from behind. "Get a hold of yourself.
What is happening to you? Gaye? Gaye!" he called to her as if
she were far away and he wanted her to come back. Hebe almost
saw her mother come back into her own eyes. They focused on her
daughter's bleeding face. She moved toward Hebe cognizant of
what she had done and filled with remorse. Hebe instinctively
moved back. Gaye got down on her knees with her finger tips to
her mouth and promised that she was not going to hurt her three
times before she could step forward to her. As they embraced,
Art took the wine bottles and threw them away. He rubbed his
forehead and gazed long and concernedly at his wife.

"Gaye, you shouldn't allow yourself to get out of control
like that. I've never seen you that way before."

She turned and Hebe saw her mother's sweet familiar face
answer, "I know. Forgive me. I don't know what came over me."

Art pulled the curtain dimming the carnival of lights from
their window and calm restored said, "Well, if you two are not
going to kill each other, I'm going back to work." He walked
over to Gaye and rubbed both of her shoulders and gazed adoringly
into her eyes. "Are you sure you're going to be all right?" She
nodded her head and he held her and spoke over her head into the
air. If I didn't know about you and your past and all that you've
been through Gaye, I swear I'd think you were just crazy." they
seem to have forgotten abut Hebe again.

"What about me and all I've been through?" she thought to
herself as she slunk up the stairs to tend to her wounds and
retreat to her room. She sat there holding her Davey Crocket

hat and her stuffed dog Rivet listening to the surf, letting the
dark fall around her. Called to dinner, she just remained seated
unwilling to move. She didn't want to see her mother, but being
a child she had no choice. Automatically, she reappeared in her
life, in her door bearing a tray with supper. It was one of her
favorites, paprika-chicken and potatoes. She didn't try to get
her to speak, but timidly sat the silver tray on the vanity, lit
a candle, turned out the light again and left her in peace. the
steam rose up in a small fog beneath the candle light and Hebe
noticed an envelope on the tray. Thinking it an apology from
Gaye, tenacity kept her from reaching for it and she closed her
eyes. The Blue Danube flowed in on the wake of a gentle flurry
redolent with Eucalyptus and the promise of rain. The gossamer,
voile curtain began lapping her face and she stood up and went to
the window where she saw her mother and Art dancing on the
terrace below. She wished she could dive from the window, an
invisible bird into their togetherness, not to break them apart,
but to dip into the love between them and catch just a few drops
on her downy wings.

She snatched the letter off tray. It wasn't from her mother
at all. It was from Brookline, Massachusetts, number 219 Warren
Street, an address she had never before seen. And when she
opened it, out fell a photograph of a motley group of people
which included her father and Hans and a couple of letters. They
wrote! They missed her! And most importantly, before the
signatures it said, "I love you." They thanked her for her
letters, and she learned that her father had joined the Merchant
Marines and had sailed on a ship to India and promised to write.
She also read that he had called, but she was always at school or
asleep. She wondered why her mother hadn't told her, but put the
question in the back of her mind in order to find their World
Atlas book.

India was on the other side of the world! She had an idea.
She would go there and meet him. In the other room she heard Jude
crying. She went to the window and called down in an angry
voice, "The baby's crying!" Art and Gaye were laughing and didn't

hear. She yelled, "Art! the baby's crying!" They got up and
walked inside.

Everything was working in her favor. Since Thanksgiving
vacation was coming up, she was told that she didn't have to go
to school the next day. She rode her bicycle into the travel
agency in town. The agent was entertained by her small client's
inquiry about passage to India and gave her all the information
she would need and told her to have her parents call when they
were ready to make the arrangements. She went to the soda
fountain at the drug store where she treated herself to rootbeer
float and tried to calculate how long it would take her to save
enough money. She sat befuddled by the figures and vowed to pay
close attention in math class. The teacher's words, "This is
something you will use in everyday life," were true after all.
She asked a man at the counter to check her calculations, and he
did. She sighed disheartened. Even if she saved every cent of
her $2.00 a week allowance, she would not have that much money
any time soon. Nevertheless, she would begin an armchair
exploration of the far off land. She decided to go to the
library.

Riding there, she thought she saw Art's big, black car
parked along the street. She rounded the corner to check because
she really wanted a lift. There he was standing with three other
men and a woman. His classic, dignified handsomeness attracted
the subtle flirtatious glimpses of a couple of women who passes
by, and he acknowledged them with a wink. She compared him to
the other men next to him who were about the same age. Although
he was certainly the best looing among them, he just didn't
appear attractive in her eyes. The images of him in Boston
sneaking in the back door, sitting in her father's chair, lying
in her father's bed had damaged her vision of him despite his
kindness to her. She was certain he would give her a ride if she
asked, so she watched waiting for a moment to interrupt. The men
shook hands and walked away.

Art opened the car door for the woman. hebe peddled as
quickly as she could and arrived on the driver's side of the car

just as he was about to pull away. The woman was sitting so
close to Art that her enormous, cartwheel hat brushed his face.
Seeing Hebe, she distanced herself by scooting toward the
passenger's side and looking away.

"Hey kiddo," he greeted her. Brushing the woman's fingers
off his arm, he introduced her, "This is my," he paused. "Um
this is one of the firm's clients, Miss Gonzales." She was quite
tan and had dramatic black eyebrows. Nodding her head slightly
in greeting, she turned up the ends of her long, full mouth in a
pleasant smile, then began nervously searching in her purse.
"Are you feeling better today?" Art asked lighting a cigarette
and tapping his ring on the steering wheel.

"Sure," Hebe answered.

"Art, do you have my lighter?" Miss Gonzales had the rich
calm voice of a pampered woman of leisure. Hebe watched her
white-gloved hand touch her stepfather's as he held his lighter
under her cigarette.

"Did your mother tell you it was o.k. to ride your bike all
this way?" Hebe looked at the ground. He reached out and patted
her hand. "We'll, if she finds out," he winked. "I'll tell her I
said it was o.k." There it was, the kindness, she thought.
Since he said he was in a hurry, she didn't ask for a ride.

"Thanks," was all she said, as she covered her eyes from the
sun to watch the car drive off.

That night, she obsessively poured over the images of India
in her library books: crowds of people, women swaddled in thin
cloth; open markets beneath dust-filled air; bony, cows ambling
in unpaved streets; words about princes and princesses; the
magnificent Taj Mahal. Then, she settled down to read about the
place she thought would be her father's new world in, Kiplings's
The Jungle Book.

Weeks and months went by with no word from her father. She
didn't even have an address for him anymore. Fearing he may have
been devoured by a ferocious Bengal tiger, or that he had quite
simply forgotten about her, she wrote to Hans.

"My Dear Little Sister," began his reply giving her the

details of his life in Boston, his new found "creative friends,"
and how wonderfully he was progressing at her father's alma
mater, MIT. The letters were kept with Gordy's in a laquered
Japanesse box which was tied up with a large pink ribbon. They
sat in plain sight on the corner of the desk under the map of her
father's destinations, all their post cards, some photographs and
a children's rhyme in Dutch.

    Hik sprik sprouw,
    Ik geef de hik aan jou;
    Geef de hik aan een ander man,
    Die de hik verdragen kan
    Iikh ben het.

Most of the cards were from Hans. There was little news of Gordy
other than Hans' comments that he remembered her and certainly
missed her. "Some people are just not writers," he once wrote.
She came to know and like Hans better and better, and her
correspondence with him bridged the incredible geographic and
temporal distance between her and Gordy which expanded through
the years.

FIVE

COMING OF AGE

"No la chava!"

San Diego, California

December 22,1957-March 13,1958

The post card she had finally received from her father in
1954 was, indeed, from India. Amazingly, it arrived on her
eighth birthday, November 30. It was a picture of a woman in a
sari. Though dated weeks or months earlier, one of his post
cards or notes always arrived on her birthday. In 1955, when she
turned nine, one arrived from Port Said, Egypt, a black and white
card of a man on a camel near the great pyramids. But in 1956,
instead of a post card, Gordy sent a note with a photograph of
himself dressed in flowing white robes in the foreground of a
vast desert. He said there had been no post cards in Ras Tanura,
Saudia Arabia. This year, 1957, for her 11th birthday, one
arrived from Port Moresby, New Guinea post marked six months
earlier. Gordy had written that it was one of the most beautiful
places he had ever seen. On the top corner of the note he had
sketched a small kangaroo and the page was covered with drawings

of butterflies. She cherished it, and wondered from where the
next one would be sent. There was no end to his cards. Each one
sent her off for more books and launched her into another armchair exploration.

For nearly three years she had been tracking her father's
voyages on the large map of the world on her wall. At one point,
she decided to tie the cards on little ribbons, so she could
reread the texts whenever she wanted. She also hung the assorted
souvenirs he occasionally sent, scarves, paper money, a lizard
pouch, even a string of bells. Taped beneath the map by her bed
were many notes and photographs from both her father and Hans.

Her favorite was a recent addition, a large black and white
picture of Gordy and Hans wearing berets and black turtle neck
sweaters. Two women, were slunk in chairs on either side of the
men. One was a young blonde sticking out her tongue, and the
other, a petite brunette blowing a kiss from her upturned palm.
A third woman was stretched out on the ground at their feet with
an artists paint brush in one hand and a cigarette holder in the
other. Everyone was smoking. Gordy, in the middle, held a book
titled, When We are Here Together by Kenneth Patchen. And that
was her favorite part of the picture, the title and the
hand-written message "We love you Hebe Jeebie. From Ali Baba's,
Charles Street, Boston, July 3, 1957. Gaye told her to take the
picture down.

"Gordy's back ther making a fool of himself, documenting it
by having his picture taken with obvious, "subversives and
beatniks." Probably reading that censured Ginsberg garbage.
'Pubic beards,' How vulgar," she nearly gargled the words sipping
back her third Bloody Mary.

"Why do you insist on bringing up Gordy? What could his
philosophy possibly matter at this point? Besides, Ginsberg
isn't censured. He won," Art informed her.

"Just because you went to Harvard, doesn't mean you know
everything."

"Gaye-Lee it was all over the press that.."

"You can't tell me."

Art knew when she was drinking, she was not to be contradicted, but he couldn't stand being wrong. When she tottered downstairs to fill her glass with more proof, he formulated his in his head and followed right along behind her.

Instead of taking the picture down, it had the most prominent place in Hebe's room because she felt very close to them. They were ever present in her, in that special place reserved for loved ones left behind. They were tangible in all the things they had sent her; books, a miniature telescope and a chart of the stars, a camera and most recently, a portable record player.

One day, she received a package marked "do not open until Christmas." Her childish enthusiasm ripped it open five minutes after she decided she would take it down and place it under the Christmas tree. It was a sweater, but she was much taller than they had guessed. Now, at eleven, she stood 5'7" in her stocking feet. Except for the too-short sleeves, it fit; she just pushed them up. It was black like the others' tops. She imagined that she would fit into the photograph perfectly; it was fabulous. Standing at the top of the stairs, she anticipated her mother's disapproval. But height had made her bold because she noticed that the taller she got the less she seemed to get hit. In addition, the half foot advantage made dodging much easier when Gaye-Lee did slap at her.

No one heard her arrival because the osterizer was crushing and whirling ice into a cocktail. The appliance was Art's early Christmas present to Gaye, and partly to himself because concoting and sampling exotic, alcoholic potions had become their new joint hobby. Hebe stood on the catwalk a quarter of the way down the forty foot room and admired the giant Christmas tree spanning to the railing and unfurling into the room. She adjusted the star on top sending a ripple down through the branches where Art was hanging tinsel and singing along to Bing Crosby's "White Christmas". Art turned his eyes upward and stopped, captivated by the stunning appearance of Hebe in this form fitting sweater and a dash of make-up. As she started down the stairs, his eyes ran over her from head to toe, then he let out a small wolf whistle. The osterizer stopped and Gaye poured the frothy, mint green cream into two glasses and said, "Black? A black sweater on a child? I think not." She didn't look at her daughter's face but at her firm young breasts. "Besides, it doesn't fit properly. Return it back to whomever you...,"

"Daddy's friend Hans sent it to me," she said modeling for Art. "You think it looks nice, don't you?"

Art flicked his glance to Gaye glaring at him then back to Hebe and shrugged.

"Would those crystal ornaments be in the box upstairs?" he asked steering clear of involvement and attempting to prevent a quarrel.

Gaye grabbed at her arm, but she pulled away "You're sending it back." She was poised for battle.

"O.K. I just want to wear it tonight," she shot out quickly before darting down to the basement level recreation room to watch Jude riding his tricycle.

He squeeled in delight to see her; he always did. They only had good times together. And she could always depend on him for a hug. Sometimes he would climb right up onto her, hold her around her neck and rest his head near her face for a very long time. Perfectly serene, they would breathe in unison. Once in a while, they would take a nap snuggled together.

Other times, they exerted their youthful energy in games of catch or tag on the beach. Jude would become so excited, he turned into an inexhaustable two-legged locomotive running wild all over the place. All she could do was sit and watch him. He enjoyed showing off for her.

"Hebe. Hebe, watch what I can do." Then, he'd throw a ball and catch it or run really fast. Whatever he did, once was never enough. To do it meant to do it again and again and again and again. Tonight, he was riding his tricycle through the room, out the doors, around the pool and back again. Everytime he went by her he'd giggle.

"Oh, Jude, that's really fast."

It sounded as if the osterizer hit the floor and she looked up at the ceiling. She wished she could say something to her mother to make her stop, anything. She never did, neither did Art. In order to keep her mother's opinions from snowballing into violent fireworks, they stifled answers, hid their true feelings and sometimes lied. Jude went by. She smiled. A shrill argumentative scream from above pierced Jude. He sat stalk still, bent his head over and began to cry.

"Don't cry Jude." She held her startled, little brother. Suddenly, Rachmaninoff was blaring through the floor and she knew it was time to go outside because he was the composer they played the most when their discussions were plastered in the house. Their voices were not obscurred by the massive, exuberant music in the least. On the contrary, their row dominated it.

"Bet you can't catch me." She called out distracting Jude from the unsettling clamor, and raced outside with Jude right on her heels. From under a piece of driftwood near the house, she pulled out a bottle of wine while Jude eagerly threw himself into running back and forth, she watched and sipped and slowly let go of the fear that had followed her from the house. It felt good to be out in the air. She wanted to take Jude, to run away somewhere, anywhere, but she couldn't.

They lived so far away from everything and everyone. None of her school relationships even had the chance to become friend- ships because they lived so far out. Declared by her mother too young to sleepover, she was cooped up on the outskirts of town. They were all mixed up in the giant osterizer of a house. How she wished some big hand would come and pour them all out, let the foam of their lives blend with that of the sea and thus be washed away, maybe to some foreign shore where she would be reunited with her father and the fairy tale life they had once upon a time.

Babysitting Jude the next morning, a chance for escape happened to ride up the in a big, red convertable with Margarita. From the front steps she watched him cooly leap out and lean over into the back and get the packages Margarita had brought. His back was as long and powerful as his legs, and his black shirt which was unbuttoned nearly to his belt was tucked in at his small waist,the short sleeves rolled up over his muscular arms. Just looking at his high cheekbones and his full square jaw, a totally new sensation flooded her body and made her blood run faster. It was like being a hot, butter-filled, baked potato, and as he strutted behind Margarita, bags in his arms she felt the oven get hotter. The distinct aroma of Agua Lavanda and bubble gum filled the air when he came near.

Margarita was all touches and kisses as she passed by and into the house. She stopped and with a wave of her rebozo gushed, "Oh Hebe. Mira, is my son, Tony. He come back from Mexico." She kissed her son's bare arm and pinched his cheek as if he were a baby. Then she gestured proudly to the car, "Si, and is the car of Tony." Tony lifted up his dark sunglasses, gazed at Hebe with his coal black eyes and reached down to shake her hand with a gentle grasp and a carress of her wrist with his thumb. And with that the potato burst and the butter seeped out. He abated his steady gum chewing long enough to say, "Mucho Gusto." Hebe remained speechless and immobile. He tipped his head allowing his sunglasses to fall back in place on his face before following his mother into the house. He paused and held the door open assuming Hebe was coming too. She stuck her chin up in the air and swished girlishly under his arm and inside. He gave out a little amused grunt. Margarita oohed and aahed at the Christmas tree exclaiming that it was the most beautiful she had ever seen in that house. "Oh Dios!" she exclaimed. "Azucar, Oh and...," she stopped and scratched several items on a piece of paper, then snapped the paper out in front of Tony. "No foolin' around. I need thees thins. Ju con right back," she started then turned to Hebe. "I wan you to go with heem." And with that order, Hebe was sent out to a new world.

With Margarita's description of exactly what she needed in her head, she excitedly bolted out to the shiny, red automobile. But she had to wait for Tony. He stepped out into the cloudy day and strutted down the walkway as if he were a movie star, turning his head casually from one side to the other to see if anyone was looking at him. There was no one around. He pulled a small comb out of his pocket and smoothed it through his thick, black hair. Boldy he placed his hands around her middle and picked her up to lower her into the passenger's seat. Another potato started cooking in Hebe's oven. Her breath disappeared as she dangled there for a second before he slowly inserted her into place with a snap of his gum. She fanned herself from the heat, and glanced up to see if the sun had come out. It hadn't.

He combed his hair again, turned the ignition, and stepped on the gas. "Oh no, wait!" she cried. He lifted up his sunglasses and waited. "I need my sunglasses," she said. He moved the car forward and popped the glove compartment open revealing two pairs. She took one and put them on.

Thrilled, she kneeled on the seat and leaned over the windshield letting the air break over her face as they sped along the road beneath the canopy of trees. The wind whipped her skirt wildly. Her little red panties caught Tony's eye. He reached over and smoothed her skirt down allowing his fingers to run over her soft-skinned thigh. She turned around. Her house was completely out of sight. Suddenly, he hit the brakes on purpose to throw her back into her seat. She went into a fit of happy laughter. Still chewing, he moved his glasses down his nose and seeing her merry reaction, broke into a full grin completely amused by her behavior. "You're nutty. I've never seen a chick wig over a car ride before. Let's do it!" He floored the accelerator and the car streaked down the highway like a stroke of delible paint. It was the first of many which began to paint her out of the dull, restrained corner of the world where she lived.

The trips that followed usually took her to Margarita's house to visit Rosalita. Though the house was small compared to her's, it was located in the middle of a street lined with pink and white houses, filled with neighbors, mostly Mexicans. Loud Spanish was tossed through the streets and the same loud voices could be heard inside of the houses above blaring televisions and

music, spicy, rythmic music that filled her body and made her
move with it. Margarita's house was overflowing with her tribe,
Tony, Rosalita, two young cousins, Chico and José and their
friends. In their presence, Hebe discovered she was shy,
especially in comparison to Rosalita. When their boyish rough
housing toppled lamps or escalated into a bonafide fight, she
only had to slap her hands together and say, "Favor!" and they
would desist.

Now that she was thirteen, Rosalita's mother banished the
male cousins to sofabeds on the porch, and gave her a room to
herself. There, she and Hebe whiled away the hours reading
magazines, doing one another's hair, sewing, or most importantly,
talking about boys. Rosalita had a crush on a high school boy, a
senior classmate of Tony's whom he introduced her to at the soda
fountain in town. She was certain he liked her simply by the way
he smiled at her. "I want him to ask me to the dance," she
gurgled applying the finishing touches to Hebe's make-up.

"What dance?" Hebe asked wincing as her eyebrows were
plucked.

"Don't be a baby," she told Hebe. "You have to get used to
little pains. It's the price we girls pay to get the boys." Then
answered her, "How do I know what dance? Any dance. I'd go dance
in the parking lot with him just to look into his pretty eyes."
And with a finishing touch of mascara, she turned Hebe around to
look at herself in the vanity mirror.

Hebe was looking into the mirror, but she didn't see
herself. In her place was an older girl, a much prettier girl.
At first she was uncomfortable. Little by little she started to
like it. "And, favor, don't sit like that all sloppy," Rosalita
advised her. She showed her how to sit and even how to hold a
guy's hand when he lit her cigarette. Even though she didn't
smoke much, she payed close attention. Her friend had a free
life, did what she wanted and had boyfriends. Hebe wanted to be
just like her.

In the family album she saw the population of Garcias: the
aunt and uncle in Mexico with whom Tony had been living;

Margarita's parents who had passed away; the paternal
grandparents who lived in Northern California; a crazy uncle; a
spinster aunt; ten married aunts and uncles and more cousins than
she could keep track of. Then there was a picture of Rosalita in
a short bride's dress. "Holy cow! were you married?"

"No," she tutted at Hebe's ignorance. "That's my
confirmation. Didn't you have a confirmation in the church?"

"No," Hebe answered a little sadly. For the first time she
lamented not saying her prayers when her mother insisted. "I'd
love to wear a dress like that."

Out of the closet it came. For fun she tried it on and
Rosalita put on the new red, ruffled dress she was making for her
fantasy date with the high school boy. Rosalita made her put the
dress on with the back zipper in front to make room for her
breasts, "You're gonna get all the boys with these boobies," she
commented making Hebe blush. Rosalita stood in seductive poses in
the mirror. "That's how you do it," she stated.

"Do what?" Hebe asked innocently.

They stole out of the room and across the hall into another.
It was dark; the windows were closed, and the stale air was a
mixture of perspiration, cigarette smoke, bubble gum and cologne,
like Tony. They were in his room. She felt his tense cool energy.
Rosalita turned the old metal key locking the door and produced a
bottle and a few magazines from under the bed. She took a
healthy gulp from the bottle and handed it to Hebe joining her on
the bed. In the bottom of the bottle there was a drowned bug, or
something. Closer examination proved it to be a swollen worm.
Repulsed, but wanting to do what her friend did, she put the
bottle to her mouth and swallowed her disgust with a mouthful of
the golden mezcal. In the Playboy magazines, she saw the
guidelines for Rosalita's poses. Liquor loosened, she posed with
her. In the dark room, they muffled their giddiness under the
quiet sighs of their dresses until their jubilant spirits
overtook them and they began dancing and ended up jumping on the
bed. Down they tumbled into an untidy heap of limbs and cloth
momentarily embracing and falling on top of each other, they

panted catching their breath, then gasped in unison.

The key clinked on the floor; Tony leaned his tall form cockily in the doorframe. The other boys in the house gaggled behind him, and he yelled at them, "I didn't invite you in here." They scrambled off, and Rosalita and Hebe tried to do the same. Rosalita made it to her room and peered out as he grabbed Hebe by her arm and held her. Feeling her fear, he loosened his grip, but he still held her firmly. "I didn' mean to scare you, Mamazita," he paused for a moment his eyes surveyed her face and moved over her body with the deliberate inspection of a rancher purchasing a colt. He leaned over and sniffed the nape of her neck. "I just want see if you are the girl I brung here."

"You see, it's me," she announced meekly.

"That's a lot of make-up," he said with his eyelashes almost touching hers. He fired a glance at Rosalita's door and she shot back inside. Finally, he let go of her arm. She didn't move. The two stood in a small magnetic field of mutual attraction. He jerked back and started putting his magazines away. "Well, I'm supposed to be take you home now."

Quickly, she washed her face and changed into her own clothes reverting back to a young girl, but Tony's earlier image of her had not left his mind. The big blade of a car ripped open the cool evening air as it tore down the street while the sinking sun casting an orange glow over them. Neither spoke. Each was surreptitiously stealing glances of the other, then they did it at the same time. In that brief moment, he smiled and Hebe saw the sun split into two stars in each of Tony's sunglass lenses. She scooted over on the seat next to him. She could hear him chewing his gum. They drove onto a small road which led to the only house around, a big, stucco mansion on top of a hill. Arriving in front of the big iron gate, he stopped. She watched his carmel mouth come closer. Just as their lips met, he slid his hand between her thighs.

"Stop," she squeeled and pulled away.

He looked surprised, "Don't you want to kiss me?"

She took his gum out of her mouth which she wiped with the

back of her arm making an unpleasant face. He laughed and honked
the horn. The gatekeeper opened the gates and they entered the
curving driveway and parked in front of the house. Immediately,
a woman appeared in the brightly lit entranceway. Tony got
several large packages from the trunk and took them into the
house. She followed him back to the car. As she stood there
telling him to have the car filled up and washed, Hebe saw her
face clearly. Her distinctive eyebrows were those of the woman
she had seen with her Art when she had ridden her bike into town
and the many times thereafter when she and her mother had dropped
by for lunch, or just money. She was never sitting behind the
desk. She always seemed to be leaving just as they were
arriving. Hebe thought she was very rude because she never spoke
to her mother.

"Hello," Hebe said. The woman acted as though she had
never laid eyes on her, just turned away, dusted Tony's shoulder,
put some money in his pocket and hurried into the house.

"That's my stepfather's client," she remarked as the drove
back through the gates.

"Mrs. Gonzales? I am not surprised. All the rich men seem
to have a service for pretty womans, especially when is the wife
of one of the wealthiest landowners in this area." Then he added
sheepishly, "In fact, this is one of her cars." He opened a new
stick of gum.

They didn't say anything for the rest of the way to her
house. When they arrived, he took his gum out of his mouth and
kissed her again by nibbling gently on her upper lip. She closed
her eyes. His hard knuckles nudge at the edge of her panties. By
the time she opened her eyes she was simmering in a delicious
steam as her body responded to his touch. He stopped her and
whispered, "How old are you anyway, Chica?"

"Eleven," she answered with a smile.

"Puta madre!" he exclaimed slamming his palms against his
cheekbones. He emitted a grunt and slumped his body forward
accidentally dropping his head on the horn. The sound snapped him
upright and he looked at the sky. "Me lleva la chingada."

"What?" she asked moving closer. He didn't touch her; he adjusted the rear view mirror.

"Well, I used to be ten," she offered sweetly. He didn't move. "So don't you like me any more?"

"Oh, mi amor. Are you kidding? Tony likes all pretty girls," he assured her placing his arm around her and repeating "eleven," several times tracing the outline of each of her breasts with his finger. "Is that you have eleven, and I have seventeen," he announced with great conviction. "I am a man."

"I have another friend who is a man." She went in her pink plastic pocketbook and pulled out a small snapshot of her and Hans in Franklin Park triggering an instant sense of possession and jealousy in his Mexican heart.

He snatched it from her. " Tha's no man! Is a woman."

She snatched it back and moved to get out of the car curtly thanking him for the ride. He quickly caught her by the waist and laughed.

"Mamasita wait. I was kidding." He checked his hair in the rear view mirror. Then he asked, "Did you ever kiss him?"

"He's my friend I told you. I never kissed any boy before. Couldn't you tell?

"Of course," he lied. "That's why I give you the kiss. I know is good if I am the first. One night we will go to the party together. But you can't tell nobody that you have only eleven, o.k. Chica?"

"I won't," she promised. Eagerly, she held her face up to be kissed again, and she got out of the car feeling more intoxicated than when she had gotten in. Her face was flush, her body glowing. She knew she must have walked up the path in order to be standing at the front door, but she didn't remember her feet touching the ground. It was as if she had floated there. She paused. She was really late. Thinking about her mother, the ground slammed up against her feet. Her shoes became two heavy weights which she dragged into the house.

She was ready for anything Gaye could have said, but Gaye didn't say anything, not one word. Hebe recognized the theme to

the television program <u>The Twighlight Zone</u>. The golden cross
around her mother's neck twinkled in the light of the television
as she sat staring at it with Jude resting his sleeping head on
her lap. Her arm moved to bring the jumbo cocktail to her lips;
her glazed eyes were riveted to the set as if she, herself were
lost in a twighlight zone. Even though she knew Gaye was aware
of her presence, she held her breath and watched her face as
closely as a rabbit passing by a mountain lion because she didn't
know if her mother was herself or the alcohol sucking beast who
lived inside of her. Since not one muscle of her face moved in
the maternal welcome she sometimes received, she decided it best
to creep past. Suddenly, the glassy, eyeballs of the monster
grew large, rolled in their sockets and landed on her. She stood
as still as the ticking clock. She didn't flinch or breathe.
She consciously tried to stop her heart from pounding for fear
that the monster would hear it and attack. Then, the eyeballs
rolled back toward the screen as if they hadn't even seen her.
Immediately, she soft-heeled up to her room.

She expected to be castigated the next day, but she wasn't.
Several days later at breakfast, Gaye still had not spoken to
her, not even to return her morning greeting. She concluded that
her mother's silence was the punishment. She asked Art what she
should do.

"I didn't notice anything odd, Kiddo. She seems her usual
self to me," he replied.

When Margarita arrived, she asked her for advice.

She listened very carefully, then offered her a riddle.
"Sometimes el antídoto para un virus es lo mismo virus. You know
the tit for the tat," she advised.

Heeding Margarita's sage words, Hebe stopped trying to talk
to her mother. For three days, they ghosted around as if
invisible to one another. Tony had gone to Mexico City, so she
was back in her corner of the world. Up in her room, she
contentedly occupied herself with her books and her new pastime,
sewing. Tony did't say exactly when he was taking her to a
party, but she wanted to be ready, so she started to make a

dress. She really missed him. She missed the warm, loving familial fold of the Garcia household; the loud, demonstrative welcome; the laughter; the harmless bickering of the boys; the big out-of-doors voices; the click of the cousins playing dominoes; the smell of tortillas and rice and beans cooking. For it was there, amid the din of life being lived with boisterous deliberation that she could make herself up in Rosalita's room, and emerge a pretty, powdered Latina to take her place in the portrait of a close, south-of the-border family. Endearingly, they called her "Hebita" and treated her like one of their extended clan. She was asked her opinion; needed to help out with cooking and cleaning; beckoned to participate in singing songs and watching their favorite television show, I Love Lucy. Whenever Ricky Ricardo spoke in rapid Spanish, they would translate for her and explain why it was funny. She was loved and cared for and had a sense of belonging.

She wished she could take them all to Boston with her, or bring her father and Hans and his little dog, Lucky to California, to have her heart in one place rather than on the two separated coasts of the country. Although, she wasn't all together certain where her father was at this time; his last post card came from Hamburg, Germany. Sewing a heart on the skirt of her yellow, dotted-Swiss, party dress she reread Han's last letter which closed with, "We're all living in a big house together now. So if you ever need a place to come. We're waiting." She let her fingers rest for a moment and listened to Margarita humming downstairs. Looking around at the memorabilia from Boston and thinking about her Mexican family could not fill the emptiness, reduce the lonliness born of being immured in her room. It was Wednesday; Saturday, Tony would return. But these few days passed as slowly as a month in which she sat and watched the hands of the clock ticking away the time second by second. An unseen hand had reached into her being and held her spirit tightly in its hand. After a while. she didn't want to sew or read or talk to her little brother, or even eat. Dutifully, she went to school where she stayed withdrawn. At home she gazed out of the window. It was as if the world had come to a stop except for the gulls screeching and diving at the sea mirroring the dismal grey, sky of eternal summer's winter.

Saturday, the hand released her spirit. Gaye spoke to her and Tony arrived; the world was spinning again. Not only did they enjoy an Elysian afternoon at the Garcia house but also he told her that this was the night for the party. Learning that Hebita was going out with her older brother, Rosalita was bubbling with excitement. Immediately, she began to see into the distant future when she would be her sister-in-law, and they would have children who would be friends. The problem was that she wasn't sure whom she wanted to marry herself; there were so many candidates. Hebe's problem was that she hadn't finished her party dress.

Wrapped up in that single thought, she had Tony drop her off, forgetting to take off her make-up and undo her French twist which she always wore at the Garcia's. No one was home when she arrived. She spurted up stairs and began stitching without a moment's delay. The main seams were done; a little hand finishing and it would be complete. She became totally absorbed in the task.

On the path outside, Jude led the way for Margarita as she escorted a cheerfully boozed up Gaye. "Now I know why that drink is a Side Car," she pointed out indicating that she was beside Margarita," who couldn't quite follow the logic since she wasn't familiar with the meaning of the word, sidecar. "Don't you get it?" she spewed. "Mar ga ri ta," she almost sang the syllables out several times. "Jude, Dahling go ride your tricycle while Mommy takes a si es ta," she checked her pronunciation with brief reference to Margarita's face which approved. While Jude ran off as requested, they trudged across the large room through the great number of rainbows made by the enormous window, and ascended the stairs. Margarita tried to guide her to her room, but seeing Hebe's door ajar Gaye pushed it open. She didn't see Hebe; she saw a stunning, young, teenage girl in a fitted green dress with her hair in a French twist sitting on her daughter's

bed sewing. Sensing trouble, Margarita tried to gently direct
her toward the master bedroom with a jovial, "Maybe Señora would
like the bath before siesta." Gaye shrugged her off and stood on
her own two feet gaping at Hebe in disbelief. Hebe kept her eyes
on a spot on the floor.

"Who are you? And what the Hell are you doing in my house!"
asked Gaye genuinely not recognizing her own daughter. "I'm
talking to you!" she commanded. Hebe raised her eyes and to her
horror, she didn't see her mother anymore than she saw her. The
flaming, green-eyed, liquor-breathing monster was frothing at the
mouth, poised in front of her cornered prey for the fusillade.
Her speech was slurred and her voice as loud as an actors in a
very large theatre as she tottered unsteadilly back and forth in
front of the young woman whom she finally saw as her daughter.

"Are you going to a costume party? Are you putting on a play
up here all by yourself? Are you playing dress up? That's what
I hope you are going to tell me. You are an eleven-year-old
girl. And to think, my mother wanted me to send you to a
finishing school back east. No one would have you. Just who the
Hell are you supposed to be?" she asked in a pitch and volume
which was straining the veins in her neck and reddening her face.

"I think she was just playing with my Rosalita, practicing
to be like the ladies....," Margarita began in attempt to defend
her.

"Ladies!" Gaye bellowed. "Of the night! Tramps. That's why
I didn't want her going over there to your house with your, your
primitives. Don't think I don't know about you people. Her
father's one of you," she threw her comment in Margarita's
direction, then looked at the wall. " She's going to have a hard
enough time being a half-breed. You see the news. You know
what's going on all across the country with the coloreds,
Lynching 'em down in Little Rock. I tried to keep her away from
that, to give her the better of her two halves, my half," she
placed her long finger near her throat and held her head up high.
"Now what am I going to do? Look at her!" She grabbed Hebe's
face and showed it to Margarita who hung her head down

subserviently mute.

A thought lifted her head and she said, "I don't know. I think los two halves are good Señora. In July, this year, the negro girl, Gibson, she won the Wimbeldon. Maybe Hebe gonna do something too. Always you say the Hebe, she is like the Maria Tallchief in,"

As she was exchanging a smile with Hebe, Gaye snapped back, "What do you know about me and my family?"

Wanting to prevent her from possibly firing Margarita again, Hebe instantly took a very deep breath, rose up to the five foot nine stature that her high heels gave her, looked down at Gaye and whispered in a meek, quavering, voice, "Mother, stop it," she paused, then added, "Please." Gaye raised both of her arms to attack, but sobriety, added to height, gave Hebe the advantage for a moment as she caught her arms and pushed her down on the bed. Margarita was pleading for them not to fight, but when Hebe, who had become enraged herself, picked up a five-pound jar of cream from her dresser to throw at her mother, Margarita screamed out, ran across the battlefield of the bedroom and stood in front of her with her stolid body.

"Hebe, ¡Déjate de eso! Control yourself. Don't do anything crazy."

Gaye was unattractively sprawled across the bed and was accidentially stuck by one of the pins in Hebe's dress. "What's this?" she asked holding up the heart-pocketed dress with an evil sneer. Without waiting for an answer, she ripped it again and again.

"No! My dress. God don't. I made it by hand," Hebe bawled as a force deep in her heart pulsed hot-blooded fury through her.

Margarita restrained Hebe, calming her with, "You have to forget about it right now. I'm so sorry. You are a smart girl. you can make another one. She is drunk, your mother." Hebe saw Margarita's kind dark face, but she didn't hear her until she started to vigorously rub her hands. A tingling sensation went through her arms, and she heard her name and Margarita urging her, "Run outside Hebe. Run!"

She kicked of her heels, and burst out of the room, out of the house down the cool, wet sand on the beach. The brisk, winter wind whipped her updo free and her hair flew out behind her. She ran herself breathless, then kicked the winter cold water and yelled at the sea. The Irish setter, she sometimes saw, charged out of nowhere and stood beside her barking at the waves and wagging his tail as if her were imitating her. Diverted by his sudden accompaniment, she bent over and patted him. He sat down and licked her face when she knelt beside his warm, furry body. He didn't bark or bolt around, but stayed panting, eyes straight ahead as if he were joining her in watching the wildly rolling sea.

That evening, much to her relief, Art was either taking Gaye to see On the Waterfront or to a company dinner, at least that's what Margarita had told her. In either case, they would be gone the entire evening, reducing the chance of another conflict. The last drink"for the road" was being crushed up in the blender when Art came to her door and lit a cigarette. He had never come to her room before. He had a vexed looked on his face as he stood there smoking. Then he gave a little chuckle and began, "I don't know what goes on around here when I'm not here. I do know it has to stop." She crossed her arms and turned to watch the water rippling in the swimming pool below as he continued. " If you can't stop upsetting your mother...," She spun around and searched for his eyes, but he kept examining the jewel of his cigarette. "Well, we're thinking it might be best for all parties concerned that you be relocated. We think, perhaps, you would get along better with Grandmother Wilkinson, in Boston." Hebe couldn't believe her ears. He cleared his throat. "Also, we think, if you do stay, you should try to cultivate friendships with some people who are," he chuckled again to himself, "more in keeping with the social position of our family. O.K. Kiddo?" And without waiting for a peep from her, he flicked his cigarette ash into his palm, then casually strolled down the hall.

Dumbfounded by his proposal, she brooded over her future. She couldn't believe they wanted to send her to Grandmother

Wilkinson, or that the grande dame would want her to come and live in her house. She shuddered envisioning marching interminably though the streets of Boston behind Grandmother Wilkinson in search of an old edition of some book, or the perfect hat, constantly banished from her conversations in counterside chairs. Since arriving on the west coast, she had only heard from her directly, once a year when she sent a birthday card. She always included her name in other holiday greetings, but had never once asked to speak to her when she called, or wrote to her personally. A mutual drowning of one another in the waters of oblivion had been permitted in light of the time and distance between them, and Grandmother Wilkinson was no more than a flourishing, falsely sentimental, signature on her cards. She didn't want to go and live with her. Clearly, if she wanted to remain in the familiar volatility of life as she knew it in California, she would have to try to avoid her mother. She remembered how smoothly all went during the days her mother had stopped talking to her. What she couldn't figure out was how to give up the place she had so joyfully filled in her surrogate family, the Garcias. She would have to keep away from them too.

At first, she wanted to because she didn't know how to tell them, face to face, that she had been asked to give them up on the grounds that they weren't considered good enough for her to socialize with. Painfully, she declined phone calls, refrained from sending messages, as she once did, and refused invitations extended by Margarita whom she still saw everyday. She attended classes, and returned home where she made an effort to be non-existant. She became but a passing shadow going to the beach or the pool, spending time with Jude, or ascending to her room where she poured over her books, corresponded to Hans and tried to forget about her friends, nearby. She took her dream coin out and put it under her pillow hoping it would call her steed to her. More than ever, she wanted to ride him through the sky, to have the exhilarating sensation of galloping in the wind. She envisioned him before she fell asleep, but he didn't come to her. In the morning when she awakened, all she remembered was darkness.

A few weeks later, she recieved a letter in the mail from
Rosalita. Amid the hand-drawn hearts and flowers was an apology
for whatever it was she had done to hurt her and make her stay
away, and expressions that told her they all loved her and missed
her and hoped to see her soon. Attempts to write back to her and
explain failed; she couldn't find the words. She decided she had
to see those who cared about her.

Friday, she called home and uneasilly lied to one of her
favorite people, Margarita, claiming her entire class had to stay
after, and she would be late. She rode the schoolbus as far as
town. There, she walked to the park to think over whether or not
she should go to Rosalita's because if she got caught, the
consequences would be very serious. Sitting on a bench a short
distance from the playground, she watched a very, old man
lumbering down the path being led by a beagle puppy which looked
just like Hans' dog, Lucky. She took out her Brownie camera
which she had brought along to take souvenir photos of her
friends on this day, probably the last day she would ever see
them. With the action of snapping a picture of the frisky pup,
the man considered himself invited to conversation. He tipped
his worn, hat. Two big, round blue eyes shone in his deeply
wrinkled face. He wheezed thanking her for interrupting the dog
from his eager trotting and started a brief history of how he had
acquired the four-legged companion when a woman walked up.

"Hello." Her voice was so soft and melodic that the word
floated from her lips and brushed Hebe's ears with the softness
of roses. It was hard to say what she looked like. Her short,
pale-blonde hair was in a flip which peeked out from beneath the
scarf covering her head. Even from behind her large, dark
glasses, she radiated an angelic quality. "Do you want me to take
a picture of you with the puppy?" she offered shyly. After
emitting a variety of noises from the strain of sitting, he posed
with Hebe holding the beagle, licking her nose.

"How about you girls together," he took the camera in his
shaky hands. The woman removed her glasses. "Everybody say

cheese, and for goodness sakes stay still. I'm going to hold my
breath to steady the camera." He did hold his breath, but his
trick didn't stop his hands from shaking. The trembled so much
that he appeared to be rattling the camera instead of taking
pcitures. He managed to fire off two. Then he shortened his
dog's leash, tipped his hat and said, "You are such gorgeous
girls, like movie stars. I'd like to ask you out. But I don't
remember where all those places are anymore. Besides, I have a
very long walk home."

The woman squirmed childishly, "Do you need any help."

"No thank you. Bye-Bye."

"Bye-Bye," she and Hebe said together.

Hebe slumped and sighed.

"I thought that was great fun, but you don't look very happy
at all."

After hearing how she had been forbidden to see her friends
she shook her head sympathetically. "It must be tough to be a
kid. What a predicament." A child's cry from the playground
snatched her head around.

"Are you children there?"

"I don't have any children yet," she lamented. "But, I want
to. They're all going to be just as smart and sweet as you."
She stroked Hebe's hair and asked, "What are you going to do
about your friends?"

"I may never see my friends again if I don't go now. I have
to see them. I just have to. The problem is, I don't have any
way to get there." She showed her the address.

"I have a swell idea." The woman sprang to her feet and
looked her right in the face. "I'll drive you. My car's right
over there."

"I don't want to take you out of your way."

"Oh, no trouble. It's no trouble at all. I just came here
to get away from it all myself. It's peaceful sitting here
watching the children playing. Well, I did. Now, I can go.
Come on!" Thrilled with her own idea, she slipped her soft,
manicured hand into Hebe's and tugged her up from the bench.

The magic of their instant mutual liking of one another made the lift a fun-filled ride. Hebe opened up to the woman who said her name was Marilyn, and told her a bit about her life. She even shared her picture of Hans and her father. Marilyn thought they were both, "dreamy" but she was curious about her father. Hebe bragged proudly about his itinerancy with the Merchant Marines, and even revealed her Indian identity which she usually kept hidden under people's assumption that she was a Mexican.

Marilyn gasped in disapproval, "That's awful. I mean, some people won't like you because of that, because they have small minds. Never mind about them. You have to be who you are because, well you can't really ever be anybody else." A small hiccup of laughter followed as if she, herself just realized the truth in her impromptu philosophy. Then she added, "A lot of people like Indians. Why, there's even a song "Cherokee Indian Love Song." She searched for the words for a moment, then sang it in a breathy feminine voice:

Sweet Indian maiden, since I first met you,
I can't forget you, Cherokee sweetheart,
Child of the Prairie, Your love keeps calling,
My heart enthralling, Cherokee.
Dreams of summertime, of lover time gone by
Throng my memory so tenderly and sigh, My sweet
Indian maiden One day I'll hold you in my arms
fold you, Cherokee Kee.

She giggled, "Isn't that romantic? Sounds to me as if someone really likes Indians a lot." She made a playful face and patted Hebe's leg. Hebe marvelled at her wise and tender-hearted companion who gave her a new found esteem. Eagerly, she sang the song again with her in an effort to commit it to memory. They sang more songs; Marilyn had quite a repetoire because she had a lot of friends in show biz.

All too soon, the strains of the sounds and music of the Garcia neighborhood interrupted their conversation. Intending a surprise visit, she exchanged a big hug with Marilyn and got out at the corner giving the requested promise that she call her

mother if it got too late. Glad to have met her and sad to see
her go, she waved until the big caddy took a turn and disappeared
from the streets and her life probably, forever.

The residual sentimentality of her meeting was burned away
moments later by the hot Garcia reception on the lawn. Seeing
her arrive though the window, they flung open the door and
streamed out to welcome her in a pool of their warm attention.
Even Tony, whose masculinity restricted his facial expressions to
tough, sexy or cool, allowed a sunny grin to cross his face
fleetingly.

Impulsively shunning their few menial responsibilities, they
all loaded themselves into Tony's big red bullet and shot
themselves down the streets in pursuit of recreation along the
roads which eventually led them across the border.

The kaleidescope of pieces of Mexico Hebe had glimpsed at in
the Garcia house multiplied and organized themselves into a
living picturesque panorama that was exploding around her in the
firecracker heat of color-festooned Tijuana as she perched on the
folded-down top of the car. Burlap bags of rice, baskets of corn
meal, beans and vegetables and hands of hanging bananas
surrounded the black-haired carmel-skinned, people carrying
protesting chickens, encouraging stubborn donkies and languishing
in the dusty market life. Bolstered by the vision of fortune,
some merchants rushed to the flashy, new, red car carefully
cruising through the peopled way with their handicrafts in their
hands. Young men shouted out in approval, or ran their
work-calloused hands over it, leering at the girls as it passed.
Fascinated, but uncomfortable and afraid she slid down into the
seat.

After they finally parked the car, the cousins announced
they were going to a relative's house and left with very little
adieu. Rosalita wanted to go and visit a boy, and she asked Hebe
to come along. Tony was leaning against the car turning his head
to and fro to see who was looking at him, as usual, and smoking a
cigarette. Hearing the invitation, he answered for her in the
form of a question, "What does she want to go there for?"

"So she can meet my friends," she answered sassily.

"She doesn't want to meet those punks," he proclaimed in a clearly possessive-cool tone and put his arm around Hebe.

"Well, maybe I'll just stay with you," she teased starting toward him. He snatched her purse

"Got any lipstick in here?

Rosalita grabbed back her purse which she always hung over her shortest forearm to make it less noticeable. After a brief search she produced three lipstick tubes and held them up for him to choose.

He took one, then proclaimed, "Rosa you gonna have a better time if you go be with your friend." She started to protest. "¡Lárgate!" he commanded so forcefully that she jumped, and after hugging Hebe scampered away. "¡Llamé Mamá!" he called after her with his hands cupped over his mouth.

Hebe was both nervous and titillated by his wanting to be alone with her. Without a thought of permission, he unbraided her hair and lovingly brushed it out into a fluffy mane. She covered her face embarrassed and blushing from his grooming. He asked her to take off her ankle socks, and put on the lipstick to give herself a little more age. She complied and succeeded. An older woman passed by with a large, carved tortoise shell comb in her smooth, oiled hair. Tony gestured to her and exchanged a few words in Spanish, but the woman kept shaking her head. He took some money out of his pocket and she reached up, took it out and exchanged the comb for the dollar bills. When he came back to Hebe, he swept one side of her hair with the comb to keep it in place. Her eyes twinkled with appreciation. He took her small hand and in a swaggering stroll paraded like a powerful lord with his girl-lady though the streets.

Hebe was just as proud to be with Tony. Being near him, she had the sensation that she had eaten sunshine. He was caring and big and strong. Many women threw various smiles his way, but he didn't return them. When they, then, shot their resentment at Hebe, she would lift up her chin and very pompously turn her lips up at the ends ever so slightly. Being there in the street was

like being at an amusement park. There was the same excitement
of the crowd and in each corner, there was something interesting
to see. Hebe snapped several shots with her camera as they went
in and out of the old wooden market stalls. Once, she posed with
an over-sized, black velvet sombrero on her head while Tony took
her picture. She threw her hands up in the air and cried,"Viva
Mexico!" The merchant was perturbed when they didn't buy it. So
to appease him, Tony bought a jangling pair of colorful earrings
for her. "That's for you Hebita. You give me a kick the way you
get so excited about things, little things."

"Maybe this is the best day of my whole life," she said
clipping on her earrings.

"Of course, mi amor. You're with me."

It was night. Hebe's promise to the beautiful Marilyn to
call home, and home itself, were pushed into the recesses of
oblivion by the power of the present moment in a land of
enchantment and mystery, being admired and very hungry. They went
into a bar for a bite to eat. Hebe was an alluring charm
dangling from Tony's arm as they moved through the bodies packing
the small place. A band was playing, dressed in ruffled shirts
and matching black suit. The vibrations sent the rythms through
her like an unexpected and lasting shudder. The rapid tongue
rolling of Spanish was a song in itself sung all around them
while they ate. She had eaten with Tony before, and it was
something she thoroughly enjoyed because he didn't follow any of
the polite restrictive dining etiquette she had been forced to
adhere to at her own table. In fact, he didn't have any manners
at all, unless she took into account the estimation made by her
mother after seeing him eat Christmas dinner at their house which
was, "He eats like a pig." His gastronomy included a good deal
of olfactory enjoyment and vocalized oral appreciation in
addition to corporeal contact with his food. When it arrived, he
hung his head over it and inhaled the aroma. He separated the
leg from the thigh of the chicken and sucked at the steam before
picking up the leg with his fingers and licking a bit of the
sauce from it, some of which ran down his chin. He had an

unusually long tongue which he frequently substituted for a
napkin. Out of his mouth it came to rescue the escaped drops.
Next, he held the leg away from his face as if he were teasing
himself before finally biting into it and devouring the juicy,
dark meat right down to the bone which he lapped and bit and
sucked the marrow from, all the while uttering a gutteral blank
verse praising it's taste. His face was annointed with sauce and
grease which his tongue cleared away before he picked up a few
strands of his spagetti with his fingers and started taking them
up from the plate with a kissing sound. Hebe, for reasons
unknown to her, got very excited witnessing this display. When
he stopped and pawed the thigh on the plate she found herself
wondering how it might feel to be chicken part. Before he began
again, he ran his muscular napkin over his face and she burst out
laughing.

"Your tongue is so big."

Pride swelled in his chest, and a broad smile slid across
his face, in acceptance of what he thought was a great
compliment.

"Gracias mi amor," then he ordered, "Ella, un Coca Cola e
para mí, ron y Coca Cola,"

"Why don't I get a rum."

"Because you are a baby," he teased. "An' I don't like girls
who drink."

"Rosalita drinks."

"Si, and I don't like it too,"

"What makes you so different?"

He rolled his eyes at her and asked, "How many times do I
have to tell you? I'm a man. The men they do many things." Her
sweet pout softened him. "O.k., you can have some of my one."

The juke-box numbers were punched to a popular tune. The
whole room let out a cry of approval. Tony extended his hand to
Hebe and escorted her to the floor. Several young men watched
with the eyes of hungry wolves witnessing their leader close in
on a delicious prey. Tony addressed them in an admonishing tone.

"Abuzados he cabrones."

She knew that meant he was watching them. That's what he had told her when he had used it before.

One of them knocked into Hebe making her drop her bag. In one swift stroke he retrieved it and placed it over her shoulder. Simultaneously Tony pulled her away and pushed his face in front of the man's. He spoke softly through a sly smile.

"Esta es mi vieja," he announced twirling her around and catching her on his powerful forearm. He held her still and turned his head to the men again. They waved him off and took their hunt across the room.

One beat later, Hebe and Tony were in the eye of the flashing lights moving in the human merry-go-round of limber figures grinding up and down and round and round to slow songs. And, to the fast ones, they rippled their bodies together and waved through the space like ribbon candy in the making. The physical sensations filled her with lightheartedness. Dancing was sensational. Hebe thought she was dreaming. Perspiring, but exhilarated, she closed her eyes when Tony drew her next to his body. His strong hands squeezed her ribs; she opened her eyes, burning from the smoke and let out a whoop. She was awake.

Several songs later, Tony led her outside so they could cool off. Only the silver wrapper of his gum crumpling in his hand and their ardent inhalation of the smokeless air interrupted the silence of the streets as Tony leaned against a post and Hebe leaned against him. Together, they let out a sigh of contentment. All of a sudden, Tony jerked away from the post and took a step forward with his eye focused down the street.

"Hey," he said in a hushed voice. "Ya valios madres," then sprinted down the road shouting, "Ya valios madres." Hebe followed him to a clearing under the trees. He threw his arms up and stomped the ground, "¡Que pedo con el coche!" he bleated. He threw his arms over his head and let out an anguished yell. "¡Ponde puta madre esta el coche! Hijos de puta!" he bellowed. She looked across the road to see if perhaps he had parked there. Such a big, red car in such a small, dark town was not easy to miss. It was nowhere. "Hijos de puta!"

She was standing a few feet away, trying to think of
something to say to stop him from shouting when several
flashlights started coming at them from behind the trees. There
were at least three policemen. They were talking to Tony in
Spanish. He put his hands in the air and one of them shined the
light on his face. The eyes were wide and the muscles were
tensed in a grimace of genuine fear. If Tony, "the man," was
afraid, she felt she was faced with serious danger. Instinct
told her to take flight, and she did. First, she heard the
policemen, then she heard Tony's scream.

"Hebita! Don't!" he shriek. His words, knotted with love
and desperation reached through the dead of night and struck her
still. "La chava no! La chava no!" he pleaded. She turned in
her tracks and saw one of the officers crouched over holding a
gun dead on her. Her mouth went dry and her knees began to knock
together. A police car had been pulled into the clearing and
they were beckoning her to come. She wanted to comply, but, at
first, her legs wouldn't move. Her knees knocked harder together
and tears spilled down her face. Tony turned and spoke to them,
then stepped forward with one of the policemen. Slowly, they
came together. She reached for his hand, but he was already in
handcuffs. He leaned down and whispered to her, "Everything's
gonna be o.k. Entiende?" She nodded. "They think I stole the
car, and **you**." Hebe gasped in terror and trembled as they tried
to put handcuffs on her. Her wrists were so small, they kept
falling off, so they tied her hands with a piece of hemp rope.
One policeman stayed behind scanning the ground with his light.
The other two ordered their prisoners not to speak and to sit
apart. As the car made a noisy start, Tony wriggled around so
they could hold hands.

"Everything's going to be o.k.," he repeated barely
audible.

Hebe believed him, but she knew this "o.k." state of affairs
could only last until Gaye was called. When they got in sight of
the border, she realized "o.k." never existed because there, in
the bright lights of the station, sat Art's caddy. She didn't

have a chance to step out of the car because Gaye had opened the
door and dragged her out. She fell to the ground. Unknown to
her, one of her earrings had fallen off. With her hands bound,
she was defenseless. He mother pulled her to her feet and slapped
her in the face. Surprised that Hebe didn't retaliate she
stepped back. In an unexpectedly sympathetic voice she said,
"What have they done to you?" And, called the cording to Art's
attention.

   "My good man, it seems you have mistakenly tied up the
girl." He glanced at Tony. "Or is that what you did when you
kidnapped her?"

   "Kidnap?" Tony began, but the guard struck him.

   Hebe ran over to the policeman and butt him in the stomach
with her head. "Oh Dios," muttered Tony, Gaye-Lee yanked her
away and slapped her until Art stepped in.

   "Perhaps you would rather stay here for the night," he
announced. She stood still and took a breath while the a
policeman's rough hands gently removed her bindings. She felt
the welts on her face. Art threatened Tony, "I pray for you
that you have not taken any liberties with her. Come along Gaye
Lee," he ordered and guided her mother to the car with one hand
on her back and one holding her arm. Hebe sensed that Art's
actions were to prevent her mother from fully venting her anger
in public and causing a bigger scene. Distressed about leaving
Tony, she turned and paused briefly to inspect the scene at the
station. In the shadows on the side of the building was not only
the big, red car, but the owner, Mrs. Gonzalez leaning on a
curvy, brown Rolls Royce smoking. Spotlighted by the outdoor
lightbulb, she saw Tony. Hebe called out, "Mi amor!" He raised
his cuffed hands over his head like a winning prize fighter and
watched her as she put a little wiggle into her step for his
benefit and got into the back seat of Art's monstrosity.

   Art's beast rumbled slowly down the black, unlit roads
heading home, and she waited tensely anticipating a row. She took
an audible breath, the first one she had been aware of since
being picked up by the police. And Art, thinking she was going

to say something, cut her off with, "I really don't believe there's anything to say right now."

There was no argument from her, there was no discussion between her parents, there was no conversation at all, not then or for the remainder of the week end which she spent in he room. Monday morning, Art knocked on her door and told her she was excused from school, and she watched from her window as he and her mother and Jude drove away.

Contemplating her fate, wondering if they would actually send her away, she restlessly began straightening up. On her vanity she came across the hair combs tony had bought for her and a lone earring; she clipped it on the side of the mirror, then resumed her meticulous cleaning. She was surprised to hear the car returning to the driveway in such a short time.

Presently, Art stood in her doorway, his hat still on his head, his condescending social expression under it. Standing there, he looked exactly as he did the day he came to their backdoor in Boston, distant and sly.

"I just stopped by to tell you the good news," he punctuated his speech by knocking his ring on the door jamb. Even though she knew Art was a bonafide snob, his arrogance had a more noticeable artificiallity at this moment. "You're going to Boston tomorrow." He slapped the jamb with his palm with a certain finality.

"Why is that good news to me?" Hebe asked dryly.

He tipped his head as if puzzled, then answered, "We had this discussion previously, Kiddo. Remember? If you don't, I think you can figure it out by the expression, 'Actions speak louder than words.' Listening to your actions, so to speak, your mother and I deduced that you wanted to go. Just for a little while. O.K. Kiddo?" Before she could object, he concluded with another pat of his hand on the wall and an annoying broad smile, "So, we'll bring some suitcases up so you can pack." He turned and left. She slipped on a sweater and tried to brush angrily passed him in the hall. He reached out to stop her, but only got a handfull of her sweater. Defiantly she pulled away. "Where do you think you're going?"

"To say good-bye to a friend," she retorted haughtily and without waiting for any further remark, bolted out of the house. Down by the sea, she hugged herself and called out for the red setter, "Here boy." At first there was no sign of him. She walked and walked wondering why they hadn't even asked her what happened, or offered her another chance, or a thousand different things which crowded her mind. Just like that, they were sending her away. Or was it just like that? She was suspicious of the speediness of their actions and decided they had been long planning her departure, and were just waiting for an excuse to get rid of her. And "What about Tony?" Max's barking snapped her out of her thoughts, and they ran toward one another. She fell to her knees, and he began licking her, washing off her grimace with slobbering affection. Several swells from the ocean broke onto the sand before a large wave crested in front of them sending droplets of water high into the air. Hebe kept her eye on one forced so far up that it hung suspended in mid-air so long that the wave it rode in on rolled to shore with out it. The droplet fell into a dark swell of unfamilar sea. Unable to fight back her bitterness she dissolved into a fit of weeping. The dog whined too; he pawed at her. "Don't you be sad too Max," she said consolingly. "You have people who love you. Let's go!" They sprinted down the beach together until Max took off up a hill near his house. "Bye, Max!" she hollered. He wagged his tail and bark before resuming his way home.

Two large, brown suitcases were standing in her room when she returned. Neatly, she filled them up with her clothes and all her special belongings; the map, the photgraphs, her Davey Crocket hat and a few books. Jude came in and playfully helped her, and asked where she was going. She told him she was "just going away for a little while," and the image of her father saying almost those exact same words before he went out to buy peach icecream flashed through her memory. "Maybe, I won't be back so soon. Maybe it will be a long, long, long time," she corrected as he wiggled his head trying to comprehend her. "But,

I will always think about you, and write to you. O.K.?"

"I love you, Hebe Jeebie," he squeeled giving her a big hug
with his small arms.

"I love you too," she responded picking his up and holding
him, holding him and holding him.

Art had brought Chinese food home for dinner. Her mother
didn't join them. When she asked about her, Art said, "Well, she
doesn't feel well. She's in a state. It's best if we just leave
her alone. She'll get over it." And the three of them sat down
to a proper meal at the table in the dining area. As Art
reminded Jude not to chew with his mouth open and not to bring
his head to the food, but to bring the fork to his mouth. Jude
tried to execute the skills he was being taught. Three forkfuls
were now in his napkin in his lap. His effort to eat, thwarted
by social grace, he gave up and innocently picked up the napkin
and sucked up the food. Art frowned disapprovingly and Jude
defended himself.

"I gave it to my mouth." Art and Hebe both laughed, and
the meal continued in reserved harmony.

Exhausted and emotionally drained, Hebe crawled into her
sheets and thought about leaving. It meant the end of endless
summer. She hung in the cottony limbo between sleep and
wakefulness hoping to both postpone the arrival of the next day
and to get her mother out of her state so she would come and
speak to her, explain why she was sending her away, why she hated
her, or even just say good-bye. From the kitchen below, she
heard the blender crushing her mother's evening meal, and for
once she was glad. Perhaps a drink might help her find her way
upstairs, might loosen her tongue enough to talk to her. She
wished she could hold onto the hands of her clock, to provide her
mother more time. Frustrated by the loud ticking announcing the
death of each second, she threw the clock, and it did stop. But,
the incessant passage of time invisibly ticking away continued.
It hadn't been enough for her mother's mood to change. The
following morning, Hebe departed without as much as a farewell
from her mother. She pretended not to notice, but she kept

looking around, longing for her to come out of her room so she
could at least see her. She did not. Sitting in the car, the
blender's whirring Gaye's breakfast turned her head and she saw
her mother's ghostly image, blurred and distorted by the patio
glass door, peeking out at the car. "Bye-bye mother," she said
outloud to herself. There was no pretending it was not the end of
the perpetual California summer anymore. Ruthlessly, she was
sent into a future partly dearly remembered, partly vaguely
recollected from her past in the Boston springtime.

SIX
GRANDMOTHER'S HOUSE
"A little neglect may breed great mischief."

Benjamin Franklin

Mt. Vernon Street, Boston
Friday, March 14,1958

Hebe was glad to feel the solid ground beneath her wobbly
legs and weakened body. The plane had rumbled and trembled so
violently before landing, she had filled up the airsickness bags
of the entire first two rows. One of her seatmates, a very nice
looking G.I., had genuine concern in his voice as he remarked to
the stewardess, "Gosh Ma'am, I think she's really sick. Even in
boot camp, I never saw anyone turn green. She's really green."

She gave a little guttural agreement and added proudly,
"It's all the take off's and landings. Next year we're going to
go straight from coast to coast," then guided Hebe down the
narrow aisle to three empty seats where she could stretch out in
comfort and throw up in private. Whenever she heard the
stewardess's tinkling, golden, charm bracelet, she would lift her
head and ask hopefully, "Now?" But after a dozen negative

response she stopped. The interminable droning of the plane echoed in her head around the noise of the wings rattling in the frigid wind outside making it impossible for her to sleep or even think in the long hours before the final landing in Boston.

Her whole body was shaking and she felt weightless, as if she had just come out of the ocean after swimming for a long time. Her teeth chattered from the cold. Everyone turned and looked at her running through the flurries across the tarmack to the terminal in her flimsy, colorful, California clothes.

Searching the warmly-hatted heads of the bundled up people in the waiting area, she didn't find her grandmother's anywhere. But, her merry, chiming voice rang in her head, "Society is always late," she hoped she would not live up to that adage tonight. Resting on a chair she read the headlines of "The Boston Daily Globe" about the snowstorm in New York. Just above it were pictures of Princess Grace who had just given birth to a baby boy to follow in the footsteps of Prince Rainier and the beautiful Queen Soraya of Iran whom the Shah was sorrowfully divorcing because she was childless. As she began to wonder about her own parents, she heard her name being called out from across the room. It was Kathleen, the maid, waving at her with a coat, marching hastily in her direction shaking out her umbrella, wearing a little half smile on her pastry puff white face that didn't hide the fact that she was very put out by the duty of picking up grandaughter Hebe in such horrible weather. Glad to see the overcoat, she mustered her strength, got up, and slipped her arms into it as the houskeeper offered her grandmother's deepest apologies for not coming herself and explained that the storm stranded her in the house on Cape Cod. She nervously lit a cigarette.

Beneath the fleecey, snow-filled dusk, they stood in front of the cab stand where Kathleen's large, round blue eyes met Hebe's for the first time, and she realized they were level with her own. Thinking she might be slouching, she righted her posture then put her shoulder next to Hebe's and noticed that the sleeves of the coat she had brought were too short.

"Sheesh, you're hardly a wee one anymore. You're a regular
lassie, you are. That's your grandmother's coat it is," she
remarked and glanced at her cigarette. "You shouldn't get too
tall you know. None of the boys 'll have nothin' to do with you.
And you won't be telling Mrs. Wilkinson, I smoke. Thank you very
much," she admonished her. In addition she pointed out that
while she had tidied up her new quarters, as requested, she had
no intention of permanently adding the task to her already taxing
list of responsibilities. As she took another breath to continue
grousing, Hebe cut her off with a smile.

"Don't worry Kathleen. I'll take care of myself here just
as much as I did in California."

"California," she echoed in a dreamy sigh. "Yes, just look
at you. You're all brown. I guess you go to the beach every day
there."

"I'm always this color. It's too cold to sunbathe now."

"Really? Still, I'd like to be going there m'self someday.
It looks so beautiful in all the photos," she remarked with
sudden interest. The cab sloshed its way through the slushy
historic gutters while Hebe gave enervated answers to Kathleen's
questions about California. Unwittingly, she endeared herself to
her by tattling Gaye's preference for her over Margarita. Pleased
by the compliment, she boasted, "Well, of course. I am very good
at what I do. I've been with your grandmother for almost ten
years now. Your father reminded me of that just last summer when
he was here."

"You've seen my father?" Hebe asked snapping to attention.

"Sure. Last summer, he come up to the house." She lowered
her voice and covered her mouth with her hand to keep her
conversation private before she began to blather, "Some lawyers
and your grandmother were meetin' about the divorce. But you're
father wasn't going to have none of that. It's so romantic.
Imagine him sitting there poor as a church mouse thumping his
nose at fifteen thousand dollars. I seen the check with my own
two eyes when I was cleaning up the table. Fifteen thousand
dollars," she repeated and paused for a moment thinking about the

money. "Laughed right in your grandmother's face, he did. Said, 'My wife and family are not for sale. I know your daughter, Gaye Lee still loves me. I can feel it here,' and he pointed to his heart, excused himself and left. Just like that. Oh, what I wouldn't do for the love of a man like that," she stated aloud causing the driver to turn around with a devilish grin. She turned red. "You need to be lookin' where you're going, now" she commanded. Then covered her mouth and whispered to Hebe, "Is that the truth? Is you mother coming back to him then?"

Hebe didn't have time to answer because the car had stopped in front of her grandmother's house on Mt. Vernon Street and Kathleen had not only already gotten out, but seemed to have also forgotten about the conversation.

By the light of the old gaslight lamp posts burning electric, the cab driver toted all her suitcases at once up the snow-dusted stairs to the first floor. Pausing to scrape his grimy shoes on the footscraper, he caught Kathleen admiring his broad shoulders and they both blushed.

He looked down at the suitcases under his arms and in his hands. "Well, there's room for you right up here on my shoulder. I could carry the both of you," he bragged in a proud, gruff, tenor voice. Kathleen blushed and giggled and slid in the small space in front of him to open the door. He placed the bags down with a thud, and pushed up his jacket sleeves flaunting his powerful forearms. "Anything else?" Before Kathleen could answer, he made the first move in the parlor game of cigarette flirtation by offering her one, which he lit while she gazed mischievously into his eyes. Hebe, debilitated from the trip, brushed passed the dallying pair.

Although she had not been in the house many years, she remembered it; the deep wooden window seats, the fancy, black fireplace fender, the richly carved window frames; the high wooden ceilings, a gloomy trunk of a place more suited for things than people. One wall was an inset bookcase filled with shelf upon shelf of old leatherbound volumes, the golden titles quite dull, not from being handled, read and enjoyed, but dull from having been ignored. They were bored books. Everything was exactly the same, as if time had stopped by one day and decided to stay. Her tired, young footsteps were smothered in the heavy valances and velvet drapes around the windows and the soft, silk orientals on the floor. The solemn oil portraits' lips, painted shut for all eternity, added to the overall resounding quietness of the house. It was overwhelmingly warm and she still had on the overcoat, but she couldn't stop shivering. She called out to Kathleen, "Where's my room please?"

"Top floor!" she sang back from the hallway.

She took the small, wooden closet of an elevator up to the fourth floor. The hall was lit by the natural light coming from one room to the left, but a whispering tintinnabulation beckoned her from behind another door, partially ajar. With hesitant curiosity she pushed it open and gasped in awe. Elegant, prismatic rainbows born of a light's gentle carress floated throughout the air and jeweled the raw, unpainted walls and storage crates of the old, wooden, attic room. The night silvered window reflected the image of her watching two rainbows mingling on her palm while hundreds of others fluttered around her from at least a dozen dust sprinkled chandeliers dangling from iron hooks above. Several large crates beneath them were adressed to her grandfather's import company. She lifted the heavy top of one scattering dust and sneezing. Packed in straw were heavy, delicately faceted presentoir, sugar-candy thin goblets trimmed in silver and blood red fruit dishes. Each entry of her hand into the packing was awarded with a new prize. The last, a box contained an unopened bottle of French cognac. It seemed unusually heavy because exhaustion had returned to her. Sneezing again and still shivering, she decided to find her room and come back the next day for the treasures, but she took one small aperitif glass and the bottle with her.

She guessed the room at the end of the hall to be her's because an old porcelain-faced doll she used to admire when she was little had been placed on the bed, and there were fresh Spring flowers in a large vase on the table by the window. In

desperate need of air, she flung the window open and tried to
gleen strength to go back downstairs to call Art and tell him
that she had safely arrived.

Perched on the edge of the bed, she opened the bottle,
poured a drink and sipped it. The stinging nectar was decidedly
delicious. She glanced up at the door, then tucked it behind the
books on the bottom of the nightstand with the empty glass. The
emotional fatigue of separating from life as she knew it and the
physically draining flight overtook her. Filled with emptiness
and more tired than she had ever been, she reclined on the bed in
a heap and was instantly snatched into the arms of a deep, hot,
black sleep.

There was no dream. There was only a pulsating, blue glow
from some unseen heat source which got hotter and hotter until
everything was flickering red and yellow. Opening her mouth to
gasp for air, the invisible heat source poured down her gullet
and she burned so hotly that riverlets of sweat ran from every
pore of her body and her hair hung in liquid scrawls around her
face and shoulders. She couldn't breathe. She thought she was
sleeping face down in her pillow and wanted to pick up her head,
but she couldn't. She tried, and searing pains shot up through
her chest from the sides of her heart to her throat. The bed
clothes were drenched. Not being able to move, she thought she
was dreaming. Her raspy wheezing and a firy burning of her
dehydrated eyes told her otherwise. Finally, she managed to open
them. She was not facedown at all, and the realization frightened
her, made her fight for even a tiny breath. The dense darkness of
a thousand northern mid-winter midnights settled around her in an
almost tangible fog making it impossible for her to see where she
was. Suffocating, she called weakly, "Mother!" Pain shot into
her throat and she wrenched her chest as she called our again.
"Mama!" For an instant, not a sound was heard. Sick and afraid,
scalding tears trickled involuntarily down her face before she
started to cry vociferously. It hurt even more, but she couldn't
stop. She pressed her hands to her lungs to try to stop the
agonizing pain as the bedroom door opened and the overhead light

was snapped on.

She squinted in the glaring light and saw Kathleen showing in a tall, slim man with thick white hair and black-rimmed eyeglasses. He was carrying a black medical bag which he brought along to the edge of her bed where he sat and spoke to her in a gentle, almost monotone voice. "I'm Dr. Ives," he said taking her pulse. "Do you remember me from yesterday? I'm a friend of your grandmother's." Hebe tried to speak, but only sent herself into a piercing coughing fit which left her shaking. He gave her an injection in her arm with the words, "This might sting a little." It didn't. She didn't feel anything, not even his hand on her arm. Her teeth began to chatter. "Yesterday?" she thought, and moving her hand to her face to cover another cough, she saw that she had been put into a night gown and there were several bottles of medicine on the table beneath the flowers. Her other small hand was perspiring into Dr. Ives' as she stopped coughing and her eyelids became very heavy.

In a whisper she asked, "What day is today?"

"It's Sunday night," she heard him say as she began to slip under the spell of the drug.

"Things are still going on in the night when I'm asleep," she thought to herself.

A truth which became more apparent to her when she regained consciousness, not in her new room, but in the hospital where she was lying inside of a huge, round, green machine. Dr. Ives was there, and he told her it was an iron lung. His voice sounded far away. Thinking she was asleep again he spoke to the nurse, "I really don't understand this one. She shouldn't still be this sick." She opened her eyes. The nurse mopped her forehead. With his soft, sure physician's touch, Dr. Ives examined her eyes closely. In his glasses, Hebe could see them herself, encircled in brown, lost in her pale, sunken, lifeless face. But Dr. Ives looked pleased. He stroked her hair. "Don't worry. We'll have you out of here and home in no time."

"Home?" she thought over and over. "Where was home?" Before she knew it, she was sitting on her old balcony in Boston, a

million needles of bright summer sunlight infusing her with
tingling warmth, watching her father come home from work.

"Daddy!" she called out.

"Hebie Jeebie!" he responded with the joy of seeing his
little daughter pulling his handsome chestnut-toned face into a
delighted grin. He held up a brown paper bag.

"You remembered. Peach icecream!" she squeeled gleefully
and ran into the house announcing with childish enthusiasm,
"Daddy's home." Her mother rushed into the foyer and checked her
appearance in the mirror next to Hebe's favorite painting, "The
Hunt" before taking her small hand and standing at attention to
greet him. "The Blue Danube Waltz" began to play. As his key
turned in the lock, her mother gave her hand a little squeeze of
excited anticipation. The door opened and rays of late afternoon
sun shot out from behind the head and shoulders of his lively
silhouette before he swept her up in his arms and pulled her
mother to him in a close familial embrace. Hebe reveled in the
special perfume of their combined fragrances, kept her eyes shut
and clung tightly to the triangular bond. A horse began to whinny
and she turned around to see that she was in the painting. Tufts
of green, wet grass tickled her bare feet. Her grandfather
reached down and put his hands around her waist to lift her onto
his noble, bay horse. The familiarity of the touch of thumbs on
her ribs transformed his face into Tony's right before her eyes
and angelic voices sang "The Cherokee Indian Love Song" as he
placed her on the horse's back, mounted himself behind her and
let his head fall tenderly against her own. Rubbing her hair on
Tony's face, she could feel the damp heat of his breath on her
neck. The sun burned brighter and brighter until its whiteness
permeated everything in sight to invisibility. The incessant whir
of a blender crushing ice over and over accompanied the sensation
of a thick cocktail washing over her in a giant wave which tossed
her to its crest, then towed her under. The sound of a faintly
ringing bell grew louder until it was right in her ear, and she
awakened.

Her arms were wrapped around her pillow and she was in her

top floor room on Mt. Vernon Street. She had to get out of bed
and reach way under it to retrieve the alarm clock where she kept
it, on Kathleen's suggestion, so she couldn't just reach over,
turn it off and go back to sleep. She had to go to school. The
new, warm clothes her grandmother had arranged for her hung
loosely on her body, still skinny from her long stay in the
hospital which, while only last week, seemed long ago.

Kathleen had come to pick her up accompanied by the cab
driver, Steven, who had taken them home from the airport. Hebe
didn't hear the reason her grandmother offered for not having
come to pick her up. She didn't want to hear about yet another
thing that had been more important than her. She had heard about
quite a few on the visiting days when her grandmother did't
appear at the hospital. Dr. Ives would enter, clear his throat
and start, "Mrs. Wilkinson sends her apologies..." She knew now
that her own delivery and installation in her grandmother's
historic house on Beacon Hill had transpired as if she were but
another objet d'art Mrs. Wilkinson had aquired at an auction.
Her grandmother had executed the extent of her responsibility by
arranging payment and leaving instructions for her proper care
with someone else. She was, however, not excluded from her
grandmother's busy social calender. There was church on Sundays
and dinner at eight on Wednesdays.

The first time she had seen her since her arrival from
California was a Wednesday. The formal table twinkled beneath
the chandelier and she and Dr. Ives were erect and quite
well-dressed for dinner. Dr. Ives was just as handsome and kind
as Hebe remembered. It was the woman, her grandmother sitting
next to him, Hebe didn't recognize immediately. She had never
seen her without a hat before. She had abundant light brown hair
which she wore swirled away from her face toward the sides of her
head. Strands of platnium delineating the direction of the
sweeps caught the light and sparkled throughout. Her porelessly
smooth, powder-puff white countenance was unwrinkled from a
lifetime of inexpression. Her large blue-violet irises and small
nose gave her otherwise sohpisticated look an innocent allure

making her a pleasant-looking, older woman.

Hebe presented herself at the door and fully expected a greeting. Instead, she received a fleeting look of astonishment because her grandmother was equally surprised to see such a tall, swarthy, string bean of a young woman in place of her little grandaughter, especially not in shorts and a black, cashmere sweater, her mane of hair frizzing disobediently around her head. Hebe?" she inquired, then quickly concealed her feelings behind her easily summoned superficiality. Still expecting some warmth and holding a tender spot in her heart for the memory of former greetings with her grandmother, Hebe was radiant and stood waiting for her to open her arms to her.

"It's nice to see you Grandmother," she said shyly, then greeted Dr. Ives.

"You're looking much better," he commented.

"Yes, well, it's nice to see you as well," began her grandmother. "But it would be nicer to see you if you were properly dressed for dinner," she added snuffing Hebe's glow. She started to move toward the dinner table, but the matriarch's cool, glaring pastel eyes stopped her. "Don't you have a dress?"

"Most of them are sleeveless," she answered softly. The icy stare gave her goosebumps which culminated on her nipples directly in her grandmother's line of vision.

"Sit down." She rang a little porcelin bell, and a servant whom she hadn't seen previously entered wearing the exact outfit her mother had tried to get Margarita to wear. "Bring Miss Gourdin the beige cardigan from my dressing room before serving dinner," she bade her without as much as a glance. Once Hebe had draped herself in the enormous garment and buttoned the top button as requested, Grandmother Wilkinson finally looked pleased to see her, "There's my girl. Now, tell us all about California," but before she could begin her grandmother turned to Dr.Ives and announced, "Gaye Lee's husband, a Harvard man, of course is..."

Dr. Ives touched her lightly on the back of her placid, white hand. "I know. You told me. Let the girl answer," and he turned to Hebe.

"Husband," flashed through Hebe's mind with Kathleen's story about the fifteen thousand dollars. And for a fraction of a second she considered bringing it up, but instead she said, "Yes California is lovely, just lovely. I'm sure mother has told you. Has she called?" Hebe asked, her heart aching to hear how Jude and the others were getting along.

Grandmother Wilkinson bristled at the insolence of her sarcasm, raised her eyebrows in disapproval and swallowed her discontent with a sip of wine before answering, "Yes, I have. She sends you her best. I believe I was asking you about the weather."

Then and there Hebe decided to adopt her grandmother's formerly frequently spoken adage, "Children should be seen and not heard." She offered no information, but answered their few questions, and remained silent while the two adults discussed, current events, literature and the fickle New England weather.

Before she went up to her room that night, Grandmother Wilkinson followed her into the hall and closed the door behind her. "Hebe, I will speak with you now?"

"Sure," she answered taking off the loaned cardigan and handing it to her.

"Yes, Grandmother will do fine," she corrected her, in her Queen of Hearts voice. Then, meticulously expressed her imperceptible outrage. "Hebe, your appearance is improper, indecent and unacceptable. Think, how embarrassed I would have been had one of the Auxillary Club members been here to witness this..." She wrang her hands and looked around as if her next words were going to be found in a vase or on the chair in the corner of the hall.

"In California," Hebe began.

"This is not California! This is Boston," she clarified with great pride and dignity. "This is my home. And for a long as you are in my home, in my charge, you will dress accordingly. And behave accordingly. Eating fish with the meat fork. The very idea. Really Hebe. It's fish, meat then salad. I know you know that. You were deliberately trying to embarrass me, weren't you?

And when is that dreadful tan going to fade? You're not wearing make-up, are you? Your mother has told me about your misbehavior and what it has done to her. You disgraced her. The tears she has wasted over you..." she stopped mid-sentence, tutted and shook her head from side to side. "I simply won't have it," she announced.

Hebe thought it best to keep her ignorance about the fork rule and the reminder that she was olive-complected to herself. She just stood unhappily learning that she had hurt her mother and realizing this to be the cause for her grandmother's distance. Though a full two inches taller than her grandmother, she felt very, very small. She stared at a pattern of flowers on the carpet.

"I'm going to call the department store tomorrow morning before I leave. You will go and pick up clothes...," she paused searching again for words, "well, more suitable for this climate, and certainly foundation garments," she concluded stealing a glimpse of Hebe's breasts. "And you will wear them. Do you understand?"

"Yes, Grandmother," Hebe answered meekly. And sans touch or parting word, her grandmother turned and walked regally back to the era from whence she came in the dining room and closed the door.

Filled with self-loathing for being such a disappointing daughter and grandaughter, Hebe went to her room. She tried to write her mother a letter to tell her that she hadn't done anything to her intentionally, to tell of the maid's rumor of her father's ever bright love for her, and to offer the promise of change, but she wasn't certain exactly what she had to change; her clothes, her table manners, the color of her face. She sat in front of the mirror. The pretty, young confident girl reflected in Rosalita's mirror had been replaced by one who was sad and sickly and deemed an incapable, miscolored misfit. She couldn't write a single word. On the radio, the announcer broadcast the big story about Lana Turner' daughter. She had stabbed her mother's boyfriend to death with a ten-inch knife.

He said everyone was shocked, but Hebe thought, "I'd like to ask her what happened." She tried to think about the fun she would have shopping the next day.

When she arrived at the store, apparently what she needed had been discussed and selected over the telephone and set aside for her to try on. There were plaid skirts with coordinated blazers in grey, navy and plaid, white blouses, woolen tights and of course the much demanded brassieres. Being told she was eleven , the saleswomen had much smaller sizes waiting in the girls' department, and in fact couldn't fit her. They had to send her to the women's department. The feel of the new clothes, the fineness of their quality and her conservative appearance pleased her because she thought it would please her grandmother. The saleswomen oohed and aahed over her figure. No one believed she was only eleven. "You could be a model," one of them said and they all agreed.

And so, she became a well-dressed, very tall fifth grader at the Prince Elementary School on Newbury Street. The New England educational system neither required nor accepted any of the mandatory physical education credits from her three years in the California school system, so she was placed back a year. In addition, her former school was small and went from kindergarten to twelfth, and the one in Boston was only a grammar school, so she was the tallest pupil in the entire school.

She liked being tall, but she hated only being with children. Her experience and her height distanced her from them. The first day she entered the room, all the other pupils shushed one another thinking she was a teacher. Discovering she was not, they made the childish assumption that the taller, older girl must be stupid, and referred to her among themselves as Big Dummy until one day while studying mountain ranges, one of the boys upon hearing Grand Tetones, turned and called her the same. The nickname stuck. She didn't protest; she forgave them their silliness. She couldn't hate them, but she did hate being there in the fifth grade in the dingy, old school. The windows were particularly offensive. There were no wayward, palm tree leaves to evict, or cotton-clouded, blue skies paving the way to daydreams. Closed against the cold and the noise, the large windows offered no more than a foreground of grime for the background of the busy, grey city. Their dirty streaks hung in front of her face like prison bars and the inmate-pupils filed from room to room as the schedule dictated and stood, sat, listened, memorized and repeated as the teacher demanded making the entire experience of school a monotonous passage of time.

Three things kept her in attendance; the desire to keep her distance from her grandmother, a healthy drink of cognac, and the promise of the lovliness of the Boston Public Garden. She had to pass through it en route to classes. In the quiet of the early mornings, the air, rich with the special freshness of new spring gently tickling the everywhereness of newly born greenery sparkling in dew invited her to linger there. On the edge of the pond the mallards would laugh and chatter quackingly greeting her and anticipating food as they waddled at her feet. Afternoons, it was filled with the noise of tourists strolling on the paths, and the voices of children scampering around to the music of their own laughter under the watchful eyes of their mothers.

Except on Wednesdays and Sundays, she ate dinner alone in the kitchen, sped through her easy assingments and escaped to the world of her room which she had decorated with her many favorite pieces from the crystal treasure chest. Instead of curtains, she had ropes of crystal prisms. Glass figurines and priceless vases filled with flowers were everywhere. Though architecturally different, it was the same as her room in California. The map of her father's trips framed by cards and souvenirs on one wall. And on the other, hung pictures and keepsakes of the Garcia family, even their letters. Rosalita's letters about boys always included notes from Margarita about Jude and the house. Apparently, Gaye-Lee was again plagued by the floor to ceiling window when the curtained had to be taken down to be cleaned. Hebe loved to receive news of her little brother's mischief. Tony didn't write much, but he sent small trinkets; a eucalyptus leaf, a half a stick of gum, cocktail napkins from places he had been and many, many pictures of himself. He even sent the earring she had dropped. It had no note, but she guessed he had found it because it still had particles of Mexican border dirt on it. She thought about what it would be like to see everyone again in June when school was over. She put on the pair of earrings and watched her face move as she acted out her fantasy reunion with him. She opened her arms wide and let him fall into her arms before she imitated his hug by wrapping her arms around herself. Behind her she saw her grandmother holding a small jar. A blush burned in her cheeks as she turned to greet her.

"Well," she began in a voice charged with assessment and judgement looking at the crystal and clasping her hands. Suddenly, one piece, a small female figurine caught her attention. Hebe watched her grandmother's icy expression melt just like a snowman's face in an unexpected sun as she picked up the glass woman. Her mouth never moved, but somehow Hebe knew she was smiling. "Your grandfather gave this to me a very, very, very long time ago," She said softly, then took a deep breath and exhaled the memory as she looked around at the other crystal spinning webs of light throughout the room. Her eyes fell on the curtains in a heap on the floor. "You should have told me the curtains fell down. I'll have someone put them back up."

"They didn't fall down. I took them down. We didn't have curtains on most of the windows in California. They shut out too much light."

"No curtains! I don't know what on earth is wrong with Gaye Lee. What must people think? No curtains. No autumn. No symphony. No clubs! Everyone wearing sunglasses, so much gaeity and frankness. California doesn't sound like my kind of place."

For the first time ever, Hebe completely agreed with her Grandmother, but she didn't dare to tell her. She knew her grandmother hadn't made the journey to the top floor to talk about California or crystal. She took a step forward toward the night stand and bent over to look at her book titles. Hebe was afraid that she would smell her secreted cognac.

"When did grandfather give you that?" she asked hoping to

divert her eyes..

Her grandmother again eyed the crystal figurine in her hand.
"I told you, a long time ago," she answered quickly without
looking at her. Then she set the jar she was holding on the
nightstand. "Here is a cream for you to use," she added with an
insincere smile sweeping her long white hand toward the wall as
if she were about to introduce someone. "You will have to clear
this wall Hebe. The French country wardrobe will be moved in
here for your winter clothes. Gaye Lee has sent your summer
things."

"But why? I thought I was going back to California in...,"
she tried to still her racing heart so as not to shout at her
grandmother.

"You wouldn't understand dear. You're much too young to
think Hebe. Children should be seen and not heard. Just do what
you are told," she ordered in a deceivingly calm voice, then
turned to walk away.

"So this means I have to stay here?" she asked unable to
cloak the stress in her voice.

No answer came from the hall. She started to dart after
her, but hearing the elevator gate squeal shut she stopped. She
picked up the curious gift of cream and read the jar. It was a
bleaching cream. "Guaranteed to fade unsightly dark skin." Angry
and hurt she threw it against the wall and began to pace the room
which, in a fragment of a second, had grown incredibly small. She
slammed the door shut and ripped all the bedding off her bed
causing the crystals to tinkle and chime. She longed to go away.
Her second bottle of cognac, stolen upon it's delivery to the
kitchen with several other bottles, was already half gone. She
drank so as to have some for another time, thus passing the night
in a thousand sips.

Several days later, she was surprised to see a young girl
sitting in the seat in front of her; it was usually empty. she
looked more mature than Hebe, herself, and she greeted her with a
warm smile as if they had been friends for a long time. During
the lesson, the girl kept giggling to herself. Though stifled,

it was contagious and Hebe couldn't help laughing along with her. During recess in the schoolyard they stood by the wall watching the other girls jumping rope. Though they hadn't yet exchanged a word, curiosity drew Hebe to her. She offered her a cigarette which she took out of her bra after snatching a look around for the teacher. In a thick Polish accent, she introduced herself, "My name is Bozena."

"I'm Hebe," she said with her own paranoid glance around the corner for the teacher. "Are you new here?"

"No. Old. I am too busy for the school.

"You'd better be careful or they will kick you out," Hebe warned.

"For this I am praying. Does not happen. They send truant officer everytime. I tell him, 'I am too busy. Many things more important than ABC's,' but Bozena is never kicked out," she exclaimed rolling her eyes at the sky and emiting a little puff of frustration.

"Just don't come."

"And go to jail?!"

"You won't go to jail."

"Sure not?"

"I've missed lots. Do I look like I am in the jail."

Bozena was very pleased with Hebe's confession. "I knew it. I knew it. I knew it. I knew you were same like me when I saw you," she said giving Hebe a little embrace. Then she began to giggle again.

"Why do you keep laughing?"

"Did you ever do it with legs on the shoulders? Is very funny," she replied and again began chuckling causing her large firm breasts to vibrate.

"Do what?"

"It," she repeated with a gesture using both of her hands that made Hebe blush.

"Oh that. Well, no," she admitted thinking Bozena would think less of her. Then she added defensively, "But, I have a friend, Rosalita in California, and she did it." A surprised look crossed Bozena's face as she inhaled deeply on her cigarette.

"You come from California?"

"Yeah!" Hebe answered sending Bozena's gaze off into space.

"Must be nice," she beamed, "legs on shoulders, warm California beach on back." She made the noise of someone eating something delicious.

"Well, I never did that on the beach. But, I've done lots of stuff on the beach and I don't know how fun that'd be 'cause, I think you'd get sand..Hey, do you understand me if I talk this fast?" she asked interrupting herself.

"I think she understand's you perfectly." Hebe spun around to the greeting of the teacher's scowling face. "Not another word out of either one of you." She stopped and gave an asthmatic gasp. Put those cigarettes out! The idea!" She watched as Hebe dropped it. The teacher looked older than Mamie Eisenhower, but was named, Miss Young and had a reputation for being quick with the rattan for punishment. Hebe felt nauseous watching as she stepped on the unfinished cigarette and stamped it out as if it were a large, poisonous, hard-shelled bug. When it was but tobacco dust she gave a little hum of satisfaction that she had properly destroyed it and said, " Follow me." She walked ahead of them in the direction of the school door. Miss Young was old and slim and slow and she wobbled in her large-fitting shoes as she went. She didn't look back, she never felt it necessary. She just assumed that respect and trepidation would keep anyone, especially little girls, in tow behind her. Hebe and Bozena followed along until they got near the steps to Newbury Street. Bozena yanked Hebe's hair and motioned with her head that they should go up the steps. A split second later, Bozena had bolted up the steps without waiting for any acknowledgement from Hebe. Impulsively, she raced up after her.

"Girls! Girls! You come back here!" Miss Young stamped her foot and her ill-fitting shoe came off. She waved it in the air.

All the children lined up at the wrought iron fence to witness the great escape. At least once or twice a month someone made the attempt, but usually fear brought them scurrying back, or the teacher posted on the corner dragged them. The teacher wasn't there this time. Fear was no where in sight either. Off they went to the cheers of the students.

"No geography class today!" yelled one of the boys.

"Why not?" asked another above the enthusiastic shouting.

"How can we have geography with no mountains?"

"Go Tetones!" shouted the amused boys in unison.

Laughter was added to the din, but the girls didn't know why. The last thing they heard was, "The truant officer will find you!"

Pink magnolia blossoms rained down on them as they breathlessly entered the floral wonderland of the Boston Garden. Hebe had never before misbehaved intentionally in public. She was giddy with the rush of adrenilin the sport sent through her. The pair giggled hysterically over their success as they walked by the swanboats. Bozena caught Hebe by the waist to slow her down. Feeling her hand around her, Hebe realized this was the first time any one had touched her since she had been in Boston except for Dr. Ives and the nurses in the hospital. She nestled closer to Bozena's soft, cozy body as they slowed to a European arm in arm gait and Bozena prattled on about her life.

She had married a few months earlier while she was in Poland. Hebe had never heard of anyone getting married at fourteen, but Bozena told her this was common in her country. Her husband Bolek was twenty-one. He worked in a meatpacking factory during the day and at a bar with her uncle during the afternoon and night. She wanted to work as well, but according to the law she had to be in school. When she arrived from Poland where she had almost finished school, she took a test which placed her into the fifth grade. "If was in Polish language I would have best score," she assured Hebe with a shrug. Bozena revealed herself to be a proud and contented young girl whose only ambition was to keep her husband healthy so he could make as much money as possible in order to buy her everything her heart desired, which didn't seem to be a great deal. She mentioned pots and pans and a new nightgown "for to keep husband interested," she pointed out with a wiggle of her high arched eyebrows.

They stopped in front of a strip joint. One of her long, blonde braids fell down from the half-circle it made around her head above her bangs. As she pinned it back in place, they looked at the nearly nude women featured in the pictures on the wall. Hebe noticed the strong smell of fried fat wafting over from the surrounding Chinese restaurants. She was embarrased to see the pictures and averted her eyes as Bozena said, "This is a terrible picture of Hope. Her behind is not so skinny like that. She has handles on hips more than me."

"Handles? Why do you call it that?"

"Now, I believe you never did something with a man. Why?"

"I'm not sure. Well, Tony's the only boy I've ever kissed. And I have to be careful not to remind him that I'm eleven, or he won't even do that." Hebe confided.

"Eleven! No kidding! You don't look like so young. Don't worry. Your secret is safe with me. You know, you will meet new boyfriend who will show you about birds and bees soon."

"But I like Tony." She showed her pictures of Tony and Hans.

"I pick this one," she said ooing over the picture of Hans.

"That's Hans. He's my penpal, a friend of my father's! Too old for me."

"Does he have a job?"

"He goes to M.I.T."

"M.I.T.? Money in future."

"It's M.I.T, not M.I.F."

"T.,F. old schmold. He's your guy. Listen to Bozena. Go with him. I will come clean big house he will buy for you. We will always be friends." She held her innocent young face in front of one of the dancer's photographs and put on her lipstick. "Bolek loves lipstick." She started into the club and Hebe held back.

"We can't go in there."

"This is where work my husband and uncle. Is his club!"

Hebe swallowed hard and followed her into the cavernous black mouth of the club belching out smoke and bump and grind music. The staff had friendly greetings for Bozena who strutted

through the mirky, pink light with ease, grinning and spinning
her fallen braids like tassles.

"He's out back, Honey!" hollered the dancer before prancing
back to the center of the stage on the tip-toes toes of her
stilettos. A drum accented her every move. The height of the
stage made her appear much larger than she was. She held onto a
fringe at the end of a thin red chord which was connected to a
triangle of red satin cloth between her legs. It matched the
huge pasties on her upward tilting breasts. Only a few men lining
the stage acted as her audience. The regulars had seen her act
so many times that they had lost sight of it, and sat blankly
nursing clinking drinks. Others were oblivious because they were
so engrossed in their conversations. She tugged and tugged at
the chord in a mock effort to remove it, and shrugged her body in
a sensuously slow motion gesture of defeat. The front row let
out a chorus of groaning disapointment. A man in a very
well-tailored suit looked up as she put her satined triangle in
front above his head and asked in a baby voice, "Could you help
me get it off, Honey?"

He looked away a moment, but his friends pushed him and
teased him until he reached up and the few people who were paying
attention applauded as he pulled the little red chord. "Oh
harder," cooed the dancer as he pulled again. "Harder!" He
snatched it off and for a split second no one seemed to breathe
anticipating the stripper's nudity. But she had on a black
triangle underneath. Hebe giggled as the customer triumphantly
waved the red triangle in the air before his shyness settled back
into him and he meekly placed it on the bar after folding it
neatly. The sticky floor, pulled at the soles of her shoes was
when she walked so she stood still. The dancer had begun a
little banter which was drowned out by the palaver of the patrons
in the rear. She put her hands on her hips, "Hey, do you mind?
I'm trying to entertain yuse up here."

"Yeah, we know. You been tryin' since the year o' two."

She jumped off the stage and stumbled halfway to the back
shouting repeatedly at the customer.

"Just what the Hell is that supposed to mean, Bob?"

"The drummer appeared with his drumsticks in his hand and herded her back toward the front. "I just wanted to know what he meant by that crack. The year o two. There isn't even any such thing. I'm workin' my ass off and,"

"Don't look that way from here," teased one of the men while approximating the width of her behind with a broad spread of his hands.

She turned to say something to him when she saw Hebe. "Hey kid who let you in? Aren't you supposed to be in school or something?" she asked placing her hands on her hips again. Before she could protest, Hebe had been lifted onto the stage.

"Hey, Bob. Community auditions."
Caught in the spotlight Hebe looked around at the spectrum of male faces from sober to drunk, from kind to lecherous. She had their full, unwanted attention.

"She gonna be a new Gypsy Rose Lee?"

"She wasn't nothin'. Sally Kieth, now she was something!" He stood up, held his hands up for breasts and twirled his fingers in opposite directions. "She could really make those tassles fly! Can you do that kid?"

Whistles, wolf calls and hand clapping flurried in the air.

"She's just a little girl," a voice called out. "Hey how old are you?"

For a moment the whole dingy room was quiet, except for the clink of glass and some one coughing. She shielded her eyes from the light and looked out among the skulking and scavenging men in the pink light and red shadows. Their lips were upturned at the ends and stretched out in moist lines across their faces as if smiles, but they were leers hung by lonliness, liquor and lust-seeking. She turned to the dancer who had joined her on the stage and looked up.

The stage hadn't made her appear big, she was huge, and much taller than Hebe. Her thick layer of makeup sat on the surface of her face like a mask. Her eyes peered out from behind it, flat, brown and lackluster, even in the shine of the spotlight.

Though no one had harmed Hebe, there was a frightening tension permeating the air which ran right through her. The ceiling fan hung miles away, as if she were standing on a stage at the bottom of a canyon. She actually wished she were safe in her room on top of her grandmother's house. The nervous knee knocking she experienced in Mexico when she saw the policeman's gun returned. A couple of voices interrupted the silence which seemed interminable, but had only lasted long enough for a stray magnolia blossom from the park to loosen itself from her hair and float to the floor.

"Hey little girl! What's 'a matta? Don't tell me you don't speak English. I got ten says your sixteen?"

"Yeah, Joe and don't forget sixteen 'll get ya twenty."
They all laughed.

"Tell 'em how old ya are," urged the dancer. "I wanna sit down my feet are killing me."

In a clear, meek voice she told the truth, "I'm eleven."

No sooner was the "n" out of her mouth and the owner whisked her back down to the floor.

"Who the Hell let you in here anyway?" he bellowed almost yanking her in the direction of the front door. He revealed his actions to be kind of a show for the others to see when he leaned over and asked in a kind voice, "Which one of these dirty bums dragged you in here? You can tell me."

"I'm Bozena's friend," she whispered. Just then Bozena's bright face appeared and took Hebe's arm protectively. Placing her lips on one side of his cheeks she dissolved his worried look. "Is problem Joe?"

"No. No problem Doll, but keep your little school friends out of here. Your going to cost me my license."

She kissed his cheek and he shuffled his feet almost bashfully. "So sorry. Never never no more again." She took Hebe's trembling arm and walking away said, "Bolek tells me I have first class talent as ass-kisser. I thought you were with me. Are you o.k.?"

"Sure," said Hebe trying to appear undaunted."

They went to Bozena's in the Back Bay whre Hebe met her
Polish clan, and later on her husband, Bolek. There were only
five members in all, but everyone had a husband, wife child or
friend over at the time of their arrival. As a result, the three
bedroom apartment was crowded with a large number of relatives
noisily busy with the caring acts which go into creating a family
and friends out of people: cleaning, arguing, smoking, talking
and laughing while preparing lunch, "Obiad,: as Bozena kept
telling her. Hebe was immediately gathered into the large
familial fold of the household the moment Bozena's big, brunette
aunt nonchalantly removed the books from her hands and replaced
them with the flatware and napkins to set the afternoon meal
table. In the warm food-scented air, she carried out her newly
assigned responsibility as if it were her daily duty. She felt
as comfortable and welcome as she did at the Garcia's.

The space between the barszcz, a beet soup, and the kompot
was filled with steaming dishes of kotlets, cabbage and mashed
potatoes smothered in the flow of a rich, Polish sauce of
confabulation. The barrier of not being able to understand was
constantly being toppled by grins and friendly pats on the arm or
strokes on the head. The aunt who buzzed around the table
catering to the meals's trivial needs was denied her own chair by
the number of diners. But, she thought nothing of scooting Hebe
over and sharing her seat. She draped her heavy, dough-colored
arm over her shoulder and cuddled her next to her much to
everyone's amusement. And, at one point, when the cheerful
conversation esclated into a heated discussion, Bozena
translated.

"They talk about two years before anti-government riots in
Poznan," she said. Then paused to listen, "What might would be
happen when Gomulka was not freed."

"Who is Gomulka?" Hebe asked.

"Is most important leader. I will tell you later," she
answered with a sigh of seriousness, then listened intently to
what was being said. Hebe tried to follow the conversation.
Eventhough she didn't know a word of Polish, she felt she could

understand some of what was being communicated by the subtle
flexes of their face muscles and the varying tones of their
voices. It was a skill she had developed sitting at her window
in California and interpreting the conversations her mother and
Art were having by the pool.

Her mind wandered from the table to her mother in Calfornia,
then to Hans and the first time she met him on her back porch.
She wondered if he would like to see her as much as she would
like to see him. The words, "Dlaczego ne?" brought her back to
the bustle of the room.

The dishes were being cleared and Uncle Przemek, a lanky,
black-haired man, asked that they remain seated, a request with
which they were incredibly eager to comply. More vodka was
served and they toasted loudly, "Na drzowie!" Hebe found herself
titillated by the contagious excitement which went around the
table as they watched him disappear into the other room. Impatiently, she glanced at Bozena for a clue to what was happening.
But before she could repsond, the uncle had returned with a cloth
and a violin and she joined in the light drizzle of clapping.
"Uncle lives in New York. Not for long time, we didn't hear
him," she explained.

Hebe listened and watched, appreciative of the music and
fascinated by Uncle Premestaw's performance. More than his
hands, he used his whole body to make the music. Oscillating his
lean, white-shirted torso, he bowed toward the floor, stretched
up on tip-toe, or stood straight in the center, furiously
vibrating his head while his right arm held the bow sewing the
notes into an invisible, ribbon of music. It unraveled over
everyone sitting at the table and even fluttered into the street
because when he stopped playing, the first pair of hands to come
together were those of a man standing with a woman by a gaslight
in the street below.

Hebe knew she should call Grandmother Wilkinson. Certainly
the school had already displeased her grandmother with a report
of her conspicuous early departure from the school that morning,
and she would be told to come straight home. Then it struck her

that not calling might just be the perfect way to transform Grandmother Wilkinson's anger into concern. A fleeting fantasy played in her head about her return home the next day.

Properly gloved and hatted, Grandmother Wilkinson would stand at the top of the Mt. Vernon Street stairs waving to Hebe, calling out to her in a voice sugared with cherishing, weak from a night of grieving for her "Little Dahling" grandaughter. As Hebe mounted the steps in her daydream her grandmother bent her head and her hat covered her face. When she lifted it again, her features were wrinkled in a subtle scowl of disapproval. As her grandmother turned and walked away, a chill came over her which carried into reality. She shivered in her chair. Eventhough, the latter reception was the more likely of the two to be actualized, she still made the deliberate decision not to call and not to return home that evening. Regardless of the consequences, she would at least be missed.

Arriving at the house the following afternoon, she was greeted neither by the angry face she anticipated nor the delighted face she had fantasized. There was nothing, no expression because her grandmother had not even been at home. In the kitchen, she found a note written to Kathleen informing her she was going to New York for two days and that she wouldn't be needed. Grandmother Wilkinson hadn't suffered over her grandaughter's absence in the least. She hadn't missed her at all. On the contrary, she seemed to have completely forgotten about her. She balled up the note and threw it at the wall.

The phone rang, and she stomped into the other room to answer it. "Wilkinson residence."

"This is Miss Young calling from the Prince School for Mrs. Wilkinson," announced her teacher on the other end.

Hebe was momentarily speechless, then she said assertively,, "Yes?" hoping she wouldn't recognize her voice.

"Is this Mrs. Wilkinson?"

"No. This is the housekeeper," she lied. "Mrs. Wilkinson is out."

"When she returns, please ask her to call me at the school."

"She's gone away until Monday."

"Her grandaughter, Hebe, was not in attendance in.."

"That's right. Hebe is with Mrs. Wilkinson."

"Oh, I see. Well," she began then hesitated.

"Is there any message?" Hebe asked politely trying not to laugh.

"No. No message. Thank you."

As soon as she replaced the heavy black receiver in its cradle, her amusement at having pulled the wool over old, Mrs. Young's eyes sent her into a powerful fit of cachination. Mirth roared from the depth of her young lungs intil her ribs ached. Giddiness sloshed onto her cheekbones and lips and splattered onto her blouse as she doubled over into a chair. Unable and unwilling to try to stem the waves of laughter, she plunked herself down. She wasn't certain if she was laughing or crying. But, when she stopped, she was filled with a sense of physical calm and psychological relief. "I'm free!" she exclaimed to the watchful eyes of the portraits of her ancestors glaring from across the carpet. "Ding Dong, the witch is dead. The wicked witch is dead!" she sang. "I can do whatever I want." Knowing that the witch wasn't really dead, but only visiting New York, she sprang to her feet and into action.

SEVEN

THE INTRODUCTION

"And what to us seems merest accident
Springs from the deepest source of destiny"

Friday: May 2,1958
Brookline, Massachussetts

The bowing, gnarled, limbs of ancient trees and overgrown
shrubs prevented the entrance to Warren Sreet from being
immediately apparent, so the cab which had jostled quickly
through the crowded, cobblestone ways of Beacon Hill lagged
along the suburban, tree-lined streets of Brookline Hills, and
the ride went on and on. Hebe rethought her impulsive decision
to find Hans as she tried to count the trees between houses.
They were very far apart. Then she saw the sign. "Look Warren
Street! Where is this place? It looks like the end of the
world?"

Warren Street was neither the end nor the beginning of a
place. It was a world unto itself, a precious, New England

treasure, tucked away in a rustling tissue of lavish greenery. It was the land of her grandmother's dreams, land of the privileged, Yankee gentry. The homes vaunted no elaborate, rococo heraldry, no vulgar, Vegas glitz, no conspicuously trimmed gables. Any fancy adornment would have been superfluous to the mansions set on the green hills back from the road. Regally, they stood in the proud, silent, simplicity of understated elegance. They were built by the refined, unpretentious progeny of nobles from old money, ducats and doubloons, golden and delicately veined with blue-blood. They were filled with possessions inherited, objects d'arts so exquisite and priceless they didn't have to shine to attract the eye or flaunt worth. Nothing was superior to the inherent fabric of their beings, the kaolin quality of earth from which God had fashioned them. Hebe squinted her eyes trying to see any sign of life as they cruised by a gigantic Southern Colonial house and let out a heavy sigh. "Gosh, that house looks bigger than my school! Maybe there's another Warren Street," she suggested shifting nervously in the back seat.

In his rearview mirror, the driver watched her counting her dollars into her lap. He didn't say anything, but he did push down the flag to turn off the meter. Finally, he steered the car under the spring canopy of branches by the Brookline Resevoir.

"What number was it again?" The driver asked searching the stone wall in front of the first house for an address.

"219," Hebe answered.

"Well, that place back there on the corner was number ninety-nine, so it should be.. Here it is!" he announced with a sigh of satisfaction. The car idled in front of the tall, wrought iron gateway to the well-maintained lawn of a hill. He eyed her dubiously from under his cap, "Are you sure it's 219?"

"See?" she held up the address flap.

"O.K. Miss, but I'm gonna wait 'til someone responds to the speaker box."

Hans hadn't been listed in the phone book and his name was not visible near the box. No one's name appeared there, only the two words "The Birches". When she announced herself on the

intercom as "Miss Hebe Jeebie Gourdin for Mr. Hans," the gate
popped open. She waved good-bye to the driver just as a large
cloud moved away from the sun. It spotlighted the land as she
made her ingress. Next to the private roadway, the soft, green
lawn lapped down one hill and up the slope of another to a grove
of gracefully arching trees concealing the manor. It was big,
but simple, like a country house on a sea of grass in the middle
of the city. "What have I done?" she thought to herself. "These
people don't even know me." Far away from anywhere, and having
already stated her name, she had to present herself. Something
shrieked from behind a tree encouraging her to walk more quickly
up the path. It was a peacock. It fanned its tail into a dark
rainbow of irridescent feathers. She couldn't believe something
so beautiful could make such an awful noise. She watched it strut
to its friend and tried to think of what to say.

Before anything came to mind, an elderly British butler
opened the door and pushed aside her fears with the greeting,
"Hello. Welcome to the Birches." His eyes had a friendly twinkle.

"Hi. I'm Hebe."

"Yes. Will mademoiselle be seated?"

"Thank you," she replied meekly.

"I will see if Mr. Van Rensselaer is at home," he said and
taking her pale, peach jacket walked away.

Unable to see in the ornate entranceway mirror which reached
several feet above a blue marble fireplace, she checked her
appearance in a small gold leaf framed mirror just to the side of
the enormous white door. She wanted to make the best impression
and show Hans how much of a young lady she had become in three
years. Employed to prove this point were all the things her
grandmother had forbidden, wearing pumps, the black cashmere
sweater and a touch of make-up. In the mirror, within the young
lady she had made of herself, reflected the girl, Hebe Jeebie.
Wide-eyed she put her face up to the glass and peered into her
own eyes to see herself. Pulling back, all that was around her
came into focus: the curving double staircases; the blue-sky
ceiling chock full of cherubs; the pink and white marble diamond

floor. It was a museum of a house. It was beautiful. It was a
place to which she hadn't been invited. She took the old letter
out of her pocket, to have something to take her mind off that
fact. While she was rereading the address, two uniformed maids
bustled by. One carried a heavy silver vase of bright red tulips
and the other, a matching tray bearing a single, purple plum.

On top of the table she saw a small framed oil painting of
what looked like Canova's statue of Hebe, but she was posed
differently. As she stood studying her, the butler returned.

"Look! It's me. Isn't it?"

The man stifled a small, amused chuckle and raised his
eyebrows. "Her name is also Hebe. The statue stands in the
museum in St. Petersberg."

"Oh. Then it isn't quite the same. Mine is in England."

"I see. Mr. Van Rensselauer will be down presently," was
all he had to add to their conversation before he left her alone
again.

Peeking into the grand room she saw several people knit
together contemplating a huge abstract oil on canvas next to the
fireplace where a small fire burned. Framed by the dark wood
doorway, standing as silent and unmoving as the painting, they
became the foreground figures of a living still life. Shyness
held her tongue, and she hoped no one would turn and see her. No
one did. Being totally absorbed in studying the painting, they
didn't even stop the record needle scratching near the label.
The fire popped. Then, a voice called out, animating the figures
and spinning her relievedly around.

"Hebe! Ik kan het niet geloof! Hebe!" repeated Hans' big,
soft voice growing nearer and nearer with the sound of his
footsteps. Excitedly, Hebe ran back to the entranceway and saw
Hans waving as he descended the wide marble staircase. At the
bottom, he lifted her in an enthusiastic embrace. "Let me look
at you," he said placing her back on the ground. "Oh, the
sweater!" She blushed but modeled it turning in childish mincing
steps. "You are beautiful, a beautiful little lady." he
exclaimed kissing her once on each cheek.

"I didn't know you had such a fabulous house."

"This demesne isn't mine."

"What's a demesne?" she asked making him laugh as she snapped her head back and forth looking for it.

"It's a lord's estate, the mansion and the land," he thought a moment and lit a cigarette. "The help who take care of it too."

"Where's your demesne?"

"In Holland. But, my father is taking care of it for me."

"Anyway, Mother would be very jealous." Her eyes took in the high bas relief ceiling of angels and clouds, much like one she had seen in a painting of a European castle in a book about Germany used to trace her father's ship up the Rhein. She tipped her head back as far as her neck would permit and added, "Maybe even my grandmother."

"Your grandmother? I don't know about that. Your daddy told me she's pretty regal.

"She likes to think that. So who does it belong to, this demesne?"

"It's Rem's, Mrs. Remington's. You'll meet her later," he confessed tugging a curl of her hair.

" So you're not mad that I came?"

" Mad? You were supposed to come. I invited you in my letter. Remember? Come on and see the place.

There were many different rooms, each with its own name and function, and for some that purpose was merely being lovely. They began in the tapestry and canvas gallery which led to the "Yellow Room" where the walls and drapes were yellow and proceeded through a rainbow of spaces before arriving at small passageway to a statuary patio leading to enormous domeshaped cloister garden. There, Hans paused to point out how well the jasmine shrubs were doing. The fragrance from the white, yellow and reddish flowers was so potent that she was certain she could see it evaporating into the air from the racemes and buds. "The root of this one," Hans began holding a yellow blossom, "makes a medicine, gelsemium."

"You can you eat the flower?" she asked amazed?

"Not this one. It's posionous. The other one you can use to make tea," Then pointed his finger to a carriage house and said, "They can tell you, or at least Jacques can. He's Japanese. Great with green stuff." Hebe, wasn't even listening. The burgeoning beauty of the greenery around her went unnoticed; she only saw Hans. Her head buzzed. She couldn't believe he was truly standing in front of her. She gave herself a good pinch on her forearm.

"Ow!" she winced.

Hans turned and paused and looked at her, then he knelt down on one knee. As if he had read her mind, he said, " You're really here, here in Boston and all grown up I wish Gordy were here too."

With this reminder of her father, her head dropped.

"Hey, no time for sad stuff. Let's go."

They walked to the other end of the cloister garden to a stone fountain covered with moss babbling like a brook. There were several tables and chairs beneeth the trees. "This is where we've been having breakfast lately." Between two angel statues were three small steps which led to a pool. It stretched under a glass enclosure through the lawn outside then went inside again.

"Those look like the people I saw when I first came in."

"They are. They're deciding whether Holly's painting will go best in white parlour or another place."

"Where was it before."

"It was up in her studio. Rem bought it from her."

Someone on the other side noticed them and waved.

"Come on!" Just as if he were in California by the sea, Hans had stripped down to his briefs. Unabashed, Hebe followed and stood in her underwear while Hans pushed a button opening the whole glass wall. Colorful spring petals bobbed on the surface around them as they swam the length of pool through the yard to the white parlor. Swimming in the wake of her long lost friend, kicking the brisk water out under the open spring air, Hebe was elated and ever so happy she had come.

On the other side which came out right into the room, they

were greeted by a round of applause and laughter from the others
who all lived in the big house. Soaking wet, she met them. Hebe
couldn't take her eyes off Mrs. Remmington, her poreless, lilly
white skin and violet eyes gave her the appearance of an angel in
a black turtle neck sweater. Hans said, "Ah, Hebe this is the
lord, well the lady-lord, of "The Birches." Hebe remembered Hans
mentioning in the letter with the picture from Ali Baba's that
she was 32, around her own mother's age, and that she danced.
Her name was Countess Clair de Lune de la Mar de Maupassant.
But, the others had decided to call her Mrs. Remmington because
she would go on and on about her nanny by that name whom she had
loved very dearly in her youth in England. She always concluded
that she hoped one day to be as " fabulous, accomplished and
independent" as she. In her direct manner of speaking, she said,
" Just Rem please." Then confessed that she found her titled
given name "most tiresome because it's already long enough and I
have to tack on the appendage of 'No relation to the writer to
assuge people's curiosity."

Her life's devotion to ballet was reflected in her
carriage. Her every gesture was as graceful as the stem of a
delphinium in a light morning breeze, yet she was remarkably
strong. That afternoon she was showing them a move in a piece
she performed a dance she had learned recently from some friends
with the Geoffrey Ballet. Hans stood tall near one corner of the
room while she stood diagonally opposite in another. She looked
across the expanse of polished wooden floor and inhaled slowly
while she brought her hands to her heart then slowly unfolded
them at her sides, fluttered them as if they were wings. She ran
toward Hans and precisely in the middle of the room vaulted into
the air and landed gently in his arms, then stretched out like a
solid silver rod. He raised his arms, and her body, now molten
melted into a river of woman which streamed around his shoulders
onto his torso and flowed down his outstretched leg into a puddle
on the floor. Everyone was very impressed. "I'm getting a little
old for this," she half-heartedly apologized. "But, that's the
idea." She rose to her feet.

"It's interesting Rem. They say the body is used to express music. But when I see you do that, I can hear music," commented Floyd. He played the saxaphone whether he had one in his hands or not. His fingers were always running up and down the keys while he tapped his foot. Those were the first words Hebe had heard him speak all day. That surprised her because Hans had also mentioned that Floyd was a writer, Oxford educated. He was in his late twenties, tall, bony and pretty-boy handsome with thick, sandy hair that hung over his brow. Hebe guessed that he let his hair hang down because, even though he was handsome, he had the wide-eyed gaze of someone who had witnessed a tragedy. He never seemed to smile, and he stammered with a slight British accent.

There to present his face to the world with a sweep of her hand in his hair, and to coax him with carresses on his neck was Holly. Holly was the diminutive female version of Floyd. They even dressed in similar clothing. Holly's was smaller, streaked with linseed oil, dabbed and fingerprinted with paint. Though petite, her footsteps thundered on the floor, and she had a great big laugh. She came from Connecticut and studied painting at the Museum School where she met Noni.

He was a green-eyed, Cuban who had the sure-footed, crotch-forward gait of an experienced dancer. He was well aware that his thin summer shirt and slacks accented the valleys and hills of his well-toned muscles. He would smile slyly and raise his eyebrows when he felt someone's eyes on him as Hebe's were. "Are you a dancer too?"

In a slightly accented, overarticulate, but beautifully, deep, satin voice he declared, "'To be, or not to be,' a dancer," then let out a dramatic sigh. "I could be, but I'm an actor, and a model for the art classes, to pick up a little extra money."

"Money? You need money?" Nell interrupted, incredulous.

"Like Rockefeller said, 'The power to make money is a gift from God.'"

"You do it to pick up girls," added Nell accusingly.

"But no. Ees just that my body, it is perfection. I am

doing a service to the artist by letting them immortalize..."

"You do it to pick up girls," interrupted Nell again and rolling her eyes. She had a little tiny child-like voice that matched her innocent face. Her features were fine and her complexion as poreless as milkglass. Though only seventeen, she was 6' tall and quite trim giving her the longest legs Hebe had ever seen on a woman. Her accent was a bit like Hans', but she wasn't from Holland; she was from Belgium.

Her self-introduction was, "I'm Nell, Hans' girlfriend."

From what Hebe had seen and heard, Nell had elevated being a girlfriend to an artform, and was unhappilly incapable of doing anything else. Whenever the conversation turned to Floyd's poetry, Holly's painting, Rem's dancing, Noni's acting or Hans' photography she would coyly point out with a great deal of eye lash fluttering, "Ya, and I am a good girlfriend." Hebe found this curious because unlike Holly and Floyd whom she had never seen separated, Hans and Nell were never once side by side though always in the same room.

The whole group moved through the house carrying out different activities in the different rooms. They exchanged ideas in the white parlor, had lunch under the trees at the tables in the arboretum, and played croquet on the lawn before retiring to their separate rooms for naps. Later, they dressed for the evening and reconvened in the green drawing room for drinks before dinner was served upon the sound of the dinner gong at 8:00 in the formal dining hall.

Together, the women had awakened Hebe to present her with a selection of dresses from which to choose. She knew which one she wanted right away. The floor-length yellow dotted Swiss with the small white collar. She felt like a princess as they fussed over her, putting her hair up and dusting her nose with powder before helping her into the dress. Wrapping the long yellow sash around her waist they tied her into the dress and into the group. She looked as leisurely elegant and pampered as they did.

The diamond sparkle of the crystal in the light of the silver candle sticks seemed to brighten with the energy of the clique as it entered the room. They bowed their heads as if to pray. From past experience, Hebe expected either grace or an argument.

"Ees my turn," announced Noni.

"Oh not some long drawn out speaking like they had at the ball," protested Nell.

"You don't miss any opportunity to bring up that Belgian ball of yours ball, do you? asked Floyd.

"Let her have her excitement," defended Rem. "A beautiful, young girl invited to the only royal ball in her country in a quarter of a century."

"There were six thousand invited guests," he pointed out dryly.

"Yes. Six thousand guests in the entire world and she was one of them." Childishly, Nell giggled and stuck out her tongue as Rem continued. "What do you have against royalty ayway?"

"I don't have anything against royalty. It's just that it was a World's Fair. The most remarkable achievements of the world were there. Van Cliburn played, and all I hear about is bloody King Baudouin's ball."

"If it makes you feel any better Floyd, I don't think the exhibits went unattended, except for all the women having flocked over to hear Van Cliburn's solo."

Before Floyd could say another word, Noni spoke up, "I have the perfect quote to begin our meal. All eyes turned to him. "'If music be the food of love, play on;'" and this made all the others laugh, so he smiled and continued. "' Give me excess of it, that surfeiting, the appetite may sicken, and so die.'"

"Well done old man," said Floyd patting him on the back.

"Truly Noni, you're the Ricky Ricardo of Shakespeare. That was, indeed, the perfect quote," Rem noted.

"Oh Contessa you honor me too much," he said picking up Rem's small fine hand and carefully placing a small kiss between her knuckles gazed longingly into her eyes.

A little embarrassed she took back her hand and remarked with a playful sparkle in her eyes "Yes, I think I do."

For the first time in her life, Hebe was seated at a table where she was expected to participate in the conversation, everyone was, and everyone did, even if only to listen and nod attentively. That was all she could do for a few minutes because the servers distracted her. After they served their dishes, they stood back from the table quiet as mannequins looking straight ahead until something was needed. The others were oblivious to them while Hebe wondered where they had come from and what they thought about while they were just standing by a table full of people eating. Nell reached over pulled her from her thoughts by feathering her hand with her fingertips and said, " I hate it when they talk politics. It always ends up in an argument." Hans, who had his fancy silver Leica on the table kept getting up and taking pictures while arguing his point and smoking. However, Rem ended Cuba's conflict between Castro and Batista by saying sweetly, "Gentlemen. Please. Let's have a topic that won't end up bloody at the dinner table."

Noni speared his rare beef and held it dripping over his plate and said, "Lociento, Señiora. Too late," They all laughed and changed the topic.

Whether the Russians or the Americans would be first to get a man on the moon was brought up and decided, "Too tedious," by Holly. Hans mentioned IBM's Ramac electronic brain which Floyd vetoed because it had been an exhibit at the World's Fair in Brussels. He mimicked Nell, "and then the king looked at me, right at me. I was sure he was going to dance with me." Nell's face flushed and she tensed her mouth, then she tossed her dinner roll at his head. Everyone laughed. Hebe leaned over to see where the roll landed. It was near Rem's foot, the one on the floor, the other bridged from her chair to Hans' where it rested between his legs. Above the table, he was talking, holding his fork in his hand as if unaware that he was running his fingers along Rem's right instep. When Hebe lifted her head, Rem smiled at her and dropped her foot all at the same time.

Slightly flustered Rem said, "Art. What about art? That's something we all know something about. And they did. In an instant, an absolutely electric discussion had begun over which was the better painter Pollock or De Kooning. Rem seemed to avert Hebe's eyes. But soon the misplaced foot incident was lost in the rage of the dinner debate and concluded with Rem snickering and suggesting that they let price be the determining factor, "Last year, I bought one of each. I paid $300 for the De Kooning, at Circle in the Square," she paused "and I don't remember where I got it, but only $75.00 for the Pollock."

"Oh tha's so Americano, measuring the success by the money," complained Noni who was clearly in favor of Pollock.

"That's a curious opinion for a budding tycoon to hold. Besides, I am a British born French citizen!" retorted Rem.

"Touché!" exclaimed Noni. "And I quote again 'Though she be but little, she is fierce,'"

Holly broke her big gaffaw, then delivered a patriotic monologue declaring abstract expressionism a holy movement because it was to the art world what jazz was to the music world, an American phenomenon. Upon hearing the word jazz Floyd smiled and his fingers began going over his invisible instrument. But everyone else agreed, except Hans and Nell who actually spoke together, "DeKooning is Dutch!"

Suddenly, Rem turned to Hebe and said, "You pick a topic." She giggled partly out of shyness and partly because she had no idea what to say. The room was completely quiet until Floyd coughed, and to make things worse, Hans got up and took her picture. Then he moved the camera away from his face, puffed on his cigarette, exhaled and froze. All eyes turned to him. They sat captivated as he spoke in the dramatic, mystical voice of a fortune teller. "This is really incredible. You know, that we seven are all here. Seven. Remember how the other night Floyd said, 'We're a special group all right. It's too bad we're not seven. Then we'd be perfect.'" They all made noises of agreement and nodded their heads. "Now we are the seven. Each of us so damn different, from so far away. Yet, we have found each other here in Brookline, in May 1958. Makes one wonder if there is something to the Buddhism, you know. If some souls are

in some cycle of death and rebirth, not alone, but as a group.
As if once upon a time, we were a little flock of birds together
somewhere that got separated. That our path of migration didn't
take us back and forth, north and south over the land together.
No! It separated us in a unique one-way migration forward in time
not to a place, but to each other again and again and again. Who
knows how many times we have met before?

"Or will meet again?" asked Rem.

"That's quite deep Hans, very beautiful," began Floyd. Then
he tossed his hair back and briefly erased his tragic gaze with a
smile. "I pass for comment. I don't believe we've had quite
enough to drink to carry on with that one. But I like the
significance of seven, cosmic bodies fallen into formation on the
earth, a Celestial Seven."

He held his glass up and they all joined him in the toast,
"To the Celestial Seven!" Almost a full minute of contemplative
silence followed. Then Rem turned to Hebe and said, "You were
going to pick a topic."

Listening to Hans made her think of travel, so she said,
"O.K., I choose faraway places."

"Oh that's a marvelous topic. Let's start in the white
parlor with coffee.

Among them, they had been all over the world. Hebe told
the story about running away to Mexico and being arrested. Hans
and Nell had met in Kenya while she was vacationing with her
parents and he was photographing zebras. No one learned much
about their introduction or adventure because they lapsed into an
unsettled argument about their missing the ride to Kilimanjaro
due to Hans being four hours late.

To the relief of all, Noni interrupted. "Kilimanjaro! I
love the mountains." And explained that he frequently visited
his grandmother who was not from Cuba, but Milan, in Northern
Italy. His family was in the gem business. The farthest he had
gone was on a ruby buying trip to Burma where he got his favorite
ring. Proudly, he removed it and held it carefully as he invited
each person to look closely at the deep bluish-red color of the

stone.

Meanwhile, Floyd and Holly reminisced about boarding school in Switzerland and a vacation they took to the Greek Islands. And finally, Rem spoke.

"I wouldn't know what to choose. You've all heard it before. Tibet on the roof of the world. We had butter tea. The Galapogos on the edge of the world. I caught one of those funny booby birds there. Sweden. Caught my first husband there."

"Si. They love the people with dark hair," Noni threw in with a twenty-four carat grin.

"And with money," she added.

"But, he was a count, wasn't he?"

"Nell, it seems they are all Counts or at leasts Barons. Maybe you should go title hunting there. Contrary to belief the men are quite affectionate."

"Not as much as Italians," she looked right at Hans. "I think Italians are the best lovers, don't you."

Unwilling to follow her into that conversation Rem said, "Well there's a life lesson for you. We paid all that money to go looking for adventure while Hebe's found hers very close to home, and for free. How frightening, to be arrested." She shuddered from the chill of the idea.

Floyd tapped the side of his glass. "Apros pos adventure," he began then played his invisible saxophone, "Tell them, Noni."

"I got the information." They applauded.

Rem leaned over and said in a low voice, "He's tracking UFO's," then asked "So when and where?"

"Near Provincetown."

"Let us know because we all want to go. This will be an adventure for certain. Hebe you'll have to come with us. We're going to be the welcome committee for little green men from outer space."

"Really. Oh I'd love to, but I don't think my grandmother would ever let me."

To her astonishment, she did. But, not for the reason she presumed which was that she had stayed out of her grandmother's

way, out of her life, a task she was able to carry out because of
the Celestial Seven. They had been picking her up after school
lately. In an attempt to quell Nell's brooding over her limited
identity as Hans' girlfriend, they were encouraging her to at
least try other things so that she might have some direction when
she returned to high school later in the year. Hebe gladly
joined them. Sitting in on classes in ballet, art, piano and
acting, she was so infrequently seen that her grandmother even
mentioned her to Kathleen. "Where is the child? She is
deliberately avoiding me. I suppose she thinks that's funny.
When you see her, tell her I want to speak with her."

There were no words of greeting, no smile, no formality of
any kind. Her grandmother's haughtiness inhibited her face from
turning toward her as she addressed her in the authoratative tone
one uses with a servant, "You were sent here, to Boston, Hebe,
because your misconduct was too much for your poor mother. But I
won't have it."

She stood bewildered trying to think of what she possibly
could have done. Then she remembered hooking school. In her mind
she had begun planning her escape as her grandmother continued.

"I don't know where you met Mrs. Maupassant or why she would
want to take you to a play all the way in Provincetown, but she
does." She eyed her with condescending suspiciousness. "Hear
this Hebe Gourdin, as far as background, hers is impeccable.
Everyone wants to be on her guest list. And she has chosen you,"
she tutted. Hebe held her breath wondering if she were going to
give her permission or not. But when she continued with, "You
should be honored," she had to stifle a little jump of gladness.
"I offered to come along. I thought perhaps her mother was in
town and we could have tea. Wouldn't that be lovely?"

"No. No that would be horrible," Hebe moaned to herself.
She didn't want her grandmother involved with her new friends,"
The Birches", from the end of the world. Her throat tense up the
way it did before she was about to cry until Mrs. Wilkinson
concluded, "Unfortunately, the contessa's mother is not here.
She mentioned her charge, some Belgian girl, yes, a Belgian, I

think she said she was. But I tell you this Hebe Gourdin, you
must behave. Remember, 'Be seen, not heard." She placed such
emphasis on the social prominence of Countess de Maupassant that
she guessed the second reason for her allowing her to go to
Provincetown was quite simply that she was impressed by the
company she was keeping. Of course, Rem had only disclosed that
they were going to a cultural event, a play, and kept secret the
actual objective of their trip, searching for a flying saucer.

None of her guesses was correct. The reason Hebe was sent
by Grandmother Wilkinson was a letter. It had come a few days
earlier from her uncle's doctor in Vienna, her parents
birthplace. She often wondered what her life would have been
like had they not left in 1914 and gone to Hong Kong where she
went to private school. After all, her great uncle was a distant
cousin of Emperor Francis II, a Hapsburg. Her whole life she
lamented not having been able to enjoy the cultural grandeur of
Vienna; the aristocratic social circles entertained by the opera,
the theatre, and of course, the spectacular winter ball season.
On countless occasions she asked her own mother why the family
had left Austria. She always received the same bitter,
misty-eyed tale.

"Schatz, we had to. As soon as your father heard about what
had happened that Sunday to Archduke Ferdinand and his belovéd
Sophia, he told me we were leaving for Victoria Peak, Hong Kong.
Imagine being thus uprooted! Believe me, embarking on an odessey
through the far east was no fantasy of mine. Nevertheless, there
we were, all because of some fool student in Sarajevo, Gavrilo
Princip. I will never forget his name. Curse his soul. Two
little bullets and time enough to blink your eyes changed
everyone's life, began a war. We had to go." Ever since hearing
the story when she was a child, Mrs. Wilkinson mourned on that
day, June 28th.

Living through the history which proved her parents decision
correct never dispelled her rankling bitterness about the path of
her life. Eventhough she had met Mr. Wilkinson in Hong Kong and
had married well, she couldn't help wondering what could have

been. She felt history had, unfairly, forced her to ride
streetcars and mingle with the lower classes. It had stripped
her of the life of privilege to which she felt entitled.
Holidays to her uncle's castle near Vienna, afforded her a taste
of how life could have been. Being his favorite niece, she was
often invited, and he shamelessly indulged her in noble luxury.
Waltzing in Vienna, her soft fingers resting on the stiff, broad
shoulder of a titled gentleman or an officer, walking in the rose
garden in a ballgown, sipping tea on her balcony with a staff
busily tending to her needs, these were the images she had wanted
to bring to fruition in her life.

        Instead, she was alone on Beacon Hill, a lonely, aging,
widow whose only daughter had further removed her from her
fantasy by marrying "a man with no background and no money, an
Indian whom she would not even have chanced to have the
misfortune of meeting if a she were brought up in Vienna." She
blamed herself for having raised a daughter who didn't use
background as the first yardstick by which to measure a potenial
husband, a daughter who married not only beneath her class, but
out of her race. After she reeled from the shock of seeing
Gordy's photograph for the first time, she begged her daughter to
tell her it was a cruel joke. "Gaye-Lee, an Indian. It can't
be! They are barbarians My mother told me she had seen one of
their chiefs on the ground at the St Louis World's Fair!"

        "The Saint Louis World's Fair! That was 1904!

        "She read about it."

        "Well, she read wrong. It wasn't the ground. It was a
blanket. Did she also read that Geronimo met Teddy Roosevelt. I
don't believe you can say you have ever met any president, not
even Roosevelt, mother."

        "I assure you that's only because the poor man is dead."
She threatened not to attend and to disown Gaye-Lee in toto.
Greatly diminishing the power of her words was the fact that her
husband had provided well for their daughter in his will.
Gaye-Lee didn't need her mother's wealth, and she made it clear
that she would marry Gordy whether her mother came or not. Of

course, she attended the wedding. Sadly, she only had two living
relatives, her uncle, far away in Vienna and her daughter. She
didn't really want to lose her Gaye-lee, so she reduced her
protest to a private visual statement. She had a dress made in a
dusty-grey lavender in order to be able to use the deep purple
bows from the mourning suit she had worn to her husband's
funeral. Of course she would still be listed in the register,
she had the right by birth as did her daughter. But Gaye would
be removed for marrying beneath her. It would be the demise of
her social reknown.

However, circumstances were giving rise to its possible
rebirth. As a mother, she knew she should have not have condoned
her daughter's illicit affair with Art, that such impropriety
should have been discouraged. In lieu of denouncement, she
offered praise, even welcomed and promoted it. Seeing Gaye-Lee
courted by a Mayflower Yankee, a Harvard man, filled her with a
sense of relief. The wrong of their relationship was a blessing
in disguise, a promise of salvation for her only child. Ever so
quietly, her money was working hard to realize a divorce between
Gaye and Gordy, to erase any trace of the mark that had blackened
her family name. It was difficult because he was at sea, but not
impossible. The only evidence to be gotten rid of would be Hebe.
She told all of her friends that Hebe was being put up for
adoption. And, if Hebe were going to stay with her much longer,
she had already secretly arranged to eliminate the necessity of
having to talk about her at all by sending her to boarding
school.

Now, the letter arrived with the news that her dear ailing
uncle was not well and needed her in Vienna. She had a great
many papers to sign and matters to which she had to attend. She
wanted them to be private. She wanted Hebe out of the way. Her
first thought was to return her to California, but it was almost
June, the end of the school year. Rem's offer to take her for a
few days couldn't have come at a more opportune time. Her dream
was near. The thought of the dainty rich, Viennese pastries and
the fragrant rosebuds caused her to give permission for Hebe to

go with impolite haste.

Her personal history and feelings were hidden in the dark recesses of her small heart along with all of the other genuine feelings she had in her life. She had many powerful, deep feelings, but her upbringing had conditioned her to keep them to herself. She believed that humans had emotions making them superior to animals and that a certain few humans were exalted over others by their ability to not express them. Having perfected the latter ability, she was perceived by Hebe and those around her, as an insensitive, uncaring old lady. But at the moment, Hebe thought she was swell and wanted to kiss her because she was letting her go to Provincetown, or P-town as everyone called it.

EIGHT

P-TOWN

A Dream Come True

The following weekend
Friday: May 8, 1958
Provincetown, Massachusetts

The women's luggage was all over everything in one of the
three small cottages on Bradford Street. Hans, unable to find
any place to sit down complained, "So what's the idea? This
cottage is for the clothes? What are we supposed to do with all
of this?

"It looks like more than it is because the driver put it all
in one cottage," Rem tossed her words out casually and shoed
Holly off her trunk.

Seeing the trunk, Hans continued, "Oh, now really, tell me
there's a spare bed in here. You can't possibly wear all of this
stuff in a week end."

"I don't intend to," Rem clarified politely whipping a
chiffon nightie from Noni's hands.

"Then, why did you bring it if you don't need it?" asked
Noni tossing a scarf in the air and holding his face under it
until it landed onto his closed eyes. "What is that flower,

Arpege?"

"Arpege is not a flower," she said, " And, I don't know what I'll feel like wearing tonight or tomorrow, or this afternoon for that matter. I brought a choice. I need a choice. O.K.?" Holly let out one of her boisterous laughs. The two men shook their heads from side to side. "Why don't you go find Floyd?" she asked just as the big sound of him warming up his saxaphone interrupted.

"Found him," Noni said with a smile, then picked up a suitcase and left. Holly and Nell put their sunglasses on as they stepped out. Hebe hung back near the only person she really knew, Hans. He started to follow then turned sheepishly to Rem and, thinking no one could see, ran his finger slowly down her ribs to her waist. Hebe had seen, but she thought nothing of it.

"Um..do you want company?" he asked almost in a whisper.

"Only my own right now," Rem answered instantly with a look of annoyance that discouraged him from asking again.

As if the leaves of a plant individually turning in a variety of positions to soak up the sun, the seven "Birches" went off to settle in or get oriented for the week-end in P-Town. The only two who remained together were Hebe and Nell. Their nimble, young legs pushed the pedals of rented bikes down the long seashore road all the way to Race Point. The thick sea air filled out their hair and kept them cool. They had to walk the bikes over the dunes to the water. For a while their was nothing to say.

They just bundled up in their sweaters and sat watching the mighty, grey deep of the Atlantic slap the face of the sand. At the same time, very quietly each began to hum. They turned, looked at each other and continued to hum, then realized they were humming the same song, The Blue Danube. In unison, they said, "I love that waltz." Then they burst out laughing. Nell was the first to get up. She bowed in front of Hebe and grinning, asked in a deep, mock male voice, "May I have the honor of this dance?" Merrily they mouthed the melody as Nell led Hebe in a zealous and graceless waltz across the sand dusted dance floor of

THE CHORUS BALL, last night, at the Coliseum, was not crowded by attendants as was the first one. There was a noticeable absence of full dress, and the promenaders presented a kaleidoscopic appearance, both the ladies and the gentlemen dressing in all kinds of styles. Nevertheless, there were many very costly and attractive costumes.

The music was excellent, as Mr. Baldwin had organized a very fine band specially for the evening which was composed of the following pieces: Fifty first violins, fifty second violins, forty violas, forty violoncellos, thirty basses, six flutes, four oboes, four bassoons, eight clarinets, six trumpets, six horns, four trombones, one bass drum, two snare drums, one pair of typani and one triangle, making in all two hundred and fifty-three instruments.

Dancing began quite generally about ten o'clock, Mr. Zerrahn at first wielding the baton. Subsequently Mr. Downing, the leader of the Ninth N. Y. Regiment Band, who has had control of the New York division of the orchestra, of which his own famous band formed a part, took the stand and conducted the music for several dances, alternating with Mr. Gilmore, who directed far into the night.

In the fourth dance Herr Strauss made his appearance, and was cordially welcomed by his friends, who have repeatedly saluted him as he has passed up and down the aisle between the great banks of singers. He assumed the baton, and conducted the orchestra as they played the "Blue Danube Waltz."

The order of dances and music was as follows:

1	Quadrille—"Bijouterie"	Strauss
2	Waltz—"Morgenblatter"	Strauss
3	Polka Redowa—Bagatelle	Strauss
4	Waltz—Blue Danube	Strauss
5	Lancers—"20th"	Weingarten
6	Waltz—Artist Life	Strauss
7	Quadrille—Bouquet	Strauss
8	Waltz—Romance of the Forest	Strauss
9	Polka Redowa—Le Chatelaine	Faust
10	Waltz—1001 Nights	Strauss
11	Lancers—"16"	Weingarten
12	Galop—Strumvogle	Faust
13	Quadrille—Mator	Strauss
14	Waltz—New Wien	Strauss
15	Lancers—"18"	Weingarten
16	Galop—Cascade	Faust

The arrangements for the supper were on the same scale as at the first ball. There was only one drawback to the enjoyment of the "poetry of motion," and that was the intense heat; although the Coliseum is about the coolest place in the city Those present did as well as could be expected under the atmospheric conditions, and remained stationary, listening to the delicious music, or promenading at their will. With a similar crowd as at the first ball, perspiring humanity could hardly have withstood the pressure. The smaller attendance was therefore a gratifying fact to chorus singers who had braved the heat. The occasion was one that will be remembered by all the participants in its fervid and glowing pleasures.

JOHANN STRAUSS.

THIS celebrated Austrian composer, whose performances at the grand Boston Jubilee have excited so much enthusiasm, is the eldest son of a man who was famous in his own generation for almost exactly the same class of dashing, delightful harmonies which have been rendered so celebrated by the son. His father, for whom he was named, prepared him for the military profession; but the boy's feeble health and the wonderful musical talents which he displayed at an early age decided his father to make a musician of him. He had excellent instructors, and already in his sixteenth year had become a virtuoso on the violin, and thoroughly familiarized himself with the art of composition and counterpoint. Several of his compositions were published and became very popular, and in his nineteenth year he resolved to form an orchestra like the one over which his father had presided so long and so creditably. The undertaking was successful, and before long young STRAUSS's orchestra became as popular as that of his father.

In 1846 he set out with his band upon a two-years' concert tour through the countries on the lower Danube, and was well received every where. In 1848 he published his famous "Radetzky March," which is now a national air in Austria, and for which he received a title and an honorable decoration. During the following fifteen years he visited nearly every capital in Europe with his orchestra, and received as many decorations as adorn the breast of a field-marshal. His greatest triumph he achieved with his band at the Paris Exhibition of 1867, where STRAUSS's concerts were one of the principal attractions.

He had meanwhile published a great many compositions, and the number of his works is now upward of six hundred. Some of his productions have had an extraordinary sale. Of his "Radetzky March" and "Annen Polka" upward of half a million copies were sold. STRAUSS receives from the copyright of his compositions fifty thousand florins annually, and is looked upon as by far the richest of the living composers of Europe.

STRAUSS, of whom we give a portrait on page 556, is a very fine-looking man, with a most expressive face, and seems considerably younger than forty-eight, which is his age.

JOHANN STRAUSS.—[SEE PAGE 555.]

A COUNTRY CONGREGATION.

WE fancy many of our readers who spend the summer months in the country will recognize the truth of the sketch on page 556, which represents the whole congregation turning round at once to see who is coming in after the minister has fairly launched out into his sermon. The effect on the late-comer, who has to face all these curious glances, may be easily imagined, and also the discomfiture of the minister, the point of whose "secondly" or "thirdly" is perhaps entirely lost in the momentary disturbance.

the balroom dunes with the wind in their hair.

"My great, great grandmother met Johann Strauss when he came
to Boston," Hebe boasted.

"Oh, that must have been the most. Tell me."

"It was a million years ago on July 1, 1872 at The Chorus
Ball at the Coliseum in Boston. We read about it in a letter she
wrote to her mother in Vienna. And when she sailed home, he was
on the same ship. I saw the photograph in my grandmother's room.
He's standing just like this." She stopped dancing and struck a
pose.

"What does he look like?"

"His hair is black, over his ears." She thought a moment.
"Oh, and he has a big black beard."

"Imagine dancing with a music man like that."

"I don't like beards so much, but I'd love to go to a ball
and dance with someone else."

"You will. Everyone does. I've been to lots. The last was
the most lovely. I just wish Hans had come. I waited and
waited." She sighed a heavy sigh that was the beginning of the
long story of her affair with Hans. She talked on and on in such
detail that Hebe found it difficult to follow. What was clear
was that they became secretly involved in the exciting and romantic setting of the Kenyian wilderness where they were travelling
with her parents, her boyfriend, Olivier and his mother. "I
think they were hoping Hans would like my mother. My father died
when I was six and everyone is always trying to put her together
with someone. But nothing happened with her and Hans. The first
night he picked up one of the African girls in a bar." She
chuckled remembering. "Oh, Everyone was so upset, and my mother.
Well, she didn't say it publically, but she was terribly
insulted. When Hans came to me, I asked him about this girl, and
he said he was just curious, that he really liked me from the
beginning. We didn't want to hurt my mother, so we kept our love
a secret." She made noises as if she were eating a creamy
pudding, then continued. "We did it while the lions were
sleeping."

"Lions?"

"Ja. Hans was hunting for pictures, special pictures
because everywhere you turn your head in Africa there is one
amazing picture waiting for you. We walked into a field where
there were all these lions lying around sleeping. He took a lot
of photos, then we decided to wait and catch them waking up. One
thing led to another and... It was so exciting making love with
the threat of death..."

"Why were you going to die?!"

"The lions, silly."

Hebe closed her eyes a moment to see a live lion.

"They didn't wake up when they smelled you."

"That's what I asked Hans! He just kept kissing me. Where's
the most interesting place you ever did it?"

"I want to hear the end of your story."

"There isn't one. I went home to Belgium. He went home to
Holland. We wrote a lot of letters which my mother found and,"

Hebe gasped in horror, "She read them?!"

"Yes," came out and one tiny tear rolled onto the bridge of
her nose. "I explained that I hadn't heard from him for a long
time. Didn't matter. Next thing I knew I was on the ship to come
and stay with Mrs. Rem."

"My mother packed me off too. But, what kind of a
punishment is it to send you to Hans?

Selfsatisfaction dawned on her face and she beamed, "That's
just it. We thought he was still in Holland. No one knew he was
here! Not her. Not me. See, it didn't end.

Hebe thought about the letters she herself had received from
Hans, and the photographs. She wondered if he would send the
photographs of the other night at dinner to someone, maybe the
black bar girl in Africa. She focused on Nell's words again.

"Well, I was so happy. Every time my old boyfriend kissed
me, I thought of Hans because, well, with Olivier, I noticed that
I didn't feel anything but our lips together. That's all just
the bodies. But with Hans it was all around, inside and out. I
felt like I was flying or something." When Mamá told me I was

going to have to spend the summer in America, I wasn't very
excited. I do adore Rem, but what about my friends, my life?
The strange thing is, Hans isn't acting the same. If I didn't
love him, I would find some Italian boy. Italian boys are really
the best." She threw her body back on the sand and let out a
frustrated little yelp. "You should know. You're boyfriend's
Mexican isn't he?"

Thankful that Nell had stopped talking about Hans, Hebe told
her about Tony. She said she could well sympathize with the
frustrations of being apart and waiting because he had joined the
army, and he wasn't a great writer.

"Sometimes I open it up and there's just a matchbook cover
from somewhere he's been, or a tiny piece of cloth from a new
shirt he wants to show me, or he'll tear a stick of gum in half
and chew half and send the other half to me."

"That's romantic," Nell said vacantly.

"Maybe. Last time, three weeks ago from boot camp he sent
me two long numbers. That's all, a piece of paper with two long
numbers."

"What were they?"

"At first I really had no idea. Wait, I think," she went
into her shorts pockets and produced the small slip of paper with
the numbers: 53310761 and 53310762 I tried them on the
telephone. I looked at a calendar. I couldn't figure it out.
Finally, Kathleen, my grandmother's housekeeper told me."

The suspense sat Nell up. "What?"

"Elvis Presley and Tony have the same draft number, except
for one digit."

"Maybe, he'll meet him. Maybe you'll meet him!" she added
excitedly. "Fall in love."

"With Elvis Presley?"

"Then, your granchildren will say l'arrière grand mère de
m'arrière grand mère met Richard Strauss and my grand mère met
Elvis Presley."

"Nell, don't be ridiculous. My grandmother probably wouldn't
even let him in her house.

"How can you be so sure?"

"Easy. I don't think Elvis anyone is in her social register."

Just then, they heard their names being shouted down the beach. Through the damp dusk they saw the rest of the group gadding over the sands towing two pungs full of supplies, a telescope and cameras. Nell's face lit up with the starlight of infatuation. "Hans!"

Hans spread his long arms to the side like a giant bird and enfolded the adoring girl in them, restoring Hebe's faith in him. She had kept quiet while Nell was explaining her situation, but Nell's implication that somehow Hans was hurting her, upset Hebe. She just couldn't believe that he would do anything to hurt anyone. He had served as her invisible, buckler against the negative forces in her life in California. No matter what confusing or harmful events had transpired, she always found comfort in the notes, post cards and photos from him which linked her to her father and days she remembered as happy. The memories of their few hours together were such a powerful elixer that they had lasted for the three and a half years they had been apart. Surely, Nell was misinterpreting his behavior. Nevertheless, she kept a casual watchful eye out during the night.

In the last light before dark, they pitched a tent which Noni kept refering to as headquarters. On the small card table inside he laid out his magazines, articles and reports and even maps tracking visitors from space. Floyd had begun to practice his sax, but it was too loud for the small, enclosed, canvas space. Preferring not to go out by the ocean and subject his instrument directly to the sea air, he sat in the corner soundlessly running his hands along the shiny yellow brass keys. Next to him Holly was heating soup on a bunson burner, and keeping time, humming along as if she were privy to his song which only they two could hear. Outside, their small fire was burning attracted several people who had driven down the road.

Some had just come out to see the view, to be surrounded by the sea, and others had come because the grapevine in town had

spread the word that there was a party at Race Point. Enticed by
news of the possibility of flying saucers arriving, most of them
stayed; even though, they were told no party had been planned.
One of them, a short middle-aged, black man in dungarees and a
beret threw himself in the sand by the fire and began beating on
a pair of bongos anyway. Catching the rythm in her hips, a
shapely brunette flung her arms over her head and began a
provocative barefooted dance. From the road came the call of a
guitar's strum introducing men in bulky sweaters with their shirt
tails hanging out and a girl with a long, fat braid carrying a
jug of wine and paper cups. The other instruments coaxed Floyd
out of his niche and sound out of his sax. Not a word was said
outloud among them. Through the special telepathic communication
of musicians and a series of looks and smiles and played notes,
they accompanied one another through a dark disconnected passage
to their syncopated, dune-top rhapsody as if they had been
rehearsing it for weeks. Out from their fingertips exploded the
blood-simmering, body-swinging, musical, Afro-Cuban firecrackers.
Ocassionally, one musician would glance at another with a
questioning look on his face trying to figure out where he was
going with the music. The listeners never saw. The spell of
music had entered their beings causing their arms to flail wildly
in the air, their fingers to snap and pop near their ears and
their torsos to girate next to each other. Hebe's native spirit
awakened by the circle of souls around the firelight and the
steady bongo's beat lifted her knees in a primitive prance around
the flickering flames. Having absorbed the intoxicated high
energy of those around her, she had to move, to whoop. She shot
her gleeful voice at the sky. Some gave sensual grunts; others
yelped and still others grinned incessantly, incapable of making
any sound at all. The prophecy of a party had fullfilled itself
and for a while everyone was caught up in the impromptu net of
revelry cast by the players. They drank and danced and wailed.

In the natural quell that follows such a release of energy,
Noni took center stage by the fire and delivered a monologue from
the play Twelfth Night for the general entertainment of all and

the particular attentions of a petite, red-haired girl with a
full mouth covered in cherry red lipstick. Hebe had seen him
perform the piece in acting class at least a dozen times, but
this was the first time he executed it with such animated
passion. Before beginning, he waved a paper in the air and
asked, "Coul' somebody just hold this for me; it's a prop." And
before anyone had the chance to refuse, he reached out and pulled
his bubbly, blushing prey to the front and said, "Maybe you will
help me." He gave a vague explanation of the setting, "Act 2,
Scene 5. Olivia's Steward is in the garden with the phony letter,
a trick," he glanced around and caught the girl's eyes. "You are
holding that prop for me, o.k."   Then he began.

> MALVOLIO:(Eyes the letter.) What employment have
> we here? (Just gingerly enough to accidentally touch her
> hand on purpose, Noni takes the letter and the girl's
> breath.) By my life, this is my lady's hand.
> These be her very c's and u's, and
> her t's, and thus make she her great
> P's. It is in contempt of question, her hand.

He continued and finished the long speech to win the
applause of all and the eagerly voluntary company of the girl.
After a modest bow, he slithered next to his compliant prey. A
voice from the crowd called out, "Maybe Tennessee Williams could
use you."
    "Oh yeah, and maybe that multi-billionaire guy on the t.v.,"
he snapped his fingers trying to remember.
    "John Beresford Tipton," shouted Hebe enthusiastically. She
had seen his show on the television, He had a 60 thousand acre
estate and he went around giving money, a million dollars, to
unsuspecting people. The show was about how the money changed
their lives. In order to receive the money, they had to agree to
keep the source secret. She used to think she'd buy a big house
for herself and her brother Jude and Margarita and her family to
live in. Now, she wasn't so sure. California seemed farther

than the stars and she had forgotten the man on TV until now.

"Yeah, John Beresford Tipton, he's is going to come to my house and give me a million dollars."

The bongo player stepped forward. "You never know Daddy-o. Tennesse Williams comes down here a lot. I even met him myself about ten years ago, him and Marlon Brando at the A- House over on Commercial."

Hebe made a mental note to go there the next day. The drip and drab appearance of people that began the party, ended it. No flying saucers from outer space had appeared. There wasn't even an unusual twinkle to remind them of why they had stayed in the first place. The cold, late hour sent the each back down the road until only the Celestial Seven remained. Much to Noni's dismay even his cherry-lipped girl had scampered off to catch a ride with the last car that left. He replaced her in his mind with space ships until the dense black of night was diminished a hue by the light fingertips of the approaching day. At 3:30 a.m. Rem was heard to say, "Wondrous cold? Isn't that what Coleridge wrote? 'And it grew wondrous cold.' Somehow I can relate to that more in the Alps in February than I can on a beach in May, wondrous cold." It was a freezing spring night and the sleeping bags lay unfolded. There were five. Holly and Floyd shared one. Nell and Rem fell asleep talking on one under another leaving Hans alone. The fifth sleeping bag lay empty. A plan for sleeping hadn't been discussed, and none of the sleeping bags belonged to Hebe confusing her as to where she was to sleep. The only one awake was Noni. Anxiety, paced him back and forth in the tent, periodically expanding his path outside to check the sky and have a cigarette. Hebe read one of his old life magazines and examined its photos of the phenomena thought to be flying saucers which had appeared over Lubbock, Texas in August,1951. They were called "The Lubbock Lights." She went outside to have a look for herself as Noni shuffled in.

The faded black velvet skirt of a sky dusted with glitter brushed its hem along the border of the world as night ambled off. Staring out into the inky vastness of the sea beneath it,

surrounded by stretches of dark dunes, she saw that her shadowy
form was no bigger than a small solitary rock. Sadness seeped
into her marrow with the damp. And she longed to go home, not to
Warren Street or Beacon Hill or sunny San Diego where there was a
room for her, but a home where there were people full of room for
her. Never having left the non-existant place, she couldn't
return. With a soft, "psst" Rem lassoed her and saved her from
drifting further out on the sea of irrational thoughts that often
rise in the predawn hours of sleepless nights. "Come inside. We
decided we may as well stay and see the sunrise. It looks a lot
better with a little bit of sleep. Besides Nelly and I need
you." She yawned and insisted on being between the two girls
because she was freezing; they all were. Noni was curled up into
a ball in his downy bedding, Holly and Floyd who had both gotten
drunk were passed out and buried in their sleeping bag and Nell's
body was shivering. Rem pointed to Hans. Unmindful of the cold,
his huge body was stretched on top of the unopened sleeping bag.
He had a pleasant smile on his face, and his hands rested on his
chest. They were steaming. "We wanted him to come and sleep with
us, but he said, 'It's too hot,'" and went back to sleep." Rem
shook her head, "Can you believe it?" She asked snuggling closely
to Hebe for warmth and, securing the coverlet around Hebe's
shoulder with a caring tuck. With a merry note in her sleepy
voice she added, "Here we are, home away from home. Sweet
dreams, dahling."

Even though it was only May, Hebe had gotten a slight
sunburn from falling back asleep on the beach after watching the
sunrise. It was spectacular! "The Birches" stood scattered
along the beachfront facing the sun as if ancients worshipping
the miracle of a rising young Phoenix. From 93,000,000 miles
away the muted yellow elliptical crescent inched up from the
horizon and radiated the dark of night away with billions of
bristles of heat, the same bristles that but lightly brushed
their faces with warmth. And when it had risen to its full
shape, they cheered and applauded. Floyd produced a small pair
of finger cymbals. Their tinkling chime summoned the family of

"The Birches" into a circle on the sand where they sat cross-legged and chanted. the day had begun.

No one cared that the only flying saucers seen were those photographed a decade ago for a magazine. Noni had had to come to see for himself, and they were there to keep him company. Whatever interest one had, they supported. Therefore, when Nell said, "It would be cool to see the sunrise," they allowed their comfortable cottages to serve as expensive closets and stayed on the beach; gladly agreed to Rem's theatre suggestion; and as Hebe wanted met before the play at the A-House, citing of Tennessee Williams and Marlon Brando. "Just wait until I write to Rosalita about being here," she mused. But when she had the pen in her hand, the crowning point of the weekend in Provincetown was not sitting on a chair possibly once used by a famous person, or even the flying saucer party. It was the play.

A most amusing work," Floyd informed her as they sat at the bar. He stared at his scotch as he spun it with a flick of his wrist. "Since we analyzed it in my Harvard theatre class, I'm the best person to turn to with any of your little questions," he continued jutting his chin out.

She had no little question, but she was eager to think up something clever. Whichever "Birch" was the expert on a subject, was expected to discuss it or be open to inquiry. If two claimed expertise on the same topic, they engaged in witty verbal duels for title to the intellectual territory. If none of them knew anything about an issue that came up, someone volunteered to look into it and report back to all. Communicating, thusly, she had discovered was the way to inclusion and acceptance by the group. Floyd and Holly rarely spoke to anyone, and neither had ever struck up a conversation with her. Now, Floyd sat across from her, his head cocked, poised for the key question to open his information bank, and she didn't have one, except about the title. "Be seen and not heard," echoed through her mind and the fear of saying something that would render her an idiot in Floyd's eyes strapped her chest so tightly that she could barely muster the breath to get the simple words out.

"Where did he get the title?"

"Good question, 'Where did he get the title?' Did you ever hear of Martial? Of course not. Well, Marcus Valerius Martialis, an ancient Roman writer, gifted, popular and, legend has it, all around funny guy," he began. Clearly, Floyd was king of the Greco-Roman influence in one act comedy as well as related triva. With only the one question, Hebe learned the details of Martial's love affair with a slave girl; the unique, male procreation process of the fable Greek Phoenix and the author's attempt to ressurect the art of verse with A Phoenix too Frequent. By the time Floyd was finished Hebe was truly well-informed and primed for the performance.

The stage was hung with blue fishnet, and there was a Roman lamp, a very simple set. A very simple play, only three actors. She laughed and she loved it. Therefore, she wrote "I loved it!" The lines! The names! The plot! She put in the notes Floyd had jotted down for her in the A-House. Dynamene, a Roman lady, who wants to be with her dead husband, for some reason, is in his tomb at Ephesus with her servant, Doto. But fortunately for her, the lady falls in love with Tegeus, the guard. So doto soesn't have to die. "Imagine being called, Doto? She drink wine, like us. She gets caught too, Rosalita." She copied the words from the the play Floyd had given to her.

Dynamene: Doto have you been drinking?

Doto: Here, madam? I coaxed some a little way towards my mouth, madam, but I scarcely swallowed except because I had to. The hiccup is from no breakfast, madam, and not meant to be funny."

Hebe grinned remembering the lines and the look on Tegeus' face when Dynamene asks, 'Is that how you look when you sleep?

Tegeus: My jaw drops down.

Dynamene: Show me how.

Tegeus: Like this.

Dynamene: It makes an irresistible moron of you. Will you waken now?

She ended up confessing that the very poetry of the play which amused her also confused her, that she depended on Noni, one of her new friends, to explain many of the lines. She hoped she would have the chance to see one again soon, and she tried to encourage Rosalita to do the same. "It isn't like being in one at school where you know everyone and all the lines and you laugh at the mistakes like when we did Romeo and Juliet at school last year. Remember? Wesley Anderson kissed Angela Harp on the lips and they wouldn't stop. A real play, where you don't know anyone is like watching people do things you are not supposed to see and seeing both people at once, the person and the actor, like my mother when she's bombed. I know she is both my beautiful mother and the ugly drunk. It's the same with actors. It must be hard to be two people, to remember all those lines. I can't even remember the pledge of allegiance! I only wish my mother could stop her act and be herself the way the actors do. I wonder what is wrong with her." Her young style was a long way from laconic, and she filled page after page trying to explain her new found excitement in the theatre only to reread it to recognize she had gone back to writing more of a letter to herself about her mother than a letter to Rosalita about the play. Frustrated, she balled up the papers and sat back in her chair at the table in the cloister garden.

Among the beautiful bravura of the hundreds of loud petals, serenity bloomed and it flowed endlessly in the gurgling water of a fountain in the corner. Driving home, Rem had given her the choice of being dropped off or spending Sunday afternoon at "The Birches", admonishing that the afternoon would probably be a solitary one because everyone had things to do. But without hesitation she chose the latter. Being alone in the lively shadows of people living life was preferable to being alone in the inert shadows of furniture collecting dust. The mere thought of her small immured room in the old, sequestered Beacon Hill home made her sad. She closed her eyes and wished to herself that she could stay at "The Birches", then she opened them and searched the sky for God and spoke to it in a clear voice, "Why

can't I live here? I have fun and I learn so much. They're all
really nice. Why do I have to be with people who hate me all the
time?" She scrunched up her face squinting at the sunny heaven
and continued, "So how's a person supposed to know if you hear
them?" The peacock screeched from its cloistered perch in the
trees rippling her skin with goosebumps.

Across the green, she saw a man riding up to the stable on
horseback. He spotted her sitting in the greehouse and trotted
the big, brown Morgan right up the green hill. "Good afternoon,"
he called out. "Did Holly ride by?" Hebe shrugged just as as
Ichi, the Japanese gardner appeared out of nowhere and began
softly scolding the rider and shaking his head as he picked up
clumps of grass which the horses shoes had dug up. She had heard
the others talking about him. He spoke English with an accent
more French than Japanese because during the war he had lived on
the Mauppasant estate in the South of France. Her in-laws knew
they wanted a gardner and he really wanted to go to America; thus
two birds were killed with one stone by presenting Ichi, who
prefered to be called Jacques, to Rem and her husband as a
wedding gift. He didn't look old enough to have been an adult
during the war. His shaggy hair was jet black and his round face
was as smooth as a country egg. He held up the wounded greens
and stood firmly encouraging the man to go to the riding rink
behind the stable with a shooing flag of his chubby arms that
waved his whole body, then shuffled into the greenhouse.

The clump of earth nearly tipped over the clay pot he threw
it in. Much to her astonishment, he plucked the head of a
chrysanthemum, dusted it off and popped it into his mouth.
Grumbling and grouching he gave the plants his passing
greenkeeper's attention, sticking his finger in the soil of one
and pinching a brown leaf from another as if he hadn't seen Hebe
sitting there. But, he turned and glanced directly at her over
his small, round gold-rimmed glasses when he said, "This house
Maupassant house, not Rockefeller house. Cos' two thousan'
dolla', pour le new glass this spring. Horses no good pour le
glass," and he bowed slightly and walked out the opposite door.

"So sorry, not able to talking maintenant," he tapped at his watch. "Time for Lone Langer." He bowed slightly and backed out of the door.

Floyd almost knocked him down as he swaggered in, a bundle of angry nerves in a rumple of wrinkles. He spoke in the slow full voice of someone who had lost count of his drinks. "They're bloody stupid animals, horses are!" He raved stealthily snatching at some leafy green plants and putting the tops in his dark satin smoking jacket pocket. "Tell Rem I won't be at dinner tonight."

His feet were positioned firmly in one place, but his body reeled unsteadily and his nasal breaths were short. "Are you sick or something," Hebe asked with such genuine concern, he paused and lowered his voice.

"Well, no. No I'm not." With these words, a boozy vapor became noticeable. "I'm working on a new poem. Thank you." Holly's big gaffaw caused him to pause and peruse her perturbedly as she posted on a proud dapple grey next to the man who had ridden across the grass. "Really stupid, they are!" he repeated, again shouting. "Aren't they? Aren't they stupid!? Answer me!" he demanded in an explosive voice.

An utter stillness came over her as it used to when her mother's 100 proof tongue fumed words. She knew well, the smallest word, even an utterance could enkindle a malefic firestorm. For this reason, she didn't even breathe. After a moment of glaring at her totally blank expression, he spun around and blew out, his loose satin jacket back flowing behind him.

Disregarding her own discomfort over the confrontation, she calmly placed another blank page of stationary in front of her concluding it easier to tell Rosalita about some of the new people in her life rather than deal with them. With so much to say, she was again at a loss for words. Mary, one of the housekeepers came in. "Miss Haley-Hill has asked me to tell you that there are clothes in her room if you would like to join her for a ride." Before sending her response, "Are you kidding?," and bolting out of the room, she made the same decision she had

made countless times before, to write later or, at least, send a
post card.

Mr. Thomas, the old, stable manager reached down and put his
hands around her waist to lift her onto the sweet, grey Welsh
pony shifting his weight on the edge of the carpet of grass. The
touch of the man's thumbs on her ribs gave her a feeling of dejá
vu and she shuddered from the eerie familiarity.

"You're not scared, are ya?" Mr. Thomas asked with concern.
"Horse knows if you're scared. He'll throw you right off," he
admonished shaking his head doubtfully and tsking.

"No. I'm O.K." Holly rode up. "You know, my grandfather
has a painting just like this," Hebe announced indicating the
scene around them.

"So does mine. I guess everyone's grandfather has one, or
did. Inevitably, one inherits it and displays it in a guest
room. She laughed outloud. Tossie and I are thought you might
like to join us." Holly introduced him as Thaddeus Oberland
Sheridan whom she knew from her boarding school days in
Switzerland. "We just call him Tossie."

"Oh, so you must know Floyd," Hebe commented.

Holly answered hesitantly facing the man, "No. I guess you'd
already gone to England by then." She then turned to Hebe and
declared, "When I'm a famous painter he'll be refered to as a
pre-Floyd piece."

He looked more at his horses mane than at Hebe when he
offered his stiff, "How do you do." His horse stepped forward,
and Holly followed. He murmered, but the wind broadcast his news
to Hebe. "Hebe. that's an unusual name for Jewess."

"She not Jewish!" she declared peeking over her shoulder
with him.

"Well, she's something?"

"Everyone is something."

"Does Rem take her to The Country Club?"

"For Heaven's sake, Tossie. I don't know."

"You should ask."

"Why would I want to waste my breath. What could it

possibly matter? She just a kid. Come on."

Hebe fell back for fear that one of Tossie's sharp words might pierce the fantasy bubble she had blown around Hans and his friends at the Birches. She cooed at her horse and stroked his warm neck. His tangible silken softness mixed her long-ago dream with the reality of riding. But the similarities were lost when the trio took off. In the dream, it was night and her stallion had galloped soundlessly on the wind. Today was Sunday afternoon, and her pony thudded onto the firm early Spring earth. He had yet to break a lope, and if he were able to, he was keeping it a well-guarded secret. Holly and Tossie cantered a path of interlocking loops in a pattern of repeated infinity symbols as they headed up the Sunday-deserted streets. She surmised that eventhough they had invited her, they wanted to be alone; they didn't slow up for her. They didn't even turn around. Still, it was pleasant to wiggle-woggle on the horse as he clopped along beneath the new leaves whispering about fresh pond scents and the bees buzzing above the grass dotted with dainty field flowers lining the road.

To ride, the horse named, Lightning was to ride a padded rocking chair 13 hands high. She considered reclinging, but the cantle of the saddle got in the way. Next, she leaned her face against his crest and let her arms drop around the base of his neck intending to ride on her stomach in order to watch his fascinating ears. They were ever-twitching. Out of nowhere a sportscar came speeding around the curve, and she sat up and held the reins securely. Lightning continued, ever unenthusiastic. Then, Holly charged directly at her with Tossie in playful pursuit. Lightning plodded steady on. "Were you just going to let them trample over you?" she asked after having tugged the rein and turned him right out of their path. Before he could whicker a reply, a harmless garter snake fell silently out of a tree and landed right on his forehead. There it clung draped over one eye. Startled, Lightning reared up squeeling in fright. Hebe managed to stay on and so did the snake. Lightening whipped his head wildly throwing the reptile back on her arms. Without

letting go of the reins, she shook them and the bright green
serpent hit the ground. There were no words or actions to calm
Lightning down. He was completely spooked and running for his
life down Dudley Street. Whipping though the air like a dry, rag
on a horse while sleeping was dreamy, actually doing it was a
nightmare! Fright-numbed his sensitivity to the bit or the reins
and he neighed as he sped out of control along the asphalt. Low
branches threatened her head, and Lightning's gigantic body
thundered so powerfully that she could barely hold on. Danger
and excitement stole her breath and all she could hear was the
sound of her heart pounding in her ears and the rapid iron
badabum, badabum, badabum, of hooves. All that was clear was
what she saw, the water, the Brookline resevoir. "Hitting the
water wouldn't hurt half as much as hitting the hard ground," she
reasoned to herself. "Come on boy. Can you swim?" She asked and
reached up and pulled on his right ear. He winced and snorted
and as she hoped veered right. Over Dudley Way, over the mound
they rode. And SPLASH! The nightmare was awash in the cool,
clear water of day. Ducks honked! Dogs barked! People yelled!

    "Hebe! Oh God! Hebe! Hebe! cried Holly alarmed. She
coughed and spat water and tried to answer, but her boots were
heavy and pulling her under the water making her fight for
breath. "Here boy," she gurgled to Lightning and tried to secure
her hold on the reigns.

    "God, I can't believe he didn't throw you! We saw the whole
thing!" Holly exclaimed from the shore.

    Water filled her boot and pulled her under. At first, she
struggled to tred water while getting them off. But below the
surface, Hebe saw the horse runnning along as if her were on a
path. The giant creature was not going to sink as she feared. He
was a good swimmer and headed for shore, so she held tightly to
the reins, relaxed and used her energy to keep her head up.

    "Tossie, help me," demanded Holly nearly hysterical from the
shore.

    "The horse is bringing her. I don't really see how I can be
of assistance?" he stated with supercilious nonchalance.

"What?!" she bellowed delicately encouraging a change in his tone.

"What is it you'd like for me to do?"

"Get down off your high horse."

Hebe arrived before his will to accomodate. Holly ran to help her out of the water and her boots. The two performed acrobatic poses in struggling to remove her stubborn footwear; they wouldn't budge. Tossie laughed from atop his steed and half-jokingly offered a suggestion.

"I say, the logical thing to do would be to simply stand on your head."

They unpretzeled thier bodies and she did. The water ran straight out and down her legs.

"Thank you. That feels much better," she gasped and wheeezed.

"You must have been terrified. It's lucky Lightning didn't throw you."

Feeling airsick Hebe leaned back on the ground and caught her breath. "Yeah, but I'm glad it happened."

"What a strange thing to say Hebe."

"Maybe. It's just that sometimes I feel a little left out. Everyone always has something important or interesting to say at dinner. Now we have a story."

"Another story. You told one about going to Mexico. But, honestly, I don't think anyone really expects you to say anything. You're just a kid."

"I guess my grandmother was right."

"About what?"

"She always says, 'Children should be seen and not heard'."

"If anything, I'd say you'd proven her wrong. Shall we head back? I'll get the horse," she offered.

"I just want to stay here a minute."

"But, Hebe your all wet."

"I know. I just want to be by myself for a minute."

"All right, but stay put until someone comes for you."

"Put two of you girls together and the conversation is

interminable. Must this conference be held here and now? Or..."

Tossie's voice snapped Holly upright and placed her hands on her hips. She cut her eyes over to him and cooly vented her revelation.

" You know, that's it! It's your God Damn insensitivity that drove me to Floyd, that's what it is."

"Popping pills, sulking and writing poetry are the thrusts that break the eighth commandment for you, are they?"

Holly threw her leg over her horse and turned her nose up in the air. "Floyd's had some difficult times. He's very good-,"

"Poor little lord Fauntleroy? Let me get out my handker-chief and weep for the man who received one of the largest inheritances of.."

"Oh is that it? You're jealous."

"Jealous? That's a laugh."

"Oh you would give anything to be able to breeze into the stables at Myopia anytime you wanted or be invited to join The Country Club,"

"Boring. Boring," he sang out and looked off into the distance.

"Fool," Holly tutted, picked up her reins and rode off with the vassal to her charms in humbled tow.

"Holly, wait!"

Hebe was glad they had ridden off. She wanted to be alone for a few minutes. The damp clothes clung to her body no matter how she squirmed, and her inner thighs were chaffed. No one seemed to be around, so she removed her pants and sat on them. The unrippling water mirrored a clear blue sky. The breeze didn't blow, no birds chirped, not even the flutter of a butterfly's wing could be heard in the humming silence of the late spring day as she closed her eyes and rested. After a moment, the swish and stomp of hurried footsteps could be heard in the grass, then the big voice of Mr. Thomas as it thundered out, "Lightning."

"Lightning! What have they done to you boy?" He repeated several times walking briskly toward the horse but looking

angrily at Hebe. "You should never leave a horse untethered.
He'll wander off. And I certainly didn't give you permission to
take him out of the riding ring! This isn't the wild west.
That's just suicide to take a horse on Warren Street!"

"I'm sorry. I didn't know."

"Those other two know better." He ran his strong hands
gently down Lightning's neck. "He might run away."

Hebe laughed. "He might walk away," she muttered.

A shiver ran through the animal's powerful muscles and he
nuzzled his giant head next to the man. "He's called Lightning
because he has a tendancy to bolt," he interrupted guiding him
off toward The Birches. "Don't worry my friend. We'll dry you
right off so you won't catch a cold."

Shivering herself, Hebe began to think that half-dressed
though she was, she should make a mad dash to the house and not
wait for anyone. An unfamiliar car approaching sent her scampering into a cluster of trees where she ran into the Japanese
gardner. He was digging in the ground. She shielded her thighs
from his eyes with her sopping jacket, but he politely focused on
his busy hands. "Why you are here in ze undressing?"

"I'm waiting."

"Waiting for what, dry cleaner?"

"No. Someone's coming for me."

"I don't think so. All people go in cars."

"They are looking for me?"

"Maybe not." He reached in a basket and took out two large
squares of cloth adorned with cranes and flowers and tied them
together. "Maybe you can walk with me." He handed the cloths to
her indicating that she should tie them around her for a skirt,
then put some of the roots he had been digging in a third cloth.
Together they started back to the Birches.

"I can't believe they'd forget about me."

"They not forget you. They not lemember you. It is a
difference special to ze selfish people."

"Han's friends are very nice to me...um... gosh, I don't
know your name."

"Easy for ze very nice people to be selfish than ze not so nice people. Ze not so nice people must to be kind or nobody is never going to like them."

Mr. Thomas waved as they passed the stable "Hi Jacques, Hebe."

"How's Lightning?" she asked peeking into the barn. Lightning's stall was almost as large as her room in California. It was a clean space full of fresh hay. A bronze name plate shone on his door. Several photographs of him and either Rem or Mr. Thomas hung on the wall. The horse snorted and blinked and leaned into the movement of Mr. Thomas' hands as he dried him off. He looked up at her.

"He's goin' to be all right."

Hebe said good-bye to Jaques in the greenhouse where she had first seen him earlier that day. Just as he said, the Birches were out. The old, English butler, Thurloe, raised his eyebrows at her wierd, wet ensemble and general water-logged appearance, but position held his tongue on comment while he delivered the message that dinner would be at eight in the cloister garden. He paused, then asked, "May anyone be of service to Mademoiselle?"

"Gee, no thanks. I'm going up to take a bath," she declared feeling a little awkward receiving such obeisance from a man old enough to be her grandfather. The busy, professinal staff dusting and cleaning, didn't even give her passing acknowledgement as she wended upstairs to the enormous guest room. The beautiful house aged in her hour of lonliness. Frayed fragments of tapestry loomed large, tarnished brass and unpainted corners were everywhere. The high ceilinged space diminished the huge bed and dwarfed her. A mirror hung high over the mantlepiece to help lighten the space. And, as she passed by on her way to bathe, she became aware that angled as it was, it provided no reflection of her. In vain, she walked by it several times, once on painful tip-toe. On the last of her trips, Rem verily danced into the room. "Hebe. Quel horreur! We were looking all over for you."

"You were?"

"Of course! Look at you. I'm so sorry."

"It was kind of fun. In fact. I think I had a dream about it a long time ago."

"Oh really?" Rem listened while Hebe recounted fragments of the dream and immersed herself in a soupy soapy bubblebath. After Rem had washed her back, she sat on the edge of the abolone tub admiring her own hands. "I need to talk to you. Your grandmother rang me today and asked me if you could stay here with us for a little while. What do you think about that?"

Hebe was incredulous, "Why?"

"She has to go to Austria."

"Probably to see her uncle, the Archduke or something?"

"An Archduke? Oh! What is he for Heaven's Sake, a Hapsburg?"

"That's what my grandmother says. Is that important?"

"Not at the moment. I guess I'm telling you that you may stay here with me until she returns."

"Do you want me here? I could go back to California if..."

"Well, how can I put this delicately? Hebe, California is not among the choices."

"Oh."

"You may stay here or you may, in fact, set sail for Europe with your Grandmamá."

"On a ship with the Queen of Hearts," she muttered to the bubbles then asked, "What would you do if you were me?"

"If I were you? Well, were I you, I guess I'd do whatever I really wanted to do."

"You don't mind that I am here?"

"Hebe, we all adore having you around, especially Hans and especially me." Rem dipped down on one knee and scrubbed one of Hebe's elbows with a pumice. "I rather like taking care of you the way Mrs. Remington took care of me."

"You are so nice to me. I wish you were my mother."

"Don't wish that."

"Why?"

"Because you wouldn't be you. and I like you just the way you are," she tossed the sponge in the bath. "It sounds to me as if it settled. Tomorrow, we'll go to the lawyer so I can sign the papers then pick up your things."

"Lawyer?"

"Yes, I have to be your legal guardian in case something happens.

"You don't want to have any children? Are you just going to dance forever? What about your husband?"

"Oh my, you are suddenly curious." She paused and stretched her arms gracefully over her head. "He's in France right now. You'll meet him one day. It's only 4:30. If you want faire la sieste, I'll have someone wake you in time to dress. It's hard to hear the dinner gong from this room."

Dinner was served in the cloister garden. It was difficult to tell where the greenery ended and where the salad began. Thousands of flower panicles hung around them, buds stood in vases on the tables and their plates were overflowing with fresh, white daisies, saffron marigolds and velvety, burgundy pansies. Hebe thought it was a lovely idea for a garnish until the hostess dribbled dressing over her salad and began eating, everyone did. Hebe felt strange spearing the delicate blossoms even with the fine silver prongs. After all, it was a flower, something one appreciated, painted, picked or presented as a gift, preferably not on a fork. "Marvelous," "Delicious," and "I've never tasted better flowers," were the words she heard, so she rained a few droplets of dressing over a tiny bouquet and placed it in her mouth. The almond oil, rosewater and lime dressing melted over the apricot-skinned texture of the petals to create an inexplicable sensation. She was speechless.

Floyd arrived late, and he occupied the empty chair next to Hans rather than the one next to Holly sending a silence of wondering around the table. Finally, Floyd looked up from his plate and began the conversation.

"Eat enough of this and you'll turn into a bloomin' idiot, say what?"

With a barely noticeable glance from Rem, a server stepped from the shadows and removed Floyds plate. Several uncomfortable seconds of silence ensued. Then, Holly tried to tactfully change the subject, "It was really great seeing Tossie and reminiscing about the..."

"Let's talk about the Belgian World's Fair, shall we?" he offered dryly cutting her off, then running his fingers up and down as if playing his sax.

"Really Floyd, how melodramatic? Tossie was just visiting. They only went riding, with Hebe," Rem pointed out."

"A useless aristocrat's day is not a palatable dinner topic, my dear," he snarled.

Hans clapped his hands lightly together. "Good that's the end of that. I have big news for Noni. You know the guy I'm always talking about at the wind tunnel at MIT?" He lowered his voice, "He's building a flying saucer." They all gasped. "And, guess where he got the blue print?"

"Tell me!" Noni ordered enthusiastically.

"Ezekiel saw the wheel...," he paused.

"No creo. The Bible?" Noni guessed.

"You're bloody joking," stated Floyd while Noni's eyes bulged and he made the sign of the cross; chest, forehead, left, right. The conversation boarded a train of cosmological theories and Mechanists Philosophy riding a fast rail of innumerable ology's and isms throughout the floral appetizer, a pâte with watercress and a tomato madrilène.

The only words Hebe even partially understood were in the form of Hans' last question.

"O.K., if you believe that Floyd, of all the countries in the world, which would you say, based on its present society, is the most philosophically evolved?"

At first, the women sat in polite silence listening to the verbal volley and fanning themselves, their faces revealing whether they were consonant with what was being said or not. Then they tried to participate, at least Holly did. "That's all very true, but don't you think it's a little unfair to exlude John Dewey? He's one of the most profound..."

Floyd whipped off the end of her sentence. "Chicks just don't know how to follow along, do you? Do you even know what wer're discussing."

"I sure don't!" Hebe blurted out innocently stemming a possible argument. Everyone chuckled.

"Apros pos of absolutely nothing," Rem began.

Noni, never missing an opportunity to compliment her, raised his glass and said, "The devil hath not in all his quiver's choice, an arrow for the heart like a sweet voice."

"Maybe I should give up photography and science. I'd like to come up with lines like that. From where do you get this poetry?" Hans asked.

"Byron, man. Hep cat's hep cat, you know?"

"Well, I thank Lord Byron and you, Noni for the compliment, But if you don't mind, before you all solve all of the world's mysteries, and have nothing left to say over the entree, as unlikely as that may seem, I would like to propose a Swedish toast to formally welcome the seventh member of our group to my home. Hebe's grandmother has asked that Hebe be my charge for the summer." Exclamations of surprise went around the table and they applauded, then raised their glasses. "Miss Hebe Gourdin, may you enjoy memororable hours here among, 'The Birches'."

She should have been happy. She had made her choice. Her P-town wish had come true. She should have been more than happy. Instead, she found herself choking back tears. She would be moving again, this time into a stranger's house. Certainly, the long lost Hans was there; however, the absence of geographical distance mysteriously separated them. No need to write, no time to spend with her. It was all passed in his darkroom developing photos, at classes in Cambridge or off with Noni and Floyd to the dark, jazz-filled, coffee houses where poetry was born through the oral birth canals of bespectacled beatsters in black. Hebe saw the places and the other people in the black and white pictures he carried around with him studying.

From time to time she had even encountered some of the subjects in person, unposed, wandering in various states of undress through The Birches locking for any number of things: a toilet, a drink of water, an earring, a way out. One skinny man

with big blue eyes held his head and said he had lost, his mind.
And there was a woman with a long waist, and long bushy brown
hair with privates to match who didn't claim to have lost
anything, but had apparently lost her way because she stepped
into Hebe's room at 3:00 a.m., stretched out next to her and went
to sleep. Hans came and fetched the noctambulatory beauty. Hebe
swallowed the question about Nell's whereabouts and feigned
sleep. Watching Hans tenderly reclaim the stray soul sent a
twinge of jealousy and resentment through her, reignited her
feelings for Tony.

She missed their continent sensuality, the warmth of his
chest against her cheek and the comfort of his soothing hands
constantly touching her, reaffirming her existence. She had no
closeness with anyone. And there was, Hans, a man whom she had
held dear to her heart over the years showering his affection on
a woman he had probably met a few hours earlier. She didn't
expect that he would fall in love with childish her. But she
didn't expect that he would be so easily distracted from her and
her new friend, Nell. Nell adored him, had followed him across
three continents. She was supposed to be his girlfriend. "How
could he hold another naked woman in the middle of the night and
flirt with Rem at the table the way he did?"

She concluded once again, as she had before when she lived
with her parents, that honesty was a two-faced myth, that people
were not truthful with each other and that at night life somehow
turned upside down causing people to live differently from the
way they lived during the day. Because it wasn't just Hans; it
was all of them. Rem explained the fun of a Swedish skoal is that
it requires each and every person at the table to exchange a long
gaze before they drink. Doing this, Hebe saw many people within
each person: horseback riders, photographers, philosophers,
artists, lovers, foreigners, musicians, dancers, friends, some
brothers and sisters, sons and daughters all. She sat more with
fifteen or eighteen people than merely six. All strangers. And,
now, she was going to live with them. The circle of people
seated at the table, the others around it serving, the globe of

the cloister garden dome and the border of the iron gate swung
around as if gimbals in a gyroscope from her science class.
There they were living an existence of lives within lives
surrounded by still other lives by the soft, green, sea of grass
beneath the rustling tissue of lavish greenery of Warren Street
at the end of the world.

NINE

Bohemian Ways

Life at the End of the World

Friday, May 2, 1958

219 Warren Street

Her decision to stay with Rem proved to be wise. The house
was full of bright, creative people who had chosen to be with one
another. Missing was the tie that binds factious family members
together, obligating them to tolerate one another in the name of
blood. Gone was the blind of requisite empty small talk drawn to
shut out conflicting points of view. In their place was a
loosely woven reticulance of ideas and information, experiences
and emotions. And, as they became familiar with her, they shared
more and more of their lives. Gradually, the six sundered plural
beings, the complete strangers whom she toasted at the table
became chosen friends close to her heart.

Within a matter of days, she had seen: Rem's dance rehearsal
at the conservatory, Noni's performance at The Sanders Theatre;
Hans' photographs at a private gallery; Holly's paintings at the
Museum School of Fine Arts; Floyd's music at a coffee house in

Cambridge; Nell's training for her desired ladyship. How many times she had gone up and down the marble staircase, chin up with a book on her head so she could perfect a confidant and elegant entrance at her next ball. Disciple to all, they taught Hebe their talents involuntarily as the carried them out in front of her, and, quite intentionally, one on one, when they invited into their rooms. Flattered by her intense interest, they answered her never ending questions, guided her young hands and used her as an assistant. The most challenging was blowing the sax, not just because it was so difficult to produce even the slightest sound, but because Floyd was so unpredictable and explosive to be around. The only things that interrupted his drinking were pills, an occasional cigarette and his sax. The only things to stop him for any length of time were sleep and Holly. Respectfully, she would muffle her country stomp and pass into Floyd's den as quietly as a chink of light. They never had to tell Hebe to leave. She would follow her own intuition out of the room, to let them be alone together. It always got quiet, and she would try to imagine what they were doing, what they were talking about.

Although volitile, Floyd was fascinating to be around. When lost in artistic thought, his cool, deep voice rumbled out of him as if he were recovering from laringitis. He'd ramble on about his good friends at Columbia University, the scene in Greenwich Village, happenings on Market Street in San Francisco, and "a little back street, on the Left Bank in Paris. Mostly, he talked about N.Y. "It's a place that almost defies description; it's so complex, so big. The number of people and the size of the buildings insist one alway feel small, but the type of smallness varies."

"How can small vary? Small is small."

"I guess a young girl would think that, but it isn't. Small can be small like a piece of hay in a pile of horse manure or like a steamy blue sequen on the crotch of a dancer's g-string. It can be something so infintesimal it's invisible to the naked eye like a," he snapped his fingers several times trying to think

of an example. "Like a, like an atom. Or small can be something
astonishingly massive," he laughed. " Like, uh, Twinkle, twinkle
little star. You dig?"

Inevitably, he talked about literature.
Snatches, although, beyond her comprehension, became memorable
catch phrases, "a conformity demanding social monster," or
"...the subversive attractions of jazz." Repeated most was
"constantly risking absurdity," which was also the name of a poem
by Lawrence Ferlinghetti Floyd shared with her. He read it
passionately. He read it slowly. He reread it after he listened
to her read it. It never made any sense to her. It didn't even
rhyme, a word which the Columbia University author misspelled,
"rime". She was very proud of herself for having found the
"mistake". But Floyd explained that Ferlinghetti was exercising
his poetic license, then read it again with great care. He sat so
close to her that she could smell his scotched persperation
through his skin. Sometimes, he coddled her in his arm as if she
were a smaller, younger little girl. He rocked gently as he
read, pausing every now and then to pop a pill in his mouth or
utter, "Wow, see? Words are amazing." Even when she didn't, she
would "M'hm," so he would continue.

The easiest apprenticeship was also the most boring,
primping with Nell and planning her wardrobe. Nell reveled in the
elegant mischief of an aspiring princess. It was her intent to
be titled, and to have the space marked occupation in her
passport read, "Lady" as Rem's did. From far across the sea in
Belgium, her mother's fingers shaped her schedule of teas,
receptions and even banquets. Since Nell's relationship with
Hans was a secret, introductions to suitable young bachelors were
also arranged, providing her with a princess' list of suitors
with which she teased her Dutchman, Hans. He showed no signs of
jealousy. In fact, he confidently encouraged her to go. She
squealed with indignant delight when she read in a letter from
home that her mother was using her social influence to
orchestrate a meeting for her with Mohammed Reza Pahlevi, The
Shah of Iran arriving for a tour of the U.S. at the end of June,

next month. Nell's mother pointed out that his sister had a
western husband, indicating that he might be open to the west.
So, if she did everything just as she was supposed to, she might
be able to step down the same royal aisle as Grace Kelly. It was
all she talked about until the following week when her mother's
disappointing letter informed Nell that the Iranian king, who was
thirty nine, was much too old for her.

However, the day before receiving the news, she was
intolerably giddy with the fantasy. Inexhaustable, she acted out
her interaction with the man while Hebe advised her on her
posture and gait. "Tell me if my hips are wiggling," Nell
commanded tucking her derrière forward."

"They're not. You're as straight as wood. You could be a
giraffe."

"You mean, gazelle," corrected Nell batting her big, bright
blue eyes and smiling prettily.

She had said what she meant, but she didn't want to hurt
Nell's feelings. She thought about Rosalita, how she
deliberately dragged her feet and shifted her weight from one leg
to the other to get as much movement from her hips as possible.
She could see her clearly sitting at her vanity spraying her
hair. With one arm shorter than the other, styling the top was
challenging and caused her to tilt her head in awkward positions.
She would just giggle. "Someday I'm going to have me somebody to
do this for me," she'd remark confidently. She never asked Hebe
for her opinion. She didn't need it. For Rosalita, handicapped
and not so cute, assumed that everyone considered her to be the
same "knock out" she considered herself. Whereas Nell had, "drop
dead gorgeous looks" in Rem's words, needed to be told and told
again that she looked, not just good, but perfect in her
different dresses from every angle. No amount of telling could
make her believe it. Hebe grew exasperated trying to convince
her, and finally, suggested that they go downstairs to Rem's
dance studio where the whole wall was mirrored so she could see
for herself.

The door was locked. The door was never locked. The door

was never even closed. Hebe put her ear to the door. "I hear someone moving around." She dropped down on her knee and peered through the keyhole. A big, muscular, white rear end was all she could see. Then, it was gone. In the blink of her eye it returned and began posting, as if riding a horse, a very fast horse. A ballet-slippered foot rested on its tailbone. Hebe pressed her face harder against the door. "I think it's Rem?"

"What is she doing?" Nell asked tipping her head to the side.

The people in the room sat up revealing the naked rear end to belong to Hans and the foot to Rem. She hesitated and stammered. "Well, it looks like some kind of dance. Come on. We'd better not disturb them. I'm a better mirror because.."

"I want to see too!" Nell demanded, gently pushing her aside. She gasped and without taking her eye away pounded on the door. "Hans! Hans Ouvre la porte!" she yelled and attacked the door with both fists. A sudden rush of blood turned her face crimson.

"Nell, take it easy," Hebe suggested kneeling down beside her. Just then, the door opened. The genuflecting pair found themselves face to face with Hans' enormous ego. Trembling and silent as Shakers they were until Hans grabbed Nell up by her elbows. Modestly, he covered himself with his hand while he tried to console her with his controlled voice.

"Nelly, Nelly, Nelly. C'est toi? Calm down. We were just dancing. It's a modern..."

"Dancing? Ou et la musique? Where is the music?" she shrieked at his nose.

"It's in our heads," Rem offered with a smile wrapping a rehearsal robe around her. Hans waved behind his back for her to be quiet. She slithered out behind them. An instant later the smell of match sulfur tickled their noses.

"Come on I'll show you." Pulling on her arm as one pulls the tether for a donkey, he tried to coax Nell into the studio. All at once, she sniffed, playfully broke free, caught Hebe by the sleeve and ran up the stairs.

"You can...dance with anybody you want. I don't want you anymore. You will be sorry when I dance with my king!" And she stomped away with a great amount of tearless boo hooing.

The very next morning, the letter from her mother came explaining that any arrangement between her and the Shah was impossible. Hebe was shocked when Nell ran crying to Hans who let her sit weeping in his lap half the afternoon. And even more amazed that evening at dinner, when Nell sought solace from Rem, resting her head sweetly on her shoulder, the "dance" apparently forgotten. Hebe thought about herself and Tony, all the girls he had gone out with when he was seeing her, how he had claimed to still love her. He said he had to go out with other girls because he was a man and he needed what they could give him, their bodies. But she knew Nell wasn't keeping her body from Hans. He must have given Nell another reason for being intimate with other women because she had obviously forgiven him.

Later that night, when she straddled the small, black seat behind Hans on his Vespa headed for a party in town, she pointed to the white dinner jacket Hans loathed to wear, but Nell had somehow gotten him to don. She gave Hebe the V-sign. Hebe was torn between two conclusions. Either Nell was really dumb enough to think Hans and Rem were sweating, naked and á bout de souffle on the floor dancing, or she was smart enough to ignore it in order to get what she wanted, Hans. After all, that was her true reason for staying in Boston in the first place.

The next few days were of some anguish for everyone. Noni suddenly suffered paralysis of the left half of his face. Unable to speak, his understudy was called in. And to make matters worse, the understudy was getting rave reviews. Doctors said the conditon, Bell's Palsey, was usually temporary, but the fear it would remain, ate at him and compelled him to try talking. When he had exasperated the Birches with his tortured grimace and slobbering pronunciation, he took to anguishing in his room with a reel of soft jazz.

Rem's grief arrived quite unexpectedly as well in the form of a tall, dashing gentleman from somewhere in the south of

France with a two steamer trunks. She hesitatingly introduced
him simply as, "Phillipe". He conversed with no one, but
followed Rem everywhere producing atmospherics throughout the
house when they weren't at "The Club." Enormous sighs were
emitted, cigarettes were lit while others were still burning,
countless phone calls were made. Under their breath with company
and at the top of their voices behind closed doors they confered,
consumed by the mysterious topic. Discussing it more than
bickering about it and occasionally kissing, led everyone to
believe they were very close friends, perhaps even lovers, and
that the matter was one of considerable gravity which concerned
them both. No amount of eavesdropping helped because no one
understood all of what they were saying. Hans claimed they were
speaking a hybrid. "Sounds like French and Spanish and Volupük
all rolled together."

Noni was oblivious to the event as he remained in
self-imposed exile in his room,. Hans guessed their interminable
tête-a-tête to be was about money, Nell about love, Hebe about
sickness and Floyd about drugs. Holly who had recently become
irritated with almost anything Floyd said, snapped "Oh that's
absurd. Why is everything about drugs?"

Without any reflection Floyd went in his pocket, put a pill
in his mouth and swallowed it down with a drink. "He's been here
forever and we don't even know his proper name. What else would
be so bleeding furtive? It has something to do with drugs."

As he swallowed, Holly turned away and winced as if watching
him take the pills hurt her. She stared out the window and
whined sarcastically, "Yes, why is everything about drugs, Mr.,
Mr. Benzedrine? Poetry by Floyd Benzedrine. Music by Floyd
Bennies. There, that would be more honest," she continued. Her
words smacked his eyes open in disbelief. Holly had been a mute
pillar of strength for Floyd. Her completely unexpected
viciousness deflated him. He sank to the ottoman and slumped
over with his terrified eyes glaring at her back. Spinning
around to see him hunched over and shaking made her swallow her
mouth full of venom. She ran to him, knelt at his feet and

placed her arm around his neck. "Oh, my God. What am I saying? I'm so sorry. I'm sorry."

With Holly at his feet, Floyd regained his strength. And when she moved her hand to his face to push his hair back, he pulled away and cleared his throat. Cooly, he looked down on her and with fully restored condescension asked, "Well, care to venture a guess on the Phillipe enigma or are you off to find your lost art?"

"My painting is not lost. It was stolen from the exhibit not.."

"Holly, seriously. No one steels a student's painting," he interrupted with obvious malice.

Hans took Holly's hand and pulled her to his chest sympathetically. "Don't pay attention to him."

Floyd's hands were trembling. He tossed back his hair and with exposed his dilated pupils. "Stiff upper lip, Holly. I'm sure your little assignment will show up. And if it doesn't.. And, if it doesn't, No great loss. God damn Holly, just from that little clipping in the paper you've sold two canvases. New York galleries...," A sinister smirk snuk onto his narrow lip.

"Christ Floyd, that's some comment from the disciple of beat?"

Attempting to prevent the conflict from escalating, Hans chimed in. "Holly he didn't mean anything. Floyd's just had a few too many. He's gone."

"Well, when you get back, you'd better knock. I don't know if I'm here for you," she flung at him before turning on her heel and storming out.

It wasn't until long after everyone had retired to their rooms that Holly's little DKW sport coupe rolled up the driveway. Hebe had been reading, a Playboy purloined from Floyd's room. Looking at it pleasantly reminded her of when she had gotten drunk with Rosalita on Tony's Tequilla in his room, the day she met him. However, trying to read the vocabulary in the hair-dressing ad unpleasantly reminded her of Floyd and his erudite babbling when she came across the words "tonsorial arrangement".

She turned the page and the abundantly built "Miss of the Month" unfolded into her lap and stared at her. Her generous, perfectly arched eyebrows were identical to those of the movie stars or Art's client in San Diego, Mrs. Gonzales. In the mirror, she practiced imitating the Playmates sultry, innocent stare of invitation. Posing didn't work. Getting naked and dimming the lights didn't either. She tried a number of facial expressions and thought she had achieved it when she was distracted by the car's motor which was still running, she looked out of her window.

The door of the car was open. Holly got out and lit a cigarette. The thick summer's air misted the smoke around her. Looking up in the direction of Floyd's window, she reached in and gave the horn a sharp tap. Hebe expected Floyd to go running down to her, or at least call out the window. He did neither. He started to play the saxaphone. Holly jumped back in her car, and nervously honked her horn a dozen times. Hans appeared and she got out. He lit cigarettes for both of them and leaned back on the car while Holly talked and flung her arm toward Floyd's window, then shook them at the sky and pulled her hair. The music made it impossible to hear what they were saying. At first, he played just to drown out Holly, but then the current of his own notes caught him and he was sailing the deep bluesy sea of improvisation. Holly dropped her head on Hans' chest and his arms fell from the roof of the car around her. They embraced. They swayed. They danced in the umbra of night. Witnessing Hans calming Holly made her proud to have a such a caring friend. He must have been helping because when he took Holly's face in his hands and kissed her goodnight she seemed assuaged. She had a big smile on her face getting back in her car and backing down the driveway. She blew him a kiss and wiggled her fingers in farewell. The red tail lights of the DKW got smaller and smaller, then disappeared behind the shadowy canopy of trees.

Hans stamped out his cigarette and gave an aggravated bellow up at the window, "Floyd! Floyd!

The music stopped, "What?"

"The music Daddy-o," He looked at his watch. "It's either a little too late, or a little too early. You don't want to get Rem on the bad side of the Vanderbildts, do you?"

"The Gardners are the ones next door."

"I mean the Vanderbuilts."

"They live way the Hell down there on the next corner."

"Yeah, they do. Get my drift?"

"So where's Holly?"

"Gone again."

"Where to?"

"I don't know," he looked down the road and back. "Her studio? Maybe you should have come and talked to her."

"I was playing for her. What's she want?"

"Words." There was a long pause, but Floyd didn't say anything else. He just stood in the window. "Don't worry. She'll be back."

The cool, damp sea air that sometimes blew in land had a powerful effect on things. Night lights became hazier and all was quieter than usual. Fragrances didn't flow away, but linger-ed near their source. The scent of the jasmine flowers Jacques had helped her select from the cloister garden hung in invisible tendrils sweetening her room, even with the window open. Beneath them were the many letters she had spent the better part of the night writing, paper full of words, not much different from those she and Hans had exchanged. Now, they lived in the same house, and some days, they hardly said one word to one another. Words. Where were they?

One afternoon a few days earlier, while Hans was giving himself the once over in the hall mirror before going out, she asked him directly why he didn't spend more time with her. The truth was, she was often left behind. He sat down on the marble stairs to wipe off his shoe, then looked at the floor for a minute. In the low rumbling voice some men use when they are asked to share their feelings, he answered, "Well, it was different before. Gordy was my friend and you were Gordy's little daughter."

"I still am!"

"That isn't what I mean." He rubbed his head frustrated that
he couldn't express himself, especially since he wasn't quite
sure of what he was trying to say. He sprang up from the step,
grabbed his jacket and exclaimed, "Oh God, I'm going to be late.
I was supposed to meet someone in Harvard Square." Then, he
tumbleweeded out of the door. Hebe didn't know why, but tears
welled up in her eyes. Hans walked back in. He lit a cigarette
as he knelt in front of her and lifted her chin. His voice was
calm and tender. "Hebe, this must be so strange for you to be
here all alone like this, kind of everybody's shadow. I hope
you're o.k. when I leave."

"Are you going away?" she asked somewhat stunned by the
thought.

"Well, I have to go home sometime," We all do. Even Rem."

"I thought this was her place, her house, her...demesne,"
she was pleased to have remembered the word.

"It is. One of many. She couldn't live here all year every
year? Oh no. She'd die from the boredom or lack of attention."

It was true. Rem's mail and calls were all to and from the
same faraway places whose labels adorned her steamer trunks:
Mombasa, Tangiers, Athens, Paris, Tokyo, New York.

"I suppose. A person lives where a person is. That's one way
to look at it. So, for the moment, well, we all live here," he
concluded. Seeing her great, liquid coal eyes stared at him
waiting for him to make sense, he realized he couldn't explain.
He hugged her, and said,"Sure, you live here. Hey, I know. You
could..."

Hebe knew he was about to invite her to join him, but she
wanted him to invite her because he really wanted her to be with
him, not just because he felt sorry for her. So she started to
shake her head. "No. Thanks."

She had tagged along once on one of his nights out. In
Cambridge, a petite, Radcliffe girl, Zelpha, met them at the door
of her apartment. Her shiny, jet black hair was pulled back in a
bun above her pink, oxford shirt collar. The first thing they

talked about was the status of the civil war in Lebanon, her
country.

"Oh my poor little Beirut. It's terrible. Things are
getting worse every day. It's all so horrible," Zelpha blurted
out in a soft voice wringing her hands.

At the Birches, Hebe had heard the war mentioned. She was
prepared to learn a lot more over dinner. They were supposed to
eat. But, soon, it became clear that Hans was the intended main
course. Zelpha kissed him and nibbled at his ear. She sucked
his knuckles and licked his neck. Hans gently pleaded, "Stop,"
pulling himself away with a minimum of enthusiasm.

Hebe tried to busy herself on the other side of the room
reading the backs of the books on the shelves. There wasn't a
sound and she turned to see them engaged in a deep kiss. It went
on and on. Embarrassed, she gently kicked the table leg to
remind them of her presence. They looked up.

"So, what are we having for dinner?" Hebe asked politely.

Zelpha confessed that she had been pouring over her books
and hadn't prepared anything, so they ordered Chinese food. Hebe
was given the task of going to pick it up. The restaraunt was
supposed to be about a block and a half away. Hebe counted six
by the time she had gotten there. She waited for the food. It
smelled delicious, and it was 10:00, well past dinner time. She
wanted to eat. She thought about snacking on one of the
eggrolls, but decided it would be better to walk more quickly
because the others were probably hungry too. She almost ran the
last block and up the four flights of stairs. Jazz was being
played so loudly that it filled the hallway. No amount of
tapping or rude clanking with the brass knocker could summon them
to the door. She heard their voices. She turned the knob and
went in.

The lights had been dimmed and the room was illuminated by
two flickering red candles. A half drunk bottle of wine stood on
the table surrounded by the crumbs of crackers and cheese. One
of the kitchen chairs was lying on its side. Some one else was
knocking on the door. She opened it and was greeted by the

angry, bony faced scowl of an old woman in a sleeping turban wiping off her eyeglasses.

"Why don't you tell me just how many of your brothers are going to have birthdays this week, so I can go and stay with my sister," she grumbled. "I told the landlord you were going to be trouble." She placed her glasses on her nose and realized she had not been addressing Zelpha. "Who are you? A sister? These people have so many children." Hebe didn't have a chance to say anything. "Well, sis. Turn that God damn music down or it won't be the landlord I call. It'll be the police."

Hebe closed the door and ran to the phonograph player to turn down the music. An enormous thud shook the floor followed by another. Thinking someone had fallen down, she called out above the music, "Is everything all right?" Over the girl's mirthful tittering, Hans let out a Tarzan yell from the other room. She didn't call out again, but turned on the light and poured herself a glass of wine. The door sprang open and out they came in a haze of energy wearing three-finger grins. Zelpha's hair hung around her bare shoulders and down her towel, which she had wrapped around her as if it were a sarong. Hans was dressed in her red, silk kimono. The couple laughed about Hans' long arms and legs sticking out of the small robe. Hebe did not. She felt very uncomfortable. Embarrassed and dissappointed she stared at the charcoal etching on the wall and mulled over her thoughts. How could he have brought her along knowing she would be in the way, knowing he was going to be unfaithful to her friend, Nell? Even if jumping into bed with his friend was more important than her, they should have been polite enough to wait until after they had eaten and sent her home in a cab. They weren't even hungry anymore. She wasn't either. Zelpha wanted them to spend the night, but Hans insisted that he had to get Hebe home. "Nell will be waiting up, I'm sure," Hebe added.

"Who's Nell?" Zelpha chimed in before Hebe could finish.

"Oh. Nell is a friend of Hebe's," Hans answered shooting a glance at her that both begged and demanded that she not

contradict him before pulling his sweater over his head. After
delivering a quick noisy kiss to his lover's waiting lips, he
ushered Hebe out to the Vespa.

"Wasn't that lovely?" he remarked apparently unaware that
she had been excluded from the good time. While he positioned
himself on the seat, she looked at him. Something was different.
He had the same face, the same eyes, the same long blond hair.
He was the man who played games with her on the back porch, who
had written to her for three years, whom she had longed to see.
He was right in front of her starting the Vespa, but he looked
like a stranger. She flung her leg over the black leather seat
and sat quietly all the way home.

She wanted to tell Hans that it was wrong for him to see
other women, for Nell's sake. She couldn't. After all, he
encouraged Nell to date. It was most fuddling. Therefore, she
promised herself never to tag along again, even if invited. So,
now that as she stood in the hall sensing that he was about to
ask she made it clear that her schedule was full.

"I really must finish my letter to my father. I told him I
was here. And the last card I got, he wrote that he might come
to Boston."

"That's terrific. If he comes by ship, we'll go to the
docks to meet him and have a big celebration dinner."

"Promise?"

"Zekker!" Hans paused at the door and added, "Don't worry
Hebe you will find your place in the world, your people." Her
face must have reflected that she had no idea what he meant
because he added, "One day you will understand. Tot ziens." Out
of the air, she picked a day, February 9, 1959, to be the much
touted one day when she would understand all the things people
had been telling her she would.

Already, she had begun to learn about communication and
distance. The farther away from people you go, the more people
stay in touch, the more you loved them. She wrote to her own
father much more when he was away at sea than she did when he was
at home. Then there was Margarita who was usually quiet while

cleaning in the kaleidescope shadows of the great colored window of the kitchen in San Diego, became a bilingual chatterbox on paper. And Holly. Holly loved Floyd, but Hebe saw her take that love and drive away. However, that logic neither explained why Tony had stopped writing, nor why her father never found time to address the questions of her letters. Human relationships confounded her. Maybe it was only a partial truth that people who got close seemed to distance themselves from one another while people who were far apart tried to get together.

Whichever it was, "It's really hard to be human," was her conclusion.

Mailing the letters gave her a reason to step out of the shade of the Birches, to have a leisurely day on her own. In the afternoon, she met Bozena at a coffee shop on Newbury Street. Bozena was glowing with happiness in a bright pink dress. She presented her with several homemade potato pancakes and a bottle of Polish potato vodka and explained that the source of her pleasure was that having recently turned sixteen she could quit school. And, Bolek, her husband, had gotten a job as a supervisor in a meat packing factory, so he didn't have to work in "uncle's girlie bar," anymore. From a patch pocket on her dress, she proudly produced her Mother Premestaw's recipie for the potato pancakes and asked Hebe to write it down in English because she wanted to give it to a neighbor.

"She is wanting to catch husband. Is best way with stomach."

Hebe told her bits and pieces about the changes in her life since moving to the Birches and some of the many things she had seen and learned. The story about riding into the resevoir made her jiggle her full form with squeels of delight. And, she was very impressed that she lived on a piece of land large enough for a flower garden and horses. But she was relieved that Hebe couldn't master the sax. With great disapproval she advised, "Give this up, Hebe. This instrument is not for girl." Hebe completely agreed with her and admitted that she wasn't planning to continue.

"I was only trying it out. I have to try everything, so I don't end up an elevator operator."

"Why you would to work elevator?"

"That's what I thought I wanted to be when I was a kid."

Bozena tossed her mane of hair over her shoulder and looked her square in the face quite amused. "Hebe, you are a kid."

"No, I'm not. I don't do any kid stuff."

"You don't make any money. And you never did love making with man."

"None of the grown ups at 'Birches' works. And, I don't think priests make love and they're grown up."

"Is true what you say. But is also true, Hebe, you have only eleven years old."

"O.k., but I don't feel like a child." She tried to change the subject and tell Bozena about her first trip on a sailboat, in Newport with the Birches. "We were bundled up, but it was freezing," she began.

Bozena kept interrupting with questions about the incident with Rem and Hans in the ballet studio. Finally, Hebe asked, "Do you think Nell should have forgiven Hans? She acts as though nothing happened."

"I'm think Nell did good decision. Nobody saw nothing. Only naked body. Tell me," she looked around the crowded restaurant, then continued in a whisper, "When he opened door and you saw his body, was ready or not ready?" She held her fingers out straight then let them go limp.

Hebe turned red., "I turned my head."

Bozena laughed. "Really?"

"Yes, really," Hebe added most defensively.

"So, you don't know nothing. Maybe was dancing."

"Do you really think so?" Hebe wanted to agree.

"Doesn't matter, dancing, not dancing. Man feels guilty. Now, he must pay too much attention to woman. I give her ten points."

"Ten points?" Hebe asked a little annoyed. "You talk about it as if it were a game."

"It is One day you will understand." Bozena fluttered her
eyes and grinned.

Since it was too hot for milk-skinned Bozena to sit in the
sun in the Public Garden where Hebe wanted to go, they went to
the library, collected several books and sat in the shade of the
courtyard. Hebe didn't consult the card catalogue and hunt for
her book. Profiles in Courage, by John F. Kennedy, was just
lying on a table. "Look, is Pulitzer Prize book," Bozena pointed
out, and Hebe picked it up. The Birches had recently discussed
"paradoxes in American politics," a topic Noni had brought up.

"El Señor, Kennedy's support of violating McCarthy's first
ammendment rights in order to shut up his embarrassing
accusations of the communism in the American government, is un
exemplo perfectamente," he began.

"Censureship in the land of free speech?" Hans added further
opening the door of The Birches critiqe of American politics.

Hebe had hoped to find some understanding of what they had
been talking about in the book, but the sunny day kept
distracting her until finally she put on her old California
sunglasses and gave it her total attention. Bozena, leaning
against a column with her river of copper-highlighted hair
flowing over her plump form onto the book in her lap, sat exuding
the joy and contentment of a person at peace. Hebe basked in her
presence and relaxed listening to her read in Polish.
Melifluously, delivering the words of her mother tongue, she
sounded like an actress. Suddenly she stopped. "Too bad you not
speak Polish. I could to tell you about Gromulka." Then she went
back to reading.

"I don't get you Bozena. I thought you didn't even like
school. Look at all those books you're taking home. I think
you're really smart."

"School? School? School has nothing to do with
intelligence, especially here. Hebe in my country I was top of my
class. Understand? Most smartest in gymnasium. I come to here,
they give me one English test and put me in one room with many
children."

"Yeah, I know it's really boring."

"I'm agree. Is stupid. First day, I told my husband, we no could believe." A glimpse at the time made her jump up because she had to go home and start dinner. She had an armful of books. Unable to decide about her book, she asked Bozena, "So what's so great about this book."

"Oh, it got big prize. And author, is dreamy, most good-looking and... Catholic," she added proudly.

Hebe already had the heavy bottle of vodka wrapped in a burlap bag. She didn't want to carry anything anything else. So, she left the book in the library and Bozena at the entrance. Her dinner invitation was tempting; she truly enjoyed Bozena's company. But all of her relatives were still strangers to her, Polish-speaking strangers. She didn't want to be lost in a roomfull of foreigners unable to understand the simplest of things. She wanted to find herself where she had left herself that morning in the familiar rooms of The Birches perfunctorily carrying out their routine. She wanted to go where she was not only expected but wanted. She wanted to go home.

"I can't tonight, Bozena. I have to go home." The very word in her brain brought a feeling of comfort. She shuffled and said it again. "They're expecting me at home."

Somewhere between Copley Square in Boston and the A & P Supermarket on the corner of Bolyston and Cypress streets in Brookline, the lovely warmth of the morning rolled into a sweltering heat, uncharacteristic for May. In the two hours she had been walking, the sun bleached the color from the world and the energy from her body. Peering down the blanched turnpike leading to the Birches, which was nowhere in sight, she realized she had drastically underestimated the distance and wondered how much farther it could be. Her legs had never ached so much before, not even when she had marched along behind her grandmother. While she sat cooling off beneath the shade of a tree, a large, black, cadillac roared quickly by, then stopped and backed up. Rem hopped out of the passenger side. An army of nettled words joined forces and were dispatched from her mouth in the name of concern while she held her graceful arms out at her sides. Hebe couldn't have asked for a better greeting.

"How can you be so selfish. You weren't in school today. You haven't called. No one knew anything. Don't you know people care about you? You must tell someone when you.." She stopped and released a charming shriek at the sky. "Hebe what are you doing out here on the side of the road anyway?"

"I was trying to walk to the Birches."

"Dahling, we have four cars among us. Someone would have come to get you. Dialing the phone is a remarkably simple procedure."

Phillipe stepped out and helped Hebe into the back of the car as Rem continued muttering her concern. Hebe thoroughly enjoyed Rem's reaction and sat without defending herself in the least. It was comforting to hear that someone cared. Someone was upset that she had done something that could have caused her harm. She felt good.

"Mademoiselle," Phillipe said kissing the back of her hand. Hebe thought then, as she had at the house, how gentle he looked, how young. His face was angular and masculine, but he didn't have the slightest trace of hair on it. And his hands, they were as soft and smooth as if he had never handled anything more roughly textured than than dandelion puffs.

"Are you comfortable back there? Then she turned to Phillipe, "Löfik, no one's back at the house yet. I don't want to leave her alone."

"E Jaques?"

"Who knows where he is. Shall we take her along."

"Löfik, we already have." he answered.

"Rem, what does it mean, Löfik?"

She and Phillipe laughed. "I didn't realize I had said it. It means 'dear' in Volapük.

"Where is that spoken?"

"I suppose only among my friends. It's our secret language. A German priest invented it as a universal language 100 years ago, yet the world continues to babbling to itself. Try this.

Tikob ofen len ols."

"Tikob ofen len ols."

"Hebe you're a natural. It means, I often think of you."
She made a telephone call from the big, car telephone. Only the
word, "Hello," passed through her lips and Hebe knew Rem was
calling Henry, chamberlain of "The Birches". Her tone was one
reserved for someone respected and trusted, as if he were a
great-uncle. No one had ever seen him, but once Rem mentioned
that he and her private secretary had been with her family for
years. She declared with great sincerity, "Henry is the wizard
of my Oz!" And this explained to Hebe why Rem often prefaced her
requests to him with the words, "I know it's impossible, but..."
There didn't seem to be much he couldn't do. And Rem claimed,
"Henry knows more about me than me." She picked up the jasper
urn on the mantel. "He knows if I brought this from the house in
France, England or Italy. He knows the staffs' backgrounds,
which charities I support, which mother-in-law's birthday I
remember, where I am supposed to be and with whom at all times."

Therefore, it was no surprise that she called him from the
car with the change of her plans. She requested that he convey
information to Thurloe, the old butler, about the new number for
dinner and that most importantly he call ahead to make the
necessary arrangements with the apartment at the Pierre Hotel.

"I know it's impossible, but we do need tickets to Carnegie,
have her name put on the Waldorf list. Hebe is coming with us to
New York." She reached back and tenderly stoked her wrist again.

Evidence of Henry's limitation was at the front desk in a
message of regret stating "Madame: Not even a solitary standing
room seat remains at Carnegie." But everything else was done.
Clothes, exactly her size, magically hung in the closet. It was
as if he had had someone raid the closet of her room on Beacon
Hill. So she found herself with her least favorite outfits in
New York, "Center of the Universe,' that's what the mayor of N.Y.
calls it," Floyd used to say.

Floyd's definition of New York and his stories always led
her to imagine it as hot-dark and colorfully noisy as a Mexican

border bar on a saturday night. And on that night, the Pierre residential hotel which was usually a quiet, elegant hide-a-way was a noisy crush of smoking reporters. Apparently, a celebrity was going to stay there. Despite the chaos, the doorman and the porters whisked their things through and paid close personal attention to Rem, as if they had known her for a long time and she lived there. As it turned out, she did. The Pierre Hotel was one of the many places she called home that Hans had mentioned. The staff addressed her, "Madame de Maupassant" and promptly carried her luggage to her room in the adjoining suites. It was a grand double suite extension of "The Birches". Conversations were held in low tones with a minimum of words. Even Rem had less to say.

She was quite different. Her ebullience, flimsy chiffon and gregarious movements had been exchanged for properly tailored ensembles. Never without gloves and her flawless strand of dark, shiny pearls, she was a picture of propriety, a complete lady.

"These look like the clothes Grandmother Wilkinson likes me to wear," Hebe complained kicking at her loafers. Rem sat on the end of her bed and put her arm around her.

"Yes, I know. They were never my favorite either. We can call and have a more dainty pair delivered. But remember, we're not at home playing dress up."

"Playing dress-up?" she echoed.

"Oh, come now Hebe. You know other eleven-year-old girls don't powder their noses and wear pumps." Hebe nodded. "But, I've never told you, you couldn't." Hebe shook her head. "No. Of course not. We were in the real world, our world, at home. It didn't matter. Now, we are in society's world. It matters a great deal. Do you think I like all this?" She lifted her skirt revealing a slip, a girdle, a garter belt and stockings. "It horrible. It's armor. I can't breathe. I can't move!"

"So why wear it?"

"What do you wear to bed?"

"Nightgown."

"Swimming?"

"Bathing suit."

"Tennis court?"

"Whites."

"A ball?"

"O.K. O.K. I get it. I'll wear them," she conceded grabbing up the clothes on the bed. "But I won't like them."

Rem patted at her hips, "We'll hate them together."

The next day the outfit, covered by a raincoat, was the farthest thing from her mind. Confetti snowed down on her and all the other people, more than she had ever seen in one place. There were thousands of them in Spring coats lightening the building-grey streets of Lower Broadway. They hung from the windows and clamored on the sidewalks. Rem and Phillipe each held one of her hands so as not to get separated in the crowd which seemed to be mostly women. Of course the cheerleaders and musicians of the parade were thrilling, but everyone was focused on the honored rider. Tall and slim and young, he sat perched on the back of the parade car waving. His eyes gleaming with amazement. Hebe was told he was the winner of the very first Tchaikovsky Piano Competition, Van Cliburn. And while she was certain that must have been a great accomplishment, she found herself stretching to be seen and jumping up and down for a completely different reason.

"He's really cute!" she shouted above the din. "I thought he was some old guy." There really wasn't anything to say to a man she had hardly heard of passing by on a car, so she just hollered, "I'm from San Diego!" and waved with such enthusiasm that he turned his head. So many people were calling out it was difficult to tell whose comment caught his ear, but for a split second everyone looked at her, including him. Swept up in the hysteria as she was it was a challenge for Rem to get her away from the parade line at the barricade.

"Hebe calm yourself. We can't have you calling out like that when he appears at the Waldorf? Oh Löfuk what are we going to do with her?"

Phillipe watched until Van Cliburn was no longer visible then

- 212 -

adjusted his coat collar. "I think the little girl is having excellent taste in men. I'm certain she will be the perfect lady at the Waldorf, won't you?"

Starstruck deaf she didn't hear the question. "Did you see his hair? Did you ever see such thick wavy hair?"

She liked everything about him. His hair, his eyes, his hands and most of all his music. At the Waldorf, she didn't scream. Her halibut got cold; she didn't eat. And, although she wanted to yell, "I'm from San Diego!" again, just to investigate whether he had in fact heard her, in particular earlier, she didn't speak. She could not. She was dizzy.

Noticing that she hadn't blinked for some time, Phillipe leaned over and buzzed into her ear, "This is Liszt, Twelve Hungarian Rhapsody, I think you say in English."

"Uh, huh," was her acknowledgement. Like many others, she was under Van Cliburn's spell. Thoroughly captivated, she sat with her elbows on the table and her chin resting on the back of her hands. His long energetic fingers thundered chords and rained a summer shower of notes on the audience, on her. In a matter of minutes, she was soaked to the bone with the pianist passionate outpouring of music. It filled her head leaving no room for thought. She trembled. The only times she had felt such an intense physical sensation was being kissed in the front seat of Tony's car, or watching Hans kiss Zelpha. And she felt that way now as if she were simlutaneously watching a seduction and being seduced. Unable to resist the lure of the ivory and ebony, their promise of satisfaction, the musician was obliged to stroke and fondle the piece, to perform. His gifted hands nimbly rippled down it and stroked it over and over and over. The only thought she had was that she wanted to bend backwards, sprout keys and receive the powerful soulful love the player lavished on his instrument. She wanted to be a piano.

The experience was so exhausting that she was relieved when Rem told her she was not expected to attend the New-York-Boston Waltz Evening at the Sheraton East that night. She was too young. So she stayed behind. Nell was the first person she called. She

was quite impressed about the Van Cliburn luncheon at the
Waldorf, and they went on in destinationless chatter for at least
an hour. Bozena would have been next on her list, but she didn't
have a phone. She called Rosalita. At first, she was screaming
in excitement, then she let open a floodgate for her Spanglish to
flow about what had been happening in her life, why she hadn't
written. By the time they hung up, Hebe knew what Rosalita had
eaten for breakfast and everything everyone in the house had been
saying for the past week about her boyfriend, John the "gorgeous
gringo" in the navy to whom she had become unofficially engaged.
She tried to butt in with a question about her brother, Jude, but
Rosalita answered her with a question, "You gonna be here for my
día de bodas?" Before she could reply, "Rosalita's mouth was off
and running about something else, then she said she had to go and
hung up. Hebe thought it might be fun for Jude to talk to her on
the telephone, so she had the operator get her number in San
Diego. It rang and rang and rang, and just as the operator told
her, "I'm sorry, there is no answer," it stopped ringing. No one
said anything, but people could be heard laughing and talking
over the loud music.

"Higgenson residence. Mrs. Higgenson speaking," she heard
her mother's voice say.

"She was speechless. When had her mother stopped using her
father's name, "Gourdin?"

"Hello?" she repeated.

"Hi. It's Hebe."

"Who?"

"Hebe," she repeated cupping her hand over the mouthpiece.

"Stevie?"

"Hebe!"

"Who is it?" she heard art whisper.

In the poorly ennunciated, slow-paced speech of someone who
had had at least three cocktails too many, she heard her mother
say, "Someone named, Eve or Steve?"

Art's voice came across the wire "Steve? Steve, you son of a
gun!" He verily roared above the party noise. "What's that you

say? I can't hear you," he complained. Hebe hadn't uttered a single word, but he continued. "Tell you what. We'll call you when we get back from Acapulco." And, "click" the connection was terminated.

"That was the wrong number," she told the operator when she came on the line to see if she could be of further assistance. "But I don't want to try again just now. Thank you." She knew very well that it was the right number, but she kept repeating to herself that it couldn't have been, that her mother would have recognized her voice, no matter how much she had had to drink. She would have wanted to talk to her. "It was the wrong number," she said outloud to herself. The call did not take place. Convincing herself was much easier after diverting her thoughts with a couple more shots of Bozena's potato vodka and a book, Phillipe's Complete Course of Volapük. The call was forgotten. She busied herself memorizing numbers in Volapük. With the fifth shot of vodka, she skipped ahead to the XI section, "Interjection". It was really easy. Oh in English was O, stop was Stopö!, help was Yufö. It was a most amusing way to spend the evening.

She hardly noticed when Rem and Phillipe came scrooping and shuffling through the door embroiled in the still-mysterious, politely muffled argument they had begun in Brookline several days ago. Curled up in the wingback chair, she was out of sight, and she knew it.

"I'll say it in English, Phillipe, Mrs. Pratt hasn't a pence more than she is owed coming to her. The old, sycophant. I know she has spent many hours with father; she is a nurse. That's her job. She is supposed to mind his body not his business. And to think she had the nerve to ask for the Gainsborough. It's been in our family since, since, well just about since he painted it! This is blackmail! It's illegal!"

"Löfik, so is marrying your brother."

At that moment, Hebe knew that not being noticed was not as good as not being there would have been. Unfortunately, there was no way to get out without being seen. She feigned sleep.

"Well, it was better than having him marry you, Phillipe! Besides, our...Well, how shall I put this? Our marriage is not as illegal as one would think. The conjointness between us is on paper sheets, not bed sheets."

"You are knowing I am living with, him. Why are you saying me this? Tell the lawyer."

"Phillipe really! The only crime was father even considering giving away his own son's fortune because..."

"Oui, Rem. Oui. We 'ave spoken this conversation combien de temps? Your father,"

"Was prepared to give the inheritance to Prince Philip's "Worldwide Fund for Nature" and the Red Cross if Etienne," she mimicked her father, "Is not married. It is the only way to save face, to disprove the rumors." she stopped. "The old puppeteer it's all his fault." She paced back and forth hauling on her cigarette, then fumed a question. "How the Hell did Pratt find out?" There was a long pause.

"Somehow, she saw your marriage certificate."

"No. That wouldn't have mattered. Mother's second husband adopted him. That's why his last name is different from mine. Well, it was."

"Etienne never proposed to me the marriage, Rem," Phillipe pouted.

"I'm sorry Dahling. Oh God. No offense Phillipe, but I can't believe I just sympathized with a man because my brother didn't ask him to be his wife." Rem threw her head back and laughed. "Which of you would have worn the gown? Never mind, I don't really want to know. I need a drink!" Emitting a heavy sigh of worry, Rem flounced herself onto the sofa in a bright taffetta heap, then gasped outloud as her eyes fell on Hebe slumped in a pose of sleep in the chair. "Shush. Don't say anything," she whispered motioning at the chair with her chin.

"Mon dieu! Do you think she heard, "

"I think she's asleep." She picked up the nearly empty glass of potato vodka and took a sip. "Or passed out. And not the first time either. I must speak with ma petite ivrognesse."

"Pas maintenant!"

"No. Of course not now, but soon."

However, to Hebe's relief, soon did not arrive in the near future as expected. After they saw Phillipe off to Europe at the New York airport, she suspected Rem would open the discussion of her drinking or inquire as to whether she had overheard the personal matter she and Phillipe had aired the night before. Neither was brought up. So she stored their secret along side the phone call she had made to her mother and hoped "soon" to be as far away as the third week of never.

TEN

Ni do aru koto wa san do aru.

Alone Again

Massachusetts, The Birches

The end of August:1958

The drama of summer 1958 was played out to Van Cliburn's recording of the Tchaikovsky Piano Concerto No. 1. Hebe listened to it daily since it's release in July. At "La Maisonette", Rem's dozen-bedroom summer cottage in Newport and at "The Birches". She played it over and over. No one was bothered. No one heard. In both places, she was afforded the privacy to do whatever she wished by reason of her spacious quarters with the en suite bathroom and the bell pull. She was her own person. If her pleasure was to be alone for a meal, drink mint tea at one a.m. or have a particular flower in her room, she simply had to inform whichever girl responded to her summons. One of them was Polish and reminded her a great deal of her friend, Bozena. She never abused the service; the young women worked so hard, sometimes until late into the night while the Birches were off, occupied with the exhausting task of entertaining themselves. Feeling

sorry for the girls, she decided to be her own lady's maid;
although, it was really an effortless responsibility. Clothes to
be washed went down the shoot on the right in the dressing room
and clothes to be dry cleaned went down on the left. A few days
later, they reappeared in the correct scented drawer or closet
ready to wear. As soon as the bright morning sunshine fell on
her face, she grinned, lolled in luxurious leisureliness, and
eventually rose to greet her day. After breakfast, she consulted
her agenda. On the green hills of Brookline, her hours were now
filled with tutors arranged by Rem: French, photography, science,
drama, tennis and riding. But the private lessons "The Birches"
taught had been suspended temporarily as they were all away.
Even Rem left briefly, confidant that, for just a few days her
home's divertissments: the library, the pool, the movie screening
room etc. and the tightly organized schedule she had supplied
would protect Hebe. And she was right. Hebe's hours revolved
around the plans and pasttimes barring the unwelcome ennui or
mischief of idleness in the house as effectively as the wrought
iron fence around the property kept out danger.

Nell was off, with mixed feelings about leaving Hans, to a
maternally arranged triste on a Greek island with an Italian
marquis. Floyd played music on the record player or his sax, and
came out of his room so infrequently that Rem once remarked to
Hans, "Sometimes, I hear him playing up there. Yet, when Thurloe
brings me my morning mail, I actually expect to find a post card
from him. The sad thing is, I don't think it would read, 'Wish
you were here'. I do think Holly should come back."

In mid-June, Holly had collected half of her things and
exiled herself to her studio in town on Saint Botolph street. In
the driveway, she supervised the attachment of her paintings to
the car; they wouldn't fit inside. One was a nude, a slim man
holding his thick penis, rendered in brassy yellow oils. Wingéd,
glycerin musical notes seemed to have flowed out of it. Halves
and quarters and wholes were everywhere, but the nude bowed his
head contemplating the one eighth note which had emerged, but
dangled by its stem from the aperture of his beautiful music

making instrument. Another eighth hung from the corner of his
eye. A hand stretched out toward him from the other canvas. It
was a woman's hand, nothing more. Holly suggested they put it on
the other side, then raised her apologetic explanation to Floyd's
window. "I'm sorry. I just have to concentrate so I can get
these finished." Hebe watched Holly looking up at his room and
waiting for a word from Floyd. None came. At that moment, Hebe
thought it was unkind, maybe even cruel for Holly to beckon Floyd
to the window because close by her was her moving-day lackey, her
chauffeur, her smug swain, Thaddeus Oberland Sheridan. He gave
her bottom a healthy giggle producing goose as she got into the
passenger side of his new gold German Daimler. He had arrived in
it at the end of Spring. As soon as Floyd laid eyes on it he
said, "Thaddeus has come into his inheritance I see." Rem
thought it "an elegant car, but not in gold. It's so
ostentatious." Hans was impressed by its balance and v-8 engine.
Noni recanted wanting to order one right away because he said,
"If I had one of these, I'd be so busy with womens I wouldn't get
nothing done." And on more than one occasion, they had heard
Holly sigh, "My dream car is a Daimler."

Her hand came through the top and pushed the little leather
sunroof aside to wave to "Floyd, I'll be back!" Then she peeked
through the window and held on tightly to the canvas musician as
the car rolled down the driveway. "Bye everyone!" And that was
the last anyone had seen of Tossie, Holly or Floyd.

Meanwhile, Hans continued experimenting with projects for
his thesis on the back green. Noni had offered to help. When
Hans presented the request to work on the property, Rem's concern
was about the noise they might make and stipulated that they not
disturb the peace. Appart from flushing the peacocks into the
open, they didn't. However, his project jutted out of the
landscape and competed with the pastoral scene of Warren Street.
It was a large, metal windmill painted in circus red and taxicab
yellow. He showed Rem how it worked so she would approve phase
two of the project.

"A windmill!"

"Ja. Isn't it beautiful?"

"Beautiful? Hans it's a windmill. Leave it to a Dutchman to travel thousands of miles across the Atlantic to attend one of the best engineering schools in the world to build, of all things, a windmill."

"But this one makes electricity."

The vanes creaked out drowning the movement of their shoes whispering through the damp morning grass. In the barn, Rem greeted the horses and stood with her hands on her hips. Hans flicked on the light and pointed to it as it brightened and dimmed to the sound of the windmill. Squeek. Squeek. Squeek. Flicker. Flicker. Flicker.

"The way I see it, the whole house can have windmill electricity."

"The house? The house! Hans the way I see it, the poor horses are going to need spectacles by the end of the month. It doesn't even light their stall lamp with dim consistency."

"Well that's because we have only put up the one windmill."

Rem's face tensed and she became very formal when she was peeved just like Grandmother Wilkinson's. "The one? Well, I'm certain you will agree Dahling, it would be more beneficial if our comfort level were not given the opportunity to become a calamitous victim of mischance. I don't remember the exact question however the exact answer must be no. You are so clever. Do pick something else."

The windmill's disassembly and removal would have involved blow torches and a flatbed truck, so Rem consented to allow the giant, machine to stand spinning its primal painted propellors to the warm zephyrs of summer. Hans already had an alternate project in mind which he promised would be out of sight as well as out of sound. It was for the most part.

The only indication anyone had that they were doing anything were the few professorial type men in khaki pants who came to camp out and work with them. Without their coming and going, one would have guessed Hans and Noni to have vanished into the woods beyond the little dale with their crew. No one saw them. No one heard them. No one knew what they were doing. The sight was off limits to everyone. But one morning, she was in the tak room and they were on the other side of the wall having coffee. She over heard Noni.

"This is grandé Daddyo. Just make sure you invite me when you win the Nobel prize for physics or whatever they give you for this. I love Swedish chicks.

"Swedish chicks? Noni, the world does not revolve around chicks?"

"Yes it does. That's what I learned when I lost my face. My life lives up to the musical, 'There is nothing like a dame'. And this idea, a flying saucer, a big dish is just what I need to catch a big dish, you know some big, blonde babies."

"So that's what they're up to, a flying saucer." Hebe was dying to share her discovered information with someone; there was no one left to tell. Rem had gone to North Africa, much to Hebe's chagrin.

"I absolutely can not take you out of the country. Well, I could, but not to Tangier. I will not. It's out of the question. It just isn't safe."

"Then why are you going?"

"The countess gives such grand parties. This may be her last there; the country is changing so much. Besides, I gave her my word that I would be in attendance. I'm expected."

"Is Phillipe going to be there?"

"Mais oui Lofök! and my husband."

She heard husband, but "What does your brother do anyway?" popped out. Rem was holding up a heavily beaded white gown. Her arm dropped. She turned pale and spun around.

"My brother?" In the second that their eyes met, Rem read Hebe's face and knew she had heard the conversation in the hotel room. "I was talking about my husband. He's a collector, abstracts mostly." She swished out another ball skirt. It was irridescent black and purple with peacock feathers all along the hem.

"Wear that one!"

"I believe I will."

"Feathers from your peacocks. Wherever did you get them?

"Afghanistan. I and my first husband were there. Fifty-
one, if I remember correctly. That's a country. Nothing tastes
quite like water from a Hindu Kush stream. Oh and the Blue
Mosque in Mazar-e-Sharif, such a work of art."

"Did you buy them at a peacock market?"

"Actually they were a gift from the king."

"The king! I wish I could travel the way you have."

"It's really very easy. You just put your passport on the
counter, buy your ticket and your off."

"Passport?"

"There's a big reason for you not to come. No passport."

Hebe dreaded the thought of Rem leaving her behind. Since
their trip to New York, she had become the constant in her life
that her mother once was. She was the first step in her daily
routine. Even if she were out, she would call just to say, "Good
morning Hebe." This was usually followed by, "Is everything in
order?" Sometimes that's all she had to say, but Hebe enjoyed
getting the call, knowing that she was on Rem's agenda. She had
seen her name written on every page. Their was a feeling of love
that came with the responsibility brought by Rem's trust in her.
Rem could count on her. She had even given her the number to
Henry's private line, "Just in case a serious matter," were to
arise and she needed help handling it.

In Rem's absence, Hebe realized how accustomed to Rem she
had become and how deep her feelings were. Because the long
week-end jaunt had already turned into two weeks. Even though
Rem called, she missed her more than she had ever missed anyone,
and she was lonely.

Though the six close friends were all far away in body or
mind, especially, Floyd, the Birches was peopled with the staff,
so she wasn't alone. But, since she had promised Rem on her
honor not to step foot beyond the gate of "The Birches", there
wasn't anyone to discuss things with, to listen to, to laugh with
in an intimate way. After her last failed phone call to

California, she didn't dare to call again. So she settled on the mute but musical and stimulating company of Van Cliburn and the deliciously numbing company of Monsieur Rothschild. Vintage 1945 was her favorite. She drank and contemplated her solitude. It was not the negligent exclusion she had with her mother or the intentional avoidance of her grandmother. It was just unfortunate circumstances. "Everyone is going to be back soon," she said outloud to herself drowning out questons she had about what was going on in California with her mother and little Jude. "You would really like it here Judey." She held the small framed picture of her brother up to the window. "See that's where the horse named Lightning lives. And smell. Isn't that beautiful? It's all those flowers drying all over the place."

The Birches was rife with giant squares of papers covered with colorful mounds of blossoms because Jacques decided to supplement his income by making potpourri. The heavy perfume snuck into the pages of books, their hair and even their mouths. Before leaving, Rem had remarked that it lent a passing air of paradise not because of how it looked, but because, "It tastes like heaven, doesn't it?" They all agreed. Traversing between rooms was a sweetly-flavored olfactory odyssey. And Jacques was forever fussing over the petals with oils to enrich the scent and layers of tulle to keep them in place.

One night, while becoming fully acquainted with a second bottle of bordeaux, she sat reading a souvenir New York Times from her trip with Rem and Phillipe. The article was about Wimbeldon banning gold lamé panties from its tennis courts. And there was a picture of the lady who wore them, Karol Fageros, "The Golden Goddess" lifting her tennis dress proudly showing off her black-lace trimmed gold lamé panties. Laughing suddenly, Hebe accidentally fell onto the tone arm badly scratching the record. She looked at her brother's photograph, "Jude, stay right here, I'll go see if I can borrow one of the others from Hans or Floyd.

The light glowing in the woods past 11:00 p.m. meant Hans and Noni were probably camping out. Unsteadily, she wove her way through the rooms to Floyd's. No light shone under the door, but

he was playing. Over and over he blew into the mouthpiece and
ran his fingers through the same few notes. It sounded as though
the sax were an extention of his own vocal aparatus. The tragic
wimpering series of crying sounds he created sent a shiver up her
spine, touched her heart and heightened her own sense of sadness.
Too much lonliness, too much wine and the eery notes sent her to
and fro in a mini semi circle of nervousness. Precipitously, the
huge distant walls appeared only a few feet away. The air had
gotten thinner making it difficult to inhale. She started for
the outdoors, but as she was heading down the staircase, the
steps began to pulsate with the lights, then everything turned
red and black and red and black.

    "Ojosan? Ojosan?" the vaguely familiar words were being
spoken into a long cardboard tube. Or were they? She opened her
eyes. There stooped the gardner, Ichi Tanaka, Jacques. His back
was to her, but she could see he was making tea on a little
burner. They were in the his living space, a simple guest house
adjacent to the cloister garden. He repeated, "Daijobu, Ojosan."

    "What are you saying?"

    "Not to worry, little one. Maybe you feel like the
butterly."

    "Butterfly?"

    He sat a cup of tea next to her. "Itsa Chinese story. Man
sleeps and dreams he the butterfly and that butterfly sleeps and
dreams he the man and wake up. Question, is he the man who dream
he the butterfly, or the butterfly dreaming he the man?" The
floor was strewn with hundreds of little cranes he had been
making out of red paper. He didn't say anything else. Deftly,
his fingers creased one fold and another and another and produced
crane after crane. Woozy and nauseated she tried to lie still by
holding onto the wall with one hand.

    "What happened?"

    "Vous missed step and tombe down stairs."

    "I fell down the stairs! I don't remember." Turning her
head she heard a crunch like autumn leaves and reached back to
pull out a handfull of dried potpourri petals from her hair.

"Sure. You said, 'I see the stars.' I don't go around in the main house. This is my house."

"It's very nice. Thank you." A small black and white cityscape was framed on the wall.

"That the my ville in Japan, the Kamakura. It's too special there right now in the August, many good things to eat and many singing insects." With a sad nod, he hung his head over his work.

"You must miss it."

Jacques offered no elaboration. She thought she had only blinked her eyes, but when she opened them again and sat up to sip her tea, it was cold. And there were about fifty more cranes.

She drank more tea to try to take away the cotton sensation in her mouth. "What are you going to do with all of those? You must have more than two hundred."

"Seven hundred and ninety eight," he said adding one more to one of the piles and starting another. As usual, Jacques wore a straight face, but he was not unfriendly. He had a serenity about him that made him comfortable to be around, especially when doing something. In the garden or tending the bushes he was focused. Information was never volunteered. But Hebe discovered that he would answer questions when he wanted and found out a few things. He had been in the Japanese military, a Lieutenant. He had fallen in love with and married a French woman which made it necessary for him to leave Japan forever. She didn't understand why, but the brief explanation made her think that his family felt the same way about his French wife that her own grandmother felt about her father.

"Itsa not too much popular the French wife in my country, so me and the Lulu, we stay in the France."

She died two years after they relocated to Europe. He never said how. But he said Lulu loved all growing greenery and trees and flowers, knew everything about them. On her deathbed he told her he would become a landscape architect so that he could create a living memorial for her. "After I dead, Lulu gonna live

forever in those green things I plant for her, in the France,
here in the Brookline. And those dry flowers, the potpourri. I
export it over the everywhere earth. Lulu always gonna bring the
beauty to everyone like she brought to my heart." Hebe was
speechless,she thought that was the most romantic story she had
ever heard. Jacques also mentioned how happy he was to be on
Warren Street so close to the former workshop of a great American
landscape designer, Frederick Law Olmsted.

"Go to the anyplace green in coast to coast United States.
He made that, itsa guarantee. Itsa special art move around the
nature, être assistant to the God. I lucky to be here near the
Olmsted's energy," he declared while placing a sapling in the
earth one afternoon. Now he was sitting cross-legged on his
floor making birds.

Picking up a piece of paper and copying his actions she
created a rather feeble, imitation. He chuckled and proceeded
more slowly the second time and even more slowly several more
times after that until she made one on her own. Periodically, he
stopped to swig his hot saké or smoke a cigarette, but she
folded incessantly determined to make one perfectly. For a
while, they worked in unison without talking which she enjoyed
partly because she really didn't have much to say and partly
because she felt as if she opened her mouth vomit would come out,
not words. Her stomach churned bringing an unpleasant bilious
flavor to the back of her tongue. She sipped her tea and tried
to wash it away. On the stove, she eyed a large pot full of
something like dirt. Jacques saw her straining to figure out
what it was.

"Must to cook the dirt to be, how you say, sterile. Good
por les flowers."

Then he dusted his hands off as if he were finished and
watched her work.

"That's one more to make senba zuru."

"What?"

"Senba zuru, the one thousand cranes."

"A thousand! No kidding. One thousand birds. A thousand!

What are they for?"

He gathered them together in an enormous wooden salad bowl.
"Non for the what. For the who? One thousand cranes make
someone well."

"Oh thank you. But, I'm not sick. Maybe I had a little
too much to drink."

"Maybe. But not you. For the Floyd. All the time in the
room. So sad, he has the big trouble."

"Yes, that's true." She wanted to tell him she agreed and
how incredibly thoughtful he was but she could only gag back the
sour taste. She hauled herself to her feet and wiggled her toes.
"Hey, where are my shoes?" Her stomach turned and she swallowed
hard. Jaques placed the large bowl in her arms and walked across
the tatami mats to get her shoes. Just then, the power of her
stomach overcame her throat and pushed out a puddle of vomit that
covered the cranes. She gasped. "Oh my God. I'm so sorry."

Jacques calmly took the bowl and rescued a few dry birds
with a subtle chuckle. "Yeah. quelquefois it happen. Here." He
handed her a damp cloth to wipe her face.

"I can make them again tomorrow, the whole thousand," she
gushed.

"Daijobu, Ojosan."

"No. I can't believe I did that. That was so stupid of me.
I will. I'll remake them. How many did I miss." Holding out her
hands for the salvaged cranes, Jacques placed them in one of her
palms. "This means I only have to make," she glanced down; there
were four little red birds. "Nine hundred and...," she started to
count on her fingers.

"Ninety-six."

"I think Rosalita would call this doing penance."

"Ojosan, we make it together. Daijobu."

In the end, she consented to let him help her. Standing at
the door, he bowed to her. She bowed back.

"Mr. Tanaka, I'm really sorry about the birds. And thank
you for bringing me here, for the tea and everything. You're the
best."

"Itsa no problem Hebe. No one going to leave you falling down on stairs. I so há-ppy to be there. Autrement, must be bad thing for you."

She bowed again. "Thanks anyway. You didn't yell or get the others and make me feel bad or threaten to tell Mrs. Remmington or anything. So thanks." Shame and embarrassment made her look away. "Funny, all the times I walked by here, I never even saw this place."

"Hanare."

"Hanare?"

"That le mot in Japanese. Guest house Mrs. Remington offer me one room in the her house, but I prefer to be in here for my Japanese style."

It was then she noticed the simplicity of the decor and the paper walls catching the birches' shadows in the rising sun. He looked at them too.

"I can to be close to the trees."

"Close to her."

"Who?"

"Lulu?"

There was a pause before he spoke. "I am há-ppy you not hurt Ojosan."

He bowed. She bowed. They bowed together.

Remaking the cranes and recovering from her hangover took almost exactly the same length of time, two days, even with the help of several others. Hans, Noni, the laundry girls, everyone who passed the large claw footed table in the dining hall where she had been working tried their hand at making a crane. As a result, some were big, some were small and some, barely cranes at all, just lumps of red folded and crushed paper. Nevertheless, there were one thousand cranes, senba zuru.

That night, she sat contemplating the bowl of paper birds as Tchaikovsky's Piano Concerto No. 1 floated through the air and pinched her attention like the aroma of a sweet dessert cooking. Following it to its source, she arrived at Floyd's door once again. It was very loud, and she knew he would never hear her

rapping, so she gently turned the knob and became the first
person to enter his room for many weeks. Except for the light
from the nubs of candles in the candelabra, it was dark. Playing
hide-n-seek with her father and Jude flashed through her mind.
But the room was not electric with the excitement of a game. It
reeked of portention. Persperation was the base odor beneath a
layer of stale cigarette butts topped off with a rich,
unidentifiable tinny top note. Hebe covered her nose and mouth
with her hand, walked to the table and set the bowl down. "Floyd
are you in here? Everybody made..," she cracked her ankle on
something and looked down to see his sax on the floor next to
Floyd's paper pale face in the flickering flame. Lighting her
way with the candelabra, she bent down to look at him and cringed
in horror. His inner arms were slashed. Ropey muscles and
ligaments spilled out from his elbows to his wrists in long red
and white strands. Babbling weakly over his skin was a brook of
blood. Instinctlively she knelt down to stop the bleeding. She
wanted to, but she didn't know how. The music halted, and the
room was dead quiet. All of a sudden his wild blue eyes blinked
open in a teary tortured stare.

"Help me," he whispered and touched the hem of her skirt
with his sanguine fingers triggering her reaction.

She flung open the shutters and her mouth at the same time.
At first she could only scream, then she formed the words, "Help!
Help! Anybody! Come quickly!" She turned around and they were
there. The whites of a dozen eyes gleemed with fear and
curiosity at Hebe holding the dripping candle over Floyd lying
lacerated and dying on the floor. The butler, Mr. Thurloe held
the servants at bay as the Birches pushed through. Hans dashed
immediately to Hebe and enfolded her in a trembling embrace.
Jacques tended to Floyd and Noni shoved back out.

"Oh Dios! Oh Dios! I gonna call the hopital, the ambulance!"

Three days later they got the news that Floyd had pulled
through. Hebe saw the senba zuru in a plastic bag outside of
Floyd's door where one of the cleaning girls had placed them
while straightening up his room. She took them back to her room,

stored them in one of her suitcases and wondered if she had delivered them just in time and saved Floyd's life or if it was just a coincidence. A heavy-hearted sorrow having dispirited her, she cancelled all of her lessons and kept to herself or sat with the old horse, Lightning.

Mr. Thomas had shown her how to groom him, and she found making him beautiful as comforting to her as it seemed to be to him. When she ran the brushes through his fell, he clopped his foot on the ground whisked his tail. Framed by the barn door, the sun-washed building of "The Birches" became an unclear impressionist painting of a quiet, empty house on the horizon. There was no music without Floyd. There was no stream of life flowing in and out. With it's curtains lapping out of the open windows of the upstairs it was a ghost ship sailing on its sea of grass. Lonliness was creeping into her soul when suddenly Lightning pushed her with his big soft muzzle. She looked into his eyes and stroked his cheek "'Ni do aru koto wa san do aru. Two things happen. There's going to be a third.' That's what Mr. Tanaka said. First I fell down, then poor Floyd. Hans thinks that's just a saying, but not Noni. He thinks something is going to happen. But what?" She sat on a stool in front of him. "What do you think? Is anything going to happen?" His reply was only a nod of his big neck with a loud whicker. Obsessively, the expression occupied her thoughts until she went to sleep at night.

"Ni do aru koto wa san do aru."

A distant dove's cooing accented the long pastorale of morning serenity that played in the air as Hebe lay awakening in her bed. As had become her habit, she listened for Lightning before she opened her eyes. His daybreak greeting to Mr. Thomas gave her a sense that all was right with the world. First she heard a seagull. "August rainstorm coming," she thought to herself. Next came the sound of water moving, the California surf. "Someone's having an early morning dip," she thought growing impatient for Lightning's special snort. Then she heard a blender. The unmistakeable whirring of the machine ripped her eyes open, and she found herself awake in her room in her mother's house. Her breath came in short gasps. Her limbs were led weights. Lifting her head, she felt her heart beating in her temples. The moist, sea air washed over her from beyond the window where she could see the beach. She couldn't beleive her eyes. "Hebe think!" She took herself through her steps. "You were in the darkroom with Hans. Yes. Marilyn Monroe. Hans developed your film and he and Noni thought those pictures of the woman in the park were of Marilyn Monroe." In the background the sound of ice being chipped and crushed in the osterizer grew louder and louder. She snapped her eyes open and saw the glossy black and white prints. There was one of the frisky Beagle puppy and two of her with Marilyn on the bench. She felt as if she were under the spell of the same drug laced sleep of sickness she had endured when she arrived in Boston. It tugged at her ability to stay awake. It muddled her thinking. She picked the photographs up from her dresser. "Where am I? The butterfly riddle came to her. "Am I awake in my dream in Brookline or awake in my dream in San Diego? I'm in Brookline of course," she concluded. The blender whirred away. "Mother turn that off!" she begged flattening her palms against her ears to no avail. It continued on high in her head. "Mother! Mother, please! Mother!" she shrieked.

"Hebe? Did you call me?" she heard.

It was true. Her grandmother, The Birches, it had all been a dream. She wanted to leap back in bed, into her dream at the end of the world, but her name was being repeated over and over and over, "Hebe?"

"Leave me alone!" she howled her shrill response closing her eyes. The bedroom door swung open. "Is that my mother or Rem?" she thought to herself. Lightning's whinny floated through the window on a summer's floral zephyr sending a shiver though her sweat drenched body.

"Hebe? What's wrong?" Rem asked sweetly placing the seersucker robe around her shoulders. She gave a tug on the bellpull and ordered mint tea to be brought up. "I know how you

feel. I know. This must be very hard for you. You'll find your
world Hebe."

"But Jude? What about my little brother, Jude?"

Rem alighted on the arm of a chair and took Hebe's hand.
"You can't do anything about that. If you feel sad, well you are
supposed to. But sooner or later we all learn that death is one
of the things that nature wills," That's what my Mrs. Remmington
told me when my mother died. Reaching up to shut the window, her
white negligee fluttered behind her in angelic billowing wings.
"The medicine the doctor gave you should help you sleep. Whatever happens, Hebe remember, you can always come back to the
Birches, to me." Then, with the grace of a nocturnal seraph
vanishing in the light of day, she floated into the hallway.

ELEVEN

DARK LIGHT

"No warmth, no cheerfulness, no healthful ease,
No comfortable feel in any member
No shade, no shine, no butterflies, no bees,
No fruits, no flowers, no leaves, no birds,
November!

No!" *(Thomas Hood 1840)*

The Hotel Del Coronado-Coronado, California - November 1, 1958

Looking through the blackest of sunglasses, the world burned with dark light. Removing them made no difference, everything appeared equally shadowy, so Hebe chose to wear them all the time, to have some external reason for the perpetual dusk which hung in the day time skies of southern California. The telegram she had received weeks earlier only read:

HEBE STOP
COME AT ONCE STOP TICKET AT PAN AMERICAN COUNTER STOP CAR WILL BE WAITING STOP

ARTHUR A. HIGGENSON

The reason it was sent was to be the third, the "san" in "Ni do aru koto wa san do aru."

Art's company car which picked her up late in the night didn't take her on the long drive home but over the nearby San Diego-Coronado Bay Bridge where the fanciful silhouette and reflecting lights of their destination greeted her. It was the Hotel Del Coronado. Whenever visitors had come from the east coast, relative, friend or colleague, Art would take them there. He loved the place. He would say. "The Del" is not a static structure which represents a particular architectural style, a relic from the past. It is like a person, yes, with a past, but ever in the present going toward the future. It's as if this building were a piece of art designed on a given day to be started, but never finished, to be forever reshaped by the hands of time and necessity, an adaptable socio-morphic structure. That's what The Hotel Del Coronado is." No matter what words he threw in between, Art always commenced and concluded with those sentences, and there always seemed to be a railing at hand on which he could knock his Harvard ring to punctuate his conclusion. Everyone he brought there was as dazzled as he had promised. Hebe thought the hotel was beautiful too, but she referred to it as, "that tiered, carrousel-cake place by the sea." Art and her mother had on occasion passed weekends there, and it was at "The Del" the family had brought in the new year of 1958 when Margarita, while offered a room, refused it and was granted her wish to go home long before midnight because she was afraid of running into the resident ghost. She said she would "Never, no, nunca, stay in the hotel."

Yet she was there next to Art in the middle of the suite's living room lined with carnations and lillies when Hebe returned to San Diego and opened the door. By their weak greetings and the flowers she knew this was not a leisurely visit, that something was terribly wrong.

"Where's my mother?" she asked right away.

Margarita tensed her brow and put her fingertips to her mouth, "No. Senior. Por favor. I can not say." She stepped out onto the balcony.

"What? Say what? Is she sick?"

"Look, Kiddo." Art grabbed at his hair, then smoothed it down with his palms. Why don't you sit down?

"What can't she say?"

He lit a cigarette and hauled on it so hard he made himself cough.

"Say what, Art?" She sat down.

"I'm sorry, but your brother passed away a few..."

She jumped up and waved her arms, "Jude? Jude? What do you mean he passed away? Was he in an accident?" Her insides turned to jelly and her skinned burned as if thrashed with thistles. "Why didn't someone tell...."

"Take it easy, Kiddo."

Bereaved, and in the process of drowning her pain, her mother leaned her shoulder against the hall wall for support and slid into the room. An empty bottle of vodka hung with the weight of a small anchor from one hand and an empty glass dangled from the other. She was haggard and wan, her inner suffering marked in broad, dark circles beneath her light green eyes. With a wave of the bottle in Margarita's direction and barely enough voice to be heard she instructed, "Please send down for tomato juice and," she paused seeing her daughter.

"Oh Mother," Hebe gushed starting to rush to her hoping to console and be consoled. Gaye Lee's glazed, unwelcoming glare halted Hebe in her path and stemmed the flow of sympathy that had welled up in her.

"What the Hell is she doing here?" she growled at Art pointing to Hebe. "I made myself perfectly clear, 'She is gone. Don't bring that girl back here.' Didn't I say that?"

"Calm down, my dear."

"Don't my dear me! Don't try to take advantage of my grief you two-timing..,"

"That girl?" Hebe said it outloud increduous that her own mother was referring to her as "that girl," while she was standing in front of her. "What did you do to Jude?" Her

accusation salted the wound of her mother's despondency and made
her wince. The bottle thudded against the wall, and the glass
dropped and shattered.

"And you wondered why I didn't want her back?" she growled
at Art.

"Let's all just remain calm. Hebe, why don't you go to your
room? It's across the hall. Number..," he looked at the key
ring.

"That's it? You tell me my brother is dead then tell me to
go to my.."

"That's a good idea. Get the girl the Hell out of my face."
Gaye said, still not acknowledging her.

"Oh and it's really nice to see you too, mother. I always
thought you left Daddy. Now I get it."

"Shut up!" Gaye interjected.

"He was probably glad to get rid of you, you and your
stinking drinks! What did you do to my brother?"

Gaye Lee pounced on Hebe without another word. Art made an
unsuccessful effort to separate them while Margarita ran out of
the room. Within seconds she returned with a man.

"Doctor, can you do something? She's hysterical! An
injection? Anything." Art pleaded exasperated.

"La señora, she drinking all the day," Margarita mentioned.
Gaye Lee got a nose bleed making the scuffle look   much more
violent than it really was. The doctor pulled a cloth from his
bag and held it over Hebe's face. That was the last thing she
remembered. When she came around it was late the following night
in her hotel room. Room service arrived at the same time as
Margarita who brought in some "make you friendly pills," as she
called them, from the doctor. Also, she had the agenda for the
funeral, the next day and a brief explanation of Jude's demise.

"He was riding the tricycle and he fell in the pool and his
pantalon, they got stuck on the peddle."

"But Jude could swim well."

"No, yes. But he had only four years old Hebe and con that
heaby thin' on his leg was impossible. Eez the reason your

mother can not to go to the house. Art and your mother, they
came to here the next day.

Hebe had little appetite and little to say. She took
another "make you friendly pill" and asked Margarita to wake her
up the next morning.

"Si, Hebita. I will call you. I don' wan' sleep here
tonight. The ghost, she for sure here.

"Oh Margarita. Do you really believe that, in spirits?"

She gave herself the sign of the cross and said, "Believe?
Hebita is not a question of to believe. Is the truth. If you
choose not to see it, o.k., but is verdad. The Kate Morgan died
here. People have seen her. She was murdered here. She no can
rest. Trust me, her spirit is here. And Jude, he is at the
house. Is why your mother don' go to there." At the door, she
stopped and turned and added. "To see your childrens die is la
mas grandé tragedy in el mundo. Your mother, she has the broken
heart. Believe me. Your mother, she is not a bad person Hebe.
Try to understand. With her, I cried and cried for the Jude, he
was the angel more sweeter as my own niños." Making the sign of
the cross over herself again she concluded, "I pray to Dios, He
don' let me feel that pain for my own blood. I am so sorry for
you the both."

Hebe lay in bed trying to forgive her mother, to believe
what Margarita had said about her brother's death being an
unpreventable accident and her mother caring. Drifting off to
sleep, she saw his innocent face beaming with glee as he zoomed
around the pool, the farthest his small legs had ever taken him
in his short life. She felt guilty that she had seen so much.
She wanted the chance to tell him about where she had been, the
Birches and all the things they had taught her. But most of all
she wanted to see how much he had grown, feel his small arms give
her a big hug. In her mind, she saw him sitting at the table
trying to eat properly, the day she left for Boston, only seven
months earlier, the fourteenth of March.

"Maybe, I won't be back so soon. Maybe it will be a long,
long, long, time. But I will always think about you," she said

outloud to the air. "I love you Jude," she whispered.

"I love you, Hebe Jeebie," she heard him say as clearly as if he were in the room with her. Goosebumps cropped up and down her arms and she clicked on the lamp.

"Jude?" She glanced around the room.

"I wish I could have been here to save you Jude. I know why mama wasn't there. Her and her God damn drinks." The urge to wail pushed at her throat, but no tears fell, not then or the next day at the funeral.

Sorrow wafted off Gaye Lee's black dress in waves of heat. Even beneath her mourning veil, one could tell her cheeks' hollows had deepened during the night. Everything about her was sad and dull and lifeless as she loop-legged a path from the car to the burial site. Everyone else looked out from behind sunglasses, all viewed the same dark light of the sunny day that a child, her angelic, baby brother Jude, was laid to rest. The "make you friendly pills" repressed everyone's volitile emotions, and the quiet funeral was conducted without incident.

In order to maintain the peace, Hebe and Margarita were not to travel to the cemetary with Gaye-lee but together in second car, as per Art's instructions. Hebe was secretly glad that Art's lamenting was limited. It meant, to her, that Jude was probably, as she had suspected all along, her full brother. At the grave, he and her mother stood facing one another. She looked at him supporting his wife, her mother who was barely able to stand. His intense feelings for her radiated from him and were almost visible there among the acres of death around them. Despite everything her mother had said to hurt her and push her away, she was still filled with the idelible, unconditional love of a child for its mother. She knew Margarita was right and that her mother was completely heartbroken. How dreadful she must have felt inside to know that she was responsible for her own son's death. She pitied her mother and was glad that she had Art. A dim smile turned up on her face which he returned when he glanced across at her over the miniature white roses and babies breath adorning the coffin.

The coffin. No one had ever seen one so small, no bigger than a hope chest. And it looked even smaller surrounded by the mourners, the family's close friends and Art's colleagues. The soft bed of earth was so narrow, Hebe and Gaye Lee could have reached across and touched their fingertips. No contact was made. It was clear that as far as Gaye Lee was concerned, Hebe had been removed from her life forever when she sent her to Boston because she didn't acknowledge her at the funeral service either. When Art introduced her to their new acquaintances, some expressed surprise that Gaye Lee had a daughter. From her room at the Hotel Del Coronado, Hebe watched Art escort the frail, fifty proof, vessel of a woman her mother had become into their suite and disappear out of sight. And that's the way it had been for the past forty seven days.

Her life went on in Coronado as it had in Brookline over the weeks everyone was away. She was in charge of herself. But it was strange to be on her own once more. Just before she left, everyone had returned. Holly had finished her unfinished painting and picked up Floyd from McLean's Hospital where he had been sent for observation. Linseed oil aromas and bluesy music wafted from their room once more. She promised "Never, ever to leave him again." Bandages were still wound around his arms, but no one mentioned his "accident" as they agreed they wouldn't before he returned. Holly's new pair of paintings hung side by side in the parlor where Hebe had first met "the Birches". The two hands of the unfinished work had been painted into a field of of hands growing in different positions of carressing toward the seated musician on the other canvas. They all stood critiquing and admiring it. Hans reported that their project in the woods was going well. Unfortunately, it had to remain a secret for a while longer. Nell kept checking for Hans' reactions while squeeling on and on in a breathy voice about Vittorio, her Italian marquis until Rem managed to slip a word in edgewise.

"Let's go into the screening room. I'm certain my movies from Tangier have been set up by now."

Filmed was a fabulous party, Rem dancing ballet in her tutu

on the sand, Rem being being kissed on the hand at least three
different times, once by a camel who then shlurped the camera
lense. And there were shots of her many friends, always with
books, always with drinks in crystal glasses whiling away the
North African sun in their caftans, in cafe's, in their cars in
unusual places, in the shade of their dark servants. At the end,
she encouraged Hebe.

"Come explore the world anytime you want to Löfuk. I'm sure
you would be welcome in any of our places. Holland, Belgium,"

"The villa in Lamu," chimed in Nel.

"Our plantation is just outside Rangoon," offered Floyd.

"I think she should start someplace much more sedate, comme
Genève," Rem concluded and with that bestowed on Hebe the gift
of her very own passport.

"A passport!? You remembered. Oh, so that's why you wanted
to get these pictures. Thank you! But how did you ever...?"

"Hebe, we musn't question the giftgiver," she reminded her.
"Don't forget to sign it."

The last thing she remembers of that day was Floyd
requesting that his most recent poem be read by Noni.

                         TIMES SQUARE
The neon sun blue red yellow
flickering fragmented spelling
words and shapes and beings overhead
casts its dim rays on the night owls
flying out of the underground smoking
in search of food for their souls
wearing berets not wearing berets
top buttons undone and their jackets
like shapely chicks hair fluttering
tattered sails catching all they can
in the dinty dingy din down under out in the open
guiding them along the invisible paths of good times
outside of Hayes Bickfords, Girlie shows, music shops
windows with quiet instruments lonely in the neon sun

flashing repeatedly brightly on the mouth of
the jazz club across the way with musical instruments
belching blue notes blues blare there
interrupted by yellow trumpets in some hot mambo red
headed and blonde and brunetts the chicks
have all forgotten their girdles and look cool
high eyes, brown maybe green beneath dark glasses
on their powdered faces and their black clothes
are canvases for the man-made neon sun is a Picasso
in the night painting innumerable borderless
not-so-abstract abstracts all over making
newspapers black and white illegible
flickering red by tired late night workers,
out of habit bypassing fabricated day shuffling
into the dingy dinty din of night under forty second street
annoyed by the festive daytime scene above
whores' legs visible to the thigh
invite, Johns bored and lonely blue splashes on taxis
"All Nude", "All Night", "Nemos" signs
catches somebodies speeding safely away from
their class routine, the usual theatre opera theme
in top hats, tuxes in taxis spreading time-lapsed yellow
stripes through the bright smoky night-people scape,
                    TIMES SQUARE

     They all loved it. Harmony had returned to the house. But
the very day following their grand reunification, Hebe received
the telegram from Art. It was her turn to leave. School days
had arrived presenting Rem with a dilemma because Hebe preferred
to continue with the tutors. Rem thought she should attend
classes at a school. The Beaver Country Day School had been
highly recommended by a New Englander, and it was nearby.
Unfortunately, she hadn't made the advance preparations to have
her admitted. Further complicating the issue was her imminent
and upcoming return to Genève.
     "I know I am not your mamá, Hebe, but I really am rather

fond of you. You remind me a bit of myself. That sounds just
self-centered and awful, I know. But, it's true. My own mother
was thoroughly dedicated to her social calendar. I had always
hoped one day to get to know her, to try."

"What happened to her?"

Rem sighed and averted her eyes to a corner and stared into
a past moment. Her voice was soft with sadness. "She refused to
believe that her precious body could possibly be host to an
illness as dreadful as Rhodesian sleeping sickness. 'I'm just
travel weary,' she claimed. But when she came back from that
trip to east Africa, she was extraordinarily tired and quite ill.
The doctor came for her, in a private car mind you. She wouldn't
have wanted the drama of an ambulance. And that was it. She
went to sleep and didn't wake up. The tragedy was my beau-père."

"What's a beau-père?"

"Mother's second husband, step father. Our father was a
romeo, and a daredevil. It is impossible to say which he loved
more women or excitement. En tout cas, when we were about ten,
he died in a car accident."

"I'm so sorry."

"Merci. It was a long time ago. Mother grieved for the
proper year, then curiously married her oldest suitor, 'He was
the least likely to wander, but most likely to die unexpectedly."
Rem trilled a little laugh. "Poor Jean Jacques had to see a
heart specialist before she would consent to marriage, and she
went first."

"Is Jean Jacques...," she hesitated to choose between dead
or alive.

"Gravely ill."

"That's awful. Then you will have lost two fathers."

"It's true. He's a very kind man, at least to me. I think
it's because I remind him of my mother. Even adopted me."

"Adopted?"

"Yes, so I would have his name, really be a part of him. He
had no children of his own."

"Now he has two, just like that."

"No, only one. Me. He didn't want my brother."

"Why not?"

Rem's answer was to light a cigarette and survey the clothes she had hung out for her wardrobe mistress to pack. "They say it's only a matter of time for him. There's only one thing we can expect to be guaranteed in life, Hebe."

"What?"

"The unexpected. L'imprévu. En tout cas Löfuk, now you know all about me." Hebe sat looking at her. "You're awfully quiet."

"Actually, I hardly know you at all, your history, I mean."

"History? A past, say past, Hebe. History ages one so."

"Does your brother look exaclty like your father?"

"Non."

"Did he do something terrible?"

"Hebe, one question is proper. Two is really considered prying, especially if the first wasn't answered."

"I was just asking."

"It's very private." She stood surveying her clothes, then removed a white velvet gown. "This is too warm for Tangier."

"You wore that in New York! I think you look very pretty in it. Not just me. No one could keep their eyes off you."

"I do love it."

"I thought you trusted me?"

"I do."

"So what could be such a big secret? I've told you all the details about my mother and my father. And what about Floyd? If you really trusted me,"

Rem stopped fussing with her clothes, dismissed the maid who had begun to pack, requested, "Close the door on your way out," and sat down next to Hebe. She lit a cigarette and looked right in her eyes. "A secret is an enormous responsibility. Once you learn it you have a powerful moral obligaton to protect it. To divulge it, alors it is betrayal. You could lose your friend."

Hebe stretched back on the bed. "Never mind."

Rem burst out laughing. "Don't you trust yourself? I thought you wanted to know."

"Why are you being so dramatic?"

"This is very serious."

"What?"

"You can never tell another soul."

"I promise."

"My brother," Rem began, "has never ever had a girlfriend."

"Is he a priest?"

"No," Rem answered amused by her guess. "He has had lovers,"

"But they were not women." Comprehension pulled a big "Oh," out of Hebe's mouth.

"Yes, that's why my stepfather did not want him."

"What about your mother?"

"She never spoke about it, but I know she knew. She passed away before he was married.

"He's married?"

You see Beau-père convinced her that she help 'Make him normal,' if she stipulated in her will that his full inheritance would only be forthcoming if her were married and remained married. Of course there is a clause to allow for a brief spell alone in the event of death or divorce." Rem flung a pair of rejected shoes in the closet. "Utterly stupid, but utterly legal.

"How did he find a wife?" She gasped. "He married a man?"

"Don't be ridiculous. Mother died so unexpectedly."

"You're right. This is serious. I won't ever tell."

"That's not the secret," Rem almost whispered."

"No?" Hebe asked surprised that there could be something greater than this to tell.

"I am the woman we found," she stated flatly to Hebe who was sitting bolt upright on the bed in amazement.

Revelation snapped Hebe's fingers. "Phillipe and your brother are.. And no one knows!?"

"Other than us, non. Well, only one,"

"Madame someone, Madame Pratt."

"Precis! We don't know how she saw the certificate. Now she is trying to buy our secret shall we say. The old bitch!"

Suddenly, she stopped and spun around. "Hebe you did hear us in New York!"

Hebe nodded and smiled proudly. "I can keep a secret."

"Indeed."

"So how did you manage it?"

"Let's change the subject, shall we? I think we were discussing your going to school, to learn about things, distant lands and languages and,"

"I am learning about things Rem. Je parle français. I know oodles about plants from Mr. Tanaka. What other girl has heard such discussions on philosophy and physics and..."

"What about people? Socializing with..."

Hebe finished Rem's sentence with a question. "People who hate me and call me names?"

"Don't be idiotic. No one calls you names. Once someone asked if you were from Spain, but other than that no one anywhere has ever said anything other than you are very pretty."

"Of course not. I was with you. This isn't the first time I went to school, you know Rem. I told you about the fight I had with that girl when I had a suntan. Besides, my grandmother told my mother 'Those schools would never have Hebe.' I heard her myself."

"Well, I heard the Beaver Country Day School is supposed to be involved with the American Field Service. They have students from Scanadinavia and Spain, I think even India! Let's just try it. If it turns out to be a disaster, we'll make other arrangements. Agreed?"

Hebe agreed with a reluctant nod of her head and an embrace. "I can't believe you and your brother are,"

"Hebe!" Rem admonished.

"I won't mention it again. So where am I going to school?"

Well, we shall have that sorted out by your return."

Returned, she hadn't. And when "going back" was mentioned to Art, he reminded her that her grandmother was still away, and appeared ignorant to the fact that Grandmother Wilkinson had given Rem guardianship. She didn't find it was necessary to tell him. It never occured to her that she would start school again in California.

Having neither finished classes in the spring nor begun in the fall, it was unclear which grade she belonged in, so they gave her a test. She did so well, they made her take it again while a teacher sat in the room. Evidently, life among the bright Celestial Seven, the Birches had been an education because she scored much higher than her grade level. The school didn't put her back in the fifth grade, as they first considered, or in the sixth where she should have been, or even in the seventh. They concluded that her scores, combined with her level of maturity, made it possible for her to fit right in with the eighth grade class.

The higher grade level and living at the Coronado had made California life less isolated than she anticipated it would be due to her only San Diego friends having moved. Rosalita had gone to Paris Island, South Carolina, "For to live with Tony and his wife," Margarita told her. "I am going to be the abuela in February" she announced proudly. First she saw the picture of Tony in his dress Marine Corps uniform. It made him look older, but very strong and smart.

"I thought Tony was in the army."

"Yes, look is already the private first class because he was the number one with the shooting."

To Margarita military was military and it didn't really matter which branch of the service Tony was in. He was gone. The next photo; the wedding ceremony. Tony and his bride stood beneath the crossed ceremonial swords of the two rows of marines in dress blues. The new Mrs. Tony Garcia, was the opposite of Hebe, a rather buxom blonde with a small nose.

"Shiela's fathers they are very good to Tony. Give to them the big house to live, and when they know is un nieto coming they send the dinero for the Rosalita to come and live with them for to help with the baby."

In Brookline, Hebe had wondered why she hadn't heard from either of them for such a long time, and she was surprised by the

news. But she wasn't upset. Her heart was in too many pieces
from life's recent powerful events: Jude's death and his little
coffin being lowered into the ground; Floyd's slashed arms; her
mother's lushy lamenting face rejecting her. These wounds were
still too painful for the loss of her puppy love boyfriend to
affect her. She almost didn't care. Unable to feel either sad
about Tony abandoning her and his obvious infidelity, or happy
for Margarita becoming a grandmother, she was afraid she was
permanently numbed and incapable of any emotion. This Saturday,
November 1, 1958 proved her wrong.

Surviving with the few things she had brought for what she
supposed would be a brief trip finally became unmanageable, and
she asked Margarita to stop by the house to pick up some clothes.
In addition to the clothes, she brought "All the mails from the
box and the desk," because the electricity had been turned off
and she thought perhaps the bill was there. Afraid to miss any
letters addressed to her, Hebe offered to take the stack.

"I'll sort it out and deliver it," she offered. Weekly, Art
held a meeting with her to check up on her activities and settle
her accounts at the hotel. Separating the letters, she opened
those addressed to her immediately. First was one expected from
Rem, written in French and Volapük as per her request. She set
it aside for later. Next was one, most unexpected, from Mr.
Tanaka. It read, "Nous vous manquez. Itsa too much quiet. Here
the butterflies for you from the favorite song." Once in the
garden they had seen a butterfly. "Cho Jo," he pointed out and
sang the little song. Everytime they had met after that, she
insisted on learning it. From a collage of butterflies and a
caligraphy of the Japanese words to "Cho Jo" he had created a
stunning work of art. She pinned it to the wall with two safety
pins, then sat staring at it, hoping she had gotten it right side
up. Admiring it, she absent-mindedly, stuck her hand into the
pile of letters and pulled out another. It was several months
old, addressed to her mother from her grandmother. Her best
ivory stationary, with the Cape Cod address, The Bogs, had been
used. Refolded and reinserted carelessly, it stuck out inviting

Hebe's curiosity.

May 1, 1958

Dear Gaye-Lee,

I was delighted to hear the news. It's unfortunate that you two
did not meet sooner. I know you agree. As I told you on the
telephone, Uncle needs me in Vienna; therefore, I can not attend,
but the Crown Room of the Coronado is a perfect choice. Be
reminded you are not a widow! You are remarrying. It would be
most improper to issue engraved announcements. There would be no
harm in writing invitations to the guests, in black on embossed
ecru, of course. But you needn't worry about that. As your
mother, this happy duty is mine. The wording is: Gaye Lee is to
be married to Arthur Askley Higgenson Saturday, July 12, at
three-thirty. The ceremony will take place in the Crown Room of
the Hotel Del Coronado, 1500 Orange Avenue, Coronado, California.
We do hope you will be able to be with us for the happy day.
R.S.V.P. Of course.
    I'm certain we will speak soon. Regards to Art.

                    Mother

The note and wedding invitation letter concretized Hebe's
suspicions that Art and her mother had gotten married. It had
been her intention to read it and put it back, but she balled it
up. Surprising herself, she sat it in an ashtray, lit it on fire
and watched it burn. Then she resumed sorting as if she had
never seen it. The pile for Art and her mother was full, no
doubt sympathy notes. There didn't seem to be any more for her
until she reached the very end. Damp and several weeks old, the
city was invisible, but the stamps read Venezuela. The letter was
from her father.
    There was no small talk. It went right to the point and
expressed sorrow over Jude's dying. "It seems like only
yesterday your mother and I brought him home from the hospital.

- 249 -

Try not to be too sad Hebe Jeebie. He has met his destiny. Your mother will drape herself in a tapestry of grief, that is her way and her right. Try to brighten her day with a dainty, lady thing for her. You know what she likes." Enclosed was a fifty dollar bill to buy it. "I would send something myself, but I don't want her to have to go to customs or anything at this difficult time." She held the bill in her hand and tried to feel his energy. He had held it in his hands, the hands she had last seen on the rear window of Art's car when they were leaving Boston. Certainly, he had held all of his notes and cards in those hands, but this was different. This one was sent from his suffering soul to her mother's through a pair of hands formed by both of them, her hands. Holding the flimsy piece of green currency sent a tremor through her being, and she began to cry. Freely ran the riverlet of grief over Jude's death, her physical separaton from her father and the Birches, her estrangement from her mother and Tony. She sniffled and caught her breath. The letter was drenched. The letter. The letter meant it was true. Her father still loved her mother. So what if she had married Art. Once, before he stole her way, she had been married to her father. Maybe she could be repossesssed and their love ressurected. Maybe some magic how, she herself, who was born of that love could bring them together again. Reading on, she learned that he was coming to San Diego! She couldn't believe it. It wouldn't be for a few months, but her father was coming.

He had instructed her to attach "the enclosed gift card." It was in a little envelope, unsealed. She couldn't resist. It read, "My most beautiful Gaye Lee, I have often wished for some word from you, but your cablegram was so sad. How could this happen? Our poor little baby boy. How could this have happened? I can only dare to imagine your grief, little mother. Deepest Sympathy. All my love, Gordy."

"All my love, Gordy," she whispered over and over. "All my love." The phrase filled her with an optimism that alleviated her mourning and gave her hope. That day, she put on her sunglasses not to hide and block out the raw glare of the sun, but to shade her eyes so she could look around. Through them she saw a beautiful dark light.

Monday she skipped school for the first time since returning to California. Hither and thither she went on buses, in taxis and on foot, in and out of shops large and small looking for le cadeau parfait for her mother. Nothing caught her eye. In her hotel room, she wracked her brain to no avail and concluded the reason she couldn't think of anything was because she was thinking too much. From her suitcase, she pulled out the brass finger cymbals she had used to meditate on the beach in Provincetown and went to find a quiet place to sit. She found one with a perfect view of the hotel's imported Dragon Tree. "A Chinese technique by a Chinese tree," she concluded and sat down to clear her mind of all thoughts except one, her self selected mantra, " A gift for my mother." She stared directly at the giant tree and tried to keep track of how many times she said the phrase, then lost count. Reuttering it thus, it became a rythmic series of sounds. She closed her eyes and let it ring in the dark of her mind until an anonymous man's voice broke her concentration calling out, "It's 4:10."

A woman's breath blew, "Hey, I know you," over her face, and she opened her eyes to see the blonde woman who everyone at the Birches thought was Marilyn Monroe. Hebe was very excited to see her again.

"Hello," she responded shyly.

"What are you doin' here? You didn't run away, did you?"

"No. I'm here with my mother. What about you?"

"A movie." Playfulness danced on her pretty face as she looked over Hebe's shoulder and pointed to a crowd of people charging in their direction. "And dodging them. Bye. It was fun running into you." Off she went with a wiggle mincing gait, her pursuers stampeding behind. The energy from the group was contagious, and for an instant she had to refrain from joining in the chase, to find out. Was she really Marilyn Monroe? She would try to find out later. At the moment, it didn't matter, nothing mattered more than her mother's gift. For a fleeting instant she thought maybe the movie star could be a gift, that she should try to invite her to tea or something. If she really were Marilyn, she wouldn't have time. What kind of a gift would that be anyway. She wanted something her mother could hold, some tangible evidence of her father's feelings for her. What?

She flopped down in a chair in the cool Grand Lobby and watched the people coming and going, in particular the women, what they were talking about buying and what they were wearing. Across from her, two East Indian women stood in shiny, saris one marigold yellow, the other jasmine red. Golden bangles jangled on their arms as they chatted cheerfully and rearranged things in one of the bags.

"Please, have this. What will I do with two the exact same," she thrust a small, flat box into her arms with a jingle.

"No. No. No. I can't go back to Dehli with one of your gifts. Then auntie will think I took it from you. And, if I confess that you gave it to me, she will think you didn't like it," she protested pushing the box back. It bent open and a gossamer piece of silky, sea-foam green fabric wafted through the opening onto the carpet. The golden emroidered borders twinkled in the light of the chandelier as the girl in yellow gathered it up in her brown hand. Shaking it out to refold it revealed shimmering silver threads. Hebe had never seen anything quite so unusual and lovely.

"Just be discreet. Don't let her see that you have it."

"How could I do that Mangala? She lives with us. You must not give it to anyone we know. It will just cause a problem. You must keep it. When you come home, leave them both. No one has to ever be any the wiser that they gave you exactly the same gift. No bother."

"It seems sad to leave it in a drawer."

Hebe was absent-mindedly jingling the cymbals together and leaning forward to better hear their conversation. Her heart was beating loudly in her ears and her hand got clammy because she was considering asking if the girl would sell her the cloth; she still had the box in her hand. She had no idea how much it would

cost, and she didn't want to insult her. They waved at a
well-dressed man at the checkout.

"Vyas is ready," the woman in jasmine said. "Let's go."

Hebe hopped up with a tintinabulation of her cymbals which
she shyly tucked in her pocket. "Excuse me, please," her voice
cracked." The women stopped and flashed her two big smiles. "I
was wondering. I have to buy a gift and," she hesitated. "Well,
could you tell me where you purchased that fabric? It's
beautiful."

"It isn't a piece of fabric," the woman in yellow began
sitting her small bag down. "It's a magic shawl."

The other clarified, "It's called that because one side is
all gold and the other all silver. You see? No strands show
though. It's like having two in one." They admired the cloud of
shawl in their hands.

"My mother would love something..."

The two women exchanged a brilliant glance communicating
that they were thinking a similar thought, and at the same time
said it outloud. "You may have it."

Hebe tried and tried to get them to take her fifty dollars,
but they refused, insisting "It would not be proper to sell a
gift," they jingle-jangle, scampered after Vyas when he stepped
outside. She must have stood there in amazement for a long time
because a bellman approached to ask if she needed anything. She
shook her head, then tapped lightly on his cuff "By the way, is
Marilyn Monroe staying here?"

He looked around and rocked heel toe a couple of times with
his hands folded behind his back. "I'm not supposed to talk
about the guests, but everybody already knows. So, I guess I can
say." He lowered his voice to a confidential volume. "The're all
here, Jack Lemmon, Tony Curtis. Haven't you seen them?

"No. But I heard."

"Yeah. They're making a movie."

"They are?"

"What'd ya just get in? The whole hotel's talking about it.
'Some Like it Hot'." A bell rang and he backed away from her with

a tip of his hat, a toothy grin and a wink of his eye. "Anything else?"

"No. Thank you." She mulled over joining the crowd that had trampled past her outside, so she could catch a glimpse of the movie making and decided to go another day. Nothing was more important than getting the gift to her mother. She wanted to hand it to her personally, to watch her reaction when she saw the gift and read the note. But, she hadn't seen her since the funeral. As she was walking by her mother's hotel door she noticed a small cosmetic case marked, Avon. A woman in white gloves and very full skirt opened the door and took it. "Avon calling. Would you like an Avon call?" chirped her soliciting voice. Under her breath she added, "Just tell me your room, and I'll drop by? I'm not supposed to do this in the hotel." Hebe hid the gift box behind her back and answered.

"If I have time, I'll stop back by and let you know. Will you be here for a while?"

"Yes, I think so."

In her room, she made herself the presentable young girl Rem had turned her into in New York. She French braided her hair and put on a simple skirt and white blouse. Next? Wrapping the gift.

She used old paper bags; her father always used them, or some newspaper. He had written that sometimes he bought things from street vendors "In these dusty corners or the world, wrapping paper is not used or unavailable." In stark contrast to the cheap, sometimes battered exterior of his packages were the fine, fancy, fragile contents: enameled Siamese silver bracelets; laquered Japanese music boxes; lacey Irish linen. The package Hebe put together looked as if it had fallen off a ship for certain.

Down the hall she marched with great deliberation so as not to turn back. She knocked on the door. It opened and her mother called out, "Mambo" with the chorus on a record and the Avon lady who was right behind her with her hands on her mother's waist. They danced passed the door. "Mambo"

"Come in," Gaye-Lee called out beckoning her with a wave.

The two women performed a few more steps of the mambo while Hebe stood near the bar covered with cosmetics for sale. She tucked the package behind it, so she could present it at just the right moment. Liquor bright-eyed, and straight from the beauty parlor, Gaye-Lee seemed again radiant despite some small lines etched across her brow by Jude's death, or perhaps drinking. The sun had streaked blonde highlights in her hair and color on her cheeks. Next to the shapely, young Avon lady, she looked thin. But she was still stunningly beautiful. As she snapped her fingers and enjoyed herself, Hebe scrutinized her face in an attempt to predict how she would react to seeing her. She was certain she hadn't seen whom she had invited in, and she doubted she would be glad to discover it was her because she had summarily dismissed her and had made no effort to see her since.

Life with the Birches had allowed her to witness and experience the full range of unpredictable, alternative person-alities spirits offered a drinker. She stood hoping it had provided one of its festive amnestic spells in order to block her mother's memory, make her glad to see her, or at least inhibit an angry outburst. When the music stopped, her chest muscles tensed up, but as quick as light she deduced they were lighthearted lushes because they continued to dance anyway.

"Mambo!" they called out in unison then both introduced her. While Gaye-Lee said, "Mrs. Jane Henry, I'd like to introduce you to my daughter, Hebe," the Avon lady announced, "This is the young woman from the hall, I told you..." They all exchanged surprised looks and laughed. And in laughing, the saleswoman revealed that she had probably passed her drink limit. A big gafaw blew out of her lungs and toppled her right off the bar stool. Hebe and her mother shared a facial gesture of amused disapproval as Jane staggered to her feet.

"Look how tall you are, Hebe. You could be a model," Gaye remarked lighting a cigarette.

Standing next to her mother, being near her for the first time in many months and receiving a compliment dispelled her fears of rejection. Cautiously, Hebe slip her arm around her

slim waist; her mother didn't pull away. Instead, she pressed
her hand closer to her ribs warm from the embers of maternal of
love still glowing within her. The tenderness of the touch made
the subtle moment one of quiet fullfillment. Mother, the
inevitably recurring image, had finally reappeared in her life.

On her feet, the Avon Lady invited herself to another shot
from the bar. She downed it, then suddenly glanced at her watch
and wended her way to the door with an overly controlled gait.

"Look at the time. My husband will be home soon."

"Mrs. Henry, what about my order?" Gaye asked.

"Order?" she asked, then scanned the nail polishes,
lipsticks, hairspray and other products scattered on almost every
flat surface in the room." Oh, just take what you want and write
it on this pad," she suggested slapping it on the table. "I'll be
back. Thank you. I can tell you are going to be one of my best
customers," she said and left.

Hebe watched as her merry mother made a Brandy Alexander.
She found an unexpected comfort in the familiar sound of blender
crushing the ice into the potion.

With a mirthful, "I just perfected it. Tell me what you
think," she placed the glass in front of her and offered her a
cigarette from the box on the coffee table.

The gesture made her realize, the ebullient hostess was not
her mother; she would never have offered her a drink and a smoke.
It was her mother's body, but it was only partly her spirit, the
other part was alcohol. Volitile, flamable, menacing, it frosted
her eyes, made them stare. Giving the gift to the monster would
be a wasted effort. So, before it inevitably drown her for the
day, she attempted to keep her afloat by mentioning the package.

"There was a box in the mail for you. I brought it by."

The waves lolled outside and the ceiling fan whirred a few
times before she responded.

"Oh really," she remarked in her distinctive, cool, British-
bent, Boston accent intimating she wasn't too many fathoms under
the surface of sobriety.

Her lips brushed a kiss on her burning cheek as she handed

her the gift then backed cautiously away. "What does it say?"

Gaye-Lee's hands began to tremble, and she turned her face up from the little letter. It's contents had melted the alcoholic monster's eyes and her own scintillated brilliantly as she spoke in a whisper, "Well, your father," she began.

Hebe ran to give her a tissue, and her mother reached out and drew her into her arms and back in time to their home in Cambridge before school days, before Art, before California, even long before Jude had been born when she and her mother would sit and wait for her father, Gordy. Hebe melted on her mother's bosom with the unrealistic hope that the action might erase the recent years. However, within a surprisingly short time, holding onto the past became uncomfortable and hurt her shoulder. She let go. Gaye dabbed away a tear and began to open the package. Hebe got up and moved out of arms length.

"Oh Gordy," Gaye-Lee whispered flushing crimson when the puffy fabric pooft into view. Scooped in her hands, it twinkled like a star dusted cloud on a foggy day and drifted down her arms. "How utterly lovely!" she gushed. "Such an unusual shawl. I've never seen anything like it. Leave it to Gordy." Her mother's spirit gleemed in her eyes and landed on the drink. She drained it. Automatically, she walked to the blender to prepare a refill.

"It is lovely," Hebe said as if she had never seen it before. This time, the sound of the blender made her nervous; she wanted to leave. The ingredients for the monster's blood slashed together over the sharp blades, frothed over the top and dribbled down Gaye-Lees hand. Sucking it daintily from her knuckle then downing the drink, vanquished Hebe's hopes of spending any more time with her mother that afternoon.

Gaye-Lee said, "That didn't taste quite right," and poured in more brandy. So obsessively involved with the preparation was she that Hebe had to raise her sad voice to bid her, "Good-bye."

"Don't leave. You really should try this."

With a heavy heart she sighed out, "No thanks mother. I have to go now." She wanted to stay, to exchange stories, just to be with her, but she didn't want to run the risk of a scene.

"Thank you for bringing the package," she called and waved.

Outside, a sense of relief and contentment swelled in her. Contact, however sad, however brief, had been reestablished with her mother. Through her black glasses, the dark light burned brightly.

TWELVE

The Law of Inertia:
Objects not acted on by a force
travel in straight lines at constant speeds.
Or if they are at rest, they stay at rest.

San Diego and La Jolla, California
Thanksgiving Dinner 1958 January 1959

Trying to catch Gaye-lee in a mood receptive enough to allow
their relationship to flourish proved as futile as trying to
predict a falling star. On occasion, they were simlutaneously,
in the hotel lobby, restaurant or shop. Sometimes they would
pass by one another, their eyes would meet, but no greeting was
given, no recognition acknowledged. Hebe was too intimidated to
attempt to initiate contact and chance being yelled at or snubbed
in public. However she did try in private, dropping by her
mother's suite from time to time. Once, after knocking
repeatedly, she opened the door to find her mother beside an

empty drink pitcher and a full jumbo cocktail facing the view
with the same comatose expression she had worn late nights in
front of the television when they were still living in the house.
To herself, Hebe referred to it as a Twilight Zone expression
because that's the program that often used to be flickering
across the screen. However, that day, instead of a screen,
Gaye's eyes were transfixed on the lively, tropical oceanscape
stretching beyond the window. Still as a cat, in the slow,
shadows of cumulus clouds passing the sun, she sat without a word
or a movement, not even when Hebe leaned over in search of life
signs. There were two: periodic eye-blinking and a pungent,
brandied-perfume breath. Hebe straightened up and stood
nervously anticipating being sent away with some objection.
Receiving none, she considered her presence sufferable, curled up
at her mother's feet, rested her head against her lap, and placed
Gaye-lee's limp, drink-free hand on her shoulder.

As if her mother were fully cognizant, she began relating
life's recent highlights in a soothing voice, "You know, I have
been selected to join the Science Honors Society at school. The
dreamiest fellow in the group selected me for his partner. His
name is Bjorn, an exchange student. From Sweden. He lives near
Stockholm someplace. They eat reindeer meat! Can you imagine
that?" She paused and mulled over whether to tell about Gordy's
promised visit, then decided to keep it a secret, to prevent a
possible disappointment in case he didn't arrive. She held up a
book. "See what Bjorn gave me for my birthday last week."

She winced as soon as the words came out of her mouth
because she didn't want to hurt her mother's feelings by bringing
up the birthday which grieving had apparently caused her to
forget. That's the explanation Mrs. Remington gave when she
called to give regards from Brookline and to make certain Hebe
had received their gift. She had, and she treasured it. From
the instant she took it from its black velvet box, she wore it, a
golden heart locket with a small ruby set in the center.

"You used to read all the time. Remember? Maybe you should
find a good book, mother. I know. I'll read to you from mine.

Would you like that? It's a science fiction love story,
<u>A Princess of Mars</u>." Without as much as a nod or moan of
affirmation, Hebe read several pages of the book to her audience
of one whose only movement was a bending of the elbow to bring
the drink to her lips. At quarter to four, she simply stopped,
got up, pecked Gaye-lee on the cheek and started for the door
announcing, "I have to meet my science study group now. I'll
come again another day."

"That would be lovely," Gaye-lee uttered faintly.

Her voice drew Hebe back to her side.

"Mother?"

Unclouded, the rays of sun glinted on the pink gold cross
around her neck and twinkled in her bright green irises awash in
tears. She continued in the soft, hesitant voice of a person
waking from a long, deep sleep. "I met your father in Stockholm.
There was a play, <u>Miss Julie</u>, by Strindberg." She paused as if
fatigued. "Funny. Swedes don't seem to notice the color of a
person's skin," she remarked, then chuckled over a past moment.
"What a time we had. Your friend must be very nice."

"He is," Hebe responded and waited for her mother to
continue. But Gaye fell silent except for a sweet, tender
sobbing that made Hebe feel instantly sad.

"What's wrong?"

"One day you will understand," was all she said before
turning away with a dismissive hand wave. That combined with the
pending study appointment discouraged her from pursuing the
questioning. At the door, she threw a "See you? Soon." over
her shoulder.

But when she returned, several days later, her mother was
quite different, animated, agitated and arguing loudly with Art.
Margarita, on her way out with the dry cleaning, stopped at the
door.

"Maybe ju should come back later, Hebe" she whispered.

"But," she began to protest.

"Did you see them together? Margarita!" Gaye yelled.

Margarita pushed into the hall passed Hebe. "Favor Hebita,

tell to her, I already gone. I do not want to be inbolbéd."

"She left," Hebe announced stepping into the room.

"Who the Hell said you could come in here?" Gaye growled freezing Hebe in her steps.

"What about the end of the story? I thought," she began, holding up A Princess of Mars to remind her of the reading.

"Get out! This doesn't concern you. Get out!"

"It isn't necessary to shout Gaye-Lee," Art muttered.

"Get out!" Gaye-Lee shrieked from the top of her lungs flinging her full cocktail at Hebe. Splattering and smashing on the door, the glass narrowly missed her head. Her hair, however, was soaked. "No! Wait!" she commanded, then snarled, "This is my daughter; she will tell me the truth. Have you ever seen Gabriella and Art together?"

Art handed her a towel. As she dried the drink from her hair, she didn't contemplate the question. Instead, she tried to think of how to get disentangled from Gaye's senseless ranting before it escalated into a broil.

"You left me, your wife, alone mourning for my little son while you went galivanting with that," Gaye-lee searched for the word. "With that man's wife!"

The powerful insinuation shocked Hebe. Hanging the towel on the back of the chair, the image of Art and Gabriella Gonzales in his car came into focus. "It's not possible," she thought.

"Answer me!" her mother cried out. "Have you seen Art with Gabriella?" She glared at her waiting for an answer while Art seemed to hold his breath beneath the pitiful, pleading countenance of a badly, misbehaved five-year-old. Of the truly infinite number of questions her mother could have posed, this was one of the few Hebe did not want to hear. Gaye's demeanor made it clear that the truth, that Hebe had seen them together, though it was months earlier, would certainly ignite contentious verbal fireworks in the room. A lie would thwart them, but put Hebe on Art's side. Maybe the woman was truly only his client and it was the illogic of liquor-thinking that brought her mother to the outrageous conclusion. And, maybe, Art was repeating the

role he had played in her mother's life with Mrs. Gonzales. She
did not want to know the answer. She did not even want to know
the question. Margarita was right.   It was better to be
"already gone". Without answering, she turned the knob behind
her and escaped into the hall. Another object crashed on the
door. At that moment, she made up her mind to accept Bjorn's
invitation to dine with him and his host family for Thanksgiving.

Thursday morning, she left a note at the front desk for Art
and Gaye advising them of her plans. She didn't know exactly
where the host family lived. It didn't matter as long as it was
far away from her mother and Art who were dining with his boss.
Mrs. Gates pointed out "La résidence de Raymond Chandler, the
famous writer," on the way, and finally they arrived at a grand,
ocean front home.

"The Windansea Beach," she announced.

Mrs. Gates, a native of Cannes, France was thrilled that
Hebe could speak a little French and insisted that she call them
Schuyler and Giselle, their first names. The opportunity to
exercise that liberty, or her French, hadn't arisen because the
woman hadn't stopped talking since they picked her up at The Del.
With a great deal of eye rolling and exaggerated facial
expressions, she dominated the conversation in the car. On and
on she droned in a heavily-accented monologue directed toward Mr.
Gates about continued problems with the Mexican staff's inability
to carry out her orders, the suffering she endured by San Diego
not having a Champs Elysees, and her astonishment that the Jewel
Ball at the La Jolla Beach and Tennis Club was held outside on
the tennis courts. The latter remark led her into a world of
criticism aimed at the lack of culture, manners, formality and
history in the United States. To support her claim, she listed
the numerous French products contributing to American upper class
style, everything from bread and wine to perfume and fashion as
well as art and love. She was of the opinion that The United
States should hire half of France's citizens to come to instruct
American citizens on how to live properly. "Then everyone would
go home," because the only place to really live was in France.

"After all, the best, you can only get it in France," she noted
several times. Periodically, Schuyler emitted a neutral grunt or
made completely unrelated comments such as, "I wonder where I
left my cigarette lighter," or "Jack and I had a couple of great
steaks for lunch last Wednesday." The stream of words pouring
down the right side of his head seemed to bypass his ear. His
inattentiveness didn't matter to Giselle; her conversation wasn't
dependant on any acknowledgement. Even when she asked a direct
question, she answered it herself.

"You find the weather here chilly après India, don't you?
Mais oui, of course you do. I don't think it ever is as hot here
as there. Quelle horreur L'Indie!" She glanced back at Hebe,
indicating she was addressing her.

"L'Indie?" she whispered quizzically to Bjorn.

"I will tell later," he whispered back.

"Je suppose, you must have people to fan you in the palace.
Or is it air-conditioned? No, I suppose that is not necessary.
The Taj Majal was so cool."

"Palace?" she again whipered. Bjorn just grinned.

"Oh and Bjorn. Poor, toi!" Giselle continued, "For you, il
doit être the opposite, comme, how do you say, vague de chaleur?"

"Heatwave," Hebe interjected.

"Yes, the heatwave. Imagine, he is coming from a little
frozen Swedish farm. Pauvre anémone. They really should do
something about the weather there, shouldn't they Schuyler.
Mais, yes."

Her husband checked the traffic in the rear-view mirror,
changed lanes and commented, "Rob got a great new set of clubs."
Shortly thereafter, they arrived.

In an atmosphere scented with sea breezes and eucalyptus,
they all say down to a formal Thanksgiving dinner. There were
several members of the Gates extended family, a handful of
European friends, Bjorn and Hebe.

"Rescued from supersitious bad luck by the princess," was
how Giselle ended the introductions referring to Hebe, "You are
the fourteenth guest."

"I'm not a princess," she protested turning bright red.

"Don't be ridiculous. Of course you are. Oh, I beg your pardon. I didn't mean to embarrass you," she stated looking straight at her for the first time, then turned to the others. "If you are having the title you can not use it when you live in America. All the royal people coming and visiting, they are staying at the only place so fantastique like their palaces, the Hotel del Coronado, comme Hebe; a Hawaiian King; Prince Albert and, of course, le roi d' Angleterre." The name tripped the motor that ran her mouth into high gear, and she told the love story of King Edward VIII of England and Wallis Spencer for whom he gave up the throne.

"She was a married woman living meters from the hotel. Imagine? You would like to see the house, yes? Oh of course you would."

Hebe had no chance to clarify her own identity. To her left sat a Spaniard who spoke some English, but didn't understand enough to have a two-way conversation, and to her right, at the head of the table, sat Mr. Gates whom she discovered could only hear as well as a marshmellow.

"Excuse me, Schuyler, but I think Giselle made a mistake. She may know many princesses, but I'm not a princess. She knows that, doesn't she?"

He sat there beaming at his petite, red-headed wife blathering vivaciously at the other end of the table and puffed up with pride. "Yes, she has many dresses. Has them done up on the Champs Elysees. Can't get that sort of cut here."

"May I have the salt please?"

He stuck his index finger out and one of the servers approached. "More sauce for the princess, and bring me a fresh glass of ice water with a little lemon in it."

Afraid of embarrassing him, she swallowed a protest and just gave Mr. Gates a smile of thanks as more bernaise sauce was dribbled over her meat and more wine was poured into her glass.

They knew she was only twelve and Bjorn seventeen. In fact, over appetizers and cocktails, a quadlingual debate which developed as to whether or not "the children," should be permitted wine with dinner had planted Bjorn and Hebe in two large rattan chairs sipping sodas. Bjorn assured her that they would have drinks one way or the other because he had "private bottles" of vodka and wine, but thought it preferable to be served like adults along with everyone else. They listened for the outcome. The Spaniard's declaration that "To eat the food without to drink the wine is to starve," and Giselle's friend's comment, "Si. In Italy is the same. When we are old enough to sit at the table, we are old enough to drink," certainly made points. But what actually doused the naysayer Americans' fiery objections were the third cocktails. Booze spoke for itself through the large, assertive voice of Mr.Gates.

"I dare anyone to come through that door and tell me what to do in my own damn house. This is the United States of America, not Russia. A little wine never hurt anyone. Wine all around."

Bjorn gave Hebe the thumbs up sign and rose out of his chair to escort his host mother to the dining room. Sitting across from one another in the Science Club afforded her a chance to study his face. It was square with chiseled features, and so fair and hairless that he was called, "pretty-boy" to his face and "queer" behind his back. Playfully slipping his hand around Giselle's waist, Hebe saw him as virile and handsome. His long back firmly stretched above his long legs to a full six foot three. He had to stride, and he did so with a quiet grace. His English was perfect, and his manner of speaking was powerful; it was slow and deliberate. A person had to wait for his words. He was one of the most intelligent boys at school, sure to graduate valedictorian. But many of the students said he was strange. They seemed afraid of him. As a result, other than Hebe, he had very few friends. As usual, those who knew one another were not seated together at the table. He was two seats down on her left between the Italian woman and Mrs. Gates, so she couldn't even exchange silly faces with him.

Her seatmates communication limitations created the perspective of chance exclusion from which she observed the strangers like players on a stage. Carefully regarding them, brought up a comparison of her first meals with the Birches and this one with the Gates. There was very little similarity. The Brookline dinner was a well-executed night of harmonious, intellectual discourse and wondrous discovery. This was one of boisterous competition for the floor and chaos brought about by Gizelle's incessant rambling and bell ringing. She had a small table bell to summon the help when anything was needed. As a result of jingling it every few minutes, there was soon no one free to respond causing her incessant chatter to be accompanied by ten straight minutes of steady pealing. The diners were too busy to let the din bother them. Across the center pieces, they added to it by flailing their foreign tongues at one another in petty, disagreements over which country had the best beach, the best wine, the best women. Giselle rang and rang. Hebe noticed at one point the string quartet which had been performing behind the laquered Chinese screen had stopped. An old man in a well-worn suit tottered out with a bow, placed his hands on his hips and cast a frustrated grimace in Giselle's direction. She rang and rang and talked and talked, oblivious to him until he took the bell from her hand and placed it on the table.

"At last!" she exclaimed. There was complete silence. She looked at him a little surprised. "Who are you?"

Quite annoyed, he tutted and held up his bow. Everyone burst out laughing, then took up where they left off except Giselle who exchanged a few words behind the Chinese screen. The musicians left. The La Jolla night of discordant unity continued. There was one striking resemblance between the nights. Everyone was having a great time.

Contemplating the Birches brought a wave of homesickness over her, not for anyone in particular, but for all of them, the distinctive aromas and sounds of the house and the schedule of life therein. At the California Thanksgiving table surrounded by people, one touching her elbow, she felt alone. Giselle announced that dessert would be served in the next room. Glowing and grinning, they rose and drifted away from the table.

Bjorn caught Hebe's sleeve, guided her in the other
direction, and ducked outside where they remained for the better
part of the night drinking and talking.

"So 'Princess'," he teased making her blush. "Don't let it
bother you. She's one of those people who only hears what she
wants to hear. A lot of people do."

"And just where did she hear I'm a princess? You?" she
challenge him somewhat vexed.

"Don't be stupid! If I wanted to convince her anyone was
royalty, it would be me. She thinks I come from a family of
farmers."

"I heard her say that. So, your father isn't a farmer!?"

"No. He is a painter, an artist."

"That's wonderful. Tell her!"

"Tell her!? I was exchanged with her stepson, Mr. Gates
son. John is living with my family in our house in the middle of
Stockholm! I think she knows. Giselle just heard that Swedes are
farmers. It stuck. As for you, well a lot of people think
you're a princess. All the kids at school,"

"They do?" she interrupted.

"Sure. Those girls you had for afternoon tea one Sunday all
gushed about it." Bjorn mimicked them in a soft girly voice 'I
was invited to the princess'. It was divine.' Well, you do live
alone in the fabulous Hotel del Coronado with a personal servant
and," he stopped when a big frown turned her face upsidedown.
"Hey what's wrong, Hebe?"

"Nothing. It's just that, I thought they really liked me."

"They do."

"No, they like who they think I am, a princess."

"That's people. You have a saying in English, 'first
impression is a lasting one' Sometimes, that impression is made
out of words or even ideas. So to some, you are what they think
you are. Listen, for months I've been telling the Gates' my
father's not a farmer. He's a painter. I showed them a book
featuring his work. One of his paintings is in the museum."

"He must be great!"

"He is."

"And, what does Mr. Gates do?"

"Garbage."

"What?"

"His big company is to collect all the garbage."

"You wouldn't know it to look at him, he doesn't look like a garbage man."

"There Hebe," Bjorn stomped one foot for emphasis. "What does a person in garbage look like anyway? Now you sound like Giselle."

From then on, the host mother's name was used to mean drawing a conclusion rooted in assumption or stereotype. "Don't be so Giselle," one would say to the other. It was the first of many words they created together. He moved over in the big white wicker porch swing in invitation for her to join him. After checking to see that she was comfortable, he pushed off with his foot. "Objects not acted on by a force travel in straight lines at constant speeds. Or if they are at rest, they stay at rest. The law of inertia is very easy, Hebe." He put his foot down abruptly stopping the swing and tossing her into his open arms.

"You don't have to trick me if you want to hold me," she announced quite happy to be curled against Bjorn's lean chest.

"Last time I tried, you protested,'I'm only twelve.' Remember?"

"I am."

"Not forever," he remarked and they gazed into one another's starlit eyes before sharing a tender, little kiss.

They added the law of inertia to their intimate rapport and swang innocently to and fro between the light of the porch and the moon.

When Rem heard that Hebe and Bjorn had spent the night in his guest house quarters unchaperoned, she expressed her chagrin. Hebe explained that the guest house had three bedrooms and that Bjorn had drunk so much that he ended up passing out on the couch, but Rem was not placated. Angrily, she reminded Hebe that she was still a child, and that regardless of her age it was not acceptable, lady-like behavior. Part of Hebe was sorry to have shared the story and made Rem cross, and part of her was glad. Though delivered on the phone, from a distance of three thousand miles, her disappointment still had a powerful message of concern and sprinkled her with a summer sun's warmth of love. It was consistent and present in every one of the many conversations they had over the weeks that followed.

Therefore, at the end of January, she nervously sought Rem's approval to go to the family house alone with Bjorn. Without it, she wouldn't go. Conducting a study of light for their science club project, the pair thought the kitchen's stainglass window to be a perfect subject.

"Your Bjorn is a regular Hans, always investigating something. And what a clever title Löfuk, "Bringing Color to Light.""

"I thought it up," Hebe stated proudly.

"The others will hear all about it at dinner this evening. If you need a scientific specialist,"

"Thanks Rem, but we're supposed to do it independantly. Besides, Bjorn knows absolutely everything."

"Well then, go to the house if you must, but it would be best not to overnight. And by all means leave word for your mother."

"Our project will be the best!"

"Bringing Color to Light" was to demonstrate certain behaviors of light waves: reflection, refraction, diffraction and interference. The models they had begun at Bjorn's Windansea Beach front home over the Christmas break were precise, but guaranteed not to catch anyone's attention.

"Good, but a bit dull," was Bjorn's summation of their work.

In order to make space, one model had to be moved across the room. All that was available to transport it was a Lazy Susan. Hebe placed it on a table where it began revolving like her old phantasmagoria flinging a luminous confetti of rainbowed refractions throughout the room, many shapes, many sizes and many colors some of which changed color and direction upon passing through crystal candlesticks and other glass objects. Bjorn held

out his hand, and one of the spectrumed fireflies alighted right
in the middle of his palm. They studied it as the sunlight
carouseled the dazzling flurry of intangible sparkles throughout
the room. "Motion!" they exclaimed together. And after a brief
tête-a-tête, they began to incorporate movement and tinted prisms
into the models to create rivers of light interupted by arcs of
rainbows.

The temperature hovered around 55 F, 13 C, according to
Bjorn. And while that would have been a warm day in Boston, it
was a winter's day in Dan Diego. The misty sea air made it feel
much cooler, a day for staying in the hotel suite. All alone,
Hebe sat lazilly observing and notating the behavior of a few
rays of light passing through a prism and a thick cube of glass.
Bjorn had claimed, "the only way to know something is to watch
it." But without him, motivation was beyond her reach.

She dipped into her small library heaped on the floor and
pulled out the book on which her hand landed. It was one of her
other birthday books, <u>Lady Chatterley's Lover</u>. An innocent
schoolbook, cover concealed it's name because students were
strictly forbidden to read it, even the shortened American
version. This was the complete, unexpurgated, British
publication which formerly belonged to Bjorn. Quite able to
replace it in Europe, he gave his copy to Hebe. It was well worn
and many passages were underlined. While reading the book, she
wondered why it was banned. Nothing about it seemed so naughty,
not even the parts which Bjorn had underscored twice. To her,
Lady Chatterley was a pitiable character, especially when first
seduced by Mellors after being in the chicken coop.

"It was more sad than anything," she reported back to Bjorn
who was surprised and amused by her complaint on the telephone.
"Their lovemaking was so quick. And they did it in the dark.
Mellors did everything. Lady Chatterley, 'She lay still, in a
kind of sleep, always in a kind of sleep.' Sleep! Is he kidding?
I've never done it, but when my boyfriend Tony used to, well,
sometimes he would, well I was never in any kind of sleep around
Tony. And I've seen people do it. It's fun. Lovers get naked

and dance into each others arms. Play music and twist their
bodies around into modern art poses. Mellors would have had more
fun with one of those chickens. Don't you think?"

Bjorn burst out laughing and answered by questioning her as
to how she had been such a lucky witness. Witholding the names,
she told him about coming across Noni and the red-haired girl on
the dunes in P-Town and peering in on Hans and Rem in the dance
studio. He pressed for more details, specific details, intimate
details.

Uncomfortable with the demand, she stammered, "You're almost
eighteen. You must have your own stories."

"Lots," he confessed with a mischievous laugh.

"So tell me one of yours, then I'll give you details. But
not over the phone," she added in order to drop the topic.

Bjorn agreed, and they planned to have the tit for tat when
they went to the house to study the window light.

Due to the fact that there was no electricity, plans had to
be written up before they went to the house. Eliminating this
step would allow them the maximum number of hours to observe the
natural light. Simply knowing what she was supposed to do hadn't
proved motivational. She just lay on top of her bed rememorizing
the Law of Inertia. "Objects not acted on by a force travel in
straight lines at constant speeds, or if they are at rest, they
stay at rest," repeated over and over in her head while she lay
half-heartedly reading the book wondering why she had suggested
telling the stories in person. How many details would he want?
Those about her and Tony were out of the question, too
embarrassing. "Objects not acted on by a force travel in
straight lines at constant speeds, or if they are at rest, they
stay at rest," echoed in her brain until her thinking switched
off and allowed her to lapse into a passive appreciation of the
simple beauty of the floating prisms reflections. The clock's
metronymic sound tick tocked into her thoughts and began to lull
her to sleep. "Objects not acted on by a force travel in
straight lines at constant speeds, or if they are at rest, they
stay at rest." She jumped up. "I can't stay at rest. I have to

wake up." She had to work on the project. "A Coca Cola will be the force to act on my drowsiness," she concluded and headed out, absent-mindedly bringing the book in her hand, Lady Chatterley.

The wet bar in her mother's room was much closer than the restaurant, but the last two visits had only brought disaster. Her mother had drunk enough not only to drown her sorrows but also the last vestiges of her personality. Maniacal and giddy for the simple reason that it was Thursday or the sun was shining one moment and the next moment violently confrontational toward whomever dared to disagree, she was no one anyone knew. She was no one anyone wanted to know or even be around.

The first time Hebe crossed Gaye-lee's threshold after Thanksgiving was the week before Christmas. Rem was certain the nuclear family would come together for the holiday. It was the first time Hebe had known Rem to be wrong. The sottish alterego of her mother made her instantly unwelcome shortly after she came through the door.

"Is that why you came in here, to ask about Christmas? Christmas is a month away!"

Trying to argue with her was like trying to argue with an angry dog. She didn't believe the calendar or understand the words spoken. Barking was the only way she could communicate until she got frustrated and struck out with her hands.

Screaming, "It's a month away," over and over, she slapped and pulled at Hebe's hair so hard that her scalp wept persperation droplets of blood over her ears and forehead. Smarting, bleeding and afraid, Hebe scrambled to her feet and down the hall to her room. If Rem hadn't insisted, she never would have returned. The fifth day of the New Year, 1959 arrived.

"I know it's difficult, but try to see your mother. Maybe she has turned over a new leaf," Rem reasoned.

At first Gaye-lee was calm and gracious; it seemed she might have turned over a new leaf. Hebe playfully presented her with a brain teaser joke from science class. "Which is heavier, a pound of feathers or a pound of nails?" Her mother guessed a pound of nails. When Hebe giggled and said, "Neither. A pound is a pound," it was clear that Gaye-lee had turned over a leaf, but not a new one. It was an old drink-doused leaf. Her soused alterego inveighed against being wrong and vollied invectives at Hebe ending with, "I know nails are heavier than feathers!" Gaye-lee railed on as she prowled toward her, "Maybe I didn't go to Harvard, but I know. I know plenty. You can't pull the wool over my eyes Mister."

"Mister? Mother? Mother what's wrong with you? It's me Hebe," she stated nimbly backing away.

"Don't you think I can see?"

Torn between the fear of being hurt and the desire to help her mother come to her senses made her tremble. Her stomach was full of bees and her legs shook as much as they had in Mexico when the policeman drew a gun on her. "Mother!" she cried out again before crouching on the floor to duck out of the way. Gaye-lee reached down and yanked at her hair. Her scalp hadn't fully healed from the last attack, and the pain was so great that instinct took over, and she retaliated. Blindly, her hands delivered slap after slap after slap, and then she grabbed her mother's arms. It was the first physical contact between them in a long time. Externally, she knew she had to push her away. Internally, she wanted more than anything to pull her toward her, to have her mother hold her. The conflicting urges pulsed through her forearms as she gripped her mother's slim wrists and attempted to restrain her. Gaye was the smaller of the two, but fueled with spirits, she was the more powerful and Hebe had to summon all of her strength to keep her in place. Staring at her mother, she saw a grimace as cold and tough and determined as Fidel Castro's. As surely as he had led his guerrillas into Havana on New Year's day, Gaye-lee would surge through Hebe's defense. Suddenly, an eerie look of maternal love skimmed across the surface of Gaye's face and Hebe weakened her grip for a split-second. That was all the time Gaye-lee needed to break free and release her force on Hebe standing still. With a Wimbeldon worthy backhand she struck her across the jaw and sent her sailing across the room. As she tried to keep from falling she heard her mother's voice calling her name, "Hebe! Oh my God! Hebe!" She struck her head hard on the floor and everything went black.

She came to in her own room. She had a large knot on her head, a black eye and a bandage on her arm covering a dozen stitches. Bjorn was sitting at the foot of the bed with some bright red flowers, "I see you have given up your princess' crown to become a sparring partner for Ingemar Johansson."

"It was an accident. I fell is all."

"I knew a girl back home who was always falling."

"What happened to her?"

"I don't know, but her Papa is in jail."

"My father would never hit me," she snapped.

"I didn't say he would."

She never mentioned the "accident" again and neither did Bjorn. But he came to keep her company every afternoon during her convalescence.

She thought about him as she hesitated in front of her mother's door. He had been a good friend and she didn't want to let him down. He was counting on her to do the model drawings. She didn't want to waste time going too far for a drink. Receiving no reply to her knock on her mother's door, she poked her head in. All was quiet. It was 4:00. Art was still at work; Gaye-lee must have gone out. The coke was cold and sweet and zesty.

A Life magazine, a few weeks old, caught her eye and she flipped it open. Illogic faced her on page 36J in two contrasted images printed one above the other. Pictured on the bottom was a policeman in Johannesburg striking a negro woman with a force so great that it raised both his feet off the ground. She was one of a group protesting the demand that negroes carry identity papers. Above it was a picture of Eartha Kitt once described by Hans as "a sexy chocolate singer." The photo had been snapped at the London Coliseum as she met England's Queen Elizabeth. Each picture had its own caption stating exactly what was happening. No comment of connection or contrast was made. Geography and time had determined that one negro woman would be very fortunate and the other unfortunate.

Hebe contemplated how her own life would have been if she, had been born a hundred years earlier, in 1846. Her much cherished passport would not have been available. Her father told her once that Indian people were allowed to become citizens of the United States until 1925. Maybe, she would have lived close to the earth, swum in waterfalls and befriended the animals, really known the traditions and language of her father's parents. She glanced in the mirror at her tanned face. Since returning to California, she hadn't considered her color. It didn't seem to be an issue. Perhaps because her address was now that of the prestigious Hotel del Coronado. There was no way to tell. But this time around, most people assumed she was an East Indian rather than a Mexican. "Being of mixed decent", Rem once pointed out, "You are neither one nor the other, but a human unique unto yourself." The word mixed reminded her that she could also have grown up in a schloss, a castle, in Austria. She gasped, "I could have been my own great-grandmother, Grandmother Wilkinson's mother!"

A few pages later were Life's pictures of John XXIII becoming the new Pope. One showed his brother wiping away tears of pride. Jude's cute face popped into her mind as he rode around on his little tricycle, and she tried to imagine what he would have grown up to be. "He loved to go so fast, maybe a race car driver. Definitely not the Pope. But what? Would he be considered lucky or unlucky?" This was much too big a question for 4:20 on a Tuesday afternoon. Had she been in Brookline, she could have presented her query, "Is a person in unfortunate circumstances unlucky? Is one in fortunate circumstances lucky? Maybe the woman being beaten would change the world. Maybe Jude would have had a horrible life," she sighed then called aloud, "Birches I miss you!"

THIRTEEN

The Dawn of Understanding

February 1959
Two weeks later:

Margarita had left the mail on the counter and Hebe shuffled
through; bills for magazines; a letter from Harvard for Art; an
invitation from the Country Club; a recent letter from Vienna,
and laying open underneath them all, one from Art's brother Phil
in Virginia. Nothing for her. However her name, "Hebe" lept off
Phil's letter to Art and pulled her nose right into the middle of
it. The words indicated that Art had written to him for
information about a "Boys'Town" for girls. He was trying to find
a place to ship her off to again. Insecurity and rejection
flooded out of her marrow and diluted her cheerfulness. In
addition to writing that he knew of no such place, Phil wrote
that "abandoning Hebe" was not a good idea. She hoped Phil was
an older brother whose opinion Art respected. A strong storm
breeze blew in whirling papers around, and she rushed to close
the windows in the suite.

In the bedroom, she stopped short. There was Gaye-Lee
stretched across the bed. Tiptoeing past, the odor of stale
liquor became noticeable, and Hebe concluded that her mother was
not napping, but passed out. Her mother's magic shawl, draped
over a nearby chair, billowed in the last gust of wind that snuck
under the window as she slid it closed. Hebe sat timidly in the
chair and watched her mother for a few minutes. It was difficult
to believe that such a lovely, peaceful woman was so filled with
sadness, could inflict so much pain. She tried to remember the
last time she had seen her awake and so serene. "Objects not
acted on by a force travel in straight lines at constant speeds,
or if they are at rest, they stay at rest," cropped up from her
subconscious. "Stay at rest," she repeated. Risking meeting her
wrath by disturbing her, she placed a tiny kiss on her cheek.

The moment filled her with so much tension that she couldn't
head straight back to her work. She headed outside to the brisk
air to settle her nerves. Jimmy, the bellman, was smoking on a
break in the shade. He smiled as she stood next to him. Since
Marilyn Monroe's departure, he had become very friendly toward
her. As she was leaving, she singled Hebe out of the small,
crowd of people for a tiny private conversation and a big hug.
After that, reporters and guests descended on her with questions
about their relationship. The manager summoned Jimmy to rescue
her and escort her safely back to her room. She didn't tell
Jimmy anything about her meetings with Marylin because there
wasn't much to tell. But in her room, he saw the private
snapshots of them together with the little dog and presumed their
relationship to be a little famial. He adored Marilyn and had
many pictures, some from an old calendar, others he had taken
during her stay at the Hotel del Coronado, one was autographed.
Marilyn's gesture of closeness toward Hebe elevated her in
everyone's eyes, but especially Jimmy's. Almost every time he
saw Hebe, he would beam and ask in a loud clear voice, "Hey
princess, everything o.k. with Marilyn Monroe? Usually he was in
a populated area such as the lobby and those standing near would
cast a casual, curious glance. Initially, Hebe insisted that she

didn't know Marilyn. "Your secret's safe with me," he assured her with a wink. But proudly he would tell people who inquired as to who she was, "Oh the little princess, she's a personal friend of Miss Monroe." Hebe found out about his gossip because once, while having a cigarette out back, a sailor told her what Jimmy had said and asked if he could take her picture. Rem laughed at the story and advised her not to waste energy attempting to figure out or alter another person's illusions. "When he asks about Marilyn, tell him the truth. You guess she's fine or something. And that will be the end of that." And that's what she did.

"Hey, Hebe. How's Marilyn Monroe."

"Oh, you know Marilyn," was an answer guaranteed to make him smile, and that was what she said chuckling to herself and lighting a cigarette.

"How's the arm."

"Getting better."

"How's your boyfriend?"

"My boyfriend?"

"That tall, blonde guy. You should'a seen his face when he came in here lookin' for ya after your, you know, thing," he pointed to the bandage on her arm.

"He's fine too."

Jimmy's eyes flicked across something in the distance then back to her. "You know there's somethin' I been wantin' to ask you," he began. "That Mr. and Mrs. Higgenson, are they your parents?

"Art's my stepfather. Why?" Her eyes followed his when they shot another glance across the lawn.

There was Art walking with Gabriella Gonzales. Not only was her arm wrapped around his back, her hand was under his jacket and her head was resting on his shoulder as they sauntered toward his car. When he deliberately brushed his cheek against her hair and kissed it, Hebe felt as if she had been punched in the stomach. Her eyes met Jimmy's.

"He's an architect. That must be one of his clients."

"Looks like he's one o' her's," he quipped, then added a
hasty, "Sorry."

"What for?" she blurted out defensively. "He's affectionate. I have to go now."

Walking down the hall she tried to erase what she had just
seen, so she could focus on her homework. A new found sympathy
paused her at her mother's door. She dismissed the urge to go to
her, went to her own room and immediately dove into her design.
By 11:00, she had finished and announced her success to Bjorn on
the telephone. The days of dreading school were long behind her
now as she lay excitedly anticipating the following day's classes
and presenting Bjorn with her updated sketches. In her mind's
eye, she could see the pleased look on his face. Then she saw
herself standing next to Bjorn on the stage where they were
accepting a science project award. She could even hear the
applause. Exhausted, but tingling with the promise of success,
she snuggled into the cool sheets and turned over into a deep
sleep.

There was shouting. There was pounding on her door. There
was the sound of the key in the latch. The lights snapped on and
Gaye-lee blasted into the room in a rage and snatched her from a
land beyond dreams by dragging her out of bed by her arm. Her
spluttering was indecipherable. Hebe was not listening. She
could not hear her yet, but her defense system had immediately
mustered waking strength to arms. She withheld nothing in
warding off Gaye-lee's attack. Pinned with her back against the
wall, she saw Jimmy dumbstruck in the doorway with his key still
in his hand. "Help me!" she cried sending him scrambling away.
Overpowering Gaye and forcing her back, she saw her banned copy
of Lady Chatterley's Lover fall from her mother's fingers and
understood it to be part of the reason for Gaye's ranting.
Gaye-lee grabbed a long, thin white belt from the back of a chair
and snapped it across Hebe's legs with the skill of a practiced,
lion tamer. It was hard and cut her. As it whipped through the
air, Hebe realized she was being hit with the buckle end. Again
and again she pleaded, "Stop! Will you stop it?!" as it smarted

and gashed her flesh. Attempting to dodge it, the buckle
cluncked into her cheek bone and sent a piercing pain into her
nose and a stream of blood down her face. Injured and facing
further danger, something inside of her broke, not a visible,
biological part or even an unseen biological part, but a tiny
piece tucked deep in the caverns of her subconscious that dams
back the mind's roaring rapids of insanity. An inhuman growl
rumbled beneath her collar bones. A bright black flashed in her
eyes, and self-salvation rushed a raw madness into her blood
stream. It burst out of her skin in a hot persperation steaming
away her fear, transforming her from prey to predator. Throwing
her hand up, she caught the belt buckle in mid air and yanked it
away. Infuriated, her mother charged. Hebe was ready to fight.
And they did.

Two large men, a security guard and a policeman separated
the women. Gaye-lee was hauled back to her room and told to stay
there or be arrested. Hebe stood against the wall quaking inside
with the belt still wrapped around her hand. The policeman tried
to get her to talk, but she was frozen. He took a cold, damp,
wash cloth from the bathroom and blotted the blood from her
cheek.

"It's o.k. She's gone now. Do you know that woman?"

Hebe took the cloth and sat down. The officer tried to get
her to sit with her head back to stop her nose from bleeding, but
she was so weak that she could't hold it up. Letting her head
drop forward, the rich metalic smell of her own blood filled her
nose, and her tears burned her cheeks. She wanted to stop
crying, but she couldn't. The cuts inflicted by her mother
penetrated the cistern of the rains of Hebe's many sadnesses.
Out spilled droplets for everything; publicly scuffling with Pia
on the playground in Boston a half a decade ago; being separated
from her father; tasting her grandmother's dislike and rejection
of her; witnessing Floyd's arm slashing; watching her brother
being buried; privately battling her mother in her own room.

The policeman was baffled and ill at ease with Hebe's
crying. He took off his hat to rub his head, righted a chair in

the room ransacked by their battle and sat opposite her.

"Can you tell me what happened? Do you want some water?"
She nodded. After she took a sip, he sat down next to her with a
piece of paper. "I know your upset, but I have to ask a couple
of questions to make a report. O.K.? Now, do you know the woman
who was," he stopped as Hebe raised her liquid, black eyes and
looked him right in the face.

"My mother."

"Sure. You want to talk to your mother?"

"No," she sobbed. "That woman **is** my mother."

He rubbed his chin and looked at the ceiling.

She didn't usually smoke in her room; she didn't like the
smell of stale cigarettes. But after the officer left, she was
afraid to go out and run into her mother. So she sat smoking and
smoking and smoking. Somehow Jimmy had gotten in touch with
Bjorn, and he came by. He didn't say much, lit her cigarettes
and let her curl up next to him in silence. His gentle presence
radiated away the negative atmosphere, until Art stopped by.
Incapable of neglecting propriety, he was cordial and greeted her
and Bjorn with his usual nod of the head and artificial smile.
Then, as if he were nonchalantly ordering a drink he spoke.

"You just couldn't leave her alone, could you?"

Hebe started to reply, but Bjorn dissuaded her with a caress
of her shoulder.

"Can't you see there's something wrong with her? Why do you
insist on upsetting your mother knowing that she is ill?"

"Oh shut up!" she snarled.

He snapped to attention. "I beg your pardon?"

"My mother is not ill! And I am not the one upsetting her!
I saw you in the parking lot with Mrs. Gonzales this afternoon."
She repeated, "**Mrs.** Gonzales."

"Yes," he acknowledged quite unruffled.

All conversation was suspeneded while he tapped a cigarette
down on his silver case and lit it. "Gabriella," he puffed,
"Mrs. Gonzales, is a client and a friend. And like it or not
Hebe, your mother is not well. But unlike you, I am not leaving.

"Leaving?"

"Yes." He turned to Bjorn and looked at his watch. "It is rather late for guests."

"I was just about to go."

"Good." Still speaking to Bjorn, he turned back to Hebe. "Take a minute. You could stay and arrange some German lessons," he smiled and simply walked away.

She wanted to point out his ignorance by informing him that Bjorn was Swedish, but she was too exhausted to be caustic.

"What is the matter with him? He didn't even ask you how you feel! And what's this about German? Do you think they'll send you away to Austria?"

Her enervated response was barely audible. "Maybe. You'd better go now, Bjorn."

When he moved toward her to kiss her good-bye, without meaning to, she flinched and backed away.

"Hebe, what are you going to do?"

"I don't know. I really don't know." She raised her hand like an indian and said, "See you."

"If anything happens..."

"It's o.k., now. Thanks."

The door closed and opened again. "I guess Jimmy thought you needed a bottle of coca-cola," Bjorn whispered and place the bottle inside.

Hebe turned out the light, took the icey bottle and placed it on her swollen face, then just stood by the window staring out at the moonless inky nothingness of 1:43 a.m. until a line of peach haze on the horizon diffused it away.

That day in school, her home room teacher, Mr. Vincent, remarked upon seeing her tired and wounded face, "What happened?" And when she didn't reply, he asked again and the whole class turned to look at her. She bowed her head in embarrassment.

"I was attacked."

"Attacked. Oh how awful."

"Everyone wanted to hear the story, but when the teacher learned that she hadn't seen a doctor, he sent her straight to the nurse who drove her to the hospital. The doctor was quite concerned and interested in many particulars.

"What did you put on the wound last night? Did your nose bleed? A little or a lot? Was the weapon made of metal?" Her answers were such vague whispers that he tipped his head like a roosting owl then asked, "Don't you remember?"

"Yes," she answered emphatically trying to figure out what to tell him. After all, the night before when the policeman learned she had been hit in the face with a metal belt buckle by her mother, he acted as though he didn't believe her. He didn't write down a single word of what she had said. He just stood dumbstruck, his head turning back and forth as he made a sympathetic tutting noise. Then he glared at her suspiciously, "You pullin' my leg?" The doctor would probably be doubtful too. Besides, she didn't think she could bear to hear the words again herself, to be reminded. She wanted to forget it. So, she decided not to tell him the painful truth, to draw attention and possible scrutiny by the authorities. It would, in her mind, only make more trouble, maybe prevent her from ever again seeing the Birches or Bjorn or, most importantly, her father. She fabricated a new story.

"Well, I fell and hit my face on a, um, on a piece of metal patio furniture. A chair. You know, the edge."

"That certainly explains the odd shape, but there are two lacerations. What did you do, fall twice?"

"Yes. I slipped in the blood after I got up."

His brow knit with skepticism as he peered at her over his glasses. Then, taking her blood pressure, he noticed the bandage on her arm. "And what happened here?"

She never did find out what had made that cut on her arm the last time she fought with her mother. She coughed and sat silently kicking her legs.

"Whatever, it needs a new dressing. Those are tiny stiches. You won't have much of a scar, not here or on your face. A couple of stiches in one and a butterfly bandage on the other, and you will be as good as new."

She looked into the hair growing in his nose as he applied the butterfly. And when she was leaving, she noticed that he also had soft black hair on the backs of his hands and growing out of his ears lending a furry kindness to his pudgy appearance. He handed her his card.

"You keep that," he told her with obvious sincerity. "And, if you have anymore of these," he stopped and put his hands in his white jacket pocket, "these unfortunate mishaps. You can call me. Don't make yourself crazy about keeping track of the card. My name is Gold, Dr. Gold. You can't forget that, now can you?" He gave her a firm pat of assurance on the shoulder, and sent her home in a cab.

Arriving at the hotel, she found Bjorn waiting to pick her up in the Gates' car. From that day forward, she kept out of her mother's way, out of harm's way by arranging to be either dropped off or picked up. A full schedule busied her. She accompanied Bjorn to tennis and proudly took lessons from him. An excellent player, he was a much sought after partner at the club. They were both in the honors science society, and she managed to talk him into ballroom dance classes. Always careful to leave a message indicating where and with whom her days were being spent, neither Art nor her mother were invited to seek her out, her life was her own. And she enjoyed spending so much of it with Bjorn. Living far away from home, from the people he loved, and distancing himself from Mr. and Mrs. Gates of whom he was not particularly fond, he had known what it was like to be an outsider, to feel alone. With Hebe everything was different. The days were somehow brighter. Giselle Gates didn't get on his nerves so much. And, things were funnier. They were in his room when Hebe asked him what he meant. He found it difficult to answer.

"I don't know. Things just seem funnier," he repeated. Before we were," he stopped.

Hebe held her breath. Secretly, she thought of herself as his girlfriend. But she wasn't sure about it in the same way that she had been with Tony. His position had been clear from the beginning by his incessant possessive touches and his boorish declarations of love, "You are mine," and "If anyone even looks to you, I will kill him!" Once, she asked what would happen if she were to look at someone else. He smiled with all of his teeth and choked out a laugh. "Tha's neber gonna happen," he began. Then roughly kissed her on the mouth and bit out, "Is it?" compelling her to agree. And when Rem had heard some of her stories about Tony, she frowned disapprovingly and stated her opinion that perhaps Hebe had not so much fallen in love, as she had been stimulated and terrified into thinking she was in love. However, learning the details of the Bjorn relationship Rem cooed, "It sounds perfectly sweet. He must really like you."

Unaccustomed to emotions expressed subtley, Hebe was very uncertain of Bjorn's feelings for her. All she knew was she felt something for him. Never had she seen him with anyone else. And their constantly being together was an often-gossiped topic at school due to the disparity in their ages and the fact that he was already in the eleventh grade while she was only in the ninth, still a junior high student. But the rumor was also, "since they're both a little strange, it's only natural for them to be a couple."

She sat on the edge of Bjorn's bed where he was reclining. He invited her to lie next to him with a pat on the pillow and said, "Before we were together,"

"Together?", she repeated her heart beating faster

He stroked her hair, smoothing it as he did so, then smooched her on her mouth, "Ja together. You are so cute sometimes, yust like a little kid. I'm glad you are here. Really glad."

"Me too." She tingled all over as she placed her head on his chest and he held her in his arms.

He pointed to the ceiling, "Watch. Up there."

She watched, but before she saw anything, she heard something softly rustling. Suddenly, a tiny, white-breasted bird fluttered around the rafters and landed next to a small hole in the wall near the ceiling. It slipped through and darted into invisibility in the white midday scene outside.

"She and I have shared this room the whole time I have been living here, but I didn't notice until I started spending time with you." Bjorn stuck his face into the petals of the potted hyacinths and jasmines Hebe had given him.

"Hey, what are you doing?" Hebe protested. "I want to smell it too! Save some for me!"

"Save some?"

"Yeah. You're sniffing all the fragrance away."

He laughed out loud at her silliness and kissed her again. "Yes, Hebe, things are funnier when you're around."

"What's so funny about that?"

"Just the idea. You know, someone coming along and sucking up all the aroma, so no one else can get any. Sounds impossible."

Smelling the flowers together, Bjorn drew her so very near to him that they were one breathing in the same beautiful floral fragrance and being warmed by the same liquid silver sunlight. The moment brimmed with joy and Hebe felt safe and loved and happy.

*****

Two days later, Margarita dropped her off in front of the old house. After glimpsing through the mail she had unstuffed from the box, she handed it to Margarita.

"I dunno, Hebita why ju wan' go to there. Is, maybe, a little dus'. I don't do nothin' much no more in the inside since your mother, she be livin' at the Coronado."

"It doesn't matter. Bjorn and I are just goin' to watch the light coming through the window."

"Thee light?"

Hebe nodded.

"Thee light?" She shook her head. "In the kitchen window? All that trouble your mother went through tryin' to cover it up and ju are coming all the way out here, only for to see it. One day ju gonna 'splain that to me. For now jus' tell me what time

- 287 -

ju want I should come back?"

"Bjorn's taking me home. He'll be here around ten."

"I know I don't have to tell to you this Hebita, but you
don' have to show your friend the whole house, jus' thee
kitchen," she admonished.

"Come on Margarita. You trust me, don't you? Bjorn and I
are just friends."

"De antecedentes humildes, from small beginnings...," she
said with an all knowing look in her eye, then drove off with a
beep and a wave.

Hebe thought about the autumn day in 1954 when she had first
seen the house, how unfamiliar and queer it had appeared, the two
A-frames standing tall all alone at the end of the road, the edge
of the beach. A gum wrapper flitted by and she realized her feet
were on the very spot where she had shared her first real kiss
with Tony. So much had happened since then, that although the
house remained structurally the same, it looked quite different.
Nevertheless, it had a sense of home about it that invited her up
the path.

Before going in, she closed her eyes and drank in the rich
sea breeze. A shiver sent goosebumps up her arms and she
thought her mind was playing tricks on her. The salty air seemed
to have been somehow laced with the freshness of her father's
agua lavanda cologne. A dog barking snapped her eyes open to the
vision of her old four-legged friend, Max charging after a stick
in the waves.

Hollering gleefully she let her limbs flail and took off for
the shore. He delivered the customary soggy doggie welcome of
shaking out all over her and slobbering on her hands and face.

"Is that your dog, Miss?"

"Daddy?" she muttered in disbelief turning around. And there
he was.

"Oh my God! It's you, Hebe."

Hebe was rendered both dumbfounded and immobile by the
unexpected sight of her father. And when she did speak, it
wasn't to say any of the clever things she had rehearsed in the

many fantasy reunions held in her head over the years. She
shaded her eyes and simply asked, "How did you get here?"

"Taxicab. He'll be back in about forty minutes."

"Forty minutes!?"

"Yes. I'm up from Venezuela on an oil tanker. We only got
an hour's shore leave. I came right here," he informed her
looking about. "Maybe, I should have telephoned." He offered
her a hand up. Even though she had grown in so many ways since
they had last seen one another, her hand was still quite small in
his. "Oh, you're so tall. Look at you. You're beautiful."

"You too," she said exchanging a long embrace. "We need more
time, Daddy."

"Oh, Hebe. Life doesn't know about time. To live is to be
river water journeying over your bed. You don't really have any
say in how much water you get or how fast it flows. You have to
go with what you've got. Go **with** the flow." His eyes followed
the dog, now playing catch the stick in the distance with another
person as they walked to the rear entrance of the house in a
peaceful quiet. By the side of the swimming pool, they came
across Jude's little, blue tricycle tipped on it's side. Gordy
knelt down spun the peddle and turned it over. "How's your
mother?"

Neither wanting to lie nor tell him the truth, she held her
tongue never imagining a silence could itself speak part of a
story. "I have a good idea," she announced avoiding the question
and scampering into the house. On her way out, she gazed through
the glass at the man, sitting on the patio. He was the Chief
Engineer on the merchant ship, and he looked so dignified in his
khaki officer's uniform. The yellow sun danced in his shiny
black Indian hair and on the high cheekbones of his august face,
strong, powerful and as berry brown as it was the last happy time
she had seen him, the summer of the hurricane on the back porch
of their house in Cambridge, the night he had brought Hans home.
Long had she hoped for this very day, their reunion, the day her
daddy would come to see his little girl. And there he was, big
as life, in person, Daddy. But his little girl was absent, her

innocence, her childhood washed over by the river of passing
time, banefully lined with rue, had carried her away; she was
forever gone. How she wished he could have witnessed the child
of her disappear into the young woman she was becoming or see his
baby son turn into a boy. The best she could do would be to show
him what he missed. She had quickly found some old photo albums.
No one had been in the house. They were exactly where she
remembered.

Working against the clock ticking urgently forward they
travelled back into the times pictured. Though, she hadn't seen
the prints for many months, they didn't interest her as much as
her father's face which she hadn't seen for years. Adoringly,
she gazed at it reacting with tenderness and amusement to the
glossy sweet irretrievable moments in the white bordered squares.

"Is that Jude?" he asked excitedly removing the photograph.

"Yes. Last summer."

His question, "Are there any more of him?" shot her in and
out of the house with a framed, desk-top portrait of Jude sitting
on his tricycle with his hands resting on the handlebars. Hebe
watched a most unusual expression cross her father's face. It
was a combination of joy and tragedy that brought tears to his
eyes while a burst of laughter coughed out of him. Following the
focus of his eyes, she saw Jude's left hand. On the back, above
his knuckles were three small, light moles which had become
noticeable when he was about two, they formed a constellation,
the same triangular constellation which could be found on Gordy's
dark hand.

After a moment, she told Gordy how everyone who met Jude had
remarked how clever he was for his age. He didn't respond. He
just took a deep breath and smiled. Carefully, she turned the
album pages passed those of Gaye-Lee and Art; nevertheless, one
fell right into his lap. It was their wedding day on the lawn of
the "Hotel Del". Hebe tried to sneak it away, but for reasons
beyond her, Gordy wanted to see that too. Blankly, he stared at
it, at him, Art, the man who was everything he was not; white,
rich, successful, married to the mother of his children, the

woman he loved who once loved him, who perhaps still did.

"Oh! Look!" Hebe cried, intentionally distracting him. "I don't believe it. Here's one of you and mother from a long time ago, a very long time ago. Her hair is so long," she exclaimed handing the yellowing photograph to him.

He gasped, held it near his heart then looked at it again. He took Hebe's hand and squeezed it with his eyes closed. Quickly, he flicked away a tear that had formed in the corner of his lower eyelashes.

"Where is that?"

He composed himself and said with a smile in his voice, "Sweden. Stockholm, at the theatre where your mother and I met. Someone took this the day after that night. We didn't have a camera. No," he chuckled, "We had a camera, but the flash didn't work, so we went back the next day." He flipped it over and read the small writing, "July 12, 1945," and fell into a heavy silence that made a few seconds seem like a half an hour.

Folding up the album, Hebe asked him to tell her about all the places he had been. He reminded her of their limited time, so she asked to hear about the place which had most fascinated her, India. His story of India was not an objective account of the food or the culture or the sights or the people. It was a personal tale of a fellow seaman who had bought a cute little monkey there and what happened after he went against all the regulations and snuck it on board the ship. Right after he began, he remembered the unhappy truthful ending, that the animal had been discovered and, of course, as per Captains orders, thrown overboard. At first, he thought to soften the monkey's demise by altering his being deliberately thrown overboard to an accident in which he was swept overboard. But her upturned face sparkling with anticipation provoked from his lips not only a changed ending, but a mini fable. Hebe giggled envisioning the burly merchant seamen teaching the cuddly creature to fluff their pillows and turn out the lights. But she laughed outloud like a child when Gordy told about the day the monkey escaped and caused chaos ringing bells, knocking down the giant pots in the galley and even standing right behind the unwitting captain and mimicking his cigar smoking with a piece of banana. In the fabled end, the monkey made it all the way to London where the seaman presented him to his aunt. She named him Collin and taught him how to dress himself in the fashionable clothes she made for him, including a tiny satin vest and a pair of purple velvet pants.

"Oh Dad, she gasped delightedly, "You're making that up."

"Well, I won't say I'm not. I'll send you a picture. You'll see," he looked at the photo of himself and Gaye-lee still in his hand.

"Don't move. I want to take a picture just like that, of you with the picture of you and mother."

Gordy sat up in the cafe style patio chair and watched proudly as Hebe adjusted the settings on the reflex camera. Humoring her, he held the picture next to his face and pointed to it with a broad grin as she clicked the button.

"That's just as much yours as mother's. You keep it."

These words turned the conversation to Gaye-Lee. Gordy, listened with great concern as she unraveled the yarn of her most serious wounds. Disquieted by it all, his eyes filled with shadows of sadness. He understood completely when she admitted that she wanted to get away, and while he wanted to help, he knew he was powerless to do anything at that moment other than offer some suggestions.

"If you were just a couple of years older, you could become legally emancipated."

"Oh yeah, if she doesn't kill me first," she quipped cynically.

"Hebe!" he exclaimed outloud, but in the back of his mind, he knew what she said could be true; nevertheless, he snapped at her, "You shouldn't say such a horrible thing. She is your mother." Then he added half to himself, "It would probably be best if you were not in her way." He tried to offer an alternative. "Is Grandma Wilkinson..." Gordy didn't bother to finish the question because the way she cut her eyes over to him

made it clear that no great bond had developed between Hebe and
Gaye-Lee's mother.

"I don't know if I want to be emancipated, Dad."

"You could be declared independant, responsible for
yourself. However, I do believe you have to prove you have
income enough to support yourself."

"I'll be thirteen at the end of this year, November. I
could find work someplace."

"Only thirteen? I don't think work is a good idea just yet.
Although, no one would guess that you're under sixteen. How did
you get to be such a grown up young lady?"

"Dad, what about your mother? Couldn't I stay with her?"

"A-gi-tsi?"

"A-gi-tsi," she repeated.

"Yes. Its Cherokee for 'my mother'."

"I thought she was Cheyenne."

"She is, but she lives with a Cherokee man on the rez in
North Carolina, dear. You need to go to school and," He paused,
then mentioned quietly, "She doesn't speak much English, you
know. She doesn't want to. That simple life would be too hard
for a little lady like you."

"Is that why I have never met her?"

He brought his face so close that she could feel the hard
edge of his officer's cap on her forehead. "There is so much you
don't know Hebe, but there just isn't time." His eyes lit up
playfully. "I guess you'll be getting married one day and you'll
have your own family to worry about."

"Married!"

"Well, sure. You're so pretty, in a few years someone will
come and take you away. You'll only visit your mother. You'll be
free."

"A few years?" she muttered to herself.

"What about living with Rem? She likes you very much."

"I know! I asked to go. Mother won't let me," she sulked.

"Try to understand, Hebe dear, regardless of what she has
done, you are still her daughter. She has already lost her son.

It must be difficult for her to loose you too."

"And what about me?" She stepped back from her father and flung her arms out. "Doesn't anyone care that I lost my little brother? **People** have to understand, I feel sad too. And I am tired of her making my life miserable, hitting me. Tired. I am very tired."

A horn blared making him snatch a peek at his watch. He didn't want to leave her with her problem unsolved, but he had no choice. He offered one final suggestion.

"Ask her again if you can join Rem. I'm sure she'll agree." Together they walked across the yard.

"I will, but," she stammered, then offered another possibility in the form of a soft wimpering plea that poked at Gordy's heart. Before him, with her Medusa curls frizzing around her head, stood his long lost little girl, Hebe Jeebie.

"Just a second," he called out to the driver. He knelt down in front of her and took her hand. From behind the grey clouds, a glint of sunlight reflected off something and stabbed her in the eye. She stared at his hand. She hadn't noticed it before. He was wearing a gleaming golden band on his finger.

"You got married!?"

"Remember, I wrote to you about her in my last letter."

"You only wrote that you had met someone in New York, a Cherokee woman, a musician named Wa-le'-la."

"Yes. Hebe, right now," he began.

Swallowing her ignorant jealousy, she unwittingly released him from his hook of awkwardness and let him swim back into the sea of irresponsibility with the cool comment, "You know, I've been to New York. I really wouldn't want to live there."

"Hey Mack! Hurry it up!" the driver bellowed stepping out of the cab. Hebe walked to him and explained they just needed one more second for him to take a picture of them together. "One quick one. He told me not to let him be late."

"We've got time," Gordy stated turning his wrist to see his watch. Then he added in a loud manly voice, "Besides, that ship is not going anywhere without me."

Hebe jutted her chin out. "He's the Chief Engineer," she remarked proudly.

"Oh yeah. Hey chief. Say cheese," he hollered pointing the camera at the pair in front of the drab February horizon. Hebe held Gordy's hand in a way that covered the ring. There was no emotional farewell, not because there was no time but because she didn't feel sad. In fact, she didn't feel a thing. He held her tightly, but she was numb. Without a smile or a tear, she watched as he jumped into the car which vanished behind a curtain of morning fog being chased out to sea by the chilly morning breeze.

When Bjorn arrived, he found her curled up in the bright, late morning sun on the chaise lounge beneath a woolen blanket. Her camera was on top of the photo album on the table. She tossed back the blanket edge sending some change clanking onto the flagstones.

"Hey, sömntuta. What's all that?"

She picked one up and flipped it to him with a big yawn. "Silver dollars. When I was a child, my father sometimes put them under my pillow."

"You must have spent a lot of time in bed," he chuckled jingling the handful of coins.

"There's only seven." She didn't want to mention the visit from her father, to have to explain its brevity or deal with the melancholy that accompanied discussing him. The number seven; however, did bring to mind those she loved to talk about, the Celestial Seven, the Birches. Heading into the house with Bjorn at her heels she blurted out, "Hey, do you want to go to Las Vegas in May?

"Hebe, what are you up to?"

"My Boston family is all going to Las Vegas. I really want to see them. So, I'm going."

Bjorn hung his mouth open in amazement in the kitchen doorway seeing the wondrous spectacle of colorful stalactites of light pouring into the room. His eyes followed a royal blue beam from the window to a yellow bottle which it had colored green before it became a purple puddle on a red cloth placemat. "Wow."

A bright yellow light settled angelically around Hebe's mane of hair and she asked, "Well, what do you think?"

"This is an experiment in light. It's great. I wish we could bring the whole window to the science fair."

"I mean about Las Vegas."

"Mr. and Mrs. Gates don't care what I do. But...,"

"Don't worry. I'm not going to ask my mother."

"Now I am worried."

"I'm going to ask Art. I already made an appointment to see him. He'll let me go. You'll see." She aimed her camera and began taking pictures of the shafts of light.

"You know, Hebe. We just might win the science club prize."

*****

Three days later she put on her conservative, east coast, school girl outfit and French braided her hair in preparation for her appointment with Art at his office. Several messages left with his secretary had gone unreturned. Once in the parking lot, she tried to talk to him, but he was hurring off to work. Not wanting to run away and certain she could obtain his permission, she was determined to speak with him. The only way she knew to secure his undivided attention was at work. He had no idea she was coming because she deliberately made the appointment with one of his partners secretaries in the name of Miss Smith. The secretary's questions regarding exactly who she was and what their meeting would be about were stemmed when Hebe, who had been imitating Rem's sophisticated accent as best she could, said, "Tell him, it's personal."

At the office, Art reluctantly had the secretary show her in, then told her, "Kelley let me know as soon as Miss Smith gets here." He went to the wall and opened a large cabinet to reveal a mirror-backed bar and clinked some ice cubes into a glass. He glanced at her reflection. "Isn't this a surprise," he began flatly. "I've never seen your school outfit most becoming, most

becoming. Would you like something to drink, juice, a Coca
Cola?" She shook her head. "Everything all right at the hotel,
you know with your mother?"

"Art, our school vacation is in May. I want to go to Las
Vegas to meet my friends. We're going to the Grand Canyon."

He sat with his profile to her slowly gliding his
well-groomed fingers over the polished surface of his desk.

"Why are you asking me? Your mother..,"

"I didn't want to upset her, to have another scene."

He sipped his drink and sternly said, "It just isn't my
decision. I'll bring it up with her tonight." He jotted a note
on the pad on his desk, then buzzed his secretary. "Any sign of
our mysterious Miss Smith yet?"

Hebe sat studying him while Kelley promised to tell him the
instant Miss Smith arrived.

"Hebe, I'm very busy, so why don't you,"

"Art," she interrupted, "I want to go to Las Vegas on school
vacation," she asserted very calmly. "If you don't give me
permission," she stopped and caught his eyes.

They stared at each other. She knew he was thinking she
would mention Mrs. Gonzales, but she didn't. When she repeated,
"If you don't give me permission," Art refilled his glass of
scotch at the bar, lit a cigarette and gave an amused chuckle.

"Not threatening me, are you?"

Putting up a thin front of innocence, she sounded hurt.
"Threaten you? What are you talking about, Art? How could I do
that? I was just going to point out that I would go anyway."

"Is that so?"

"Yes, that's so."

"And I believe you would, wouldn't you?"

A Cheshire cat's grin flashed across her face. "Look. If
I'm not here, I can't upset my mother, now can I? I doubt she'll
notice I'm gone, but if she does, you could tell her I went on a
school trip."

Miffed at being manipulated, he ran his hand through his
hair and warned her to "Be sure and leave your friends names, the

hotels, phone numbers, every last detail, or I'll have the
authorities pick you up."

Secure in the knowledge that he wouldn't call anyone for the
simple reason that he didn't want to have his well-organized life
disrupted, she strode confidently out with a proper, "Thank you
Art. I'll send you a post card," and almost ran down to the
waiting car to tell Bjorn.

FOURTEEN

Las Vegas Vicissitudes

The Periwinkle Moon

Las Vegas
Late May 1959

Women's nipples became the object of her contemplation as
she sat in a dressing room backstage at the Dunes. She hadn't
expected to see them. A minaret-sized Alladin in flowing Arabian
regalia was standing on the roof of the big-top-like entrance to
the resort and had deceived her into thinking they would be
treated to some sort of circus entertainment. Nell claimed her
cousin, Marina, a modern dancer, could "do amazing things with
her body," and that a man who had seen her perform while she was
on the road in Denmark had offered her a stint at a Vegas club.
Hebe put it all together to mean she was an acrobat. Watching
Marina balance a two foot high crown of lavender ostrich plumes
on her head and simultaneously manoeuvre a cape of matching
chiffon several yards wide proved her to be partially right.
Watching her do it in very high heels wearing nothing else,

except a pair of long gloves and two smaller pubic plumes, she realized Marina was more of a showgirl. Nell's idea had been that the Birches collectively fly out to Las Vegas to offer her cousin moral support. Coincidentally, Rem was headed that way to meet a gentleman admirer, so she was all for it. The others followed. But Holly stayed behind with Floyd who was being seen as an out patient at the hospital and not up to the trip. Rem, Hans, Nell and Noni had already been in Vegas for almost three weeks. They picked up Hebe and Bjorn and took them on a brief tour of town before heading over to the club for Marina's rehearsal and a quick backstage peek. It turned into a long visit when Nell asked if she could try on one of the plumed, costumes. As usual, all got involved and flocked to another dressing room in search of more lavender feathers. Hans loaded his Leica and Noni adjusted his pants before bringing up the rear of the line of ladies filing out. Rem had instantly supported Hebe's disinterest in donning a downy g-string. Nell called her a prude and declared, "Americans are so ridiculously modest."

"I do believe most of the showgirls here are American. She is expressing her choice," Rem defended.

"If you want to go with them Bjorn, you should go," Hebe encouraged. But just at that moment, five statuesque girls, equally gorgeous, entered the dressing room.

"No. No. Here is good," he remarked his eyes darting among the pretty faces of wonderment.

After Hebe explained that she and Bjorn were Marina's friends, the girls casually got undressed and started to make themselves up. Modestly, Hebe kept averting her glance to the colorful cosmetics in front of the vanity mirror, and wouldn't have noticed the vaiety of nipples at all had it not been for Bjorn. He was all eyes as he relaxed with his hands folded behind his head. First Hebe gave him a kick to get his attention. Then, she gave him a jealous glare.

"What?"

"You don't have to stare."

"I'm not."

"Yes, you are."

He didn't defend himself further, but asked her, "How old do you think they are?"

"Certainly much older than you."

"Maybe this is a competition."

"What?"

"Marina was all in lavender. These girls are all in green. You know, like teams."

"Teams?" She snapped her head away with a tiny angry tut and he reached over and held her fingers. The woman seated next to her began rubbing lotion on her skin making her nipples contract. Hebe scanned the room in vain for a visual divertissement. In the crowded space, filled with mostly nude women, flesh and nipples were everywhere. She marveled at the diversity of sizes, shapes and colors. Marina returned and offered a "Hi everyone," to the girls.

Rem ducked under her feathers and went straight for Bjorn's cigarette pocket "Do you mind?" she asked helping herself. He lit her cigarette with his lighter. She took it from him and read, "S.L.? I thought you were B.L.".

"Sven Lagerkvist. It's my father's," he explained while Nell struggling to balance the headpiece strutted ostrich-like into the room and tipped over onto a stool right next to Bjorn. Everyone laughed.

From the corner where she sat alone, an auburn-haired, green-gloved girl sang out, "It's not as easy as it looks, is it Blondie?"

Noni caught the ladies' attention by swaggering dramatically into the middle of the dressing room. "O.K., guess who I am? he asked directing a look at the redhead. He gestured to those wearing feathers with one hand and those without with the other and quoted, "'We must divide the biped class into featherless and feathered.' Who am I?"

Two girls' answers were fast and incorrect; "That actor, José Ferrer," one snapped with her gum. Another raised her hand, "Chicken farmer?" Then la rousse guessed "Darwin?"

Noni fell on his knees and prayed to her. "Oh mi amor," he exclaimed while the others clapped.

"I'm right? she repeated aglow with self satisfaction.

"I don't believe a woman as beautiful as you could ever be wrong," Noni began then recited 'And wisdom's self

    Oft seeks to sweet retired solitude,

    Where with her best nurse Contemplation,

    She plumes her feathers, and lets grow her wings.'"

He rose to his feet, leaned and whispered something apparently very effective into her hair because before she left to warm up, he had written her number on a matchbook cover.

Hebe heard Hans tell Noni, "Darwin? You mean, Plato."

"Sure. <u>The Statesman</u>. I don't think she'll figure it out before tomorrow night.

The men laughed and shook hands over his success.

Then Rem turned to Bjorn remembering something, "Some years ago, I knew a Sven Lagerkvist? Count Lagerkvist, the artist?"

Nell's ears pricked up hearing the title, "Count".

"Ja. Dat's my papa," Bjorn announced thickening up his Swedish accent for Nell's benefit."

Nell who, upon being introduced to Bjorn at the airport, had mumbled to Rem, "A little thin for a dreamboat," suddenly fluttered her eyelashes at him, inflated her bosom by inhaling a big breath and let it out with, "That would mean you are a count, Count Bjorn."

Hebe held Bjorn's hand, but Nell held his libido. An electric magnetism sparked in the air between them which was visible to everyone present. Suddenly aware of the power of his title he got up, took Nell's hand and kissed it.

"Oh brother," Hebe mumbled and sized up the pair. She had never seen Bjorn moon over anyone, she thought he was behaving foolishly. And Nell? Five months of geographic separation had apparently separated them emotionally because she carried on as if Hebe, her friend, were not there. Nell was, indeed, a knockout, pretty as always and in the showgirl feathers, very very sexy, something, Hebe, had never considered herself. It

dawned on her that while Bjorn thought she was clever and cute,
their petting had never gone beyond a few, simple kisses. And
he had certainly never gaped lustfully at her as he did Nell.
She released the edge of his jacket which she had subconsciously
been holding onto, but Nell held firmly onto his attention.

"Wow! Maybe you should apply for her job," he complimented
Nell moving his eyes to a calendar pin up of Miss Atomic Blast on
the wall by her head. She struck the same pose and Bjorn studied
her like a contestant judge.

Hebe joined Rem standing on one side of the bleached, white
band of desert light that sliced through the open door to the
outside.

"Hey Bjorn. We're leaving now," Hebe called out sweetly, but
he didn't budge.

"Bjorn?" Rem tried. "Do come along. Bob will be waiting."

Nell, watching Hans in the chorus line of girls teaching him
to kick, humpfed audibly and spun around to Bjorn. "Oh, don't
you want to stay?" She cooed plucking a lavender fluff from her
g-string and tickling his ear. "We're going to have great fun."

A cat's cradle of confused loyalties, dissapointment,
selfishness and sympathy threaded through the eyes of Bjorn,
Hebe, Nell and Rem as they waited for him to make up his mind.
Hebe knew Bjorn was going to stay. In order to avoid hearing the
sound of their bond breaking by listening to him admit his
preference for remaining with Nell and the others, she bolted out
into the dusty-yellow day. Bjorn called out from the dark
doorway. Thinking she hadn't heard him, Rem said, "Bjorn is
calling you."

Every hair on her body had become a thorn of indifference
within the few seconds it took for her to flick her ponytail and
turn around. She was numb. Without a smile or a tear, her eyes
blankly met his before she turned and calmly rushed to catch Rem.

"Hebe," and "Wait," Bjorn called out several times. She
refused to hear. He did not run after her. She did not care.

Apathy filling her soul somehow emptied her heart and her
senses of feeling. Life became mediocre. The desert sun

coloring the clouds apricot descended unseen before her gazing
eyes into a radiant magenta twilight. The succulent snails
dripping with rich garlic butter slid untasted down her throat.
Bob's gift, the dazzling diamond and emerald encrusted bracelet
went unremarked upon from Harry Winston's box to Rem's wrist.
She knew he was the best of the best jewelers. She saw the warm
thank you on Rem's face and knew she should say something other
than, "It's nice," but she just couldn't. As Rem fawned her
appreciation over her generous sodalis, Hebe turned away. Their
display of love and affection annoyed her. It was just the three
of them, so she tried to watch the floor show. But the dismal
emptiness which had crested behind her eyes did not subside.
Claiming to have a headache, she excused herself.

She felt at ease in the dark and decided not to turn on the
light. However, unlit, the vanity mirror,in the corner held no
image of her, like the mirror in her bedroom at Rem's. She turned
on the lamp and sat down. The mischevious little Hebe who once
played dress-up in her mother's gowns in Cambridge was not there,
nor the pretty Chicana she liked to see at Rosalita's in San
Diego, or the sparkling sylph who always had a smile for her at
Rem's in Brookline. Instead, a quasi-stranger slouched on the
bench, the dark, dispirited girl with the flat black eyes of an
old mare she had seen once or twice at Grandmother Wilkinson's.
With a quick click of the switch, she managed to snap her from
sight, but not from her soul.

The morning brought a new, hot, dry, desert day. She felt
the same. Not even the slightest anticipation stirred in her for
the plane ride into the Grand Canyon for a picnic with Rem and
her Bob White. In fact, she was dreading going since it would
still only be the three of them. All the others had joined Noni
on a wild two night sojourn into the desert for a UFO sighting
campfire party. Hebe didn't want to go, to see Bjorn with Nell,
and she didn't want to be the third wheel with Rem and Bob.
Planning to stay behind, she remained in her room at breakfast,
but Rem sought her out.

"I thought you wanted to spend your vacation here us."

"I do."

"Well, Löfuk, look around. We are not in your room. Za, no esäkob nog ole liko fat olik studom."

The meaning of the words was not clear, she had not heard Volapük for a long time. It reminded her of their trip to New York and the many good times they had had together, the laughter and the trust. A random answer, "Labob penedi," was emitted with a flicker of cheer.

Kindled by Rem's caring, the flicker brightened to a small flame of lightheartedness. However, her spirits remained a bit dim. It wasn't until she threw up over the Grand Canyon that she felt completely herself again. A bag couldn't be found quickly enough, and since they were coming in for a landing and near the ground of their destination, Quarter Master Mesa, the pilot suggested, "There is the window." The thin, bilious glue of her breakfast poured through the sky and dropped down to the canyon. Embarrassed, she didn't want to pull her head in, but she didn't have a choice. A hand placed a cool damp checkered napkin in her lap and the plane jostled and rolled to a halt on the earthen landing strip.

"Well, that's one way to feed the wildlife," Bob shouted with a grin above the droning of the engine dismissing her embarassment.

The mesa which was below the rim, but still a few thousand feet above the river was nestled within the canyon, a most remarkable spot for a picnic. She was really glad Rem had encouraged her to come. Over champagne and crab legs, she learned that Rem was in Vegas to divorce Etienne and marry Bob. They had met in Paris last fall, and by Valentine's Day, he had proposed. Her mien was that of a woman in love. In Bob's company, she was less a mistress-of-the-manor lady and very much a dainty ballerina, often in his lap. Hebe was pleased to see her with someone who cared about her so deeply and proud to be trusted with the secret of their pending marriage. She figured, she was the only Birch told so far because no one else was privy to the fraternal nature of Rem's former marital union, a fact Rem obviously wished to remain private.

"If everyone knows about the wedding and something goes wrong with the divorce," she began. "Well, providing all goes well, we will have a reception at La Maisonette."

"Newport? I thought we decided on The Country Club, Rem."

"It's half the price to have it at home. And we can't have it at The Birches there was a little flood and the main floor is being resanded. There's so much dust, Dahling."

"That's my girl."

Curosity compelled Hebe to inquire, "What about your brother, Etienne? Doesn't he have to be.." She stopped, thinking she might reveal the secret to Bob.

"Married he will be Hebe. He stunned everyone and got down on bended knee to Penelope, a second cousin. Quite well off," she explained. "Just not, the belle of the ball. Poor thing. She must be well over thirty by now."

"Does Penelope know your brother, her cousin," Hebe started to ask about Etienne's lover, but hesitated again.

"I don't believe he did mention Phillipe," Bob said, and she realized he probably knew all of Rem's secrets.

Rem, chewing, shook her head and swallowed. "Now you know why we didn't want to go camping with the others." Then exchanging a gaze of adoration with Bob continued, "We shall be married tomorrow. And, of course, you are coming, Hebe. But you musn't say a word."

"Just like the movie stars" she blurted out.

"Hebe what are you talking about?"

I heard that Eddie Fischer and Elizabeth Taylor got married in Las Vegas just two weeks ago. And Sammy Davis Jr. This is swell." Sensifacient again, everything glowed beautifully in Hebe's eyes; the day, the food, the bugs, the news. She threw her arms around Rem then Bob. "I'm so happy for you."

She sat back and scrutinized him, Rem's future husband, her third. The first, she had married because he had an impeccable background, "Well, we both did," was the way she had put it last year when, after a rare night of too much bubbly, she shared a heart-to-heart with Hebe. "On paper, we were perfect. And, we were a stunning couple. He was quite handsome. Still is. Too handsome. He never missed a performance of mine, no matter how little my role. And flowers! The other dancers secretly hated me. Hated me, and I later found out loved him. At least two. How he found the time to sneak around I'll never know. Our social calendar was booked solid! That fool. He actually thought my upbringing would force me to protect our projected illusion of perfection no matter what. Of course, I was prepared for the expected continental infidelities, but not with a child! She was seventeen, and he was forty two! 'I can't just end it,' he told me. 'I'm her first; she loves me! Try to remember when you were young.' I thought my feet might give out by twenty-five, but not the rest of me. I vowed never to marry again. Then, the situation with my brother. It was only meant to be temporary, you know Hebe. The doctors gave my father a few weeks. That was months ago! Doesn't matter. No one knows. We could carry on this way forever, unless something beyond the bounds of possiblity happens; I fall in love with someone utterly wonderful and want to marry him."

And there he sat, someone "utterly wonderful", Bob White, whom Rem would marry for love. He was a big man, at least three times the size of Rem, maybe in his late fifties, a man of considerable charm, puissance and physical strength. He had easily beaten Hans at tennis early in the morning before they left. His thick shock of white hair was cast with the subtle memory of chestnut tones which made his green eyes twinkle. He was, indeed, distinguished with a melifluous voice, obviously, a powerful and auspicious business man. After all, they were delivered to their luncheon in his private plane, and he mention-ed finalizing a deal in Vegas with the Summa Corporation, a company Art had brought up on occasion; it was owned by Howard Hughes. And yet, the curt, tense business demeanor Hebe had seen in Art's friends was missing. Bob White was mellow, kind and relaxed. She couldn't picture him in clothes other than tennis whites or the chinos and beige sweater he wore.

The enchanted expression of a found soul that Bob reflected in Rem's presence was one Hebe had never seen before. She didn't know how to define it, but she thought to herself that it should be placed in a museum near the words, **true love**. Within the second it took Rem and Bob to exchange their smile, a bewitching, ocean of rapture began to ebb and flow between the shores of their beings.

"How poetic you are Remy. It really is a terrific idea. Shall we come back here to the mesa?"

"No. On the canyon floor. Maybe near a waterfall."

"We could take one of the trails down tomorrow morning."

"On horseback?" Hebe asked clapping her hands?

His jovial, "Of course," delighted her.

By evening, all the arrangements had been made for a predawn departure. The early start was necessary because the trek down on the horses would take several hours. The plane had brought them near the spot where they rendezvoused with the horses and their group: an old minister; a doctoral student in anthropology from Columbia University, Julie; her husband, Buck, an archeologist cum tour guide and his friend; Murphy, a Hualapai Indian who lived in the Grand Canyon and knew it very well.

Upon seeing Hebe, Murphy looked right in her eyes, smiled in greeting and spoke in his language. He gestured with his hand toward the rocky path leading down the steep hill into the canyon, said something else and gave her a leg up.

"I'm afraid I don't understand you."

"But, you are Indian."

She was stunned. Not, colored, not Mexican, not Persian or Greek or East Indian, but Indian, he guessed. Murphy had looked into her face and seen the blood invisible to others. As flustered as if he had accidentally seen up her dress, she blushed and eyed him with suspicion.

"Did Rem tell you that?"

He shook his gleeming head of shoulder length, black hair while he adjusted the girth on her horse. "Your mother didn't have to tell me," he commented scanning her face. "It is there," he pointed at her nose, "in those flashing black eyes."

"My mother?"

"Yes. Mrs. Rem has same voice, same gestures."

"But not my mother. She's in California. She's white; my father is Cheyenne. I'm half."

"Half is sometimes the whole story," he remarked and fell silent. Descending through the forested path, she tried to figure out what he meant until the beauty of the surroundings completed distracted her and Murphy stopped her Pinto. Placing his forefinger to his lips for quiet, then extending it out to the side, he guided her eyes beneath the aspen leaves. There as still as stones, posed a doe and her deer mother listening intently. Satisfied they were alone, they nibbled on some leaves and finally wandered away. Hebe was thrilled. Continuing down the path, he treated her to the glimpses of wild creatures his experienced eyes caught; chubby squirrels, a waddling porcupine and many types of birds and a mountain lion. Though she didn't really see the cat, she said she did because after the eighth time he whispered, "Right there," she felt a little ridiculous. Searching the leaves for an animal flitting or sitting in hiding, also took her mind off the steep dirt trail the horses were carefully clomping down. She was certain she would fall which she almost did, but not on a count of the four-footed transportation.

As her horse found his footing to the clearing where the others were waiting, someone, called, "Hebe! Over here." It was Julie aiming a noisy motion picture camera in her direction. Clowning around and waving with both hands, Hebe nearly lost her balance. Julie clicked her pulling herself back into the saddle, and, in fact, documented all the day's events: the wedding party trying to straighten out their saddle sore legs upon dismounting, their various bodies swimming in the river and relaxing on blankets; Buck and Murphy smoking and building a fire; the minister with one of the wild flowers he was picking stuck in his lapel; an ancient adobe house; the waterfall bursting white into the rushing river, then Hebe at the side of the ruins of the house, her hands cupped around her mouth.

"Ready when you are."

The bride, who had not changed into a wedding gown or even a fancy dress, was wearing her old charm bracelet, a new pair of white linen slacks and a borrowed white shirt from Bob which she tied at the waist. Blue Delphiniums hung in a lei from her neck.

"It's so nice that you fell in love again, so you can get married," Hebe told her.

"Oh my precious Hebe. One doesn't get married when one falls in love," she exclaimed vigorously brushing her short hair.

"Oh, no?"

"No. If everone were to marry whom one loved, I'm afraid, many people in the world would first have to get divorced. One marries when one is young and idealistic. One marries when middle-aged and pessimistic, lonely or afraid of being lonely," she concluded powdering her nose then continued. Once in a blue moon, no, a periwinkle moon, one marries for love. But more often than not one marries for status or money, or pregnancy, or convenience, or control, or money. Did I say money already? Well, throw spite in there," she laughed.

"So which is it for you?"

Rem leaned over, tied her white sneaker and gazed down at Bob waiting by the waterfall. He had changed into a creamy, embroidered Cossack shirt he had displayed earlier at the end of a rousing adventure story of his journey to Odessa in the Ukraine. "Cossack is a Turkic word that means free man."

"Then," Buck laughed, "that's a strange choice for a wedding shirt, man."

Bob pulled Rem into his arms and kissed her. "If you knew Rem, you would know it is the perfect shirt in which to marry her."

Before answering Hebe, she admired Bob "He is so many things, wise and patient and thoughtful. I want to believe we could make the forever fantasy work, but I don't know. Maybe I am marrying him for curiosity." She had not taken her eyes off the groom. She sighed. "No. Truthfully Löfuk," she hesitated.

Bob happened to glance up at Rem while she was looking down at him. The enchanted spell of their cherishing enveloped them though they were yards apart. By chance, Hebe kicked over a cup which startled some birds, but not Rem. Amour had reserved her senses for Bob alone as they indulged in a moment of mutual serenity. She broke the gaze to check her appearance in the hand mirror propped against the tree.

"Rem?"

"Yes, Dahling."

"Maybe you think you're getting married for curiosity. I think it's the periwinkle moon."

"Yes, I suppose it is the periwinkle moon," she echoed holding her in her arms. Hebe acted as flower girl and strewed red petals in Rem's path on the narrow, earthen aisle leading to the stone altar. Listening to the wind blown waterfall, Hebe tipped her head and heard it cascading in the rythm of the Wedding march.

Several hours later, the short, sweet, simple ceremony was no more than a sparkling, collective memory, one of many reels of film in Julie's pack which now sat on a terra cotta floor. All were in Murphy's village for an unexpected, impromptu reception. No one mentioned whose house they were in, but it was clear the wedding party was quite welcomed by the warmth with which they were greeted, and their hosts setting to immediate action preparing the table, stoking the fire and offering them blankets and towels. The native people said little beyond what was needed to complete the tasks they were performing. They were humble, industrious and good-natured. She watched them interacting with each other, treading lightly, some humming softly to themselves and wondered what exactly Grandmother Wilkinson found so objectionable, so "savage" about indians. To her, they exuded the gentility and grace of the deer she and Murphy had seen earlier. Several older native women, whom she thought Murphy had introduced as his grandmother and her sisters, prepared meat and beans, fire-roasted corn, frybread and, at Hebe's, request tea brewed with water she had collected from the waterfalls.

Everything smelled delicious. And, except for the pilot, who had slept in waiting all day, everyone was famished and suffering from physical exhaustion. The fatigue was intensified by the warm food and fire, and twice during dinner, Rem had to nudge Hebe seconds before her nose was in her plate. Hunger gnawed and grumbled audibly in her stomach, but she only managed to take a few bites; she was too tired to eat.

"It's a pity we have to go back tonight," Rem's lament sounded muffled and distant to Hebe as she put her plate down, involuntarily dropped her eyelids and fell into a deep sleep. Projected through the hot blackness, her legs began girating; peddling furiously; running. But she didn't feel anything beneath her feet. Each step simply collided with molecules of space as she ran deeper and deeper into a tunnel. She heard her mother's voice "Hebe!" it repeated over and over as she plummeted through the bible black nothingness. The tinkling of brass bells brought a floating rain of bright lavender down fluffs and orange poppy petals. Quick and glaring as a camera light, Tony flashed into view on the Mexican border. He raised his hands over his head like a winning prize fighter and bellowed, "Mi amor!" Dizzy, she reached for something to hold, but there was nothing. In the breezy black abyss, she rode airwave after airwave straining her eyes to see. In another flash she saw her father's hand on the rear window glass of Art's car in Harvard Square. His tenor pitched voice sang out, "Bye Hebe Jeebie," over and over and over as she leaned her cheek next to the pane then jerked away; it was ice cold. "Bye Hebe Jeebie," faded away while her mother chanted her name as if she were desperately searching for her. Bjorn flashed into view and from the dark Las Vegas doorway yelled, "Hebe, wait!" then vanished and drown in the waterfall's roar which whirred and whirred into the sound of a giant blender. Her mother's voice was again clear, "Hebe. Hebe come back!" And she saw her in a huge ghostly image as blurred and distorted as a reflection in a silver Christmas tree ornament. Reaching for it, filled her hands with the white gown of her dreams while she dropped her onto the Birches horse.

Lightning whinnied a greeting, tossed his head and trotted around a wide circle of flames on the periphery of reality. Her mouth and cheeks grew parched and very hot. Relaxed and safe upon her velvetty felled friend, she leaned forward onto his mane and closed her eyes.

She opened them to a glowing yellow fire burning under a black cauldron and thought she had awakened in dreamland until one of the native women leaned over to stir the pot.

With a friendly twinkle, she said, "Oh, hello."

"Hello," Hebe repeated.

"Your mother went with the others filming and digging."

Much too groggy to clarify her relationship with Rem, she let the comment go with a, "Thank you," until after she had washed up. Helping fold up the blankets and cot where she had slept in the kitchen not far from the dinner table, she explained and discovered it was already mid-morning. Outside, she saw Murphy saddling up his Appaloosa named, Him, and getting ready to take another group into the canyon.

"Sleep good?"

"Yeah. I don't usually sleep this late. Hope I'm not coming down with something."

"Believe me you're not. It's the exercise. Exercise and air. If you really want to sleep even better, sleep outside, near the ground."

"The ground?"

"Sure. I slept right there last night. Your feet are in my bed," he pointed where she was standing and she hopped off the spot. "See, outside, you are truly on the bosom of earth mother. She will hold you in her arms and blow night music through the rocks and trees, lull you to sleep." He closed his eyes.

"I slept outside on the beach in Provincetown, and I almost froze to death."

Murphy laughed. "By the sea? No wonder. Too damp. When its dry there is no fog. The sky is clear, so clear that you think you will see all the planets. You look. Maybe you will see the Constellation Crater," he took a stick and outlined a drum shape in the sand.

"How do you know all of that."

"Astronomy was my minor at the university."

"You went to college!" she exclaimed in an unexpectedly
surprised tone.

"Sure. Berkley California. Why?"

She didn't want to hurt Murphy's feelings telling him he
pronounced his words a little strangely for an educated man, or
by asking if he were one of the fortunate few reservation indians
she had heard about who were sponsored in government schools. It
was too personal. But she really wondered why, with his great
education, he wasting time riding a horse and taking people into
the Grand Canyon instead of getting a good job. Something about
her thoughts sounded so very wrong that she refused to let them
out of her mouth which caused a stammered, "I," to keep repeating
itself. Murphy read her mind and chuckled to himself.

"I got their paper award, their degree for their white paper
education, their white paper information from their university."
He spoke calmly and slowly. "I learned many things. I was
offered many jobs. But I don't want to sleep in a building up in
the air and run around chasing the minute hand of Europe-made
time," he tapped his watchless wrist. I prefer the sun."

"So, what time is it right now?" Hebe interjected with
innocent curiosity.

Without a second's hesitation, he peered directly into her
eyes and answered, "11:10." He didn't wait for her to confirm;
he knew he was right. Hebe glanced at her watch. Right he was.
11:10 on the nose. He continued, slightly annoyed. "But what
does ten minutes matter among trees?" He spread his arms out and
up toward the sky in a gesture of native worship, then dropped
them. What good is Latin or Greek or French out here. What
good are words? What good are facts? What important information
you," he pointed at her, "going to tell to a rock, thousands of
years old? What is the white paper history to Him?" he patted
his horse. The way they recorded it, there was nothing here
until they found our wilderness and created their civilization.

The truth is, there was everything until they got lost in our world and destroyed it trying to make it look like theirs," he sighed. "Indians are bad in white paper fables, researched and written." Then he threw his head back and laughed. "But Whites are worse in our stories. They were documented by the eyes of our ancestors. Our truth breathes by mouth to mouth resuscitation."

Hebe heard his words, but she felt awkward; comprehension eluded her during his speech. Her father was a Cheyenne, so she was Indian. Her reasoning told her what Murphy said should have held great meaning for her; she should have been able to agree or disagree, comment in some way. She couldn't. Suddenly, his expression turned solemn and sour; his eyes stared at the horizon.

"We are supposed to assimilate, to forgive, to forget the pain to forget who we are." His words came out through his teeth and under his breath. "Never? We better follow the example of the Jewish. Never forgive. Never forget. And never let the persecutors forget. Remind them daily. When they are dead, remind their children. Trail of Tears did not end in 1839. They are still forcing us to walk, not to a place. No, to a barren wasteland in a corner in society's mind, out of sight," his eyes fell on her bewildered brow, and he stopped abruptly, then grinned. "Oh, I'm so sorry. That was a very long answer for a question that was not asked, wasn't it?"

"Yes, it certainly was. You seem so angry."

He shook his head amused by her honesty and mounted with the kind, sagacious words, "When you figure it out, you will be angry too. And you will, figure it out." Before trotting off, he pointed to the earth, "Sleep on it Coal Eyes."

Dumbfounded by the interaction with Murphy, she stood as quiet as a flower watching him ride away as the jeep pulled up, Bob at the wheel. The pilot got out first and went inside. Then Buck and Julie scrambled out in a romantic romp.

"Everything O.K. Hebe," Julie asked noticing the serious look on her face.

"Yeah. Sure. I was just talking to Murphy and,"

"Oh no. Did he give you his spiel?" She turned to Buck and they went back and forth imitating Murphy, "What good are words?"

"What good are facts?"

Then a duet, "What important information you," they both pointed at her as Murphy had, "going to tell to a rock, thousands of years old?" They laughed.

"I didn't think it was funny," Hebe noted halting their amusement.

"Well, it isn't. But don't let him get to you," Julie suggested heading toward the house. "Sometimes, he gets in a mood."

Buck lit a cigarette. "But the mood does have a point."

"Did I say it didn't? I was," Julie started.

"Picking on my friend."

"I am not," was her sweet, wounded return.

"Are to," he answered childishly and chased her inside where she shrieked delightedly.

"Hey Hebe, I'm going to give you a book for your road trip.

"Trip?"

When Rem spoke, it became clear. She and Bob decided to honeymoon in Hawaii, but first wanted to drive to California via Yosemite. Buck had rented them the jeep, and they couldn't think of any good reason to return to Las Vegas. Hebe had three options: return to Vegas; fly back to San Diego or accompany Rem and Bob in the jeep. The latter was bound to be the most fun, but she wasn't sure if the newlyweds would really want her along. Nevertheless, she blurted out, "I want to be with you."

Bob dispelled any doubts with, "Terrific. I knew you were a trooper. Let's go."

He gave the pilot some instructions and Julie gave Hebe a book, <u>Coming of Age in Samoa</u> by Margaret Mead. "It's yours. I have two copies. It's interesting, true stories. It's always best to have a book. Believe it or not, beautiful scenery can get a little boring.

Julie's words didn't ring true until days later when they

were leaving Yosemite and on the highway heading down to San
Diego. The powerful visions of the park hung in her mind like
thick Spanish moss: The Grizzly Giant Tree, thirty-four feet in
diameter in the Mariposa Sequoia Grove; the infinite spectrum of
lush and needled greens showered in sun yellows in the Yosemite
Valley; the crystal clear lakes at the foot of the great, jagged
moutains on the High Sierra; the cute bear cubs she saw tumbling
around there and, of course, Rem and Bob kissing in front of the
misty veil of water blown from the cliff of Bridalveil Falls.
After a few days, mustering up appreciative admiration for even
one more breathtaking scene had become unthinkable, and she was
glad to have the book. It opened to a chapter entitled, "The
Experience and Individuality of the Average Girl" and she was
immediately captivated by Dr. Mead's Samoan account. Even though
her vocabulary was difficult, "salacious," and "insouciance" for
example; the observations she recorded read like scholarly, small
talk. Everyone's relationship with everyone else was discussed
in detail. Young Samoan girls were named by name and their
habits tattled: who had dirty children; a good nature; a painful
menstruation; who masturbated and who had begun having sex!
Everything. For a while, Hebe forgot completely about the
scenery passing by and got lost in Margaret Mead's Samoa. If
only she had her dictionary. She was glad they were on the
highway home; eventhough the grand old Ahwahnee Hotel was just as
comfortable. Rem too, apparently, was eager to get back to
civilization. When they were leaving she tried to discourage Bob
from taking "one last" photograph.

"Oh please. Let's not stop now," she pleaded to no avail.

He aimed his camera, put his arms down, held his breath and
snapped several shots.

"I guess this is what it's like to be married to Ansel
Adams."

"Perhaps. But the magic Remy is that my prints will allow
you to see through my eyes. Really see what I see."

What Bob saw, it turned out, was impressively similar to
what Ansel Adams saw, but markedly different from what Hebe saw.

She was surprised and quite dissappointed because at times she had been photographing right next to Bob. Yet her pictures were, as Rem put it, "pretty good," while Bob's were stupendous.

Rem and Bob who were staying with one of his friends not too far from Bjorn's, had stopped by the Hotel Del to give Hebe her own pictures and to let her see Bob's. Assorted guests passing by their table at the pool paused in awe, but he was quite modest about his talent and claimed, "It's good, but not quite what I was after."

And when Rem implied that, "Joseph might display them in his gallery in New York."

"Don't be ridiculous Remy dear," was his response.

Hebe kept an anxious watch for her mother. Bob wanted to meet her parents, and she wanted more than anything to introduce her generous chaperone to a man and wife who were thankful for the care and adventure he had shown their clever girl, a man and wife who certainly were not Gaye-Lee and Art. Still, she didn't wish to give the impression that they were ungrateful, so she lied and told him Art had an important meeting and her mother was out shopping. The truth was she had not asked Art, and her mother was on her second pitcher of drinks, maundering to Margarita about the television drama, The Guiding Light. Her only audible words were, "Fool. Isn't she a fool?." Afraid her unpredictable behavior might bring her outside unexpectedly, she kept scanning the area. She was no where to be seen or heard.

"So you ran off to Yosemite. The concierge just said you had gone." It was Bjorn. His eyes met Hebe's and he smiled. It was the first time she had seen him since the last time when she left him outside in the shadows of the dressing room in Vegas. And because of the exquisite and exciting events of the past week with Bob and Rem, she had scarcely thought of him. Having made up her mind not to speak with him about anything other than their science project for the fair, she didn't want to return the smile. But Bob had already given him a big hug and a pat on the back, and Rem had kissed him on the cheek. She permitted a polite smile to slip through her lips. Seeing through her insincerity, he hung his head, a gesture that poked at her heart. Curious about what the others had done, she asked, "How was Las Vegas?"

From behind his back, he produced a large, green, ostrich feather fan which made Rem squeel with delight, "Oh what fun."

Hebe took it with a "Thanks," and eyed him suspicously. "Which one of the girls gave you this?"

"The one in the shop where I bought it," he told her pricking a tiny pin hole in the big balloon of defense she had blown up around herself. The slowly escaping air hissed a little faster when he stole a kiss and told her, "I have to give a tennis lesson. I'll call you later. Good-bye," he said to everyone.

Bob gathered up the photos and hugged Hebe. "I'll see you in Brookline then?" He raised his eyebrows quizzically at Rem who confirmed with a nod.

"Yes, I will speak with her parents on the return trip while you are off building your empire Dahling," she informed Bob with a smooch.

Permission to go one state away for one week was an easy demand to present to Art on her own. However, she knew full well that permission to go across the states for the whole summer was going to be difficult, not because he cared; he did not. But she was his wife's daughter, and he was unable to transcend propriety's dictate that he, at least, give the impression that he cared which is exactly what he did two weeks later when he met with Rem. He claimed it was "a big decision," and he would, "have to discuss it at length with Hebe's mother." However, Rem subtlely flaunted her obvious charms and, more importantly, her background and connections, and before she left, he had agreed to her propositon.

Hebe was ecstatic with her departure date, June 21st. The approach of the first day of summer, brought many good things. For one, she and Bjorn had come to an understanding about the Las Vegas trip. He invited her to the Gates' for "a little sip of champagne," before he went to a senior party to which she was too young to be invited. Three things were toasted: their third place Science Fair Award for creativity in physics; Hebe's continuation with honors to the ninth grade and Bjorn's graduation. He explained that nothing had happened between him and Nell. Apparently, as usual, she was only trying to make Hans jealous. "I was just playing a little game with her when I saw she was impressed by the title. Hebe, I know many artificial girls like her Hebe. I was surprised that you left. I always thought we, you and me, we are friends," he contemplated his glass, finished it, filled it with Akvavit twice, and added, "very good friends; very, very, good friends." He drank again. "You are the only one who understood me in the whole fördömd school. I like you too much," he told her. And when she asked why "too much," he answered in a loud half-drunk voice, "Well, I can't like you any more until you are older."

"Older? Bjorn, I am twelve years old," she said proudly. "Bjorn, I want champagne. This is too strong." Then she picked up Coming of Age in Samoa, which she had been telling him about. Tipsy courage enabled her to read aloud while she walked toward him backing away, struggling with the cork. "To be a virgin's first lover was considered the high point of pleasure and amorous virtuosity." Just then the cork exploded out of the bottle. Bjorn laughed nervously and snatched up a glass, but she only paused and raised her molten black eyes, "I told you it was better than Lady Chatterly." She continued forward and he stumbled over the chaise lounge and fell. Kneeling beside him she finished, "A girl's first lover was not a boy of her own age," she concluded stretching out on top of his long, lean body. She experienced the sensation of being bubbles on a glass of Bjorn champagne.

"No more champagne for you," he teased.

Rubbing her nose on his she informed him, "That's how they kiss in Samoa."

He drew her hot face close to his and kissed her again and again and again; her eyes, her cheeks, her nose and her lips, first the upper, then the lower and finally their passion steamed into a beautiful full mouthed baiser.

"Well dat's how ve kiss in Swe-den."

His national pride swelled beneath her just before he laid
her on her back and kissing his way along her torso stroked her
with his broad, strong hands. His silky hair lightly brushed her
stomach. Aroused and frustrated, he gave a shout, scrambled to
his feet, downed another shot of Akvavit and stated, "Olycksalig,
this is not Sweden." Glowing, her moist lips all a tingle, she
leaned on her elbows.

"Well, let's pretend it's Samoa," she suggested eagerly.

"Hebe we are very, very, very, good friends." He poured her
a shot and they headed for the bottom of the bottle dancing
wildly and bellowing with the songs on the radio: "Hot Diggity",
"Mack the Knife" and finally "Love me Tender." It brought them
together in a silly slow dance parodoy which quickly became a
tantalizing passion play enacted poolside. Bjorn resisted his
urges as long as he could. While Elvis was still crooning, he
dropped Hebe's hand, leaned backwards and fell into the cold pool
white dinner jacket shoes and all.

"Oh fyfan!" he yelped. "I've got the Hebe Jeebies!"

"Oh no Bjorn, your jacket, your shoes. How are you going to
go to your party."

"Det gör ingenting. This is the party. You are the party."
He made the funniest wide-eyed goofy face she had ever seen and
they continued to pass the night cruising through the planes of
inebriation: mirth; madness; maudlin confabulations and confes-
sions which led them to the conclusion that not only were they
best friends but that they would be forever.

At the airport two days later, he read her address outloud
before folding it and putting it in his pocket. "219 Warren
Street, Brookline Massachusetts, USA. Are you sure you're going
to be there on the East Coast?"

"Positive."

In front of his host parents, he shyly gave her a little
hug, shook hands with Mr. and Mrs. Gates and headed home for
Stockholm.

The following week, his "goofy face" shot into mind and cheered her up as she waited with Art at the airport for her flight.

"It's a pity your mother wasn't feeling well."

"Yes, a pity," she echoed flatly.

Art tapped down a cigarette and lit it. Then he did something she could not remember him ever having done before. He made direct eye contact. "Hebe, I'm sorry things are, well, the way things are. Your mother just needs time. A few more weeks and we will be out dancing and," his voice faded out and came back in, and each time it did, she heard a word or two, "Club," "Garden party," "Normal," "Fine." At first, she didn't know why his sentences kept cutting in and out. She closed her eyes and heard the sharp cries of a left-alone puppy and saw herself as a little girl bawling her eyes out somewhere in the dark. But on the outside, she, herself was was quite collected. The little girl's gasps for air, took away her hearing. Before she left the Del, she had stopped by to say, "Good-bye" because she knew her mother would not take the first step. She stood there unable to say anything. Gaye-Lee did not recognize her. She thought she was someone from the jewelry repair shop who had come to pick up her golden cross. It needed a new clasp. Hebe was stunned, and she held Gaye-lee's lilly-soft hand while she placed the cross in her palm.

"Mother?" she whispered. "Are you OK?

Their faces couldn't have been more than six inches apart. There was no mistaken; she was not herself. She was not even her drunken self. She was quiet and her dazzling green eyes were a lackluster hazel shade.

"Thank you very much," she said politely and walked away.

Hebe tried to be thankful she had, at least, seen her, that they hadn't argued before she left. During the ride out to the airport, she was deeply concerned about her mother's strange behavior. But now, Art was telling her that, in a few weeks, her mother would be "over it," as if "it" were nothing more than the flu. The little girl inside took a deep breath and let out a scream which escaped through Hebe's mouth in an angry mumbled question. "Why don't you do something?"

"About what?"

"She didn't even know who I was this,"

"Of course she did," he interrupted with a, "Pshaw. She was tired." People were climbing the stairs to the plane. "All aboard then, kiddo," he announced like a train conductor.

"Art, you've got to help her," she pleaded in a voice loud enough to interest a couple halfway down the tarmac.

"We are doing the best we can," he assured her and tapped his ring on a railing. "Oh I almost forgot, Margarita brought your mail from the house. At the foot of the boarding stairs, he searched his inside pocket.

It was a post card from London, a little monkey dressed in a suit. The message read simply, "Love Collin." She threw her arms around Art, gave him a hug meant for her father, then hugged him once for him before climbing the stairs of the plane.

Fighting back tears and trying to make sense of her confusion, she took her seat. For the first time, she did not want to leave her mother. She wanted to stay. She rapped on the window, "Wait. Art." She knocked harder. He saw her and waved. She got up, but the plane was rolling forward. She looked out again. Art was gone.

"You'd better put on your seat belt." The jolly old man next to her handed her the strap. "Is that your dad?"

Swallowing the lump in her throat, she managed to get out a, "Yes." The truth was temporarily unimportant because she knew if she started to talk, to explain, she would cry and make a scene. She stuck her monkey post card in Coming of Age in Samoa and began reading that page, "...but Fitu felt that their mother and their home were unusual and demanded more than the average service and devotion. She and her mother were like a pair of comrades, and Fitu bossed and joked with her mother in a fashion shocking to all Samoan onlookers. If Fitu was away at night, her mother went herself to look for her...," the words were blurry. The page was covered with tears.

The man put his hand on hers. "Don't be afraid. Soon as we get in the sky, we'll get that gal to bring you some ice water."

"I'm o.k."

"Well sure you are. And if you're not, just grab on to my hand. Don't be shy. I have a daughter just about you age. What are you about sixteen?" Hebe shook her head, hiccupped a tiny giggle and sniffed. "Well you're not supposed to ask a lady her age. Maybe I can guess what you do. Model? Actress?" He took the book from her lap and read slowly. "<u>Coming of Age in Samoa:</u> <u>A Psychological Study of Primitive Youth for Western Civilisation</u> by Margaret Mead. Psychological study," he repeated closing the cover. "You're pretty enough to be a psychologist. Those people will come in, take one look at your pretty face," he clapped. "Problem solved. Not that I've ever been to one of them. Don't need 'em. Life has taught me, if you're patient, most problems solve themselves." He leaned over and spoke right into her ear in a confidential tone, "For example, I can't help noticing, you're not crying anymore." She smiled. He clapped his hands, "You see? Just like that. Problem solved. Next stop? Boston."

FIFTEEN

La Maisonette

July 2, 1959
Newport. Rhode Island

Many relatives, in addition to all the Birches, were in
Newport for the wedding reception. It was not held on the first
day of summer as Rem and Bob had planned because Rem wanted
lillies, "the best in the world," she declared. Jacques took her
literally, and he ordered them from a man he once knew in the
south of France who had a brother in Morroco with a connection
in the Nile. The first week of July being the soonest they could
arrive, the ceremony was moved to The Fourth of July, a festive
time when calendars were certain to be clear; however, the harbor
was not. It was filled with ships great and small from ports
near and far for The Fourth of July activities in Newport Harbor;
their presence was making delivery of the precious Egyptian cargo
difficult. Hebe heard Rem lament into the phone to her estates'
chamberlain, Henry, "My poor lillies are stranded at sea. We must
rescue them."

Henry pulled every string he had, and apparently one was well-connected because within hours, the old ship of gay flowers was receiving a Naval escort to Bailey's beach, near enough so that La Maisonette's yacht crew could ferry the blooms to the house. Before dawn, accompanied by Jacques and the gardners, they began the first of countless trips back and forth to the ship to bring the flowers ashore.

By mid morning, a few members of the Spouting Rock Beach Association could be seen assembling on the shore basking in the breeze and discreetly observing the ferrying of the flowers. On the other hand, children of guests staying at La Maisonette were on the beach with two nannies swimming in the lillies from three crates of the giant white blooms which had by chance toppled from the sailors' hands into the morning tide. All seven girls and boys had at least one behind an ear. But Burleigh, Rem's little, six-year-old Godson had hung seaweed from his swimming trunks, adorned his skirt with many lillies and stuck another in his curly locks. Very pleased with his ensemble, he scrambled over the sand to the nannies declaring loudly, "Hey everyone! Look! Here comes the bride! Here comes the bride!" As soon as she saw him, a shiver of enthusiasm blew a joyful, "Jude," out of Hebe's heart and soul and mouth and raised her hand in the air in a vigorous wave. Almost as quickly as it happened, she shyly retracted her arm and looked around to see if anyone had heard her mistake. The vision of Jude's grave flickered in space for an instant, but vanished with the sound of Burleigh crying out again, "Here comes the bride." Stifling their amusement, the nannies disrobed him of his green sea garment and tried to convince him to be the groom by draping the seaweed in a dripping shoulder sash with a boutonnieère the size of a large corsage. "No! No! No!" he protested wiggling away to salvage his gown from the simmering summer depths of Baily's Beach. Dressed again to his own satisfaction, he ran right into Rem and Hebe shouting, "Here comes the bride! Here comes the bride!"

"I say. Look at my Godson. Perhaps flower boys run in the family," Rem joked in a whisper to Hebe then knelt down to the child, "How smashing you look in your Neptune costume Dahling."

"Neptune? No. I'm the bride," he corrected rubbing his tan tummy while modeling his seaweed in a quick, clumsy spin.

"My dear little Burleigh, this is only half a dress. A bride should not traipse about half nude. Should you be Neptune, that attire would be acceptable. After all, he is the lord of all the seas."

"A lord?"

"Yes."

"King of all the people? Even them?" he asked pointing to the nannies and children.

"If they are in your sea, they are your subjects."

Instantly inspired, he strode toward the others repeating in his biggest little voice, "Hey subjects, those are my flowers, Give them to me. I'm the lord of the sea. I'm lord of the sea."

From the hill above, Bob came striding. His long strong legs brought him swiftly to Rem's side. "The men have this under control. Come inside. I am hungry." Rem's twinkling glance of inquiry caused him to conclude, "You know how I dislike eating with an empty chair."

"Doesn't it look like Giverny?" she asked lifting one of the lillies from the water.

"I've never been."

Rem gasped, "Never? Oh Robert, you have a shortcoming."

"Only the one, I assure you. I should have told you. Is it over between us so soon?"

"You shan't be that easily rid of me," she bubbled and nuzzled up to his neck. "But truly, not to see Giverny is not to have lived."

"Hmm," Bob rocked back and forth on his toes. "I would have said that about Culpepper Island."

Rem laughed and delivered a dainty slap to his cheek. "One simply must see Giverny."

He wrapped his arm around her slim shoulders, the surf of blossoms swirling around their feet. "Yes, but only with someone they love. Fortunately, I met you Remy or I may never have had a reason to see it."

"So quick with a sweet retort, Bob. I adore you for that."
She turned to Hebe to invite her to eat with them and found her
lost in thought gazing at the ocean.

Unlike the ever blue Pacific, the Atlantic appeared grey,
even on this summer's day. A twinge of homesickness gnawed in
her stomach as she watched the combers rushing to the sand. San
Diego was on her mind, yet she asked "Which way is Sweden?"

Bob looked left, then right and stretched his arm out
diagonally, "In that direction," he announced confidently, then
stamped to lend a hand to the men with the most recent batch of
flowers. "Careful, there. We don't want to lose any more."

"Have you heard from Bjorn?" Rem blurted out excitedly.

"Remember, I read the part about," she began.

"Ingemar Johansson knocking out Floyd Patterson in Yankee
Stadium," they said together.

"And his decision to become a nuclear physicist. Remember?"

"Of course." Quickly changing the subject she asked, "Have
you had Mr. Downey check the guest list to make certain that your
friend Anne was invited along with her parents?"

"No, but I will," she answered finally snapping out of her
daze. "Thank you," she added.

"And if there is anyone else you would like to invite, you
needn't secure my,"

Suddenly, Hebe began to cry.

"Why Hebe, what is the matter?"

"I don't know. I guess, I'm wondering what I will do. Where
will I go next? What will become of me now that I'm losing you
to Bob, to your marriage. Nevermind. That was a stupid thing to
say, thinking about myself at this happy time for you."

"Dahling, we are all selfish, egocentic and survivor alike.
It's simply that one chooses to think only of himself, the other
must. Both are selfish. All of us. I would say it is quite
human. And we are all trying to figure out where we are going,
but one mustn't overinvest in sorting out the destination and
details; the adventure is in getting there," her long slim arms

swept up to the sky and down. "You are on your adventure." She took the lilly Bob had given her and twined it into Hebe's hair.

"My mother needs me. I left her, and she needs me."

"She needs herself, Hebe. She has lost herself. How can a person who is not there need another? You are the child; you are her responsibility, not the other way around. She has Art. When I met with him to make arrangements for you to come here, we had a long chat. He does love her. They chose one another."

Hebe did not respond. She just stood there listening to Rem's words, trying to accept them. "Well my father," Hebe began causing Rem to throw her arms up in a gesture of defeat.

With as much kindness as she could muster, Rem explained, "Hebe, your father." Harsh words crowding her throat came out in a mutter, "There's egocentric selfish for you." Then she spoke up. "Gordy is certainly off reveling in his fancies as if he hadn't a care in the world, doing what he,"

"You don't even know him!" She shouted, surprising herself and lowering her voice. "My father loves me!"

"You forget. It was I in those pictures in front of Ali Baba's on Charles Street. A million years ago it seems. I do know Gordy. I did. And we all heard about you, his beautiful little girl, how proud he was of you. But Hebe, love is not just a sensation one feels or words one speaks. It is the expression of that feeling in gestures, in sharing, in understanding, in caring. It is a wonderful mystery that draws people together, keeps them in touch. Nothing is written demanding they must, not even a father and daughter. Where are your father's letters to you? In all the months that you have lived with me, he has yet to ring you up. I dare say, he probably does not even know where you are right now."

"Because he is away at sea."

"Not with his new wife?"

Hebe was stunned. Several seagulls screeched as the ocean foamed over their feet. Their eyes met, "I never thought you would be mean to me."

"I am not being mean."

"Why did you bring her up."

"You seem to think your father is going to come sailing up on a ship with your mother and take you back in time to an isle of happiness that was but a fleeting moment in your life Hebe." The wind blew hard on the beach causing them to shout.

"My father loves me."

"So does your mother. The odd thing is, she hurts you by being with you, and he hurts you by being away." Shielding themselves from the wind, they wrapped their arms around one another.

"Look Bob is waving."

The mere sight of him lit up Rem's face. "Coming." She returned his wave with childish glee," and turned to Hebe. "He is so adorable when he pouts. He enjoys my running after him. Such silliness from Bob." She caught Hebe's hand. "Join us for brunch," she cooed softly. Hebe nodded as Rem took a step away then turned and said, "Sometimes water is thicker than blood."

"What does that mean?"

With a driftwood stick, she drew a pair of hearts in the sand. "Let's just say, I hope you know I love you, Hebe Jeebie." She tossed her head to Bob. "We love you. We hope you will be able to stay with us for a long long time. If you were to lose me to marriage, you should still be in the Grande Canyon now."

"Remy!" Bob called impatiently and tugged the band of his pants away from his waist as if to indicate he were dropping pounds while waiting.

They tittered together, then without waiting for comment from Hebe, Rem pranced gracefully over the lillies of the surf after him. Burleigh's husky voice ground out, "Here comes the bride. Here comes the bride," and Hebe looked to see him again dressed in his seaweed gown.

By midday, a full half of the lillies had been brought into the chateau and set beside the crates of bright, blue daisies; red honeysuckles and Madagscar Jasmine awaiting arrangement. The scheme of red white and blue for the Fourth of July wedding was lovely, but the scent of the ship of flowers combined with the

hundreds delivered by the florist produced a powerful fragrance
which seemed to have a mildly intoxicating effect on the staff.
Nell giggled incessantly, performed clumsy, amateur, ballet steps
and complained of light-headedness. Everyone seemed giddy. Then
Janet, one of the upstairs maids, swooned and fainted into Bob's
unsuspecting arms with a smile on her lips.

"Oh dear," Rem sighed. "It appears my lillies are transforming la Maisonette into the land of the Lotus-Eaters."

"Nature, once again, reminding the world of her powers," Bob
grunted struggling to lay the large girl on a sofa beneath the
palms on the piazza facing the sea. "She'll be fine."

He ordered drinks brought upstairs and led Rem away by her
hand leaving Hebe to wait for Darcy, another of the upstairs
maids who had been sent to fetch a cup of water. Watching the
uniformed pastry puff form of Janet, she noticed how much the
maid's appearance had changed since last year at The Birches.
Shortly, Darcy returned, courtsied to Hebe and gave the glass to
her woozy friend. But the only clue she had that Darcy was Darcy
was that Mr. Downey called her by that name. The Darcy she had
known was a gangly girl, fair with hardly any eyebrows at all.
This one was swarthy and rather hairy. She got up straightened
out her skirt, declared herself, "Quite all right," then flumped
into the shadows of the house on the other girl's arm.

"Janet and Darcy look completely different from,"

"They are Patricia and Lilly," Mr. Downey pointed out
flatly.

"You called them Janet and Darcy."

"Of course. The Countess' upstairs maids are named Janet
and Darcy and Meg whether the house is in Brookline, Newport,
Pairs, Tangiers or London. Chauffeurs; Smithers and Dobbs and,"

"That hardly seems considerate of people. Why?"

"It is a system Madamoiselle, one which was begun by the
countess'great-grandmother, I believe. When one has so many
residences with such a large revolving staff; fifteen upstairs
maids, at least ten chauffeurs and on and on. The name of the
first person to have held the position is handed down. It is

most convenient. The name becomes the title, an honor. Which would madamoiselle prefer, the upstairs maid or Janet?"

"Neither, thank you very much," she declared and scrutinized Mr. Downey to see if he were the same secretary, Downey, from Brookline.

Feeling her eyes going over him, he said, "There is only one Downey. Now then," he tapped his pen on his clip board full of papers curled up from the pressure of his tense handwriting, then ran his pen down a list. "Miss Anne Atkinson is the young lady in question. There she is." He tapped the board with satisfaction. "Be assured that Miss Atkinson was both placed on the list and included in her parents hand-delivered invitation. Is there any one else madamoiselle wishes to include."

"Thank you, no. Have Thurloe send the car around, the convertable. I have to go in town," she ordered politely and went outside.

Awaiting the car in the breezeway provided relief from the powerful fragrance of the flowers and the din of the preparatory wedding chaos. Briefly under no ones management, delivery men and anyone else who saw the large doors open, trudged right in. The regular staff and an army of assistants stumbled over one another and the field of crated flowers in order to carry out their tasks, polishing chandeliers and silverware, finding place for the stacks of china and the crystal condiment ferris wheels, one hundred and fifty of them which had to be assembled. In one corner, a stout, ruddy complected man in a tuxedo was already on the second step of a ladder finishing one of the two champagne glass pyramids Rem requested. In the middle of the dual curving marble staircases, Jaques stood with three women showing them how to secure the first completed garland for the winding banisters. The crew was still going to and fro leaving large containers of lillies and larger puddles of the Atlantic on the marble floor. As a result, all those present tred in the balancing acrobatic steps of tightrope walkers. Caterers trying to find the kitchen moved in slow motion with their enormous racks of quails, dozens of them. And they dragged in burlap sacks of rose petals and

garlic and bushels of cactus fruit along with mountains of
carefully pressed deep crimson linens, all mistakenly being
brought straight through the gaping mouth of the mansion. One
mischievous gull went unnoticed eventhough it rode boldy atop a
silver candelabra. Searching for an opportunity to snatch a
delicacy it sat tipping its head at the sound of Floyd's sax and
Hans' mock renditon of the opera song, "Cara Mia". His rich
voice rang out, "Cara mia mine," which he rhymed with, "Kiss my
behind." Entering via the balcony overlooking the interior, he
held his note long and loud and clearly to the everyone's
amusement, but had his performance cut short when two news
reporters rushed in. One slipped on the floor, and one snapped
an explosive flash. Above the screams of aggravation and
surprise, the reporter on the floor still managed to pose his
question to Darcy, "Has Miss Duke arrived?"

Clipboard in hand, Downey answered dryly, "The only one to
have arrived sir is you who is on his way out."

Another flash went off as the photographer snapped the guest
list. Hans charged down the stairs and chased the two out of the
house declaring, "I'm de only photographer invited here."

"I had hoped we could do without gendarmes," Rem sighed out
from the top of the balcony. "Thurloe!"

"I am already on the phone with the authorities, Madame."

"Doris Duke? Really Bob. Why should I invite her?"

"Doesn't she live in The Crossways?

"No that would be the Mahers. Rough Point, on Bellevue, on
the curve behind us. That's hers. Whether she actually resides
there..." she shrugged. "This is dreadful. I wanted an event,
not a circus."

"There is a Chinese proverb? 'Bad beginning, good ending.'
I'd say from the looks of things, our event shall most certainly
turn out perfectly."

As the couple disappeared behind the large French doors off
the balcony, the sea gull saw its opportunity and dove at one of
the passing trays of quail. And the hubub began. All blindly
pursued the bird and tried to keep it from flying into the other

rooms. There was a flurry of small projectiles and a waving of towels and arms before the gull circled and landed on the very top, the three hundredth crystal glass of the finished pyramid. There was a huge collective gasp. No one moved. Hebe peered into the grand entrance hall at the frozen pandemonium of people whose eyes were focused on the bird. Framed by the enormous front doors, standing as silent and unmoving as a sculpture garden, they became the figures in a live painting, a humanscape of chaos. The gull blinked, the innocent little Burleigh popped up on the upper balcony in his oceanic bridal wear, flung his arms in the air and giggled out a husky, "Here comes the bride," sending the bird into flight and the hall population into fresh calamity. Hebe winced, turned her head and moved away from the heavy door allowing it to swing slowly shut on the sounds: CRASH! SQUAWK! CACHUNK! BOOM BANG! She dashed to the car.

Riding along Ocean Drive in the back with the sea breeze in her hair always offered a pleasant diversion from life's little bothers. In the middle of the week, with so little traffic, it was a peaceful place to think, just what she felt she needed to do. Part of her wanted to know that her mother was no longer in the trance she had seen her in when she tried to say good-bye. Part of her wanted to forget about her mother, never speak to her again and stay with Rem and Bob. The soft leathered womb of the car invited her to snuggle in the corner and study the clouds in the sky. Just then a horn blared.

Peering over the back, she saw a bright red Mercedes roaring up behind them. Beep! Beep! The driver, a blonde with a straw hat battened down on her head with a blue scarf, was at the wheel next to an old man. She got up on her knees to have a closer look. Beep! Beep! "Hebe!" It was Anne. She blinked her eyes in disbelief. Anne was driving the car!

Fortuitously, life had brought the two girls back together again on Hebe's second day in Newport when she and Rem attended a lunch at the Newport Country Club. Having been seated apart from Anne during the affair, there had been little opportunity to exchange more than a few words of surprise recognition and

"Hello." Giving Hebe no way of knowing whether or not Anne had turned out to be as immature as some of the other daughters of Rem's friends who only discussed their dolls and dresses. Anne was now fourteen, quite attractive with cornsilk hair and sky blue eyes, and she was much taller than any of those girls, even taller than Hebe herself who was now a full 5'8". Hebe equated height with maturity because most people looked up at her, then down at her shapely bosom and quickly assumed she was at least sixteen instead of twelve and a half which had forced her to both behave like more of an adult and to be accepted by them as older. She hoped Anne had had the same experience so their friendship could be rekindled. When Mrs. Atkinson invited Rem to her house for cocktails, Anne rolled her eyes to Hebe and in unison, they mouthed the words, "Bo-ring."

"Mother, we will go in town for a while," she stated.

Mrs. Atkinson had a tense, unsmiling face with a small red mouth barely big enough to let words out. But her tone implied that these particular words had been forced through the rouged chink in her face many times before as she explained her child's authoritative manner of speaking to her to Rem, "Anne was away in Europe until recently. She doesn't seem to think she should ask my permission any more," she concluded with a false laugh, then turned to Anne. "Where in town?"

"Maybe we'll watch tennis at the Casino."

Rem sped up their departure. "Linda, do come along. It is stifling in the car. The girls will be fine."

They had Anne's driver, Cobb drop them off on Bellevue in front of the Casino, but as soon as the car was out of sight, Anne grabbed Hebe and steered her down William Street toward Thames. Hebe stopped and pointed to the lovely shingle-style rust and green buildings which made up the Casino.

"Wait. I thought we were going to the Tennis Hall of Fame? I saw a photograph in Hans' studio of Rem with a movie star here. Grace Kelly, I think."

"Well my mother met President Eisenhower last summer at the country club, but you don't see me hanging around there."

"Grace Kelly is hardly President Eisenhower."

"That's true, but come on."

Hebe hesitated with a little look of yearning on her face and emitted a sad little sigh. "You know I used to watch my father play tennis. It was most engaging."

"My dad will be here this weekend; you can watch him play," she offered pushing her down the street. "And besides, I'm sure your mother will drag you here for some other some reason just as mine does; a lunch, a flower show, an art exhibit, Viennese night, invitational golf, invitational tennis, invitational invitations, all kinds of stuff."

Hebe hesitated.

"Now let's go."

Fresh from the country club, overly groomed in white gloves, Hebe and Anne stuck out among the many sailors drifting up and down the streets and in and out of bars. But Anne walked with the confidence of someone who knew exactly where she was going. From across the way, someone whistled, and a young man wearing chinos and a t-strap t-shirt stepped forward. His toussled hair blew about his bronzed face, and every inch of his frame was stretched with powerful lean muscles.

"Steven!" she gushed and emitted an almost visible stardust from her eyes.

"Jeepers. Who is that?"

"Steven, one of our yacht crew, and the crew for that boat too, the Princess. I always look for it whenever I'm in town."

"You mean you look for him." Anne laughed nervously. "Are you going to go over?"

"Are you kidding. My mother's eyes are all over this street. I can only talk to him when we go sailing. He is showing me how to make knots. See." From her pocketbook she produced several small pieces of knotted chord and cradled them in her hand as if they were rare gems. Tenderly, she held each one up to identify it, "This is a square knot, a figure eight, a bow line," then she pulled out her key. "And this," she pointed to the blue ribbon looped through the key, "is a lark's head."

Steven whistled again as he hopped onto the vessel and below, out of view. Anne flicked her head up and the key tumbled to the ground with a clink-clink. Two scruffy young townies passing by noticed and stopped. "Miss, you dropped something," one said giving his companion a devilish elbow in the ribs. "Let me get it for you."

"Thank you," Anne said, her eyes still fixed on the spot where Steven had been standing.

When the boy stooped down to pick it up, he deliberately lingered on the ground looking up her dress while his friend stood yukking. Hebe scuffed her foot at him with a "Hey!"

"Oh you little pig snot!" Anne demurely pushed her petticoat closer to her with one hand and opened the other in front of the boy dangling her key in her face. "I will have that."

He put his face right up to Anne's and mocked her prim voice, "I will have that. O.K. Preemer donut, for a kiss." He puckered up while his friend continued yukking.

Hebe's knees started to knock. Anne turned bright red, and her eyelashes began to flutter as if she were going to explode. She did! Quicker than the eye, Anne walloped the boy in the head and knocked him to the ground sending his friend into stitches.

Hebe squinted her eyes at him, stood tall and quieted him with, "You shall be next."

"The words, for your information," Anne informed the boy while bending over him, "are prima donna, not preemer donut." She snatched the key.

Humiliated, he jumped up and snatched it right back. She let out a surprised scream, but was ready to bop him again. Steven reappeared on the deck of the ship and stood as stiff-backed as Superman with his hands on his hips. Spying the boy running and Anne pointing, he bolted down the street to her.

"He has my key." A large smudge of dirt was on her glove from hitting his face. She took it off. While rubbing her knuckles, her eyes met Hebe's and twinkled. "Nobody can call you a sissy!"

"You either!" Hebe exclaimed.

"Well the nerve. To even think I would kiss him. I wasn't
going to let him get the best of an Atkinson.

They exchanged a long look filled with the mutual admiration
and liking that comes in the moment friendship is discovered.

"It's too bad about your glove," Hebe symapthized.

"Yes, and my key!"

"Anne! Anne!" Steven was sprinting back up the street
twirling the key over his head.

Hebe stepped aside and went to look at nothing particular in
a window so they could have a moment alone. Steven moved very
close to Anne and without a word, stretched out her fingers and
placed the key in her palm. Hebe saw Anne's legs wobble. Still
panting from the chase, he bent down and placed a kiss on her
cheek and dashed back to the boat. Captivated with her mouth
agape, she held her hand over her heart, the key clenched tightly
in her fist. When Hebe approached and called her name, "Anne!"
There was no acknowledgment. "Oh my God. You've got it bad.
Let's walk." She hooked her arm in Anne's.

Finally, Anne spoke. "Isn't this turning out to be a real
red letter day? He kissed me. Steven Vernon Anderson kissed
me." She touched her cheek then took Hebe's hand, "And we met
again. I wondered why I never saw you again. I told everyone I
had met a fairy. The girl on the shore."

"Me too. You were the girl in the row boat."

"That was a lovely day."

"This is a lovely day! The summer of 1959 will be great."

"Yes," Anne agreed giving Hebe a firm side hug. "The most."

Hebe pulled away and looked at Anne with a crooked smile,
"So where do you think you will pop up next in my life?"

The question was answered a week later when she went on a
yachting picnic with "The Birches" in their vessel, L'Arc, and
two others. When they arrived at Block Island, someone let out a
whoop, dove right off one of the other ships into the water and
swam to shore. It was Anne. Several days later, she strode out
of the the dress shop in town in a gown she was modeling for her
mother. And now, today, Anne was blaring her horn behind Hebe's

car on Ocean Drive. "Smithers, pull over!" she demanded
excitedly. He did. The girls called out what had become their
perfunctory greeting, "Preemer Donut," and hugged while the
baffled chauffeurs strolled to the cliffs by the shore and lit
cigarettes. Anne explained that it hadn't been difficult to
convince their chauffeur, Cobb, to let her drive since he had
revealed he had begun driving at the age of only eleven. It just
wouldn't be allowed in town. "And besides, I've been taking
lessons," she admitted with a wiggle of her eyebrows. First they
sat in Hebe's car, Rem's convertable Rolls, which had a bar in
the back. Hebe took a drink while Anne kept an eye out for the
drivers.

"Are they coming?"

"No, not even looking. The coast is clear. In fact, they're
heading around the rocks."

Hebe peeked for herself, gave Anne a most playful glance and
said, "Shall we go for a ride?"

Anne's reply was to dash to the Mercedes and get in the
driver's seat. As soon as the chauffeurs heard the engine turn
over, they appeared from behind the cliffs and started to run
back toward the Rolls. The wind carried Cobb's cracked, old
voice hollering, "Miss Atkinson, do stop or it will be necessary
to inform your mother!"

"They're coming after us!" Hebe remarked alarmed.

"Don't worry. That car was built for comfort." She shifted.
"This one was built for speed." She stepped on the gas and took
off down Ocean Drive. "Isn't this divine?" she shouted above the
air blasting over their heads. Hebe nodded. Anne pulled over at
the curve in the road before the Castle Hill lighthouse.

"Where did you learn to drive like that? Cobb?"

"No." A big grin crossed her face. She looked at her lap,
then announced, "Steven." Hebe squeeled with happiness for her.
"Get out! Get out! she ordered as Smithers and Cobb zoomed over
the gravel into the dirt parking spot with their arms flailing.
"We'll be ready to go shortly," she called out with a wave and
sauntered toward the water with Hebe in tow.

"Aren't you afraid he'll tell?"

"Tell? Tell about what?" she asked pulling a puzzled look onto Hebe's face. "I find it best to act as if nothing were wrong, when something extraordinary happens, don't you? It isn't as if it's going to come up in conversation." She mimicked her mother's tight-mouthed manner of speaking, "How are you? By the way, Cobb, did you notice Anne driving the car today?"

"Drive? Drive? Anne can you drive?," Hebe gasped so seriously, Anne was momentarily perplexed.

"What are you talking," she stopped. Realizing Hebe was kidding, she threw her arm around her shoulder, her mirthful laughter joining Hebe's in a gleeful, minimelody of comradery.

"Great. Hebe you are great! I wish you attended my school. We'd have a marvelous time.

"Where is it?"

"It's Ecole Lémania in Lausanne."

"You mean in Switzerland?!"

"Oui en Suisse. I've been going there for two years. Last year, one of my classmates was a princess, from India! She was my roommate when we went skiing and my entire class went to Spain on a field trip! Barcelona and Madrid." She struck the pose of a Flamenco dancer with her hand up high. "Come on." Slowly, she drew her hand toward her mouth then behind her back. "You pick the fruit, eat it and throw it away." She watched as Hebe did it. "Perfect." She hummed while they repeated the gesture and patted their feet in an attempt at Spanish dancing barefoot on the sands of Newport.

In unison, they cried out "Olé!"

"We'd have such fun, you and I! Promise me you'll ask."

Hebe nodded and inhaled the primrose perfumed seabreeze as they strolled by the monarch butterflies sampling the bright, yellow and pink wild flowers. Perhaps Anne's casual suggestion of school in Switzerland would solve the problem her own presence seemed to be to her mother and, at the same time, provide her with friends and a place to which she could belong.

"I'll ask."

"No don't! Tell you parents. That way they don't have to think about it. I always get what I want. Actually," she grinned from ear to ear, "I think they love me too much to deny me anything. But, Hebe, you must tell soon soon. There's the application and all."

"After the wedding party. I'll ask then."

* * * * * * *

The wedding party was, as Bob predicted, perfection. Rows of eight foot torches enclosed in red, white and blue glass covers lit part of the street and the path leading to the house steaming with the scent of flowers from every opened window and door. A large striped tent hung over the orchestra behind the chateau and three smaller ones housed the guards posted at the corner of the property and the front gate. Anyone not on the guest list or without an invitation was turned away. So far there had been three. With each new set of headlights, Hebe rushed down the curving staircase in her blue velvet evening slippers several times to see if it were the Atkinson's car.

She loved the rustling sound of the voluminous petticoats under her red, silk taffeta skirt. It scrooped when she moved and when a person brushed passed her which everyone did because it was so full. She beamed at each who nodded in going by. And she noticed how attractive they all were. It seemed Rem only knew beautiful people; distinguished men and elegant women percolated through the rooms of La Maisonette in the rythmic placid movement of pretty merry-go-round ponies. She herself went up and down and up and down the stairs so many times she began to perspire.

Upstairs, Rem's wardrobe mistress patted the glow from her face, sprayed her French twist in place again and suggested that she "calm down." After quietly sipping some mineral water, she descended for the seventh time and ran right into Anne's parents, Dr. and Mrs. Atkinson.

"Good evening. Where's Anne?"

A space the thickness of a book jacket opened between her

lips to release her soft response, "Anne is in her room. She
will not be in attendance this evening." Then she glared at her,
and Hebe knew her mother must have found out about their joy
ride. She gave a quick superficial smile and walked into the sea
of lovely people gathered outside by the fountain. And there was
Anne. She spoke so quickly that within a minute Hebe learned
that Mrs. Atkinson had found about the ride from a neighbor who
had passed them, that Anne was wearing a dress borrowed from her
mother and that she had convinced Steven to come as her escort.
Her name was on the list and he posed as her chauffeur, so no
questions were asked about him. It was her intention to avoid
her mother but enjoy the party. Steven walked over with two
drinks. His pretty face made him look younger than the sixteen
or seventeen he was supposed to be, and must have been. He did
have a driver's license.

"Good evening Hebe. Lovely party. Manhattans. I said they
were for my parents."

Anne saw her mother heading their way, and the cat and mouse
game was on. Hebe knew every hidden nook and passageway in the
large old chateau, so it was easy to steer clear of Anne's
parents but difficult to predict where they would go. Twice, they
all ended up in the same place, the screening room first. Only
flickering film light lapped their faces at the showing of the
wedding ceremony from the Grand Canyon; they were safe. Even
after the lights had been fully illuminated for Rem to make her
grand theatrical entrance in her House of Worth gown on Bob's
arm, they were safe. The three hundred standing guests were
focused on the couple repeating their vows beneath the arbor of
roses and lillies. The second time the cats and mice were
together was in the oak music room; there was a concert. The
violin soloist was mysteriously hidden by double screens. All
stood watching and listening to the first notes of the smooth
passage as the screens were parted. There she was, the musician
with no violin. Instead, her instrument was her voice which she
bowed with her throat. In amazement, the onlookers shared their
surprised reactions with one another. That's when Mrs. Atkinson

glanced at Hebe, at Anne, at someone else and at another someone else before awareness snapped her head back to where Anne should have been. But she had ducked down with Steven and managed to weave and bob out the doors to the gardens. Hebe's was the only head Mrs. Atkinson saw offering a nod of acknowledgement. And Hebe quickly returned her full attention to the violinless violinist. As soon as the performer stopped, Mrs. Atkinson pointed at her and Dr. Atkinson craned his neck in Hebe's direction. Applause thundered, and she wiggled her fingers at him and dashed out. After searching a while in vain for Anne and Steven, the annual Fourth's sizzling sparks spangled the sky and lit the grounds. Anne was not to be seen. She had vanished. Where had she gone?

Hebe was aching to find out, but she didn't dare call and chance questioning by Mrs. Atkinson. She waited to hear from Anne whom she suspected to be serving a brief sentence in her room. After a week with no word, unable to stand it anymore, she called and heard, "Miss Atkinson is not here." Incredulous and disappointed, she had Smithers drive her up to the mansion on Ocean Drive where she found the gate shut, a sign, Anne revealed indicating all the Atkinsons to be away. Nevertheless, she got out and peered through the bars hoping to catch some sign of her friend. None. In her heart, she was hopeful Anne would pop up, as always, when least expected. Everywhere she went, she found herself peeking around anticipating Anne.

Another week went by with no word. Except for Holly and Floyd, everyone offered an explanation for Anne's disappearance at breakfast one morning.

Nell was first with, "Anne eloped with Steven."

Hans laughed, "You mean he ran away, and she ran after him."

"It was a flying saucer," Noni began dramatically. "Silent, swift. And who would notice with all those fireworks?"

"Ever consider writing instead of acting?" Bob asked Noni casually as he lifted his head from the newspaper and adjusted his glasses on his nose.

"I told you before," Rem clarified, "Todd and Linda probably

took her to the townhouse in New York. After all, Todd is a
psychiatrist, not the best a profession to carry on from one's
vacation home."

Hebe sighed and stared blankly past the screens around the
sunroom facing the sea where Holly was crouched by the ocean
watching Floyd playing his sax. Upon seeing him again, Hebe was
surprised by his normal demeanor. He even smiled once or twice,
something she had formerly never seen him do. "McLean's magic,"
the others called it referring to the therapy he had been
receiving at that hospital. But Hebe told them she thought it
was more a "Holly healing," because he really lit up when she was
around. They were inseparable. Hebe noticed that each of them
was paired with another. Rem was on a cushion on the floor
reading part of the paper, resting her head on Bob's knee. Nell,
perched on Hans' lap while he ate breakfast. And Darcy dawdled
over the flowers by Noni permitting him to surreptitiously stroke
the back of her leg. Again and again, she flicked her eyes at
him and her brown feather duster over the same spot. Hebe saw
her own reflection in the window. Her chair was a teeny island
with a population of one in the middle of the large room until a
few minutes later after all had left except Hans and Nell. Way
over she stretched in order to get Hebe's attention, then made a
sad face in front of her.

"What's de madder?"

Her Dutch accent and sweet childish expression lured a smile
to Hebe's lips. "Something is wrong. I just know it. If Anne
were in New York, she would have called. Everyone I ever make
friends with goes away."

Hans stopped crunching his toast. "We are your friends and
we are here. Well, I'm not sure of Nelly, but I am here."

"Yes, now. But you were away when I was in California."
She crossed over and gave them both a hug, then stood back and
observed Nell cuddled up to Hans. "So, you are back together?"

Nell gave an audible sigh which slumped her forward. "He's
all I got." She toyed with the miniature crystal and silver
ferris wheel party favor from Rem's wedding reception. "I'm never

going to a wedding with a prince."

Hans choked on his coffee. "What? Two days before you got here, you went to Prince Albert's affair in the Empire Salon."

"Ja, and he married Princess Paola, not me," she retorted with a feisty slap. "I want to be the bride." Hans pulled her toward him and kissed her bare shoulder as she whined. "Look at Steven Rockefeller. He would have been perfect. He's going to marry a Norwegian girl. Nineteen! Younger than me."

"An' thee maid," Noni pointed out emphatically walking back in, a dusting of feather-duster feathers clinging to his shirt and oiled hair.

"Rockefeller isn't a prince Nell. There are no princes in America," Hans corrected her with another kiss, then picked up his bowl and drank the remaining cereal milk.

"Well, if they had princes, he would be one. That's good enough for me." She let out a little angry woof and almost whispered, "You know, in April, the Japanese Crown Prince, Akihito wedded."

"No princess either," Noni chimed in. "Some Japanese Wallis Simpson type." He shuddered, spun one of the feathers between his fingers and muttered to himself. "I couldn't go out with a chick named Wallis."

"What if she let you call her Maria?" Hans asked.

Noni shook his head, "No. Nunca, man. That's my mother's name. Marta would be good." He glanced at the hall and added, "Or Darcy," and peacocked in front of the door while she dusted the door frame.

Nell boo hooed, "Oh Hans. All the good princes are gone. I should have married Albert or even Akihito."

"Nelly, for God sake! A Nederlander princess of Japan?" he asked furling her brow in thought.

Hebe lent her support. "Well, it isn't unthinkable. The Swedish royals are French, descendants of Charles the fourteenth who was General Bernadotte of France, and"

"And the Antilles had a Dutch queen," Nell announced as if she were a game show contestant.

"Not as a result of any amicable conjugal union," retorted Hans again confusing Nell.

"Oh so! The Shah was with a lot of girls. None Persian. Besides, a Japanese girl was picked to be Miss Universe this year," she concluded with a pout.

Hans burst out laughing and held her tightly, "God, you are adorable when you are stupid," compelling her to start slapping him lightly on his hair. He turned to Noni. "What am I to do with her?"

Noni stroked his chin and thought, then said, "King Henry has your answer. 'She's beautiful; and therefore to be woo'd,'" he gave Darcy a wink, and when she walked away from the door he followed, but stuck his head back in to conclude, "'She is a woman; therefore to be won.'"

"I don't know Nelly. I think we are Love's Labor's Lost."

"I am not a stupid," she wimpered.

"Oh so dat's de problem. Pardon. I mean irrational."

"Well. O.K."

They engaged in a kiss, and Hebe headed for her room to check her agenda. "Riding with Anne"; Tennis with Anne"; "Sailing with Anne"; and "Lunch with Anne," had been written across many dates in July and August. Without the contribution of her companion's daring devil may care attitude and joie de vivre, events would again be reduced to simply events. Things weren't going to be the same without her. She reclined on the day bed to contemplate cancelling the lesson when her eyes fell right on her. There was Anne. She sat on her telephone table in the form of an ecru letter from Switzerland which unraveled the mystery. She had decided staying at the party too risky and asked Steven to take her home. Nervously, they sat in the car "forever" talking under the stars. As he kissed her goodnight, on the cheek, which she underlined three times, her parents drove up. Right then, her father fired him from the yacht crew and advised him not to attempt to see her because, "She won't be here. She will be in Switzerland." The letter ended apologizing for not having said goodbye and reminding her of her promise to come. The P.S begged her to keep her word.

It was not difficult to persuade Rem. She knew the school well and had a very high opinion of it. In addition, she pointed out that she and Bob were going to Switzerland; Hans and Nell would be relatively nearby in the Netherlands and Holly and Floyd had planned to visit Noni in Italy, so Hebe would have plenty of visitors. "Ecole Lémania? What a perfectly wonderful idea!" A few days later, she added, "Your stepfather has agreed. You may go!" Hebe was jumping for joy. "I have already booked a call to Anne in Switzerland, so you can tell her yourself Lofök."

"Oh Thank you!" Hebe exclaimed and wildly flung her arms around Rem as the telephone rang. The operator announced her call, and she heard Anne's voice. "Anne?"

Their shrill young voices joined in an enthusiastic duet of "Preemer Donut!" which Rem claimed, "was most certainly heard far and wide on both sides of the Atlantic."

"I can come. I can come to Switzerland!"

Count Etienne Marie d'Entrecoeur

SIXTEEN
Remembrance of Things Past

Mt. Vernon Street
Boston, Massachusetts
July 20, 1959

        Back and forth she sauntered in front of their old place on
Hawthorne Street. The house wasn't on her list of things to do,
but Harvard was. Rem and Bob had dropped her off in the square
to collect Floyd's mail from the philosophy department. The house
was so close, she succumbed to curiosity and impulse and followed
her feet over the red brick paths to her childhood neighborhood.
It was exactly as she remembered, as if time had forgotten to
pass that way. The deep gash from the bolt of lightning was
healing in the large tree. Its boughs teased the windows of the
big yellow French doors on the second story, her former window to
the world. Mrs. Clunes' big beetle of a black Packard was parked
out front; perhaps she had returned from England. "The woman has
endless breath, talk-talk, talk-talk talk-talk talk all the live
long day. She could have been an opera singer," she remembered
her grandmother saying and refrained from knocking. There was no

time to dawdle. Books about Switzerland and precious things left
behind last year at on Mt. Vernon Street had to be located and
packed before she went to Warren Street for dinner. "No later
than 7:00," Rem and Bob told her. As she was walking away,
something glinted on the ground by the white fence. Intermingled
with the crystalline glimmerings of dew captured in a spider's
web in the shrubs were speckles of hobby glitter. With a touch
of determination and a bobby pin, she unearthed the dingy tube of
it held by her Valentines box so many years ago. A wave of
memories kept her kneeling so long that Mrs. Clunes came out to
inquire, "What are you doing?" In the manner of a confused dog,
the old woman tipped her head from side to side, "Heavens me.
You are the very image of a little girl who lived upstairs."
Squinting her eyes shut, she searched the archives of her mind
murmuring, "Let me see. Lynn? Eve? Evelyn?" Opening her eyes
she spoke up, "Well, she was Mrs. Wilkinson's granddaughter!"
    "I am. My name is Hebe." she corrected with a heave on the
"H" in her name. "How do you do?"
    "Well I'll be. How do you do? Eve, I'm so sorry about your
grandmother," she began, her voice dimming with sympathy. Such a
tragedy. And your poor mother," she continued unaware of Hebe's
ignorance of the news. "I know how it is, believe you me. When
we lost our mother, I didn't eat a meal for a month. Completely
forgot about it. Not Grace, my sister. She ate what I didn't.
Heavens, she put on at least thirty pounds. It affects everyone
different. Oh and the children! They adored their grandmother."
Her eyes were squeezed shut again as she imitated one, "'When are
we going to heaven to visit gran'ma?' Laura asked. They don't
understand at all. No ma'am, it is never an easy topic for young
people." She was eye to eye with Hebe. "It's uncanny how like
your pictures you are, but I thought you were a little girl. You
look at least fourteen," her eyes ran over Hebe's shapely figure
and repeated, "At least. How can that be?" She started a finger
calculation.
    Though flabbergasted by the rumor of her grandmother's
death, an automatic "I'm only twelve and a half," floated out.

"I suppose you're right. What do I know, I've only seen your picture. By the way, Eve, do you know? Will your mother put the house up for sale? I'm only mentioning it because I would like for her to know, I am an interested party. I've lived here for years. A place grows on you. Why, in January of 53 when my own mother passed and I had to go to England to settle her affairs, your grandmother had a dickens of a time convincing me to let that man, Mr. Higginson, live in my house."

"Convince you?"

"Yes. Men are so messy, smoking and drinking and leaving laundry and dishes all over the place. And girls!" she added. But when she mentioned her daughter's fiancé, well.."

"So you have never ever met my mother," was all Hebe uttered because she was stunned and fascinated, by her story, and wanted to allow Mrs. Clunes to let the wind out of her sails.

"I met the Smiths! They were upstairs before I went to England. They had the noisiest puppy, a cocker spaniel. It scratched up all the floors. They had to be sanded so your mother could move in with you, and by the time I returned, you had all already moved to California. But I was invited to the wedding. The Hotel del Coronado! I couldn't go. I did see the pictures. Pretty as a princess, your mother was. I'm sure you know. See how the Lord works, Eve, lining every cloud with silver." Bestowing a consoling pat on Hebe's shoulder, she cast her eyes skyward, "May your grandmother rest in peace. I was,"

"Excuse me, Mrs. Clunes. It was very nice to meet you, but I do have some errands to run in Harvard Square and,"

"Oh, of course you do. Do give my best to your mother," she patted her shoulder again. "Oh Heavens, your poor mother."

"Oh your poor mother," Hebe repeated mimicking the neighbor while sorting through the mound of mail on the dining room table. The neighbors words spun around in her head like ten balls on a roulette wheel. They didn't make sense. Her mother couldn't have been engaged to Art in 1953. That was the year before they went to California. And if her grandmother had died, Art would have told her. Mrs. Clunes was a lonely, old widow who filled

her uneventful life with other people's stories. Finding a post
card several weeks old to Kathleen from her grandmother, Hebe
balked at the the tale.

"Grandmother dead. I wish," she mumbled outloud to the
ticking clock slapping another pile of the mail down dispersing
the thin layer of dust which had accumulated on all the surfaces
in the room. "Kathleen where have you been?" she asked as it all
settled. Her eyes fell on the always-locked liquor cabinet which
was open. "So there you have been. Tsk-tsk," she giggled and
peeked in expecting to see the carefully marked decanters and
bottles. There were none. It was completely empty! Finger marks
streaked through the dust on top. The silver candlesticks and
knick-knacks displayed ruled out robbery and caused Hebe to
wonder how the mail had gotten from the floor by the door mail
slot to the table. Suddenly, a shudder ran down her back to her
toes, and she had the feeling she was not alone in the old house.
The German clock's pendulum swung to a halt and filled the room
with a vast silence heightening each creak of wood, each crinkle
of balled up paper, each wheezy breath the stuffy building fifed
through its many drafts. Blood pulsed visibly in her wrist. The
drawn window shades filtered the bright late-summer afternoon
into an eery dark gold light which spilled into the room around
the undulating shadows of clouds and trees. Shuddering again,
she quickly rifled through the correspondence, snatched out those
addressed to her and shot upstairs to the little room she once
occupied.

Crystals from the window, the Davy Crockett hat, the Mexican
earrings on her vanity, silver dollars from her father and notes
from Tony all went into the cloth, Dutch shopping bag she had
taken out of her purse. Nell lent it to her and said, "For only
a few things you don't have to lug around a valise. In Europe we
do with one of these." Using the pretty floral bag, she felt as
if she were already in Switzerland. Swinging it on her arm, she
smiled and trilled out a cheerful, "Bonjour," and saw herself in
front of Ecole Lémania with Anne. The fit of frights had melted
into a wave of excitement, and she sat on the edge of her bed and

pulled out her passport. She wore it in a silk holder around her neck partly for safe keeping and partly to see what it felt like to have official identification, even on the short national trip from Newport to Boston. She knew it wasn't required, but enjoyed possessing the distinguished document carried by mature worldly individuals. When Rem presented it to her last year, she never dreamed the opportunity would arise to use it so soon, to go so far. The power of the booklet tingled in her hands. It was her passport to the many countries about which she had read over the years tracing her father's voyages. It was her passport to adventures in friendship with dear Anne in Lausanne and the Birches in their native lands. It was her passport to freedom. She kissed it and noticed the time on her watch. Scanning for treasures previously overlooked, she was surprised to find that the items she had already selected were all she wanted, except for the navy blue cashmere blazer her grandmother had ordered for earlier school days. She draped it over her arm, shut the window and peered into the portentous dark of the musky upstairs hall. There was no other way out except the fire escape. Donning her Davy Crockett hat for courage, she began a bolt down the eerie narrow stairs. But on the landing, the area rug slipped and tumbled her to the floor. As she was getting to her feet, a muffled, "Kathleen?" arrested her. Unstirring as a tiny mouse catching the scent of a cat, she tried to decide whether to respond.

"Kathleen, I am calling you," her grandmother bellowed with urgency, and still not a muscle moved. But when she screamed, "Kathleen!" the third time, the tone was so exigent and desperate that human instinct drew her toward her grandmother's room. The glass knob was cool on her palm as she turned it and pushed the door open. The room was in a terrrible upside down whirlwind state. A lava of clothes spilled out of dressers onto mountains of other clothes covering every piece of furniture. The peaks jutting up here and there were empty booze bottles, glasses and a blender. Shoes, coat hangers and boxes were spewing out of the closet. Inside, on the floor, she found not her grandmother but the fiery volcano of her mother, Gaye-Lee. Her hair stuck out in the untidy mane of a lion returning from an unsuccessful hunt, her green eyes, wild with grief and intoxication, were encircled with deep purple shadows above her protruding cheekbones. As soon as Hebe's eyes fell on her, she knew Mrs. Clunes gossip had not been idle chatter. Her grandmother was dead. Her mother's condition pressed hard on the soft spot of her heart which unlike the one on a child's head never grows strong, but remains forever tender to its mother's image and feelings.

"Oh my God," she whispered, tears washing precipitately down her face.

"Margareta, refill please," Gaye demanded holding out the glass for an instant before draining another drop from it.

Exasperated before she began, Hebe said, "Mother, it's me, Hebe."

Failing to steady herself by grabbing onto the clothes, she staggered into her daughter. "What? Don't correct me God damn it. Where is the liqour cabinet around here?" Feeling her mother's warm arms enfold her, inhaling her unique aroma, she couldn't resist loitering in her embrace, but Gaye-lee pushed her away. "How dare you!" she protested. "How dare you put your filthy hands on me!"

"It's me, Hebe," she repeated several times watching the bedroom library of books being pulled out one by one so her mother could search the back of the shelves. "Oh my God. Oh my God. What should I do?" she asked herself outloud and started searching the mess for the telephone as Gaye-Lee slid down the side of the empty case to the floor and began to bawl. Hebe balled up a clean lacey pillow case, plunged it in the ice bucket and dabbed it on her mother's face.

Suddenly, fully cognizant, Gaye picked up the edge of the case bearing her own parents' initial "W", looked her daughter right in the face and sobbed out, "My mother is gone, little girl. There were so many things I wanted to tell her. So many things I wanted to ask her." Exhaling and chilling her face, she began to resemble herself. Hebe knelt down and Gaye seized her blouse and shot a soulful stare directly into her child's heart. "Please don't ever leave me," she pleaded stealing her breath away. Hebe shut her eyes and laid her head on her mother's bosom clattering the contents of the European shopping bag still slung over her arm.

"Oh, my poor mother," she whispered as Gaye-lee stroked her hair. Hebe's spontaneous, "I love you," was followed by a sad, enervating silence rather than a much desired echo.

Suddenly, she brushed Hebe off as one would a cat, fumbled around for the radio and snapped it on. "Mack the Knife" cut through the tense atmosphere. Her glass held high, she sang out mirthfully, "Get me a drink!" The change in her demeanor was astounding. Her personality was that of a Jack-in-the-box full of enormously different Jacks. One never knew which would pop up; this one, the violent, temperamental, drinker, Hebe knew too well, so she moved to comply with the request in order not to rouse her wrath. To her disappointment, the blender was half full. Reluctantly, she mixed the potion and served it to her mother dancing in front of the door and singing along with the blaring radio. Confusion and the walls started close in around Hebe. She wanted air. She wanted help. She wanted out. On the way, she crossed into Gaye-Lee's dance steps and got twirled right to the door. The knob in her hand again gave her a sense of relief.

Safely outside in the hall, she heard her mother apparently partying with no one. "O.k. Let's dance!" And she broke down and cried for her mother who she deduced had lost her mind. No sane person would behave this way, especially not in the face of her mother's death. Guilt swelled up inside her chest because of her earlier wish that Grandmother Wilkinson were dead. "What a stupid thing to say." She wanted to run down the flights of stairs, run from the feeling, run out of the house and away from her mother so she would never have to see her mother as boozy Jack again. She would go to the Birches then to Switzerland and never mention this. But hearing the sound of her mother's voice in the other room made her decide to first call Doctor Ives. The door opened,

"Kathleen! We want fresh glasses," her mother hollered, pitching a series of them out in a shower of drinks and slamming the door. "Good-bye Mother," she whispered. Thousands of needles prickled up Hebe's legs, and a wave of nausea and numbness washed over her as she hurried down the stairs. For some reason, by the time she reached the next landing, she could barely stand. The remains of the potion had splashed her, and at the top of the last flight of stairs she bent down to wipe it from her leg. Panic forced out a swift, shrill scream. Lodged in her left calf was an enormous shard of one of the shattered crystal glasses. Her leg smarted and her sock was drenched in the blood throbbing from the wound. Hissing in pain, she pulled it out and unwittingly uncorked the femoral artery it had hit sending a geyser of hot, young blood over her ancestors portraits on the wall. The top step suddenly met her bottom. She thought she shouted, "Mama!" but her voice was faint. Everything began spinning round and round and round as the tune "Mack the Knife" played repeatedly on a slow speed in her head. Weakly holding onto the bannister, she tried "Mama!" once more. The effort tumbled her head over heels down to the first landing. Thousands of rainbowed chandeliers shifted and slid in blinking kaleidoscopic patterns as she lay in a heap on the cool planks of the hardwood floor. Though panicked and numb, she summoned the strength to exhale a fully alarmed "Mother!" All sound ceased to exist, and she turned her head to see added to the multiple images one of her mother at the top of the stairs reeling down the hall calling, "Hebe?" Hebe attempted to lift up her head. It seemed very heavy. Her lips moved with the mute message, "Here. I'm down here." And she watched as the thousand fragments of her mother slowly disappeared from the picture and all the chandeliers brightened into a singular white star which flickered in front of her eyes then dimmed to black to the fading beat of her heart.

Sirens droned behind a cacaphonous choral repetition of her name which ended in a softly cooed solo.

"Hebe? Hebe, can you hear me?" it asked in a cool-roast, British-bent, Boston accent. Hebe opened her eyes. Silhouetted

by the sterile white hospital enrivonment was the inky blur of
woman in a black summer dress and hat. Coming to, she recognized
the dress immediately; she had stared at it at Jude's funeral.
And the hat, one she had seen Grandmother Wilkinson model on one
of their shopping excursions. Gaye-lee lifted her head. The
buzzing overhead lights illuminated the blonde hairs on her milky
cheek and formed fuzzy rainbows in the beads of laquer holding
her hair in place. Though beauty parlor fresh, she did not
radiate. Placing a hesitant hand on Hebe's arm, she bowed her
head again. When she raised it, Hebe saw the liquid, lachrymose
eyes of her mother, a child who had lost a mother, a mother who
had lost a child and wounded another. From under the dusting of
powder covering her grey grief and remorse, she managed to turn
up half her mouth in a faint superficial smile. After a few
long, uncomfortable moments, the silence was broken by the rustle
of tissue paper as she unwrapped a doll. Her voice was soft and
low as she presented it to Hebe with, "I.., that is Margareta and
I thought you might like some company."

Hebe could not remember the last time her mother had given
her anything, and she was deeply touched by the gesture. "Thank
you." It had the figure and odor of a Barbie, but looked unlike
any other she had ever seen. The doll's hair had been died black
and braided into two long braids held together with a red ribbon.
The blue eyes had been replaced with miniscule jet black beads.
And she wore a dainty off-the-shoulder Mexican style dress with a
rebozo identical to Margareta's. Hebe snickered because now she
owned the doll she had made fun of other girls for having, and
her doll, her custom fashioned Mexican Barbie was really pretty.

"Barbita," she named her.

"Hebe," Gaye-lee began neither remarking on the doll nor
looking at her daughter. "Art and I have a new house, and really
think it would be best if you came home with me. I have some
matters to attend to here, then..."

Hebe reminded her mother that Art had given permission for
her to go to Switzerland to study with Anne at Ecole Lémania.

"Things have changed."

Hebe tried to stem a brook of anger by pressing her lips together, but the words sputtered through her teeth. "Things? I don't know about things. Maybe they have changed." Her eyes cut from Barbita to her mother. "You have not,"

"What?"

"You know what!" Cautiously, she held her hand up to her face mimicking a person taking a drink.

"How dare you! That will be quite enough!" Gaye-lee snapped. "Whatever happened to children should be seen and...?"

"Oh its' still there Mama, but the children are gone."

"Don't babble at me in riddles, Hebe."

"Riddles? Mother half the time you don't know who I am. The other half you don't care. I would like to see you just one time and not have you throw something."

"Throw things? I don't throw things."

Hebe's jaw dropped, and she emitted a gutteral sound of disbelief, then she flung back the covers and pointed to the bloody bandage around her lower leg. "A hundred and twenty three stiches!" The truth moved Gaye-lee into wordless action gathering her purse and gloves, and she threw her a wounded stare rousing guilt in Hebe's chest. "I'm sorry. I'm sorry, but why can't you just be my mother again?" she pleaded. "Remember that lovely Christmas when we went to Canada?"

Gaye-lee's matter-of-fact response came with a sigh. "That was nineteen fifty. How could you possibly remember that?"

As if in a dream, her words rambled out, "You watched Daddy pulling me on a sled. We went in a circle around you, and we were all throwing snow at each other and laughing. I had on a squeeky blue snowsuit. A big brown dog appeared out of nowhere and tore after me snapping his teeth. Daddy stopped and chased it away. You fell on your knees and caught me in your arms 'cause I almost fell over. 'Mama's got you, doesn't she?" you said. "Mama got her Hebe Jeebie.' You gave me that name, you know, not Daddy as you always say." She searched Gaye's face for acknowledgement.

"Brown dog? I don't recall there being a brown dog," she confessed flatly, and without looking at her again went to the door. "I'll be back in a while. I have some business with the attorneys."

As she was leaving, Rem and Bob were coming in with the nurse, two men and a woman whom Hebe had never seen before. Gaye-lee turned on her heel and putting her hand in her glove snarled, "From whom you will certainly hear Mrs. Maupassant or Remmington or whatever the Hell your name is."

"Mrs. White," the ever unruffled Rem informed her. While she and her mother were standing near one another, Hebe noticed how alike they were, both had petite frames and similar skin and hair color; they could have been sisters. Rem and Bob headed in Hebe's direction, and the two men blocked Gaye from following.

"Hebe is my daughter," she announced exiting in a huff then returning for the purpose of deliberately slamming the door.

Sitting smack in the middle of the wide, grey puddle of a boundary that spills between love and hate, Hebe was sad and glad that her mother had come and gone as the cheery nurse struck up a conversation.

"You're a lucky little girl. If you had lost just a couple more drops of blood..." Knitting her brow, she picked up the doll and scrutinized it. "Well, you wouldn't have met your Barbie?" She fluffed her pillow and left.

Hebe released all of her emotional energy into a big hug she exchanged with Rem. "Allow me to introduce Mr. Wesley Tibbles, one of our attorneys, his secretary Miss Armand and," she pulled the last man from behind them, "My brother, Etienne." He was a tall, refined man with light brown hair and eyes, a soft, gentle being whose shy energy moved him around as gracefully as Rem.

After they exchanged a "pleased to meet you," he leaned over, took Hebe's hand and kissed each of her cheeks tickling her face with his mustache.

"I thought I was going to get to go home now. This looks like some sort of conference." Hebe noted modestly pulling up the covers.

Rem held her hand. "The doctor should be in shortly to check your leg. Then you may go home."

"We are here to determine where home shall be," the lawyer told her taking several papers from the secretary. "And in order to do that we will need proof that,"

Bob rolled up his sleeve and flaunted the white bandage on the inside of his arm. "Proof? There's proof. I had to give the girl blood. Had we not gone to collect her from that house, she would have bled to death while,"

"While the mother was inebriated upstairs," concluded the lawyer.

The offensive implications made about Gaye-lee caused her to declare in her mother's defense, "No. That's not true." They all turned to her. "She looked for me, but she didn't see me." In her head she could see her mother searching for her in the upstairs hall after she fell, and she could hear her pleading, "Please don't ever leave me."

"Hebe I can appreciate your trying to protect your mother, but we are trying to help you."

"Help me what?"

"Do what you want. Go to Switzerland. Be with us," Rem looked at Bob.

"I am going to Switzerland!" she insisted." They gave me permission. You did! You're my guardian."

"Lofik your mother is challenging that. She is your mother! And the custody was intended to be temporary, you know. It shall be easily revoked. Taking you out of the country under such cicumstances should be..," she turned to attorney Tibbles.

And he added, "Tantamount to kidnapping."

"I'll run away."

"And if you stay with Madame," the lawyer gestured to Rem, "You will get her into great trouble," then he laughed. "It's too bad you are not married. You would be emancipated and rich."

Etienne went out to find a pack of cigarettes while attorney Tibbles explained that much of her grandmother's wealth had come largely from her grandfather's will, a copy of which he acquired along with her grandmother's when their executor contacted him. "Since you are in Mrs. White's custody, they contacted her and

since you are a minor," he bowed. "I am your representative."
Miss Armand handed him a document. He cleared his throat, "'I
give devise and bequeath my estate and property of every kind and
description, real or personal, unto my wife,'" he stopped, ran
his finger down the page, tapped it and continued. "'In the event
of her death, then thereafter, one third of said net income shall
be paid to, Gaye-lee Wilkinson, my only child, until her fortieth
birthday. Upon,'" he stopped and skipped again. "Here it is. 'I
give devise and bequeath the remaining two thirds of my entire
estate to Hebe Gourdin, my granddaughter, and the First National
Bank in trust to hold the same with full power to invest,
reinvest,' or otherwise make money," the attorney interjected,
"'until her 21st birthday or her marriage whichever occurs first.
Upon either date, the two thirds of the principal or corpus of
said entire trust estate then in the hands of my trustees, shall
vest absolutely, and shall be accordingly paid over. The latter
provision made by this will for my granddaughter is intended as a
dowry.' etcetera etcetera..."

"Yes, but Hebe is only twelve," Rem reminded him.

"Twelve and a half," she corrected.

"It just isn't done," Bob objected.

Mr. Tibbles assured them, "There are court consent orders to
allow such marriages. Twelve is, in fact, legal. It is rare for
someone so young. Usually the girls are around fifteen, fourteen
isn't unheard of.."

"Like Holly Go Lightly!" Hebe chimed in.

"Oh I loved Breakfast at Tiffany's! Then of course there is
Shakespeare's Juliet, only twelve." Rem added.

"This is hardly Elizbethan England Remy. Even if it were
possible," Bob began. That's an enormous favor. Whom would we
get to play Romeo on such short notice?"

As soon as the word was out of his mouth, Rem's brother,
Etienne, strolled back in with his cigarettes.

"Argh. American cigarettes. I don't know which is worse
these or the coffee," he joked and noticed all eyes on him.

"But he married cousin Penelope," Hebe whispered.

"She eloped with her riding instructor."

Light-heartedly, Rem gave a little sing-song. "A willing groom, the law, a generous inheritance plus a marriage would emancipation make," and smiled.

"I just don't want to," she reiterated to Rem again at the Birches. Gaye-lee had not returned to the hospital, yet Hebe felt it was she who was abandoning Gaye-lee. "Mother knows you have custody of me; that's why she didn't return. She is fighting for me. Maybe she really loves me," she argued half to herself.

Rem did not wish to convince her of anything, but brought up the truth. "The point is, the status quo has been irrevocably challenged not only by your mother but by circumstance as well. The Birches will be bare for the winter this year. We're all going away. And while I would be happy to stay here and defend my right to maintain custody of you Hebe, I fear the outcome should deem your mother..,"

"I know," Hebe blurted out. "I know." She felt dizzy and weak, but when the doctor arrived to sign the release paper she mustered a perky twinkle and said, "I feel fine." She wanted to go home to "The Birches," and she did.

There in the magical calm of her room she set up a candle in front of the Tibetan wish flag Noni had given her and repeated the mantra, "OM AH HUM VAJRA GURU PADMA SIDDHI HUNG." Her wish was for the answer to come to her. It was a huge step to take all alone, to get married and leave the country. What if it were a terrible mistake? Little by little the spirit of peace began to consume her worried thought, and soon she had no thoughts at all. Filled with a great sense of calm, she stopped chanting and opened her eyes. She glanced around the room for some sign of the answer, but there was none. Then she heard the resonating glong of the first dinner gong, and she realized she had been sitting for a full three hours. The whole time she was showering and dressing for dinner, she kept wondering how the answer would come if it did. It didn't, and she complained to Floyd in the hall on the way down to dinner. "I guess that prayer flag doesn't work unless it's in Tibet. I wished for an answer for three hours and I didn't get one."

He emitted a burst of laughter which ended in a big sigh. "Hebe meditating is neither instantaneous nor guaranteed," he placed a soothing hand on her shoulder when he saw her embarrased glow. "Don't feel badly. If you are going to do it, you should know how it functions. It soothes and centers one, clears the mind, allows one to make level-headed decisions."

She asked him not to mention her question, and he promised he wouldn't. Since coming back from the hospital, Floyd was a changed man, less abrupt and arrogant and more congenial. He offered her his arm and escorted her down to the dining room. Over dinner, the words just came out of Hebe's mouth. She told Rem to go ahead with the marriage arrangements but also to set up a meeting with her mother so that she might make a conscious and deliberate descision about the feelings she and her mother had for one another, to determine whether or not it would be at all possible for them to have a fresh start.

Rem chose the neutral ground of the Ritz Carlton, saturday. Within an evening hour in the dining room, all was clear. In front of Rem, Bob, Hans, Nell, Noni and two attorneys, Gaye-lee transfused her blood with Bloody Marys' which transformed her from an elegant woman wrought with grief over her mother's death and concern for her daughter into a tight tempest. Hebe noticed the pink gold cross dangling over her collar bones because she kept stroking it or twirling it around her finger while vascillating from sullen rudeness to effervescent obnoxiousness. Mortifyed to the brink of tears, Hebe had almost made up her mind to agree to the marriage. But when Gaye-lee rose from the table announcing she was leaving, the invisible umbilical cord between child and mother brought Hebe to her feet; she followed her. She wanted to assuage the painful need to talk to her mother whom she knew was no longer in the body that tottered across the marble floor in front of her. Maintaining her distance, she shadowed her hoping she would suddenly, miraculously turn around and again be her mother. Time passed slowly as Gaye-lee wended her way to the lobby and outside. The doorman nodded, then took her arm and

steadied her as he blew his whistle for a taxicab. Hebe stood by
her. The Birches who had exited by the side entrance in order to
allow her a moment with her mother, watched from the Newbury
Street corner.

Spying a cab directly in front of the door, Gaye slurred,
"You jackass. There's a cab right there!"

"The driver's gettin' coffee Ma'am. If you..."

"I want that cab!" she declared bolting toward it.

Hebe tried unsuccessfully to catch her by the arm.

The doorman smiled. "Let her sit there the driver will be,"
but before he could finish, before anyone noticed, Gaye-lee was
behind the wheel of the cab blasting it down Arlington Street.
Hebe charged after it with Hans and Noni on her heels.

"Mother stop! Mother!" she screamed above the honking horns
in the middle of the street. "Mother!" came as a blood curdling
cry halting, the horns' blare, people's clamor, birds' flight,
even the leaves' flutter.

From the long silence grew the wail of a police siren. At her
feet, Hebe saw the golden cross glinting in the sun. Dazed, she
held it in her palm, her mother's warmth.

"Watch out!" Hans called out, plucked her out of the path of
a car and lifted her in his arms, then planted her in the middle
of the human grove of the Birches on the curb.

"Oh my God! What's wrong with her?" she beseeched them
thrusting her arms out to the side, her trembling body.

"She just had a few too many." he stretched above the crowd
which had gathered. "I see. They've got her! She's going to be
OK Hebe," he assured drawing her toward him.

"Oh God," she sobbed. "This is the end."

"No. I don't think so," Rem stated soothingly then cast a
glance at the doorman who summoned her car. With Hans, Nell and
Noni, Hebe got in and tried to compose herself. Everyone looked
uncomfortable and tense. Through the window Hebe watched as the
attorneys tagged after Bob and the cynosure of Rem mincing toward
the scene. She paused and gestured for the others not to wait.

Driving off, Gaye-lee's loud protest, "Get your hands off

me," sent a shiver down Hebe's spine.

"Why did this happen?" she quietly implored.

"Well I think," Noni began

Hans exploded in an aggravated interruption, "What do you know? What does anyone know?

"I'm trying to 'splain,"

"There is nothing to explain. Sometimes "why" has no answer. Sometimes, it's best not to find out why. So just hou up."

"But tha's what I was saying, Daddy'o."

"Don't pay any attention to them, Hebe," Nell advised.

Hebe just held her face in her hands and looked out of the window. Except for the sound of the two men smoking, the car was quiet, briefly.

Noni turned to Hans with a wry smile, "You know man. You're kind of cute when you're mad."

The ensuing light-hearted laughter caused the dissilition of the Ritz scene, and they rode home in intermittent flurries of small talk. At one point, Hebe winced from a familiar pain in her head. Over time, she had come to believe it was the murky grey recesses of her brain protectively unfolding to swallow the sad, painful experiences and feelings she had. It passed. The incident tucked away, she tried to tune into the Noni's animated tale about a "too skinny wife," who was a successsful flirt due to her indiscretions literally being carried out behind the back of her "too fat husband." Everyone was laughing but Hebe whom they thought didn't get it. So Noni retold the story. It was very funny, but she didn't laugh. She couldn't; she couldn't even smile. She nodded her head in understanding and toyed with her mother's golden cross. Nell scooted over on the seat and playfuly nudged her. All at once Hebe realized, her wish had been answered and she made her decison. She looked into Nell's sparkling glycerin blue eyes and asked, "Nell would you like to be my bridesmaid?"

"Oh zekker!" she squeeled with delight.

"It is probably for the best, Hebe," Hans stated.

"Yes. I know. I know."

SEVENTEEN

THE BEGINNING

"There could be worse things than be a swinger of birches"
Robert Frost

219 Warren Street
Brookline Massachusetts
September 9, 1959

Here and there fall had begun flashing a fruit stand of colored leaves, a spray of crabapple here, a sprig of apricot there, a single leaf in tangerine high in the tree tops waving farewell to summer. Hebe closed her eyes and tried to fix their image in her mind while she bade them a silent good-bye. She had no idea of where she would be next year. Her husband was going to Denmark with Phillipe, Rem planned to estivate abroad, Italy perhaps, and she was invited to go with both. With them or not, she, herself, would most likely not return to the trees to the house where she felt her life had begun at the end of the world. The sweet floral-scented crackling tinkling of the foliage in the night wind had often lulled a prelude to dreams behind Floyd's sax or the Birches' chorus of merry confabulations of learnings and living. She would miss those nights and the glorious sun-drenched summer days of the Birches; still is she was looking forward to meeting Anne in Lausanne, to starting school.

Earlier, at dinner, Nell had slunk kittenishly onto Hans' lap and purred, "This has been one of my.. No. This has been the one best summer of my life."

"So far," Hans added stroking her long blonde hair.

"So far," they added collectively and drank a toast.

Then Hans announced, "And for the highlight of the evening," he paused while Noni tapped a drumroll on the table cloth, "You are all invited to see the project Noni and I have been working on."

Every one applauded. And everyone applauded again when he stood in front of the fence in the back woods near the pond, held up a brass object and declared, "The key to the distant future."

"It looks like the key to a fence I don't remember giving you permission to build," Rem said half jokingly.

"You were in Las Vegas and,"

"And these signs. They're awful. 'Keep out,'" she read. "I hope they aren't visible from the road. What in the world could you two have in here Hans?"

With grand dramatic gestures he swung open the gate, led them in and guided them to an enormous eliptical tarp, about ten feet in diameter and four feet high. "Before I, well, we," he corrected turning to Noni.

"No it's yours man," Noni insisted. "I only had the idea."

Hans shook his head and stated, "You must all swear to keep it a secret," then waited for them to swear.

"Oh for Christ's sake's Hans. Stop playing games. Just show us if you're going to show us," Bob demanded.

Hebe had noticed over the weeks that Bob and Hans, both very handsome, both intellectual and both photographers, had little patience for one another. Hans had used "pensive, erudite and perfectionist," to describe Bob who insisted Hans was simply, "full of himself."

Before they could engage in what Rem referred to as "their p'tit masculine power struggle," she offered, "On behalf of all of us, I promise. No one will breathe a word."

Following a nodding of all heads, but Bob's, the tarp was
folded aside to reveal a large black object shaped like two
gigantic tea saucers sealed together at the rims to create a tea
saucer container. It was metal, painted flat black. Glowing
crystal rocks were mounted at close intervals in a circle all
around the upper saucer. Noni, electric with excitement, opened
his arms and said, "Ta da," while Hans folded his arms over his
big chest and beamed with pride.

"This is the big mystery?" Bob scoffed and humpfed.

"Some sort of sculpture?" Holly guessed, and Floyd agreed.

"Oh no, do we have to guess," Nell fretted biting her lip
and flitting her big blue eyes over the dusk-fogged horizon for
an answer.

"Hans," Rem whined. "It really is lovely, but I could
appreciate it so much more if it were on someone else's lawn."

"Don't worry. We're taking it to MIT tomorrow."

Hebe was elated, but fighting with herself so as not to take
the wind out of their sails by blurting out the answer. When she
heard them planning to build it, she never thought they would.

"It's a flying saucer," Noni announced inititating a series
of skeptical laughs, gasps and dubious glances amoung them. After
handing out welding goggles, he directed them behind a blind set
up at the edge of the clearing. Hans pushed the button of a
remote, and it began to spin and emit a high pitched sound not
ulike the emergency broadcast signal which, seconds later,
increased to a pitch audible only to animals, evidenced by the
sudden outburst of dog barks, horse whinneys and birdcalls,
especially the peacocks which were screeching.

"It isn't hurting their ears, is it?" Rem asked.

"No. Watch or you'll miss it," Hans told her.

The only sound that could be heard was that of a whirling
wind. Then, right before their dubious eyes, the saucer rose a
couple of feet in the air and hovered silently in place.

Nell sucked in an audible breath of astonishment. Floyd
chucked his drink down, glass and all, then took Holly's hand.
His "Wow!" was the only word spoken. Bob's eyes suspicously

searched the air around the object for some sign of trickery while the rest the Birches trilled in frightened nervous giggles one second and gawked in awe the next. Gyrating faster and faster, the crystals melded into a glowing neon tube and the phenomenon dervishly ascended another foot. Then, ever so slowly, it wound to a dead stop. Suspended in space, it wiggle woggled.

"Oh vervloekt! Die vervloekte ding," Hans yelled, alarmed.

"What did you do? Habla English." Noni replied.

"Look out! Duck down! Duck down! Duck down!"

It spun right at them. They dropped to the earth and covered their heads. But instead of passing over them, it returned to position, sputtered and sparked like a child's toy top then clunked to a metalic halt on its perch in a burst of dust and leaves. Hans ran toward it, but the Birches remained bent and peeking under their limbs.

Rising to his feet, Bob lent a hand to Rem. "Nothing like a little after dinner magic," he gloated softly at Hans' side.

"Magic!" Hans shot back at him snapping around.

Rem wriggled between their powerful chests, placed one palm up to Bob's and the other to Hans'. "Gentlemen. May I suggest that we carry on inside?" Neither man budged as if the first to move would be conceding. "Oh men!" Rem exclaimed, gently pushing them both away. "You are impossible. Do what you want. Thank you Hans for the demonstration," she said politely and headed for the house with the others right behind.

Hebe watched the chattering, black paper doll silhouette of the Birches file along against the orange hued sky. Noni guided Holly holding Floyd extending a hand to Rem, fingers locked with Bob reaching for Nell pulling Hans. Staring, then shutting her eyes tightly, she shot them into an infrangible image in her mind's album never to be forgotten. Drinking in the rich aroma of earth and grass, she closed her eyes again and heard someone running toward her.

"Hey. You should get a sweater if you are going to stay out," Hans told her.

"Oh Hans!" she exclaimed embracing him enthusiastically. "You're going to win first prize for your project, I'm sure. May I tell just one person, Bjorn? Is it really a flying saucer? Do you think there are people on the moon or someplace who have them too? This is so..."

He laughed and interrupted her excitement induced rambling. "So many questions. Help me with the tarp. I will let you know when you can tell Bjorn. But it is not really a flying saucer." He tied the tarp rope. "It is more of a wingless plane."

"You mean it won't go to outer space, be found by Martians?"

"Hebe, you saw. The thing could not even go up to the top of the trees." He wrapped his jacket around her shoulders. "A married lady and still just a kid." He lit a cigarette.

"I am not. I am almost thirteen," she protested. "I'll be in later. I want to say bye to Lightning."

Halfway down the hill he called down a reminder, "Don't tell anyone."

"Don't worry. Hey Hans?

"Ja?"

"Ik houd van jou."

"Ik ook snoes. I love you too."

Hebe was enjoying the different sound of her steps smoothing through the grass in quick whisks when a, "Psst," came out of the grey dark near the barn.

"Who's there?"

"Itsa me, the Jacques."

Jacques walked her to the door where he and Mr. Thomas presented her with a dilemma by asking what had been going on back in the woods because she liked them both and really itched to tell someone.

"It's an experiment Hans and Noni made for MIT."

"What kind of experiment?" Mr. Thomas asked his pale eyes dancing with curiosity. Just then, Lightning innocently released a gust of stomach gas with a flick of his tail.

"A wind thing," Hebe summarized hoping they would be satisfied. They were not, but the odor Lightning contributed caused Jacques to cover his face and politely step outside.

"You must to dit au revoir before to go Hebe."

"I will," she said putting a hand up to her face.

Mr. Thomas didn't seem affected by the odor, but flapped at
the air and asked Lightning, "What have they done to your feed,
boy?" Then he turned back to Hebe and drew his own conclusion
about the goings on in the field. "So it's another wind mill,
then. I knew it. Electric?"

"Yes, but flat. That's it. It is a flat windmill," she
demonstrated by holding her hand straight out.

"A horizontal windmill? Why all the fuss over a windmill?"

"You know, I would tell you if I could Mr. Thomas. But I
can't because I really don't know," she shrugged innocently.

"You were right there."

"Yes, but it didn't work."

Lightning gave a whinny and noisily infused more effluvium
into the hay sweet air sending Mr. Thomas to the other end of the
barn to open the back door to create a draft.

"Well, that Hans is a smart man. He'll get it going. I have
to be off. Millie is waiting dinner for me," he announced in a
voice indicating she should go, so he could close up.

"I'll shut the doors and everything," she assured him. "I
want to sit with Lightning for a while."

"Don't give him anything to eat," he admonished.

"I won't." Without any word of parting, he clomped into the
night. "Hey, wait." He didn't look back. "Good-bye, Mr. Thomas."

From the shadows, he called, "Yeah yeah. You're only going
to Switzerland, not the moon. Don't forget to turn out the side
light."

Lightning neighed. Stepping in, she kissed at Lord Chambers,
another of the horses. Lightning neighed louder, then reared up
and and emitted a loud whinney and a snort. "Why Ning, you are
jealous." He whickered. "I love you," she told him, and blew
gently into his apricot-fuzzy nostrils. With her cheek against
his warm velvety neck, she emptied her heart of troubles and
plans, and even relieved herself of the need to speak about the

"wingless plane" before she lowered her voice and told him, "I
consider you to be sort of a relative, you know. I used to dream
about you a long time ago." Looking closely into his huge black
eyeball she saw a tiny reflected of herself. "Did you used to
dream about me too? We are just alike, both special orphans.
You know, the kind who have parents but who don't see them for
one reason or another. So no good-bye's here. OK? Let's hope
Mr. Thomas is right, that we will see one another again one day."
Draping her arm around his neck, she leaned for the longest time
staring through his little window overlooking the black canvas of
sky sprinkled with pulsing stars.

Later, upon entering the screening room of the Birches, she
compared the unlit room dark to night dark and noted there was
always light outside, always energy, always life and concluded
that comradery of nature, to be the reason she never felt alone
or afraid outside. She fiddled with the projector and switched
on its miniature sun to bring to life the images of her marriage
reception.

The events of that day were fragmented by nerves, fogged by
champagne and made invisible by the fact of her own participation
in them, so she was glad the Birches had filmed it. Only a few
guests were aware that there had been a wedding. The invitations
Rem had sent did not read wedding reception but, " Dreams come
True," on the outside and "A Farewell to Summer Party" inside.
Guests were requested to wear white, so Hebe could wear her gown
all afternoon as she wished. The silent film whirred and flickered out Jacques bowing after speaking with a Japanese woman.
She then remembered him approaching her with sweaty fingertips to
say, "She looks like the Toshiko Akiyoshi, most famous Japanese
bandleader. Goes to the Berklee School in the Boston." Then she
laughed at her own unexpected entrance into the house mounted on
Lightning. The same pink and yellow flowers and ribbons which
hung from the garland on her head, adorned his tail and mane.
She didn't know whether she had lost control ofLightning by
losing the reins beneath her gown or if he just wanted to see the
party up close for himself. Whichever, he clopped directly into

- 371 -

the white room to everyone's amusement. Bob stepped through the
guests encircling them, found the reins and led them back outside. All the guests took this as a cue to sally forth onto the
green Brookline Hills their various stages of sobriety flaunted
in their gaits, some stiff and sober, some stiff and not, others
wriggling their shoulders and swaying their hips. One woman ran
out with mirthful shrieks fluttering her hem waist high with a
gentleman in desirous pursuit who was being ever so careful not
spill his brandy. Then the white grand piano was rolled out
under the supervision of a tiny ballerina comfortably perched on
top sipping champagne. Jaques appeared from nowhere, held up a
clump of grass and ordered them away from the lawn. An enormous
carpet was unrolled and many people sat down to enjoy the duet of
dancer and pianist.

Each of the Birches had taken a turn behind the camera, so
she tried to figure out who had taken what pictures. Certainly
the trio of Rem, Etienne and Phillipe blowing her kisses against
the backdrop of approaching autumn had been captured by Bob. But
there was a montage: a woman's rouged lips enfolding a luschious
strawberry; red lacquered fingertips smoothing a nylon stocking;
blonde hair cascading down bare petal white shoulders; a shapely
brunette's bouncing derrière; a calm red-head sitting as placidly
as the Mona Lisa; a woman in a hat flirting with the cameraman
through the lense. "Noni or Hans," Hebe decided. "But which?"
Suddenly the camera spun to the side, went out of focus on the
floor, then panned up into focus on Nell planted firmly in front
of the lens with her hands on her hips. "Hans," she mouthed
clearly with a frown. On the floor behind her was the woman in
the hat being helped to her feet by Noni. Hebe chuckled to
herself.

Her favorite sequence was the dance; she had no idea who
took it. The men formed a row on one side, the women on the
other. And there she was, herself, flanked by Rosalita and
Bozena, who acted as if they had been best friends their whole
lives. Holly and Nell stood on either side of them. Then Rem
minced across the floor to join the line, and they all fell into

a fluttering feminine embrace of chiffon and tulle and smiles.
When the music began, they stepped forward to their partners and
into a waltz. Even though the film was silent, Strauss echoed
loudly in Hebe's head as all the people she had come to know
one-two-threed in and out of focus. And she wondered which of
them she would ever see again in her life and she began to feel
very sad. The film went black. Then, as a static shot of the
Hebe at Chatsworth came on, a creak in the back of the room sent
her hand up to pause the film.

Floyd slipped in and slid into the seat next to her. She
looked around for Holly because she had not seen him without her
since she had come back from California. "Holly will be, be
here, in a minute," he stammered, pushing his hair back from his
eyes. "Like it?" he asked pointing to the statue wavering on the
screen. "That shot was Hans' idea. I think he should make more
films, like Godard. You saw "Breathless" with us, didn't you?"
She nodded. His eyes darted in the dark corners of the room,
then he picked up one of the envelopes in the box. It was one of
several "Dreams Come True" invitations. Only the name Gordy
Gourdin was written on it. "Why didn't you send it?"

Hebe shrugged, "Where to? I haven't heard from my father
for a long time."

"It must be difficult from a ship. He knows you are here,
doesn't he?" She nodded. "Well if he writes, when he writes,"
he corrected, "in addition to sending the note to you, I should
write back to him straight away and give him your new adress. Is
this it?" He picked up one of the change of address cards Rem
had had made for Hebe.

"Oh yes, please. That would be wonderful. Thank you."

Gaye-lee's pink gold cross necklace laying on top dangled
from its edge as he read aloud, **"Residence la Fleur. Route de
la Capite. Cologny, Suisse.** La fleur. How like Rem. Probably
some enormous hand-me-down castle, four hundred years old with a
hundred cold rooms." His wild wide-open eyes stared into hers.
"Actually, Hebe, I came here to thank you." Uncertainty tipped
her head. "You know, for, when," he glanced at his arms. Hebe,

at a loss for words, gently squeezed his hand. He shifted in his
chair. "I am sorry it had to be you. A little girl should not
have to see," He stopped, opened her hand and dropped the cross
into it. Neither spoke as they sat in a *L*ong empathetic silence.
Carefully, she let the necklace clinkle onto the cards.

"Why don't you wear it?" he asked without looking at her.

"The clasp is broken. It's my mother's. I had it fixed and
I sent it to her. But, it broke again, the other day." She held
her face in her hands and sighed, "If she could just keep it,"

Floyd flicked a look of curiosity, "What?"

"Maybe. Well, I think she believes in it. It could help.."

"It won't. The tangible manifestations of religious beliefs
have been hung in the most sepsistic and destitude corners of the
world, Hebe. They've been hanging there for centuries offering
hope, giving nothing."

"Nothing you can see maybe," she argued.

He gave a little chuckle, "Touché. I'm just bitter because
I'm too smart to believe in anything or too cynical to try."

"It looks really pretty on her. I'm going to give it to her
when I see her again. If I see her again."

"You will." He felt her eyes on his arms and he raised his
voice. "No. They say women don't do it like that. That it's too
ugly." Lifting her chin, he looked right at her. "I won't lie
to you. She might give in. Nobody can ever really know another
persons thoughts and limitations." He spelled, "L-i-f-e, life,
offers the agony-ecstacy duality of other four letter words like
fuck and even love."

Hearing "fuck," Hebe tittered and reminded him of her age
and pointed out, "Floyd love is not a four-letter-word?"

"Oh Hebe Hebe. Listen. I'm trying to say you will always see
your mother even if you never meet her again. Mothers have a way
about them. They magically recur in life, not just in person or
telephone calls or letters. They show up in aromas and flowers,
the shapes of sapphires, even the feel of a fabric or napkin
folds." He let out a laugh. "A mother shows up in the shade of
another woman's hair color, or gestures, the tone of her voice.

She is everywhere even though she is nowhere. But I think you shall see your mother again in person."

"I really hope so?"

"I'd bet my sax on it," he declared and Hebe's face lit up.

Holly came in and flounced down next to Floyd exchanging an indecipherable couples' glance of communication with him. From behind her back, she produced a present in a long blue velvet box, "This is from us. Bon voyage, Hebe."

A dainty golden wrist watch gleemed in the projector light. "Oh you didn't have to do that," Hebe whispered. Thank you."

Floyd smiled at Holly pleased by Hebe's reaction. "Tick tock, tick tock, a tiny clock, bad times and good times rhyme, remind you of us left behind. Your wrist clock, tick tock, tick tock chime for the future, for gay Swiss times." He handed one of the address cards to Holly and she slipped in her pocket.

"See, it is already set for Geneve time."

"I love it," Hebe gushed giving Holly a hug. "I'll be sure to think of you all the time," she emphasized the word "time."

Holly smiled and pushed Hebe's hair away from her face then remarked, "Look Floyd. This is the pin I was telling you about."

"It's a wedding present from Rem," Hebe announced turning proudly to display her Cartier brooch, a little American Indian squaw made of enameled gold. Flinging her hair over her other shoulder, she revealed a second brooch, a chief. "And this is the one she gave to my husband." Hebe stopped. It was the first time she had used the words, "my husband."

His gentle image filled her mind. On their wedding night, they had sauntered around the Birches' pond side by side saying nothing. But when they sat by the illuminated blue waters of the pool, he took her hand and stroked her fingers. Tittering, he remarked, "Your eyes are so big and so black they are reflecting the stars, one in each. Makes you looks even more pretty."

"You think I'm pretty?" she asked somewhat amazed.

"Yes, and you are. Why? Oh la la. You think I can't like a girl?" Hebe nodded and he laughed outloud. "I'm not blind. You, yourself, you can see that Nell is pretty and Remy?"

"Well, yes. I've just never met anyone like you before."

"Nor I you." He unpinned the Cartier chief from his lapel and put it on her dress next to the squaw while she protested. He shushed her. "Listen. This is my wedding present to you, not for this one, but for the real one you will have one day with someone who really loves you. That man should wear this, not me. I don't think you can truly understand what you have given me. And I promise you, you will never regret it, never."

"Thank you. They are so lovely, and they look spectacular together." She adjusted the pins and when she raised her head she was a little startled to see Floyd because she had been quite lost for a spell in the daydream.

"We're going to the gallery for a reading. Coming?"

"Sure."

Everyone read a poem. Hebe went last. "I would like to share, half a poem. I think, I hope, the reasons for that are self explanatory." After a nervous giggle, she began.

So was I once myself a swinger of birches.
And so I dream of going back to be.
It's when I'm weary of considerations,
And life is too much like a pathless wood
Where your face burns and tickles with the cobwebs
Broken across it, and one eye is weeping
From a twig's having lashed across it open.
I'd like to get away from earth awhile
And then come back to it and begin over.
May no fate willfully misunderstand me
And half grant me what I wish and snatch me away
Not to return. Earth's the right place for love:
I don't know where it's likely to go better,
I'd like to go by climbing a birch tree,
And climb black branches up a snow-white trunk
Toward heaven till the tree could bear no more,
But dipped its top and set me down again.
That would be good, both going and coming back.
One could do worse than be a swinger of birches.

The people Birches showered a multilingual rain of pleasure over being alluded to in her selection of Robert Frost's poem and they clapped and laughed and called, "Bravo." Thus complimented, Hebe blushed, but stood absorbing their attention recalling the many frustrating hours spent in Rem's library pouring over books for something perfect for this occasion, how she had almost given up, and the agony she suffered over whether or not they would be dissatisfied with only part of a poem. She reveled in their reward of warmly expressed delight. Finally, she gave a tiny curtsy, took her place and turned to Bob who was seated at the grand piano.

"Thank you for that marvelous and appropriate reading, Hebe. I dare say, Frost himself would have been flattered by your.."

Hebe blushed again as Rem interrupted softly, "Dahling, if I did not know you better I should say you are stalling. Play."

"Yes. Well, I'm not very good," he muttered modestly.

"If you don't want to play," Hans began and was immediately stopped mid-sentence by a glare Rem slapped across his face. Everyone fell into a pre-concert hush. Bob looked right at Hebe.

With a gentle grin he announced, "This one's for you." His manly hands stroked her favorite, Tchaikovsky's Piano Concerto No.1 from the keys. Tears welled up in Hebe's eyes as the notes penetrated her being and magically dispelled both sad events of the past and anxious thoughts of the uncertain future. Brimming with the gift of music in the womb of Rem's home, flowing with the love of her friends, Hebe experienced a moment of unfettered joy. It was as sweet and comfortable as relaxing on giant heated marshmallow bed, yet it seemed to originate from somewhere within. Sensing this complete happiness to be inside, she sighed contentedly and again turned to the concert. She didn't want to miss Bob's precious gift of played music. "Hardly a gift to be unwrapped later or held in the hand or tucked away for postponed savoring," she thought. "It's here. It's now. It's right now, passing away in irretrievable seconds. It's just like life," she concluded with an uttered, "Huh," of revelation. Then she sank back into her delicious moment to be consumed by the concerto.

THE END

About the Author:

WINCHINCHALA's mother was of European descent; her father is Council Chief of the Chappaquiddick Wampanoag's; and she claims a Cape Verdian in the mix added, "more than a bit of fluff to my hair." Foreign languages are one of her hobbies, and, it seems, only His Royal Highness Prince Charles has seen more of the world than she. No wonder Joseph P. Kahn placed the professor of english and film in the "native habitat" of "Multicultural center" in his *"highly selective field guide to writers on New England campuses." Expatiating the globe first "a runaway, then a hippie working in factories, taking it all in," led her to study cultural anthropology. Indeed, she is one of the new breed of degreed writers, for she continued at Columbia University in the School of the Arts film program Directed by Milos Forman and tutored by Frank Daniel. She earned an MFA and won a Warner Brother's award for **The Tea Party.**
    It is the second screenplay in her body of writing. Her poetry; **Bohemian Blue, Sexy Red and Crazy Yellow** is now available. **Pondering Purple**, the 4th volume of **Primary Poetry** and **Only Human Short Stories** are due in '99. As for being a writer on a campus, (Berklee College of Music) she states, "Not only am I affecting the future but also I get to be in touch with the curiosity, rebeliousness and dreams of the younger generation. Even if **Remote Man** or **Saving Grace** (favorite screenplays) get going, or I get to direct, I hope to return to teaching. My students' are great. I push them to learn; they push me to succeed. If they know I'm holding back on shootin' for a star, they'll tell me, 'You suck!'. Young people reflect who we used to be emotionally and spiritually. It's so easy to lose that fire. So I'm doing 'whatever' to go public with my soul. And believe me, after a certain age and professional achievement, the idea of mass rejection is scary. But it's like a hair do. You do your best to satisfy yourself. If someone let's you know s/he doesn't like it, you feel crummy. But if you let fear glue your hat to your head, you'll never hear any compliments. **Hebe Jeebie** is hats off for me."

* Kahn, Joseph P. "Writers in Residence" **The Boston Globe** Oct. 27, 1996

For additional copies of **Hebe Jeebie** or other PWW books contact your local book store or: PEOPLE WITH WINGS PRODUCTIONS fon/fax (617) 738-0355

ordering:
1234 Commonwealth Avenue Suite 7
Boston, Massachusetts 02134

Hebe Jeebie   isbn 1-889768-29-4 $19.99
Sexy Red: Poetry   isbn 1-889768-25-1 $9.99
Crazy Yellow: Poetry   isbn 1-889768-26-x $9.99
Bohemian Blue: Poetry   isbn 1-889768-27-8 $9.99
Pondering Purple: Poetry   isbn 1-889768-30-8 $10.99 (due in 99)
Only Human Short Stories   isbn 1-889768-30-6 &21.99 (due in 99)
                                        + $.500 shipping.
Hebe Jeebie souvenir pack (engraved invitation to "Jubilation of Summer Ball", bookmark and matchbook)$5.99 (+$1.00 shipping). Send check or money order only payable to People with Wings. Allow 4-6 weeks for delivery.

Note: Your copy of **Hebe Jeebie** is one of the limited 1,500 first editions produced to the writer's specifications regarding cover and photos. To further preserve the work as a product of the artist, the orignal manuscript has not been copy edited. Any handwritten notes or changes are those of the author.